D1396895

ADVANCE PRAISE FOR
THE NIGHT ARCHER

"Historian and diplomat Michael Oren has at long last returned to fiction with an extraordinary collection of stories that sparkle with wit, intelligence, tenderness, and penetrating honesty. The luminous prose is best savored slowly, but most readers will undoubtedly devour *The Night Archer* in a single sitting and then eagerly await Oren's next offering."

—DANIEL SILVA, *New York Times* #1 bestselling author

"That hum you hear when you read Michael Oren's gorgeous short stories is the song of humanity pushing against all of its innate limitations. Oren delivers a heartfelt and heartbreaking account of who we are as a species—flawed, fearful, and lonely but always open-hearted, always trusting that transcendence is possible, if not imminent. This is what optimism for adults looks like, and this is the book you should read if you need a dose of unfettered hope."

—LIEL LEIBOVITZ, author of A *Broken Hallelujah: Rock and Roll, Redemption, and the Life of Leonard Cohen*

THE
NIGHT
ARCHER

and Other Stories

New York Times bestselling author
MICHAEL OREN

WS

A WICKED SON BOOK
An Imprint of Post Hill Press
ISBN: 978-1-64293-578-3
ISBN (eBook): 978-1-64293-579-0

Cover art by Cody Corcoran

This book is a work of fiction. People, places, events, and situations are the product of the author's imagination. Any resemblance to actual persons, living or dead, or historical events, is purely coincidental.

Post Hill Press
New York • Nashville
posthillpress.com

Published in the United States of America

For Leslie
Mentor, muse, beloved

CONTENTS

Introduction

Coming home from school one day when I was twelve, sitting at my desk and pulling out pen and paper, I suddenly discovered freedom. It came in the form of a poem, "Who cries for the soul of the pigeon?" What freedom! But while reveling in it, I also encountered a truth. That poetry was not a ramble of unbridled thoughts, but a vision bound by structure, meter, and rhyme. Real freedom, I internalized even then, was only attainable through limits.

That paradox has generated friction, even conflict, throughout much of recorded history and is still destabilizing today. But controversy cannot detract from the timeless need to counterbalance liberty with law. Overly fettered freedom is tyranny, but untethered freedom is chaos. And as in society, so, too, it is with art. A symphony, a novel, or a sculpture becomes transcendent precisely by remaining within its framework, its tempo, genre, and space.

As a beginning poet, I understood that writing free verse meant first mastering form. Many years would pass, though, before I realized that achieving freedom through confinement was more than just a method. Rather, like monotheism and universal morality, it was an eminently Jewish idea.

It is an idea enshrined in Exodus, the story of the Jewish people's liberation from slavery in Egypt. No sooner do we escape then we lapse into debauchery and golden calf-building. Not until Moses receives the law on Mount Sinai and imposes it on our people is our freedom fully guaranteed. Consequently, the Jews dedicate an entire holiday to free-dom—Passover—but celebrate it with strict ritual and dietary rules. For that reason, the Hebrew language has as many words for freedom (*hofesh, herut, dror*) as it does for law (*hok, din, mishpat*). For Jews, *mitz-vah* means both commandment and blessing.

The freedom-limit paradox can be confounding but also intoxicat-ing. A friend who was born Jewish but hated his heritage accompanied me once to synagogue. It was the holiday of Simchat Torah, marking the conclusion of the year-long Torah reading, when Jews dance and sing while embracing the scrolls. My friend was flummoxed. "They're cele-brating a book that tells them all these things they *can't* do?" he asked. "I don't get it." For days he walked around bewildered, unable to grasp the contradiction. Finally, in desperation, he began to study the Bible and then the Talmud, and eventually became observant.

The paradox was yet another Jewish gift to civilization. It deeply influenced the Founding Fathers who hardwired it into their Consti-tution and the system of checks and balances. Along with proscribing absolute power and protecting the weak—two more Biblical concepts—it laid the basis of American democracy. But it also informed Zionism. While aspiring to transform the Jews into a "free people in our own land," as we sing in Israel's *Hatikvah* anthem, Zionism also worked to curb that freedom with statutes. Perhaps that was why I was drawn to Israel at the same age that I began to write poetry. I wanted the dizziness of freedom along with its sovereign responsibilities.

In Israel, I indeed found freedom but also accepted limits, paying taxes and obeying the national rules. I continued to write poetry and fiction, and, with increasing frequency, history. Writing history, I found, could be a liberating experience, provided it complied with the stan-dards of accuracy and notation. The best compliment I received for my history books was that they read like novels.

But Israeli life often restrained my freedom. For years, I was a soldier, carrying out orders, unable to do or even dress as I chose. And then I entered government service, first as an ambassador and later as an elected official. I forfeited not only my independence but the right to speak my mind entirely. Israeli law, much like its American counterpart, forbids certain representatives from publishing books while in office. Yet nothing prohibited me from writing, and I did so virtually every morning before work. Much of this collection was written then, as a personal assertion of freedom.

If, as a preteen, poetry was my gateway to expression, now I found the same route through stories. Much like verse, short fiction imposes draconian strictures on the author, necessitating constant discipline. A writer must present fully-drawn characters, a developed plot, a resolution and meaning—within as little as a single page. But while relentlessly confining, stories afford a vast creative scope. I could be anywhere—on a New England beach, an Asian jungle or a spaceship. I could be a homicide detective or a Holocaust survivor, a conquistador or a hitman, a human or an animal. I could be an adult or a child, woman or man, living today or thousands of years ago. What exhilarating freedom!

But what control. The result is stories which aspire to be both concise and audacious, structured yet wild. They are American in their candor and Israeli in their zeal, yet always, paradoxically, Jewish. They are my way of celebrating the end of slavery but also of accepting the law. They are the way I embrace limitation while dancing and singing unchained.

Michael Oren
Tel Aviv, 2020

Ruin

First off, we don't boo. We don't rattle chains or—give me a break—wear sheets. We can't move things, not books or candlesticks, not even the skateboard that some idiot teenager left at the top of the stairs. All that we can do is watch, silently, powerlessly, at most raising a few cold bumps on your skin. Sorry if this sounds disappointing. We don't shriek, we don't whimper. We merely observe and bear witness.

Ghosts, you see, aren't scary. People are scary. Walter Ackerman, for example. Wally. With his hairy shoulders and rolls of neck, arm, and belly fat. Observe him bouncing up and down on Sylvia Ricco, also known as his sister-in-law, whose butt reminds me of a half-deflated basketball. And not in the dark, either. No, these two ghouls go at it in the early afternoon when the wife and kids are safely out of the house, when no one can hear his snorting or her screeching like a cat becoming roadkill—when every vein and every pimple is hideously displayed, and every wattle highlighted. Frightened by nights of the living dead? Try seeing days of the dead living.

For that's what Wally and his family are, suburban zombies. Alice, a.k.a. Mrs. Ackerman, with her two-bottle-a-day Chardonnay habit and her bustling schedule of therapists, new age spiritualists, and Corsican golf instructors. The children, Pace and Jason, the first a community college drop-out and tattoo parlor apprentice with a magenta Mohawk and more body piercings than St. Sebastian, and the second, a zitty seventeen-year-old geek more concerned with code than with girls or his own cleanliness. A typically damaged family in a rather undistinguished aluminum-sided house that just happens to be haunted.

How I got here is a mystery. I know nothing of my previous life or lives, no sense of where I came from. Yet clearly there's forethought involved. I'm culturally appropriate, not haunting some hut in Somalia, God forbid, or an igloo. All I know is my name, Ruin, which I suppose means something, but I'd rather not contemplate it. I'd prefer, in fact, to think that it's actually Rouen, like that pretty town in France, but that's just a poltergeist's quirk.

No, the Ackermans are familiar to me, almost kin, and I can sympathize with Wally's need to pawn his mother's jewelry to pay off gambling debts or his deepening flirtation with the mob. I can understand why, when he's not snorting up or bonking Sylvia, he's locked in the bathroom weeping and bashing his head against the sink. Life is not what you think, I'd like to whisper to him. And guess what, neither is death.

For the inescapable truth is that there is no truth. At least not as humans perceive it. If one ghost exists, then there must be millions. And not only ghosts but fairies, brownies, genies, and nymphs. Throw in leprechauns, too. If reality is a skein and its fabric gossamer, then all people fret about—mortgages, stature, security, orgasms—is chimerical. If Ruin roams the Ackerman house, then countless other homes are similarly possessed and by ominously-named apparitions.

And so, I filter. Up to the attic where Wally's degrees—duly framed by his father—are kept in a dust-encrusted locker. Around the garage and the garbage bags in which, under the camouflage of crumbled napkins and soda cans, Alice disposes her bottles. The closets are fun but could be more so if I could access Pace's stash. I could infiltrate Jason's computer if I wanted to, tinker with its code—who knows, maybe erase his hard disk. Ruin runs ramshackle everywhere in the Ackerman abode, all except for the basement.

That's the one place even I'm afraid to visit. With those spooky jars of screws and nails, the rusted toboggans, the soup tureens and bowling trophies shrouded in cobwebs. The basement: home to the sump pump and the boiler, the thermostat and the fuse-box, its ceiling scored with drippy pipes and long-dead electrical wires. You know a place is creepy when it even gives ghosts the creeps. Wally, I notice, also avoids the basement, as if there were too many memories hovering there, and one too many temptations.

I long to tell Walter that all is not lost, that he hasn't squandered his youthful promise and sold his soul to thugs. Perhaps there's no cure for the male pattern baldness, I imagine explaining, but you still have your heart and other vital organs, your brain, and the occasional erection. And you're not devoid of kindness. There's your support for the local little league, the weekly visits to your mother in the home, though it's years since she's recognized you. Redemption is possible, Wally, I want to say, and the chance you have is as least as good as a ghost's. I yearn to impart these wisdoms because somehow, I know him and feel I can help him exorcize.

But, alas, I'm incapable of a boo and can't prevent his self-devastation. I cannot deter him from sniffing the last of his blow, from leaving Sylvia's panties for Alice to find, and from telling his loan shark to fuck off. When he drifts into his children's empty rooms and wails over their childhood mementos, I'm floating behind him, helpless. I'm fluttering above him still as he opens the basement door and descends the shrieking steps. Into the dark and miasma of moldy wicker and mouse droppings. If sheets were indeed my wardrobe, I'd be shaking them now, and rattling the clunkiest of chains. I'd pull the chair out as he climbed onto its seat and clip the wire looped around his throat.

Howling, I'd pull at his threadbare shirt and shiny trousers, hold him under the armpits as the chair tipped away and he plummeted. His gagging and gurgling would be mine, if only I could possess them. Silently, Walter swings, and powerlessly I witness. The meaning of Ruin is known to me now and the purpose of this particular assignment. More horrific than a thump in the night or a hatchet in the back is the specter of human anguish. Ghosts do not in fact visit households. On the contrary, it's the living who haunt the dead.

Liberation

Confined by tubes, strapped down and caged to prevent him from falling off, Lev Levitsky lay wheezing. Radar-like, monitors tracked his departure from life. Above the bleeps, though, through strata of consciousness, he could hear his doctors consulting. The issue wasn't medical, it seemed, but promotional. Never had they treated a man so revered. Not only a literary colossus but a moral giant whose existence justified everyone's. The pluses for the hospital were obvious.

"We could hold a press conference," one of the physicians was saying. "Release a statement."

But a second doctor objected. "No, we've got to keep the press away. Some jerk's liable to get in here with a camera, and nobody should ever see him like this. Least of all them."

"Them," Levitsky understood, referred to the patient's admirers peering through the ward's porthole window, crowding the hallway and the staircase and spilling outside into the hospital's parking lot. All they wanted was a final word from him confirming that evil would not, in the end, triumph, and was simply no match for love.

"Ironic, though," yet another voice—younger, Levitsky judged, a resident's—remarked. "He looks just like he does in that picture."

The picture he referred to, a photograph actually, was taken of Levitsky more than seventy years earlier, at the Ohrdruf concentration camp. Though only sixteen at the time, he looked ancient, desiccated, rags scarcely binding his bones. More mummy than man. The hollow eyes, the gaping mouth—a face that witnessed the unwatchable. Yet the expression he brought toward the camera showed more than horror. There was also gratitude and, beyond that, an indomitable conviction. "There is goodness in the world," his gaunt, shit-streaked cheeks improbably insisted. "I still believe in people."

The resident would never know the irony of that image. No one would. Only Levitsky, tied to his bed and only intermittently awake, could confess that he had not been gazing at the photographer at all that day but at the soldier standing behind him. A burly American sergeant, florid-faced beneath his helmet, a Tommy-gun slung on his arm, smiled at the prisoner and pointed at the barbed-wire gates. They parted, revealing pastures and forests, a sapphire sky, and the sun like a diadem. "Hey, buddy, look," the sergeant called out to Levitsky. "You're free!"

He stumbled out of those gates and into a world that was anything but dazzling. A mortally wounded world, it oozed with people much like him. Aimless, alone, uncertain of how or why to live. He staggered through the ruins of once-quaint cities, picking up debris that might be sold on quirky post-war markets or odd jobs with the various Occupations. He acquired languages as well, and with an ease that surprised him as much as it did the local editors who began buying his articles.

He had never written a paragraph before and yet they, too, came naturally. The first were merely news items—the defusing of an unexploded bomb, the reunion of siblings long presumed dead. But then came more thoughtful pieces. Half-baked views on life spiked with his own experiences in the camp.

Such stories were especially lucrative. Like the demand for black market soap and scrap metal, Levitsky learned, people craved hope. They could read about his parents being shot in front of him or how many of the survivors' stomachs burst when first filled with G.I. milk, just as long as they also heard tales of compassion. The former prize fighter who shared his rind of bread with a starving orphan, the women who, against maniacal odds, managed to nurse a baby born in their barracks. Throw in a little midrash, a little Buber and Buddha, even—he dared not admit it—some Christ, and, *voila*, he had a sale.

If his approach seemed cynical, the world, he reasoned, deserved it. In the camps, he stole, he groveled, and writhed maggot-like in the mud, yet he survived. So who was anyone to judge him now that he made money tweaking people's emotions?

And so, cynically, he wrote. In his oversized clothes and unkempt hair, a cigarette pasted on his lip, he frequented the cheaper Paris cafes. He drank and womanized with abandon.

Levitsky might have persisted like that, destroying his body as not even the Nazis could, sullying his soul. And perhaps that would have granted him forgetfulness. He might have died on his own terms, dissipated but free.

Then, five years after liberation, he wrote a book. Not a novel, exactly, or a memoir, but an extended version of one of his articles. Mass death combined with a singular humanity, barbarism with grace. "Dusk," he called it, evoking the interface between radiance and darkness. Told in hauntingly simple language, detached yet gripping. The publication, he imagined, might pay for some of his bar bills. Within hours, though, the first edition sold out.

And, overnight, Levitsky became an icon. He found himself suddenly a source of wisdom for countless people he'd never met, a wellspring of righteousness. Letters poured in from bereaved parents, jilted lovers, the lonely and oppressed. Celebrities boasted of corresponding with him, and school children crayoned little notes of thanks. Duly, he replied to each one, reiterating his faithful message, afraid of letting them down. Unable, he realized, to let himself out.

It soon became clear that he could never go back to his bohemian lifestyle, never return to being Lev Levitsky, freelance nihilist, the drifter in charge of his fate. Once an assertion of liberty, his shabbiness was now a brand. His suffering, formerly a license for indulgence, sentenced him to virtue. Fame and admiration impounded him.

Relocating to Manhattan, Levitsky found himself at the head of Upper East Side guest lists, a speaker in constant demand. In a voice barely audible over the praise, he affirmed his gospel of rebirth. Perhaps, too, he began to believe it, or at least to forget the time when believing or not was an assertion of will.

At one gala reception, he was introduced to Vera. Terribly thin and quiet, Vera, despite Auschwitz, retained a ghost of her former beauty.

Saintly Vera, the ideal partner for Levitsky, the sage. Their wedding, attended by religious leaders and toasted by the mayor, was newsworthy. The couple's book-insulated salon on York Avenue served as a hub for truth-seekers. More bestsellers followed, more tributes that stifled his walls, two introverted children, and a reputation for rectitude which—according to a *Time* magazine cover-story—rivalled the Pope's.

Here is Levitsky at sixty-five: rich, celebrated, sought out by global leaders. At home, Vera stood sentry-like over their lives, over their bed, it seemed, allowing no passion to enter. Each morning, he locked himself in his office, alone except for the assistants who kept his desk spotless and penciled in every hour of his day. The morning bagel they brought was toasted just right and the coffee exactingly sweetened. His writing time—between eight and two—was sacred.

At 2:01, precisely, each day one of those assistants stuck a head into his door and asked if he needed anything. And just as invariably he shook his now peppery flop, "No, thank you, no."

Only once did the answer differ. One time, he did not even get a chance to respond. Rather, the assistant—an unpaid intern, he later discovered—marched into his office, planted herself in front of him and asked, "My God, how do you stand this?"

Levitsky, dumbfounded, shrugged.

"This," she said and drew a hand over the barrenness of his desk. "Not a paper, not even a paper*clip* out of place. I'd go nuts."

Strangely, in a voice he scarcely remembered, he sighed, "What makes you think I have not?"

A second passed, an endless second in which the two of them gazed at each other. The wizened writer in his gray, out-of-date clothes, and the intern, short and compact yet jack-in-the-box sprightly and keen. They stared and then, with uncanny coordination, they laughed. They roared while the intern spread papers, bagel wrappers, and half-empty coffee cups before him. "There!" she trumpeted. "Now we know, a human being works here."

They were chuckling still when one of the regular assistants appeared and, with arms akimbo, barked, "Sidney!"

"A nice Jewish name," she explained the following day, after he hired her. "But you can call me Sid."

"Sid," he repeated, as if trying on some new-fashioned suit. "Sid…"

No more than his, her own clothing never varied. High-end jeans and close-fitting sweaters that outlined her buxomness. Pumps or sneakers that seemed to him too tiny to actually contain feet. Soon, though, he stopped noticing such things. In time, there was only her eyes and lips, green and crimson, and her puggish nose that shed freckles across her cheeks with the slightest smile. And her hair. Especially her hair at which braids and clips flung themselves trying to contain an auburn vastness in which pencils—imaginably even hand tools—vanished.

"Sid," he'd call out, usually for no specific reason, and instantly she'd come bouncing. "Sid," he'd chuckle. "Mess up my desk."

A clever, intuitive girl, she knew to retire in Vera's presence, deferring to her imperious gloom. She hung back when Levitsky's grandchildren played tag around his office. Grasping authority, she kept the other staff in line and for the most part out of his sight. Days could pass with just the two of them alone—Sid or, frequently, "my Sid," and "Leave," as she insisted on mispronouncing his first name, as if to command or beg him.

That relationship continued uninterrupted until the evening when the rest of the staff had already gone home. Set to receive yet another honorary doctorate, Levitsky stood in front of her and jokingly asked, "How do I look?"

She replied, "Seriously? You stand hunched over with your fingers tucked into fists. Like you were carrying two heavy suitcases or something. Your hair is a mess, your ears and nose need clipping. And this thing—*this*…" She pinched the lapel pin that signaled some government's highest esteem. "It's going to fall off any minute."

She re-fixed the pin, aligning her nose with his Adam's apple and then, looking up, took in the sorrows of his eyes. Then, on sneaker tips, she rose and kissed him. He kissed her back, kissed as he never had, even in his Paris days, insatiably. Somehow, a sweater came off releasing upturned breasts. Supple legs escaped from jeans. Tie, vest, a worsted suit—all flung to the floor—and papers seesawed above the desk on which the two of them first made love.

The next times would be in her apartment, amid the high school and college mementos, or in the hotels where their rooms were routinely adjacent. No one suspected. Here was a man nearly old enough to be her grandfather, and not just any man but one almost unanimously deemed above reproach and therefore beyond desire.

Yet the desire became boundless and so, too, did Levitsky. Lying beside her, filing his fingers through her uncontained hair, he for the first time vented his rage at those who had stolen his youth and butchered his family. He wept for the parents he still believed—irrationally—he could have saved. Howling, he unleashed the passions imprisoned inside him for years. Ear on her breast, he recalled the thump of approaching Allied artillery and the dream that someday his captivity would end.

And soon it would, he promised her. He would divorce Vera, give up the titles and the accolades, and escape into the world beside her. "Think about it," he said with his head still on Sid's chest and his hand sunk in her hair. "We could go to restaurants together. Movies. Take a cruise!"

Expectantly, they set a date. Days passed, together with dozens of loving notes. The office functioned as usual. Until word arrived—by special courier—that Levitsky was to receive the President's Freedom Prize. The press headlined the news. Congratulations gushed in and well-wishers gathered on the street below.

"How can we do this now?" Sidney asked in tears. "To her. To *them*?"

His voice also cracked. "How can we *not* do this? For *us*."

The night arrived, the White House aglow with personages and photographers. A famous violinist performed Mendelssohn and a choir of Yeshiva boys sang dolorously in Yiddish. Vera looked grave but elegant while Levitsky, wan in black tie, could have passed for both undertaker and corpse. The President gushed about the author's gift for inspiring millions, his irrepressible faith and belief in the human heart. The medallion, which Levitsky accepted with a dip of his disheveled head, reminded him of the sun he once saw beaming just beyond the gates of the camp.

They were scheduled to meet the following Monday, at the sole time not penciled in. But, though he asked and asked, no one had seen Sidney at the office. The phone in her apartment went to voicemail, her doorbell rang unanswered. Levitsky was clueless about texting—Sid always ribbed him—yet he tried that too, futilely.

That Monday passed, and many more after, and still the cubicle outside his office remained vacant. Trapped behind his immaculate desk, Levitsky wrote nothing and spoke to no one. The lines that crisscrossed his face deepened and his suits hung rag-like from his frame. His coffee and bagel grew cold.

His fame, though, only blossomed. More state visits, more schools and scholarships inscribed with his name. Twenty years on, he was accepting some of the world's most illustrious prizes for the second time when news came of a different distinction. Even his disease was unique.

"So it's decided, then," one of the doctors was saying. "No press conference. No photos. We release a statement, period."

"Period. You write it up."

The voice Levitsky assumed was the resident's protested, "Why me?"

"Because you're the last one here to take freshman lit," the senior physician snapped. "You probably even read his books."

And then there was silence, except for the chirp of his monitor. Only some time later, as the bleeps stretched into a drone, did he feel another presence in the room. Not Vera, he knew, who died a half-decade earlier, or his grandchildren who were somewhere off at college.

Levitsky fought for awareness. Perhaps she'd come back to him after all. Choking on his oxygen tube, straining at the straps on his bed, he managed to open his eyes. Yet what he saw hardly surprised him. After all, Sid must be a middle-aged woman by now, living on the other side of the country—he vaguely recalled hearing—with a husband and three teenaged kids.

Instead of sneakers and jeans and exuberant hair, there appeared before him a helmet and tommy-gun. Light spangled through the porthole in the ward's doorway which silently swung open. With a meaty thumb, the sergeant gestured toward a landscape greener than any Levitsky could bear. "Hey, look, buddy," the soldier informed him. "You're free."

D

Pressing his face between the slats of the wooden play bridge, he smiles. At least I think he smiles, or I prefer to believe it. In fact, he may have grimaced or merely screwed up his face for some inscrutable, mechanical reason, and the expression—smile, grimace, whatever—was not meant for me at all or even intentional. It could be that Douglas, who has now stomped along the bridge and barreled into the bright orange bulb that serves as the terminus for several slides and ladders, does not even notice that I am looking at him. It could be that he is utterly unaware of his father's presence.

What does awareness mean for him, I wonder? Not, certainly, of the other six-year old boy he pushes past, sending him plopping hard on his butt. Does he hear the kid's bawling, I ask myself, or the shriek of the girl whose ponytail he yanks so that he can replace her at the top of the slide? I watch and want to say something, if for no purpose than to pacify the parents who may also be looking on and getting angry. But I see that Dougie's naughtiness has gone unnoticed. The plastic playhouse becomes an echo-chamber of cries that he flees with a high-pitched wail of his own.

What is his world like—confused, indecipherable, ironic? He's grinning still as he scampers past me on route to the sandbox. His blue ski jacket, unzipped, flails behind him, as does his strawberry blonde hair. A hailstorm of freckles, fists like wind gusts pounding the air. So I experience him at that moment, a freaky turn of weather. Other times he's ice and others still he's fire. And always I feel off-guard, exposed and inappropriately attired.

Douglas, Dougie, or merely D—these are the names I call him, though I'm not sure he knows them completely or understands that they signify him. Other words have been attached to him, strangely beautiful words like "echolalia" and "spectrum," and he is strangely beautiful in his detachment. Just look at him, clutching handfuls of some preschoolers' castles and launching them skyward, inscribing sand angels above his head. Look at him circling the box, first clockwise then counter, his orbit recorded by untied shoes.

And what am I supposed to feel? Devotion, of course, flesh of my flesh and all. Love, though love like a shout, bellowed urgently over a canyon that swallows it without a murmur. Anger? Resentment? Fear? Or is it like on those college exams: D, all of the above? And yet every emotion ends with guilt. For I made him, and Dougie is what he is and will be, long after I can no longer look after him on the playground.

Today, though, I track Douglas's peregrinations, from the sandbox to the swings and then to a type of whirligig, a carousel powered by little feet or weary parents. None of these attractions holds his interest, though; none, perhaps, has an existence beyond his mysterious own. For me, they are merely hazards that could swipe Douglas's head or pitch him face-first into rubbered turf. Or opportunities for hurting others, children who come to the playground to play, innocent of the dangers posed by a seemingly harmless peer who sees them not as beings or even things but, I believe, images that take up space. They are not separate from him but part of a larger, undefinable whole, an impenetrable *is-ness* that exists without dimension or feeling.

For Douglas does not feel, not entirely. He runs, he falls, stands and trips again, his shoulder ramming a sliding pole with a force that would send most children screaming. Yet he does not sob, not even a whimper. He does not grind his eyes and raise his tear-glistened cheeks to the darkest clouds and howl out loud for his father.

For if he did, I would come racing. I would sweep him into my arms and hug the hurt and loneliness out of him. I would kiss each freckle and rustle that strawberry hair, zip his jacket and double-knot his shoes.

I love you, Douglas, I would whisper first in one button ear then the other. I love you, Dougie. I love you, D. And he would say, I love you, too, Daddy, and grace me with a real son's smile.

Fossils

Two sets of footprints, one wide, deep, and purposeful, and the other meandering and petite, trailed them on the beach.

"If you were a painter, what colors would you choose for that?" Beatrice asked, sweeping her hand across the horizon.

Eleanor shrugged. "Pearl-gray, I guess. Metallic." She eyed her companion peevishly. "That is such a *you* question."

But Beatrice went on, still wielding an imaginary brush. "Oh, if only I'd been an artist. Capturing the blue-green of the sea, the beige of this sand—the essence of it all. If only I'd been talented in something."

"You were a teacher," Eleanor snapped. "Not a brilliant one, maybe, but good enough."

"And you were a fine principal. Dedicated if sometimes waffley."

The peevish look turned querulous. "What do you mean, 'waffley?'"

"You know, discipline-wise."

"Discipline-wise," Eleanor stiffened, "I was a rock."

Beatrice bent down to pick up a shell. She collected shells, pretty stones, pinecones, all of which, she knew, annoyed her partner. "Rock, really?" she questioned, examining a tiny conch and depositing it in her pocket. "How about the time with that Horenstein boy?"

"He was a special case."

"He was a pain in the rump. Always pinching the girls and getting into fights during recess. You should have suspended him, expelled him, but, no, you had a soft spot for the little brat, didn't you?"

Eleanor huffed. She often huffed when defensive. "He showed promise."

"He showed," Beatrice needled her, "disrespect."

"I suppose today they'd call it creativity. Initiative. Innovation, whatever." Eleanor gazed at the waves as they rose expectantly and crashed. She squinted down the beach, empty at this late afternoon hour. "Today, they'd give it some fancy medical name, AD something or other. What did we know back then?"

"I wonder what he's doing now?"

"Who?"

"The Horenstein boy?"

"Pumping gas, probably," Eleanor chortled. "Or making movies."

The old women glanced at each other, smiled almost, and kept ambling. The one block-shaped with her steel wool hair cut short—too butch for Beatrice's taste—and the other painfully thin with great wisps of gray whirling around her head. While they both wore muumuus, Eleanor's was the duller and more shopworn. She never minded how she dressed, even as a principal. Always the same brown houndstooth suits, the same square-toed flats. Beatrice, though, displayed a weakness for fashion—for tight-fitting, above-the-knee skirts, and heels that clacked on the school's linoleum floors. Her blouses tended to accentuate her bust, which required no emphasis.

Perhaps that contrast, far more than their kindred desires, united them. Beatrice, a timid substitute just out of a Catholic junior college, terrified enough by the thought of a classroom of unruly fourth graders but also grappling with urges she could neither condone nor define. And Eleanor, ten years her senior, seemingly sure of herself and of the façades she needed to maintain.

So did the entire staff of Pleasantdale Elementary, all of them women except for the sixth grade's Mr. Hatchwell, who was actually more womanly than the rest. The oldest were holdovers from the Depression years, when schools hired only single people who did not have spouses to support them. This left the unmarried women—spinsters, society branded them—who, behind the blackboards, forged secret, desperate, bonds.

And none was faster or more frenzied than Beatrice and Eleanor's. The principal promptly took the newcomer under her protection and, eventually, during one drizzly Christmas break, into her bed. The flattery, if not the attraction, was mutual. If not drawn physically to the short, broad-hipped Eleanor, her features strictly functional, Beatrice admired her authority. She envied the diplomas on the principal's office walls that boasted of a real education. But what Beatrice brought to the bed surpassed any stature or pedigree. She brought youth—sprightly, innocent, curious—and a thirst for untapped intimacies.

So it continued for many years, the two of them keeping proper distances during the school day and, on the weekends, slipping away to a bungalow in the mountains. There were some trips abroad—to Spain and the Grecian Islands—and many Thanksgiving dinners. Yet the most cherished passage of their lives came at the end of each summer, at the beach where the other vacationers had already fled the too-cold water. Often, they were the only couple strolling there, with no one to bother them or to wonder why two retired schoolteachers, their age difference now undiscernible, would sometimes hold hands.

And sometimes, too, they would argue. Bicker, mostly, but occasionally Beatrice would berate Eleanor for her slovenliness and Eleanor would dismiss her younger friend as immature. They could raise their voices, even swear at one another—not that it mattered, as nobody was likely to hear.

No one heard, then, when Eleanor, after several moments' silence, sneered, "If I was less than a rock, you were...chalk dust."

Beatrice laughed. She could still chuckle like a schoolgirl. "Why, because after that first year, I wasn't afraid of you?"

"No." A wave sucked loudly as it folded, lowering Eleanor's tone. "Because you couldn't resist her."

"Oh, please, not her again."

Eleanor bent, filled her fists with sand, and in front of Beatrice's face, opened them. "In her hands, that's just what you were. Dust."

The "her" was Melanie. Another junior college graduate, complete with mini-skirt and beehive hairdo, vinyl boots and lip gloss, assigned to the second grade. Eleanor had her down as a ditz, convinced she wouldn't last the year. But others hoped she would—most visibly Beatrice. Suddenly, the principal noticed, both women were missing from the teachers' room. Little notes, even gifts—hairbands, Troll dolls—were left in their mailboxes. The small, black dents that Beatrice's heels made in the linoleum lead straight to Melanie's classroom, long after the recess bell.

Eleanor's suspicions were justified. Beatrice was in love, or so she fantasized. Furtive embraces in the supply room, urgent stares at lunch; she and Melanie mimicked a romance. Over the phone, whispering on the weekends so that Eleanor wouldn't hear, Beatrice would plan Melanie's escape. The two of them would resign from Pleasantdale and move to Canada, to some small, ice-bound town where the locals would revere them as educators and never ask a question.

The date was fixed for the following summer, still several months away. But then Eleanor stepped in. It began with a summons to the principal's office. Melanie's dress was utterly inappropriate for the school, she was scolded, and would she kindly wear a colorless bra. Later, into her file went a complaint, purportedly submitted by a parent, alleging unspecified yet unbecoming activities. Other teachers started gossiping, and soon the young woman was all but banished from the coffee lounge.

No longer so innocent, Beatrice knew exactly what Eleanor was up to, yet she could say nothing. And didn't, not even when Melanie failed to show up for school for an entire week, and another week after that. A month passed, and it was clear to everyone, above all Beatrice, that the student teacher had left town. Perhaps to that little schoolhouse in Canada. Beatrice might have followed her, tried to track her down. But perhaps she was not as in love, or not as grown up, as she assumed. Instead, she remained at Pleasantdale and, that summer, reunited with Eleanor on the beach.

"Chalk dust, indeed," Eleanor triumphed. "And I, I was a rock."

Beatrice watched a seagull skimming the surf. What was one woman's love—all human love—compared to the ocean's vastness, she wondered. "Yeah, a rock," she sighed, and picked up something from the beach. "Well, will you look what I found."

Eleanor did not look. Still, Beatrice in her old teacher's voice, pronounced, "A fossil is the petrified remains of a prehistoric plant or animal."

"What are you babbling about?"

"Over vast stretches of time, tissues are replaced by minerals. The result is a record of that organism which is no longer alive but is now much harder."

"Let me see that." Eleanor snatched an eraser-sized object from Beatrice's grip and studied it. Embedded in the coral-colored brick was a coiled shell whose contours were intricately preserved.

"Maybe I should save it to show my class," Beatrice giggled.

"Maybe," Eleanor snorted. "You should grow up."

Beatrice went silent. She let the fossil drop from her hand and fall between the twin stitching of their footprints. Her bare feet, toes painted, dragged in the sand for a pace or two, until they touched another precious shell. Crouching, she retrieved it and brushed it clean. "I wonder what color I'd paint this?" she asked, seemingly to Eleanor, but really to herself. "Cobalt? Robin's egg?"

"Cobalt." Eleanor answered from several steps behind. Her own feet—ungainly, misshapen—had ceased leaving prints. Her thick hands reached down. "Cobalt, definitely," she repeated as she retrieved the fossil and secreted it away in her smock.

Afikomen

The light in our living room looks as yellow as the little prayer books I can't wait to get through. The pages are stained—bright red with horseradish, brown with gravy, and purple with the wine we guzzle this time every year. Passover? Passed out is more like it, from the shit-shaped piece of fish I can't bear to look at much less eat, and the matzah I can't swallow. And parsley? Supposed to remind us of the bitterness of Egypt, they say. Well, it does the trick. Stuck at this table, waiting too long to be served too much crappy food and forced to read words I can't understand and listen to conversations I wish I didn't, that's just what I feel like. A slave.

Why is this night different from any other night? I'll tell you why. On all other nights, my rich uncle is too much of a bigshot to sit with my father, who my mother just usually ignores. And Dad does his best to come home late. On other nights, I can watch Star Trek reruns or play with the model cars I steal just about every week from the department store but which no one around here ever asks me about. On other nights, I can press my ear to the bathroom door to listen in on what my sixteen-year-old sister, Carol, is doing in there with her dumbass boyfriend, or sneak outside and meet up with Randy and spray-paint stuff on the sidewalk. But instead of doing anything cool, tonight I have to sit here while dorky cousin Steven—thank God he's younger than me—stands on his chair and sings the Four Questions.

Why is this night different from all other nights, he croaks, and I'm dying to answer him. 'Cause this night truly sucks.

There are some fun things, though. I can pretend to drop my napkin and reach under the table to get a peek at Cousin Marjorie, who's fourteen and wears mini-skirts so mini her panties practically hang out. I can drink glass after glass of Manischewitz without anybody counting or dip my finger inside and zap the Egyptians with plagues. But the best part comes at the end, when my sister and my cousins and me go off looking for a broken piece of matzah that my mother hides somewhere in the house. I have no idea why we do this, only that my dad has to buy it back from whichever kid finds it. He has to "redeem" that cracker—so the prayer book says—for five or even ten bucks.

The matzah hunt feels like hours away and, until then, I have to sit here while Uncle Harold rails on and on about Watergate.

"He's a fascist, that's what our president is. A fascist *and* a crook." He slams a fist on the table next to my dad's fork, making it jump. "And *you* voted for him."

Auntie Rita, Harold's wife, looks on nodding while Mom spoons another matzah ball into her husband's soup. Yet Dad doesn't touch it. He doesn't say a word but drinks his wine even faster than I do and gazes into the candles.

"A fascist, a crook, *and* an anti-Semite, if you ask me," Uncle Harold's still shouting. "Haldeman, Ehrlichman—sounds like the goddamn Nazi party. Except for that Kissinger shmuck, the ass-licker. Feel good about that, Artie? That's who you wanted in the White House?"

And still no answer from Dad. Instead, he slumps further down on his chair. The prayer book says we're supposed to do that, slump, or at least lean, for some reason to remind us how free we are. But Dad's not looking too free. He's looking caught between his brother whaling on him and his wife heaping a second lump of fish on his plate.

I look at my dad and feel funny about him. Sad and angry. Embarrassed and afraid. In old photographs yellower than these prayer books, he looks a lot like me. Not too tall but no shrimp, either. No fatso, quick with any ball, probably, or at sneaking model cars under his sweatshirt. Same hair, shorter maybe, but just as kinky, and the nose like a tipped-over question mark. Not the kind of kid who Laurie Finkelstein would go steady with, no way, but no one you'd want to piss off.

Then why is everyone messing with my father? Is it because his belly's gotten bigger, the nose, too, while the kinks are mostly gone, his head shining in the candlelight? Why, when Uncle Harold yells at bad guys in court, does my dad get yelled at when all he wants to do is sell furniture? And why does my Mom, every night except this one when she has to put on a show for the relatives, treat him like Laurie Finkelstein does me, like he doesn't deserve to breathe?

Those are *my* four questions, but no one bothers to answer them or even listen. Uncle Harold's still ranting, "Invaded Cambodia. Fire-bombed Hanoi. *Fire-bombed*—what are we, in the Middle Ages?" His face is the color of those stains in our prayer books. "All that you've got on your conscience."

Dad takes another gulp of wine and nods at me. "Your turn to read," he says, and from too much wine, maybe, I groan.

"No, please," he practically begs me and for a second sits up in his chair. For a second, he looks almost happy, the candles for once sparkling in his eyes. "You've got a Bar Mitzvah coming up in a year or so. It's good practice."

I think about the Bar Mitzvah, all the gifts I'll get and the chance to slow-dance with Laurie. Shrugging, I read. I read about the wise son and the simple son and the son who did not know how to ask. I can't really tell the difference between them—they all sound clueless about what we were doing around that table talking about plagues and eating crackers. Which was why I kind of liked the wicked son, the only one with guts. "What's all this weirdness about," he wants to know, "and do I really have to put up with it?"

Finally, it's mealtime. Chicken with matzah stuffing that makes the chicken taste like talcum powder. Dad hardly touches it but that doesn't stop Mom from giving him second helpings, even thirds. More wine. Auntie Rita, making moon-shaped motions with her pocket-mirror, checks her hairdo and makeup. Carol and Marjorie play with one another's hair, whisper to each other, and giggle. Steven's curled up in a corner—six years old and still sucking on his thumb. Jesus. And I'm about to conk out myself, thanks to Mr. Manischewitz. Thank God, then, when Mom announces that it's time to search for the matzah.

Stevie's a no-show, and the girls complain that they're too old for silliness, but I'm already hunting. Behind the couches, under cushions, inside the magazine rack. Mom may not do much during the day—she's a secretary who can type, she says, eighty words a minute—but she's a demon at hiding matzahs. Once, I found one lying beneath the television antenna only to have her tell me that she hid it there two years ago.

I pretty much cover the dining room and kitchen and so make my way up to the bedrooms. There's Carol's with its pink telephone and posters of the Grateful Dead and my own, a mess of empty spray cans and broken model cars that I'm always being told to clean up. Not even Mom would think of stashing things there. Which leaves my parents' room.

The satin blanket, the puffed-up pillows, the lamps growing out of vases and the corner's porcelain dog—nothing looks disturbed. I go through their drawers only to come up with socks and t-shirts and Fruit of the Loom underwear. But no matzah and no five or ten bucks to redeem it. So I set to work on the closets.

Mom's rattles as I open it, with the belts and necklaces hung on the back of the door. She's got a jungle of dresses in there that are thick with her smell but nothing else. Dad's closet, on the other hand, brings up this cool pair of army binoculars, a wooden box of tie-clips and cufflinks, and piles of sweaters he never wears. Climbing up the cubby holes on the far wall, I reach the highest shelf. Here he keeps his high school album and a bowling ball and then, under some old furniture catalogues, a leather folder.

Magazines. That's what's inside. Two fistfuls of magazines with crinkled covers and a couple pages that are hard to separate. Picture magazines of men without clothes on and doing things that I imagine Carol and her boyfriend do in the bathroom. Things I can't even daydream about doing with Laurie. But these are men and the magazines are in a folder way in the back of Dad's shelf.

My head feels like it's spinning. Not from the wine anymore but something else. Confusion. Excitement. I want to look longer and don't want to look at all, ever, and while I'm deciding, I hear my name being called.

Back into the folder the magazines go, but not before I tear out a single page and fold it into my pocket. How much would that be worth, I wonder. Fifty dollars? One hundred? My name gets hollered again and I holler back, "All right, already, I'm coming!" and head downstairs.

I'm already thinking about the model cars I can buy for once and not steal, and a charm bracelet for Laurie. I'm thinking about my father's face when later, after everyone's gone home, I show him what I've got in my pocket. I'm thinking about it still when I enter the dining room and its stained, yellowed light.

They sit there—Mom and Uncle Harold, Auntie Rita and the girls— all growling. Tired, bored, too full and drunk to move, but desperate to get it over with. Only my father smiles at me as he places his wallet on the table.

"What've you found, my little man?" he asks me. "And how much will it cost me to redeem?"

Metaxis

C aptain A. Biddle, at Skookum Bend, To Samuel Rutledge, Colonel in command of Fort Prudence. Dispatch communicating details of the Caracal Canyon massacre.
Headquarters of the Blackstone Redoubt

March 30, 1841

Sir—I have the honor, if such a word here applies, to record the events surrounding the arcane case of the mountain man Howell, an innominate being, and the deaths of eight of my men.

The concatenation began approximately three months ago, in the depths of a winter dark even for these crepuscular regions and cold enough to freeze one's bones. Shortly after reveille, I was bestirred from my quarters by the westward watch. Scaling the stockade, still buttoning my tunic, I refused the picket's offer of a glass. What I saw was easily ascertainable by the naked—I might say denuded—eye.

It was a mule, Sir. A scrofulous animal favored by the natives as well as by those misanthropes who prefer primitivity to civilization and the company of varmints to people. Only this mule was unlike any I had seen and hoped never again to witness.

Spasmodically it whirled, pasterns kicking up snow, snorting steam and sprouting white beards of foam from its muzzle. The eyes, if not anchored by their cords, might well have leapt from their sockets. Admitting such a brute within our confines was unthinkable and, fearing some rabid contagion, I ordered it destroyed. A single ball from Pvt. Keaton, by far the garrison's best shot, straight to the heart at one hundred yards, sufficed to fulfill my command.

The incident might have been forgotten, even in the lassitude of this post, but for another that fell upon us some evenings later. Once more the sentry's bell sounded and drove me from my bunk. Once more, I gained the parapet to peer through the ramparts and espy yet another four-legged creature wobbling from the tree-line and into our field of fire. The mist that nightly shrouds the mountains served to obscure my vision but only for moments before I discerned that here was not another raving ass but a pair of savages staggering across the snow.

Buckskinned beggars, they were, from one of the surviving tribes in these ranges, sickly and starving and with none of the nobility imagined them by people back East. Except for some off-beam missionary, they endangered nobody and certainly not the town of Blackstone, whose inhabitants I often wished scalped.

Nevertheless, in accordance with our orders, Sgt. Moriarty called the men to arms. The dragoons mounted and the infantry, all twelve of them, stood with rifles presented as I motioned for the gates to open. Into the compound, barefoot and blue from the cold, the Indians shuffled.

Like the mule before them, they appeared deranged. Eyes bulging, bodies twitching, their mouths no longer instruments for communicating but caves from which ghostly wheezes rose. No sense could be made of their stammering, not even by Crow, our Shoshone scout. Yet one word kept repeating itself, and that barely intelligible.

Maxemista, or so it sounded. *Maxemista*, the redskins babbled, which Sgt. Moriarty, also present at the interrogation, promptly Hibernicized into MacMaster. The name caught on with the men, and I confess to likewise citing MacMaster when addressing them. Intimately, in my own mind, though, I recalled long ago one of my father's lengthy lessons. From the Greek, cited in Plato's Symposium. Metaxis.

Do not, Sir, conclude that by drawing on this text I, in any way, wish to flaunt my classical education. My father, a beacon of our faith, countenanced nothing else outside of Scripture. Later, seeking asylum from those bonds in the ranks of another, exchanging preacher black for martial blue, I would gladly have bartered my learning for some such as yours, gleaned at the Academy. Yet there is little escape from notions implanted in the cradle. So, Metaxis it remained and thus shall persist throughout this dispatch as it recounts what subsequently ensued from the woods.

Animals—deer, boar, even an elderly she-bear—all frothing, limbs a-jerk, skittered forward. Their manifest aim was the Skookum River immediately to our rear, to salve their frenzy or drown it. Pvt. Keaton ensured that none reached the banks, much less this post, with numerous well-aimed balls. The sole survivors were three execrable squaws who arrived clutching their papooses, teetering and sputtering those same inscrutable syllables which the troops once again rendered MacMaster and their commander, discretely, Metaxis.

So it continued for well over a month, each day yielding aberrant processions. I had no choice but to double the watch with muskets loaded and primed. Respectful of the days' exertions, I retired early but in full battle dress with nothing but a brazier and bottle as solace. I lay listening to the roof beams crackle under the weight of the snow and the wind which, howling, can drive even mountain men berserk. Proof of that arrived one moonless February night when my solitude was once again interrupted.

Another figure was approaching the stockade, reeling and shrieking. A bison, it seemed, at first inspection, but at closer range was discerned to be a man. A trapper, if such can indeed be called a man for he, alone among the Lord's creation, is devoted to the killing, skinning, and fleshing of fellow beings solely for the pleasure of those who shall never know the carnage involved or the loathsome ogres committing it. Though often hearing of such hunters, I rarely laid eyes on one myself and then only fleetingly. Their custom was to bypass the post and ford the Skookum to Blackstone, there to trade their pelts for victuals and liquor, powder and chaw, and spend the remainder at establishments off-limits to my soldiery. This trapper was headed not for Blackstone, though, nor even for the Skookum. He limped, rather, right up to the gates and with unquotable indelicacy ordered them opened.

A horned man, fittingly, but one whose cornets fell along with his buffalo robe once he was warmed by our fire. That light illumed a specimen of indescribable filth, char-fingered and yellow-toothed, his beard a gallery of all that he had eaten or spewed. The hides he wore were of such a state as would scandalize their original owners. Only his eyes showed signs of humanity and those, through red-rims and rheum, appeared to have glimpsed the inhuman.

Inquiring of his name and the whereabouts of his weapon, I learned that Filkins dwelt in the barrens beyond Hoatson's Gulch and there remained his piece, his bear's claws and snares, none of which were of any use. Not against that. Defining what *that* meant, however, required further probing, lubricated by stew and long draughts of rum.

That, Filkins, plate and flagon trembling, admitted, was like *nothing I never gandered 'fore, not nigh thirty years in these here hills.* Neither man nor beast but something betwixt and bigger, a behemoth. Hair, fangs, and hunger but not for food, Filkins said, but for the butchering of it. For what it killed, it left to rot, with neither meat nor pelage taken, and the dead no longer recognizable as once living. *No carcasses just...muck.* Without a roar or the softest growl, nothing to warn its victims, only a trail of viscous liquid the color of pus and a breath like hellish zephyrs.

Harkening to this tale, as yet remaining speechless, I glanced in Sgt. Moriarty's direction. That strong-jawed face, unschooled but wise, and projecting a power I often envied, fathomed my meaning at once. MacMaster, he said aloud, and I must have murmured Metaxis for Filkins's utensils at once clattered to the floor. Skeletal hands groped for his robe and his head, too, looked skull-like, stripped and blanched by fear. His eyes, reflecting the flames, blazed terror.

Howell, he stammered. Howell, the spelling of which is my conjecture, another recluse of his ilk but more isolated yet, setting his traps above Hoatson's Gulch, in the barrens where no white man ever hazarded, nor red man either. Caracal Canyon, mountain folks called it, though never penetrating it themselves. Too many bobcats, Filkins claimed, chasms and deadfalls. Only Howell, deprived of Christian name and any civil intercourse, remained, season after season, alone. Surely now, though, he would have company and of the most abominable sort.

Save him, General, Filkins pleaded, woefully inflating my rank. *Save him while ye kin.*

The sergeant and I again exchanged expressions. A solitary question seized our minds: to what extent our duty? Situated on the banks of the Skookum, protecting the civilians within its bend, our redoubt was not designed with rescue in mind and certainly not of the nature suggested by Filkins. Yet thinking of that sinkhole, as I often did, that denizen of cardsharps and cutpurses, rapscallions and curs; thinking of Blackstone, like a sluice gate collecting the impurities leaking West, I wondered who was protecting whom and from what—the townsfolk from the forest or the wilderness from the wild?

Another exchange with Sgt. Moriarty, no less resolute for its silence, supplied the answer. Thus it transpired, Colonel, that at sunrise the next day, three of my dragoons and five of my foot stood for inspection. The force, I deemed, was more than adequate for our mission, to remove this Howell from any danger and meet all threats, hominid or other. To this end, I placed Moriarty in command, brevetting him to third lieutenant, and included Pvt. Keaton, the marksman, in his party. In addition to caplock rifles and pistols, carbines and swords, the detail bore the redoubt's deadliest ordnance—a blunderbuss which, though antique, expended canister with withering impact.

From the stockade I watched as, through the enveloping mist, Crow guided the expedition toward the tree line. From there it would follow the Nonoma Trace to Hoatson's Gulch and, from there, up the mountain passes to the canyon. Duties required me to remain at the redoubt, otherwise I would have gladly ridden at the head. Nevertheless, I remained sanguine that the troop would return well before drawing its full week of rations. Of the forty cartridges in each man's pouch, none, I reckoned, would be fired.

For whether we called it MacMaster or Metaxis, such fantastical creatures did not, in fact, exist. Of that I was certain. Tethered from birth to two traditions, the Christian and the classical, revelatory and rational, I elected for the latter, much to my father's distress. Logic can lead to a better life, Agathon, he lectured me, but God alone admits you to Heaven. Right though he was, alas, dreams of paradise have little place in a presidio or barracks nor, I imagine, on the battlefield, and even less on this frontier where detachment from reality can prove fatal. No, phantasms and reveries are luxuries reserved for our countrymen back home, secure before their hearths and pulpits. Here, there is only survival and death and the thinnest string dividing them. In the mountains, I knew, there was a grizzly on the loose or a masqueraded shaman, a medicine man turned murderous by his peyote. Mexican bandits, French marauders—numerous candidates arose—rather than incubi and spirits. Whether ursine or outlaw, this Metaxis was assuredly mortal.

Firm in that conviction, I listened daily for the sentry's bell and at night frequented the stockade, with glass to eye searching for the troopers' return. Yet there was only the mist, pierced here and there by conifers, and the hoots and caws of the forest. Seven days passed and as many sleepless nights, and still not a token. With nearly two weeks gone, I had no choice but to contemplate mounting a search. Before I could, though, one evening whilst reading my Plato, a singular commotion aroused me. Hastening out to the compound, I beheld the ghastliest sight.

Crow, or who I presently deduced was Crow, appeared at first as a blood-soaked totem, torn and lacerated, with scarcely a patch of unmutilated skin. Lips shredded, nose reduced to a stubble, and his remaining eye staring blank. At once, I sent a rider to Blackstone, there to fetch the doctor who was no doubt lying drunk across some billiards table and who, in any case, was unlikely to arrive in time. In the dwindling hours, perhaps minutes, of his life, our faithful scout must speak.

Laying him before the fire, infusing him from my personal flask, I knelt beside this once stalwart brave. Courageous he remained, mustering his terminal breaths to relate the details of the expedition's end. His gasping echoed my own.

Through Nonoma Trace and then up Hoatson's Gulch, the company passed without incident, not even encountering predators. Indeed, the entire forest seemed divested of life, with neither wolves nor deer nor pronghorns in evidence, as if driven off by scourge. No lynx observed the soldiers' ascent into Caracal Canyon, though Crow sensed they were being followed. Something, someone amid the height-stunted trees, behind the snaggletooth rocks, this Howell, perhaps. Testaments to a trapper's presence soon surfaced, in the form of stretching hoops and a pot of the beaver brains used for tanning. A streak of purulent liquid and a foul-smelling odor were remarked upon, but of the man himself, no sign.

It came, Crow panted, *fast*. I lifted his head toward mine and peered into that surviving eye. It? The word he uttered sounded like Maxemista or perhaps MacMaster, but it was lost in his subsequent screams. From these, I pieced together a sequence of horrendous shrieks, of horses neighing and men beseeching God, gunshots bursting haphazardly. Only Sgt. Moriarty retained his composure, Crow said, ordering his men into a firing line and commanding Pvt. Keaton to aim straight for the heart, which he did. But it had no heart. No body, either, only fur and fangs and an unquenchable craving to kill. How many? I pressed him, mercilessly shaking that head as the last of the air rattled out of him. He managed one word, *All*.

There comes a time in any officer's life, as you, Colonel, undoubtedly know, when circumstances dictate decisions. Mine was made by Metaxis. Without the month it would take to bring reinforcements from your fort, I ordered the bulk of my troops to gird. The others, mostly invalids, would be left behind to man the stockades and appear to guard Blackstone, which had nothing to fear but itself.

At dawn we set out, the undersigned on his trusty roan, followed by dragoons and infantry, all exceedingly armed. Without a scout but guided by the signs of the previous patrol, I led my men into the mist and beyond the tree line, along the trace and past the gulch to the foot of Caracal Canyon. Contrary to the Eden that our transcendental Emerson envisions, or his bright-eyed epigone Thoreau, the forest teems with ravenousness and cruelty, a perdition painted green. This forest in particular. As poor Crow described, no wildlife was observed, nor life of any kind, the snow unbroken by paws. The sky, too, seemed swept of birds, with only the badlands rising above.

As a man, I am not gifted like some, such as you, Colonel, with inordinate courage, and many months' desuetude strained my uniform's cut. Yet, at this point in the anabasis, there was no choice but to dismount and lead my troupe on foot. Into the canyon we trekked, single file and disciplined, until we neared the trapper's camp. The smell was to be expected, of rancid meat, but this stench was especially sinister, and the snow stippled greenish yellow. Unsheathing my sword, I ordered all weapons cocked. Such accouterments were useless, alas, against the nightmare we next encountered.

Blood, deep, clotted pools of it, further thickened with flesh. Call it fiendishness, call it horror, but our language lacks adequate words. A kidney there, and a liver, and an eyeball glaring from the gore, and bones, a great profusion of them, but scrambled. Buttons with eagles, forage caps emblazoned with stars, spurs, bridles, belt buckles, and boots, but not an individual in sight nor anything reconstructible as one.

The slaughter caused the loss of many a soldier's stomach, but I managed to retain mine, along with the wits to examine the scattered guns. Most had been discharged, among them the blunderbuss, but none appeared to have found a target. The danger, whatever it was, lurked still. I rallied the few not retching and led them, at saber and pistol-point, onward.

Within a stand of junipers, beneath a granite crop, I descried an abandoned camp—or so it at first appeared. Several paces further revealed a figure seated Indian-style and swathed in skins. The usual beaver, of course, but also muskrat, otter, and goat—so many furs that it was difficult to determine where the animals ended and the mountain man commenced. I could distinguish pallid cheeks between his ringtail cap and whiskers, his lavender lips, and extremities turned to ice. Shaking him to consciousness was futile. Yet he breathed still, I saw, and instructed him raised, blanketed, and cross-saddled. I was determined to revive him, Sir, to learn first-hand the gruesome fate befallen my squad, and unveil the identity of Metaxis.

Thus it transpired that the person I assumed was Howell entered our redoubt. I had him berthed in the blockhouse, the warmest of its ramshackle structures and the most secure. Hot food, fresh clothing, and a constant fire were provided him, and a pistol for his own protection. Whatever fortuitous stroke had spared him, there was no telling how long it would last or whether, denied this final victim, with the scent of his blood in its snout, Metaxis might seek him out.

Days passed. I did not summon the doctor, or rather, could not, that vile inebriate having been caught cheating at cards and Bowied in the thorax. Filkins, who might have confirmed whether my guest was in fact his friend, was last seen slumped in one of the town's saloons and had been thrown insensate into the street. It fell to me to nurse the patient back to health, or at least to intelligibility, depleting my own stock of spirits.

Hope had nearly deserted me when, a week or more later, alone in my quarters, my candle mysteriously snuffed out. Thinking my door ajar, I rose to find it opening to a moonless, windless night and the dusky umbra of thieves. Or what I thought were robbers. Lunging for my sidearm, I aimed and made to pull the trigger. My finger froze, fortunately, at the sound of my name. *Pray do not shoot me, Captain Biddle*, exclaimed a calm, cultured voice. *I've come to convey my gratitude.*

Into my billet he stepped, in borrowed civilian garb—double-breasted frockcoat, trousers, cravat—cleanshaven and combed, as if attending a soiree. A contemporary of mine, roughly my height, if comelier and trim, and the accent of a fellow Easterner: Howell. Apologizing for nearly drilling him, I pulled up a stool, relit the candle, and offered him my only tin cup. The rest of the night and throughout several pleasant evenings thereafter, I tipped that vessel and sipped from my flask while hearing a most hair-raising tale.

Our origins, I learned, were similar as well. Schooled in Latin and Greek, undiluted except by the Bible, torn between temple and church, Howell also had an imperious father. A man of the cloth, like mine, but a seller of it by the bolt, a merchant of self-hewn accomplishments who expected his son to expand them. Howell, though, wanted a different life, not of serge and crinoline but of manliness and adventure, of freedom. And so, at the age that I forfeited my liberty to the service, he reached for his with gambrels and fleshing tools, headed West and sought out the rockiest mountains. Instead of silk, he now wore rawhide, ate what he shot and commixed with nature as it really was, not recreated in some city park or romanticized in books, cold, hale, and refreshingly brutal.

And lonely, Howell soon discovered. For the rigors of pioneer life, he was thoroughly prepared, but not, as it happened, for solitude. The interminable days, the even longer nights, with nothing but a coyote's yelp or eagle's screeching to call company, the rare encounters with Filkins, and those mostly silent. Thoughts, especially, plagued him, as he gutted the critters he caught, their entrails oozing through his hands. Worse than any carnivore, he ruminated, for he killed not chiefly for food but for profit, and yet what, exactly, still defined him as a man? Gazing at the piles of viscera, he began to suspect he was no longer either beast or homo sapiens, but something less than each.

At this point, Howell might have jettisoned his backwoods dreams, hoisted his pelt packs and traded them in at Blackstone. Instead, he ascended. Higher and higher, he trudged, reaching these craggily summits where the air is slender and treetops dwarfed, and only the lions dare perch. *Why?* I asked and Howell smiled shyly. He pointed at the Plato laid beside my bunk, touched fingertips to its cracked leather binding. *The cave*, he whispered, and I at once muttered *of course*.

Again, Colonel Rutledge, it is not my purpose to impugn your familiarity with certain volumes or to presume what our Academy does or does not teach. I merely want to indicate that, from the outset, Howell and I shared a certain sensibility, an unspoken tongue, if you will. His reference, I gathered, was to Plato's metaphor of a man held since birth in a cave, who knows only shadows and simulacra and so confuses them with the world. Only when he escapes his confinement and surfaces into the sun does he confront the ultimate Truth. That is what Howell sought at the top of Caracal Canyon, the truth about himself.

All this I learned over the course of several nights of genial conversation and many more cups of brandy. I cannot speak for every man, but I could not help but be drawn to Howell. The fineness of his features, that firmity of chin and fullness of mouth, hair the color of goldenrod, he might have sat for a medieval master, a Holbein or Donatello. His eyes, feline green, exercised particular magnetism. I felt, nonetheless, that these very blessings disguised some internal curse. With the last of my bottles near emptied, the time had come for Metaxis.

I recounted the entire history, starting with that raging mule, the blathering savages and the half-dead Filkins, culminating in the crimson slurry that was all that remained of my men. Howell nodded knowingly, as though none of this were news, and anticipated my question with his own: *You've read from the dark bard of Baltimore?* Indeed, I confessed, and was grateful to Mr. Poe for vivifying some dreary frontier hours. *Then you fear neither the grotesque nor the arabesque.* Howell smiled again, inscrutably. *Or the malevolent.*

His story began some months ago, in the thickest of winter, with a ferocious attack. Howell was setting one of his traps beside a stream in which he could see his image and suddenly another behind it, but too late. The cougar was upon him, claws and canines sinking into his neck and shoulder. Resisting was useless. Blinded by blood, he collapsed into the water and awaited his demise. His very last thought was *Justice.*

Yet then came a second disturbance, more violent still, and the cat released its grip. Through his half-consciousness, Howell sensed a diabolical presence, a power of outrageous scope, but at that point he passed out. Awakening some time later, he rose dripping by the stream and saw the fang-cuts in his cheek. A clavicle was bored as well, but his body was otherwise whole, which was more than could be said for the cougar's. Eviscerated and split, it lay shredded across several yards. The scene neither gladdened nor disgusted him; rather, shaken and in pain, he dragged himself through the swill and back to his camp, there to minister to his wounds.

Death did not leave him, though. Suppurating, his injuries prevented him for scrounging for food and exposed him to other carnivores. Each night he dozed, feverish and chilled, expecting to be frozen before daylight or devoured, but then awakened to find his fire refueled and nourishment provided, flayed and disemboweled and ready for his spit. Thus, his health resuscitated but so, too, did his fear. Howell was no longer alone.

He paused at this point to regain his composure and to accept a cheroot, yet another of my frontier vices. Raising the candle to its tip, I again took stock of his face which was indeed appealing but also, I saw, strained. As if the wear of those desolate months in the woods still weighed on him, and the knowledge of who, or what, had nurtured him back to life. Howell inhaled deeply and blew the smoke, firebreather-like, up to the rafters. His ominous Iliad resumed.

He never saw it. Or perhaps once, and then only fleetingly, a formless hulk of black, knotted hair which presumably allowed for consumption and sight, though neither mouth nor eyes were indicated. Only a fetor, of which Howell became increasingly aware, and the putrid marks dotting the snow. Of the butchery around him he was ignorant. Not until he regained his mobility and ventured out of camp, not until he came upon the innards and the strewn-about bones, the skulls and sinews, did a grim understanding dawn. An evil was unleashed in the forest around him, ancient and insatiable.

Yet an evil, he believed, with a weakness, and that foible was none other than him, Howell. With no evidence to adduce other than the food and fire provided during his convalescence, and the fact that he was still alive, he came to suspect that the creature harbored some feelings for him, an ardor, perhaps. Why else would he be succored and spared?

Why else, indeed? I wondered out loud, and at once regretted it. Howell glowered at me perturbed or worse, incensed, and for the first time I felt my skin prickling. Why, I wanted to press him, did he not descend from the canyon at that point, escape this demon or whatever it was, seek and receive shelter in our fort? Howell seemed to intuit all this, and without being asked, restoring his composure, furnished me with answers.

He plotted his flight carefully, purposely appearing insouciant, going off to check his traps, replenish bait, & etc. The plan was to wait just before nightfall, the hour when the mountain itself seemed to sleep, to tend to his camp and unfurl his bedding, and slip away in the twilight. He had scarcely concluded these preparations, though, when a gunshot rang through the rocks. Then another, then a great many, followed by what sounded like a cannon. Horrid screams, equine and human, desperate pleas for mercy, and then…silence.

This is all my fault. That is what Howell thought, standing over my troopers' remains. The being, if that was what he could call it, was protecting him, but from what? He had no answer, only the thought to remove the object of sentiment. So he squatted cross-legged in the snow, defenseless to the elements, and waited determinedly for death.

We found him first, though Howell wished we hadn't. *It will not surrender*, he said with a desperate pull on his cigar. Its embers glowed luridly, winking in the dwindling light of my billet and exposing eyes narrowed with pain or, perhaps, rage. The brandy was low, the candle almost extinguished, and I sorely desired Howell's exit. He must have deduced this as well and presently took his leave, but not before once more pointing at my anthology of the first philosopher's works. *Ask Diotima*, he whispered. *She knew.*

I might have pondered this cryptic remark and found a route to Howell's decipherment, but as the door creaked closed, leaving me in gloom, I thought only of Metaxis. What if, rather than follow its beloved here, it was, itself, ensconced? What if I, oblivious as any fur-accursed creature, had stumbled into a trap?

Post haste, I ordered the stockade double-bolted, the blockhouse as well. The reason given was the snowstorm rolling over the mountains, hopefully the season's last. I battened my door as well, with lock, trunk, and table. Such obstructions would prove feeble, I gathered, should Metaxis choose to gain entry. Still, I huddled in my bunk, in battle dress under my blanket and a loaded Colt beneath my head. I lay there awake and shivering, listening to the tempest yowling.

Snow, sleet, thunder and flashes, the storm was the winter's revenge, a parting shot before spring. Limitless hours passed before my door was at last pierced by what I at first took for horns or talons but were soon comprehended as rays. Removing the barricade, I stepped out into a sun not seen for months in these parts, blinding and revealing at once. It was in that truthful light, I realized my foolishness and ran, hands still shielding my eyes, to the blockhouse.

The door remained locked, I happily discovered, but my relief ended upon entry. A hole slightly bigger than a man had been burst through a back wall leading to another aperture, much larger, in the stockade behind it. No remainder of Howell, not even his pistol. Only that smell, that infernal smell, and a wicked excretion in the snow.

The trail led straight for Blackstone and my first thought was the same as Howell's last, *Justice*. Imagine Metaxis amuck in the flophouses, the bordellos, and watering holes, tearing its ruffians to pieces, purging them from this earth. The image entered my mind and then fled it as I remembered our mission: to defend the townsfolk from harm.

Tracking Howell was not difficult, even in the melting snow. I had merely to follow my nose, so to speak, to the very banks of the Skookum. Yet there the evidence ceased. Smoke was rising from the chimneys of Blackstone and the settlement looked undisturbed. Like many a crazed animal before him, I reckoned, Howell had chosen to salve his madness and drown it in the river's depths.

There was nothing to do but return to the redoubt, to begin writing this dispatch, and wait for the mountains to dry. My intention was to undertake another expedition, more heavily armed if possible, retrieving the effects of the fallen and burying whatever might still be interred. The Ides of March came and vanished, and the mud solidified to earth. Once again, with nary a picket to man the parapets, I set out at the head of my troops.

Life had returned to the forest, with elk and moose grazing along the trace and eagles circling the gulch. Even the canyon contained signs of the cats for which it was named. Advancing to that summit, I ordered bayonets fixed. If Metaxis was still in the vicinity, we should fight it with every armament, I resolved, with fire and steel and bare knuckles.

Metaxis did not materialize, providentially, only a hodgepodge of bones. Massive femurs, tibia, and vertebrae, a mandible that might have been a mammoth's or a whale's, teeth as long as tusks. The other remains, to tell by the tatters left by the scavengers that picked them, belonged to Howell. His were jumbled up with the monster's, melded with them, it seemed, except for the hole blasted in the back of the skull and the pistol still wedged in its jaws.

Now, bound inside the redoubt, in my quarters with quill in hand, I reluctantly conclude this report. I say reluctantly for it does not contain conclusions. The events described have made me question my appropriateness for this role, to ponder whether I might be more suitable educating in some small Eastern college or, believing in infamy if not rectitude, inheriting my father's manse. I remember Howell, poor tortured Howell, and the last words I heard him say. *Ask Diotima. She knew.*

Their meaning occurred to me that same day, descending the mountain. No sooner dismounted then I rushed to consult my Plato. I found it, perforce, in the Symposium. "What is not fair is not of necessity foul or what is not good is evil," Diotima tells Socrates. "Love is a great spirit"—a *daimon*, in Greek—"and like all spirits an intermediate between the mortal and divine." Diotima, the prophetess of Mantinea, the philosopher of human half-ness and the battle between our bifurcated selves. Of minotaurs and satyrs, centaurs and pans: the never-ending struggle she called metaxis.

I wish to thank you, Colonel, for the recently received consignment of sugar and coffee, the fourteen barrels of salted pork and the extra drams of rum. While considered commonplace back home, such comestibles, here in this wild, are godsends.

I am, Sir, respectfully, your obedient servant,

A. Biddle, Captain

Day Eight

And God rose from resting and looked upon the world he created to affirm Himself. Gazing admiringly at its surface, he saw that the heavens and earth remained separated, the seas and the land, all swarming, soaring, and crawling with life. The light was still light. "Great," He pronounced.

But, "Not so fast," warned Satan.

A gnarly digit pointed toward a certain cave and the creatures dwelling within. Cowering was more like it, naked and reeking, squabbling over rancid scraps and squirming in their own filth. Partaking of flesh for both pleasure and food. The sounds they made—grunts, growls, whimpers—shamed the glory of birdsong, the royal lions' roar. Even insects had hives and purpose, but not these beings, whose sole objective was to eat, shit, and fornicate throughout this day without a thought for the next. Satan sneered, "Kind of blew that one, didn't you?"

God grimaced and the universe crimped. Of his arsenal of floods and thunderbolts, He chose one and prepared to uncreate.

Yet again, "Why be hasty?" asked Satan. "Perhaps there are things you could do."

Clouds rose in curiosity.

"First, you can give them consciousness. Enable them to distinguish between themselves and the world around them, even from one another. Make them aware of powers greater than theirs. They will know that they are living. They, alone, will know they will die."

Galaxies glistened—God's way of saying, "go on."

"Give them hate," Satan obliged. "So they can fight for reasons other than resources. But grant them also love, the ability to care beyond instinct, not only to nurture but to adore. And with love comes loss. Just watch how these creatures wail once their affections are rejected. See them beg in the face of death. See how, in all their torments, they turn to…"

Comets curled in question marks.

"Of course, to you. For help and deliverance. For peace."

Convinced, God stretched out His mighty hand to make it happen, but Satan once again stayed it. "Hold on." Seems he was just warming up.

"We must also give them fear." Not of the elements or of wilder animals, but of infinite unknowns. Of humiliation and failure, impotence and infertility. Satan cackled. The list was that delicious. "Of mortality and the meaninglessness of life."

If God thought this was over-the-top, that his antithesis—whom He also created—had gone too far, the universe remained silent. The truth was beginning to sink in. Any being so fearful, maddened with hatred and agonized by love, could again appeal only to Him.

"Wonder at the stars. Guilt at not being one. Longing, suffering, hope!" Satan was in a zone. "Each of them leading to you-know-where." The same crooked digit pointed upward.

"And one more thing. A trifle," Satan lied. "Good and evil." To understand that the world is not only rocks and mountains, forests and seas, but a range for working out morality. "A testing ground, if you will." For learning that children are good in a way that rocks are not and pelting them with rocks cannot be. That meeting hate with love is always good but hating love is sinful.

"In short," Satan sighed, "we'll have to give them souls."

For in guiding the soul, what better source could there be than the Lord of All Creation? The horizon, in acknowledgement, blushed. God had heard enough. Eschewing floods and thunderbolts, He merely quoted Himself. "And let there be…"

And there was. As the ninth dawn brightened, the creatures emerged from the cave. Surrounded by others that they now knew to be their neighbors, their mates, and offspring, they covered their nakedness in shame. Freed from memories of squalor, yearning suddenly for Eden, they blinked into the sunlight and threw back their shoulders to the sky.

"Thank you," they said in the first words ever spoken. For God had given them those as well, a language to evoke their love and hatred, to express their fears, and to describe both good and evil. A voice for their incipient souls.

"Thank you," they sang and, "thank you," they cried, and God heard their prayers but with difficulty. Drowning them out was a cacophony of birds and the braying of lions, laced with satanic chuckles.

The Old Osifegus

"When're we gonna get there? When're we gonna get there?" I sang and bounced up and down on the seat, just as I'd seen other kids do on TV. Their moms sometimes got angry with them, but not mine. This was just one of our games—we had a roomful, she said—and instead of yelling at me, she just leaned into the steering wheel and smiled.

"When are we going to get there, Pickle?" she asked without taking her eyes off the road. "Never."

"And how far is never?"

"Forever and back again."

I was still bouncing. "And how far is forever?"

And so it went for maybe an hour or more every day, until we had to stop for gas or use the bathrooms. We ate, when we ate, good food, Mom promised me, not highway crap. And once in a while we stopped in a place with a real bed, a TV, and one time even a pool that I stayed in for hours. My lips, she said, were bluer than my eyes, if that was possible.

Otherwise, we kept to the road. Obeying the speed limit and the other rules because the last thing we needed was a ticket. "A ticket to what?" I wanted to joke, "the movies?" but didn't. One thing was too serious for Mom—the need to stay moving as fast and as far as possible, so it couldn't catch up with us. The Old Osifegus.

"Tell me what it is again."

"What?"

"The Old Osifegus."

Mom squinted up at the rearview mirror and sneered at the idiot tailgating us.

"Is it a person? Is it a thing?" I could be very stubborn.

But Mom just shrugged. "Trust me. If it ever catches up to you, you'll know.

So we drove, mostly in the summer, heading north where Mom said the nights were cooler. Winters, we turned around and headed the other way. I never liked that way. That way was always some school where Mom sent me each morning in itchy clothes and a bookbag that hurt my shoulders. That way were strange kids who stared at me weirdly and asked mean questions like "where do you live?" and "what color's your house?" and "how come we never see your mom?"

"Tell them the truth," Mom said while putting on her lipstick in the mirror. "Tell them you live at 2002 Corolla Court and that your house is Impulse Red. Tell them your mother works in the restaurant business."

These were good suggestions, I knew, but I never took them. I never answered those mean questions but just got off the school bus at some stop where the houses looked nice and then doubled back to the diner where my mom in a white apron snuck me sandwiches. Later, alone, I did my homework.

"There's nothing shameful living like we do," Mom told me. She sounded serious now, brushing the hair from my forehead and kissing it. "I was born on wheels. I grew up on 'em. Many people do and it don't make us any less good. Remember that, Pumpkin."

I did remember it, and sometimes I thought that I was the luckiest girl in the world, driving with my Mom all day and sleeping next to her each night. Well, not next to her, really. She slept in the front seat and I laid down in what we called my bedroom. Some nights, if she wasn't too tired from driving, she'd crawl back and read me books. My favorite was about a girl my age but living a long time ago, going West in a covered wagon.

"Just like us!" I'd shout.

"Yeah, Princess, but we go West *and* East. North *and* South. Everywhere."

"But am I like the girl, Mom?" I'd want to know. "Am I like the girl—what does she call it—a homesteader?"

"You betcha." Her hands cupped my chin and rolled it this way and that. "We have this instead of a home."

After that, I pretended to fall asleep while mom climbed outside for a cigarette. That was the only time she kept the windows open, when she sat on the hood, smoking. Peeking over my blanket, I liked to watch the red dot burn brightly at first and then glow softly in the dark.

I'd wait for her to come back inside and tuck the blanket under my chin. I could smell her sharp-sweet smell and hear a sound like a little cry. Only then would she turn out the lights and lock the doors tight, safe against the Old Osifegus.

Mornings, we'd start out again.

"Where to, Perry-berry?"

"Atlantis!" I'd holler. "The moon!"

"The moon it is," she said, releasing the brake and turning out of the rest area. "First stop, though, Atlantis."

My mom drives hunched a bit, her eyes almost even with the steering wheel. Her hair is cut short like a boy's, with a color much like our car's. She wears ear studs and jeans and sleeveless shirts that show her tattoos—three hearts nearly broken in half.

"Why only three?" I'd always ask.

"I ran out of arm."

"And why broken?"

"Cause hearts are like eggs with little baby birds inside them. One day they hatch and fly, Penelope."

I like it when she calls me by my real name. The name, Mom said, of a woman she'd heard about when she was a kid, maybe from her own mother. This lady lived long ago—longer even than that little girl in the wagon—and waited many, many years for her husband to return from sailing around the world. I liked the name but wondered if Mom got it backwards. Weren't we the ones traveling? And who was waiting for us?

"Nobody, except for you-know-who, and no way we're hanging around for him." I could feel her stepping on the gas a bit and was frightened she'd get a ticket. "We'll keep moving, you and me, and you'll always be my little girl."

"And you'll be twice as old as me."

"Which means that when you're twenty I'll be, let's see, forty." Mom pouted at me but said to the dashboard. "And when you're forty, I'll be…driving."

But I didn't want to grow up. I didn't want to own a car and wash my kid in public bathrooms. I wanted to stay just as I was, gazing out of the back window at the white highway lines trailing behind us like smoke puffs from a train. I liked riding beside my mom, listening to her stories about real-life cowboys and soldiers who never came back from the war. Not once did I feel fear or a need to protect her, not until that night near the ocean.

She promised me we'd see it, when the sun shone through the windshield. Sand, waves, water, she said, bluer than my eyes, if that was possible. But before we could park, the car began to wobble. Mom held the steering wheel real tight and grumbled one of those words she never said around me. Then, nicer, she said, "No problem, Pip, it's only a flat tire."

She told me to sit tight and not open the door for anyone, just before locking me in. I heard her fiddling around in the trunk—the basement, we called it—and slamming it shut. Some clangy noises followed and I felt the car rise and fall. What fun, I thought, until our car suddenly filled up with light.

I pulled down the rearview mirror and saw two headlights like scary eyes pull up behind us. Then the lights went out leaving a burning red dot, just like my mom's cigarette, only I didn't think it was hers.

And then, nothing. I sat there for I don't know how long, wanting to bawl, wanting to holler for her and run out of the car. But I didn't. No, I just sat and played with the dials, imagining I was watching TV. I waited and waited until my cheeks got wet and my legs started shaking. But there was no sign of her, not even a red dot. Only quiet.

Then, suddenly, her door opened, and Mom fell in. She was breathing hard and smelling strong—not only her smells but some others.

"Mom?" I asked, because she didn't brush my forehead like she usually did and kiss it. "Mom?" because she didn't call me Poppy or Pooh

Bear or even Penelope. But she just sat there breathing for a while before finally turning the key.

That's when I saw it. In the glow of the dashboard, on her arm and sprinkled around those broken hearts, blood.

I cried, "Are you okay?"

She looked down at her arm and, with her other hand, rubbed the arm clean. "Fine. No problem."

"What happened?"

"Nothing. Nothing." She turned on the car and swung back onto the road. "The Old Osifegus."

I slept that night to a crashing sound that in the morning I saw was waves. The sand was very white and the water shiny but not as blue, Mom said, as my eyes.

And for the first time I thought: someday I will grow up. I'll get a job and make lots of money and buy us a real home with real beds, TVs, and a pool. Mom won't have to drive anymore, won't have to run away. We can lock the doors at night, the windows, too. Nothing will ever catch up to us.

"Well, looks like we've run out of country," Mom laughed a bit and hit the wheel with her palms. "Looks like we'll just have to turn around."

Now it was my turn to pout.

"Alright, Pepper, you win." She brushed the hair from my forehead. "But first, we'll go for a swim."

Surprise Inspection

With two fingers on each side of its brim, Hardet straightened his drill sergeant's hat. He stuffed his shirt tight inside his canvas web belt and shot out his military cuffs. Looking down, he inspected the stripes on his sleeves and the crease in his trousers. His shoes vaguely reflected his face—the heatless blue eyes, the functional nose and mouth, chin like a mallet. Only when assured that his appearance was in terrifying order, did he hit the power switch, push open the door, and storm inside the barracks.

"Lights on, limp dicks! Up and out! And I mean fucking *now*!" he shouted in a clipped cadence, heels percussing each bark. "Attennnn-*hut*!"

But Company A was already out of its bunks, on its feet, and standing pillar-like.

Hardet stood silent for a second, just long enough to glance up and down the row of t-shirts and skivvies. The underclothes, like their wearers' hair and skin, gleamed under the naked bulbs. Hoisting his most pissed-off scowl, the sergeant resumed:

"Tell me I'm wrong, *please*, but you are the sorriest lump of duck shit I have ever seen. You're worse than duck shit. You're snake shit. Fuck, you're *widget* shit."

No one in the unit flinched, much less shivered. Not even the first turtle-head who remained motionless while Hardet squared off in front of him, rose on spit-shined shoe-tips, and hollered, "You *are* widget shit, aren't you, Private?"

"Yes, Sergeant!"

"Yes, Sergeant," Hardet mimicked him, falsetto at first, then roared, "Yes, Sergeant *what*?"

The joe replied without hesitation—without, Hardet noted, a blink. "Yes, I am widget shit, Sergeant!"

"As you were."

If the enlisted man eased, Hardet didn't perceive it. He was already pouncing on the next one.

"And you, rust-bait, what's your number?"

"3335335."

"Holy mother of twat, what do we have here, a fucking vibrator?"

"Sorry, Sergeant." The cherry repeated and roared. "3335335!"

Hardet snorted and moved on.

"And you, junk heap, where the fuck are you from?"

"I'm from Sunnyvale, Sergeant."

"Sunnyvale? Sounds like some senior citizens' whorehouse." Hardet pouted and puckered his lips like some old, sad man. "It does, don't it? Like poon town for geezers."

Nobody spoke. Nobody nodded or laughed, certainly.

"Not funny?" Hardet asked the barracks. "Not funny, microwave?" He turned to another cherry. "And what junk yard are you from?"

"I'm from Sunnyvale, too, Sergeant."

A voice at the end of the row volunteered, "We're all from Sunnyvale. Sergeant."

The pucker vanished from Hardet's mouth, along with his anger. "All from Sunnyvale," he said under his breath. "Course you are."

Another silent moment followed, different from the first. Hardet gazed not at the sprogs but at the caged lights and the whitewashed walls that had witnessed so many inspections like this and so many green recruits. But now there were no more chinks or spics or jiggaboos. No bible thumpers or bagel biters. Hayseeds or sewer rats. No one to dub four-eyes or pizza-face. And no flabby lumps of duck shit to forge, through brutal discipline and training, into soldiers.

Hardet planted one toe behind a heel and pivoted. Back straight, head pinioned, he marched at precisely thirty inches per step, arms fast at his sides. Past the line of t-shirts and skivvies, wheaten hair and blemishless skin, he strode, but paused at the open door.

"You, A Company, I know that A stands for Androids," he said without about-facing. "And I don't give a fuck. Wherever you come from, whoever made you, you're mine now and I will break you. I will break you, day and night, until broke feels like fixed. And then I will build you, from scrap if I have to, into men. Fighting men. Real men."

Pinching his hat brim, stiffening, Hardet uttered, "That's all," and exited. He closed the door behind him and stood alone in the darkness. Then, with a sigh, he hit the switch, and powered down his company for the night.

The Scar

"I think I like the macramé."

He listened as a siren revolved in the night, spinning down Amsterdam Avenue. Blue and red lights, like trapped tropical birds, darted around the walls.

"Did you hear me? The macramé, I said."

The siren rounded 110th Street, he reckoned, out of earshot. The colors seemed to escape through the open window.

"You didn't. You didn't hear a word."

He caressed the cleft of her back, tense where her thin shoulders met the spine. "I am. I am listening."

"What did I say, then?" He could feel her flanks contract.

"About the invitations…"

"What *about* the invitations?"

"You liked the design we saw today."

"Yes, but which one of them?"

He remained silent, stroking some moles, reading her body's braille. He felt her sigh.

"The macramé background, I said. It'll make the lettering stand out. You don't want people to look and just think, 'yeah, your run-of-the-mill wedding.'"

"No, course not." He patted the back of her hair. Longish, dark, worn straight the way he preferred, though someday—after their first child, he assumed—she'd cut it.

"Macramé it is, then."

He did not argue with her often. An honest, level-headed, woman, a stable woman—in truth, she was almost always right. It was one of the qualities he admired most. That and her values—those counted, didn't they?—her work ethic. Inexperienced when they'd met, she seemed capable, he believed, of someday satisfying him. Meanwhile, there were her parents who loved him, and his parents who loved her, responding to the news with a joy so deafening he had to jerk the receiver from his ear. They deserved that after all he'd put them through. Difficult child, untethered adult. He liked the feeling that all their travails had been, in the end, rewarded.

He looped his arm around a ribcage, fit his body into the curve of hers, and embraced her so tightly his shoulder pressed against her cheek. In the fractured light that escaped their blinds, he could detect the strict ridge of her jaw, the outline of an ear that he secretly associated with furry animals. Her neck was thin but not so thin that he feared hurting her while resting his chin in its crook. Firm enough breasts that could be grasped but not too hard, she'd once scolded him. So, sometimes the hard way, he'd learned her limits.

Another siren whirled. Their two-room apartment came without appliances, without anything really, but especially without air conditioning, which meant they slept with the window open to summer nights like this. City smells—hot sidewalk, pizza, faint garbage—melded with the scents of hairspray and lubricant heavy above their bed. Four floors below, a man cursed loudly in Spanish.

"Jesus, what's that?"

He shrugged, "somebody's mighty pissed off."

"No, *this*." Her cheek tapped the ball of his shoulder, which was still raised in shrug. "I've never noticed *that* before."

Perhaps it was her modesty or his own embarrassment, but they'd rarely seen one another fully unclothed, confining their lovemaking to darkness. Furtively, she undressed each morning, allowing him merely glimpses of a body slim, even bony, well-proportioned, womanly. In time he'd come to know it better, he told himself. Someday, they'd explore.

"That what?"

"This thing you have on your skin here. It's a scar?"

His chin pivoted to let him see what she had; the old wound framed in a random patch of light. He nodded into her neck.

"How come you never told me about it?"

"You never asked."

"Well, I'm asking."

Now it was his turn to sigh. His pelvis pushed and retreated from the back of her thighs, skin sticky with sweat. "Must I?"

"Yeah-uh."

"Alright." He brought his wrist up to her lips so that she could kiss it. He needed that encouragement before returning to that place. The kiss he received was perfunctory, meaning he had to begin.

"I grew up in a tough neighborhood. I *did* tell you that. Tough kids, big kids and I was, well, different. Kind of fat, kind of klutzy. Bully bait. They used to wait for me when I got off the school bus. Gang up on me. I tried to run. There was a neighbor, a Mrs. Vogt, who lived a few houses from the stop. If I could reach her front door before they did, she'd let me in. But I wasn't a fast-enough runner. Most days, they caught me before her driveway. They beat me up pretty bad. Gary Prezzisosi kicked me in the kidneys. Buddy Edmundson broke my nose."

She shifted faintly beneath the sheet. "And the scar?"

For a second, he considered turning on the light. He could show it to her in more detail. The ragged curlicue, thickening and swelling as it twirled. His fault, actually. If only he'd showed it to his parents right away instead of keeping it hidden for days, weeping through the band aids and his shirts. By the time they noticed it, the mark was permanent.

"They caught me one day. Not even halfway to Mrs. Vogt's, they caught me and put me up against a tree. They got hold of some horse rope and tied me to it."

"Horse rope?"

"I don't know. It's just what we called it. I guess they used it for horses. But a real thick rope and long. It wrapped around me and the tree with plenty left over."

"And then?"

"Then?" His body stiffened, his chin burrowed into her nape. "Then they whipped me. With the end of the horse rope. Ten, twenty times, I don't know. All I remember is that it hurt more than anything I'd ever felt. That I screamed and howled. I can still see the bark of the tree in front of my eyes."

"How terrible..."

"I cried for help. I begged them to stop. But they just went on whipping me. I could feel the rope cutting into my skin, across my back. On my shoulder..."

A car with a broken fuselage clacked down the avenue. More cursing in Spanish, from two men now: an argument.

"I can feel the pain and worse than the pain."

Her head motioned side to side, dislodging his chin, forcing him to continue. "The humiliation. It's why I never told my parents. Never told anyone, ever, about any of this. The humiliation..."

The bed was shivering, vaguely at first but then with a rocking motion that revealed its uneven legs. For a detached moment he thought how interesting it was that their bed reacted the same way to sex.

"Don't you see?"

She didn't, apparently. Or maybe she did.

"The whole time I was tied up, the whole time I was being whipped, I knew that I could have escaped. I knew it. I knew it."

He knew it several more times, he told her, but she couldn't hear him because his words were lost in his sobs. His face slid downward, replacing the sharp chin with wetness. He cried into her sinews.

"The shame of it. The shame..."

He cried and if she moved at all it was into herself. Knees subtly folding, forearms shielding her breasts. No matter, he assured himself. In time she would learn to cope with such things and in her stable, level-headed way.

A third man joined the argument downstairs and a siren tumbled toward them. The reds and blues again fluttered through the blinds and into the walls.

And he would find a place for the past, safe behind Mrs. Vogt's doorway. The scar would deepen, darken, fade maybe. Or maybe not. Either way, she would never ask him about it again.

The Man in the Deerstalker Hat

In the last booth in the back of the bar, where the reek of stale beer and cigarettes mixed with stink from the john, he waited for me as planned. The bar was the cheapest in town and dim, the booth feebly lit by an old pinball machine that nobody bothered to unplug. Yet, even there, he pressed himself into the darkness of the corner. No matter. He knew who I was and why I'd come. Precisely in places like these, he knew, deadly contracts are signed.

I slid onto the opposite bench. "Name's Ray," I said stupidly, and then looked stupider still. "You?" In the depth of shadows, I thought I discerned a smirk.

"Ray," he said after a pause.

"Thank you," I said, trying to control my nerves. "You can't imagine how long I've waited for this. How long I've scrimped."

The man stayed silent. He didn't shake my hand. And still I babbled. "We're talking about someone who ruined my life. He ran our business into the ground. He stole, he embezzled. He destroyed me."

The man interrupted me, "Let's get down to it."

"Yes, of course. It."

From my jacket pocket, I extracted an envelope so stuffed it had to be rubber banded, placed it on the table and pushed it toward him. The hand that took the payment was surprisingly delicate—an artist's hand.

I was expecting something meatier and scarred. The grip, though, was steady and the movement, sweeping it from the sticky table top, graceful. But then I recalled: the guy was a professional.

"Gambling, whoring, booze, drugs. He did it all."

"When?" the man asked.

"His entire life."

"No," the man named Ray grunted. "When?"

I cringed at my own clumsiness. "Tomorrow afternoon," I answered. "Quarter after twelve, on the dot."

"On the dot. Yes. And where?"

I produced a slip of paper which he snatched from my grip and held up to the flickering light. Green and purple played on his wrist.

"Easy location," I offered. "A few blocks' walk from here."

"Thank you. I'll drive."

I continued, "On the street corner there's this round antique clock. You know, the kind that they used to put up outside of pharmacies and such. Still keeps time, still rings a bell exactly on the hour—you can hear it all over town. And fifteen minutes after that clock strikes twelve, that man will be standing in front of it."

"You sound very sure."

"Oh, I'm sure alright. You see, it wasn't enough to wreck me financially and poison my name, now he's extorting me." Elbows on the table, I leaned forward and rasped. "We set up a meeting for that time, right in front of the clock. He thinks he's getting paid."

"And I'll know him how?"

"Easy. The bastard's a dandy. Always wears a deerstalker hat, even in winter." I allowed myself a laugh. "You can't miss him."

"No," he responded. "I won't."

From somewhere in the gloom, a nod. I felt he was starting to rise and almost reached out to stop him.

"I had no choice, you understand. There's only so much humiliation that one man can bear, so much hate." I heard my voice growing louder, paused, and suppressed it back to a whisper. "We're not talking vengeance anymore. It's justice."

He moved, then, shifting from one end of the bench to the other and yet managing to dodge the ricochets of light. All I saw was the sleeve of a military-style jacket and a curl of boyish blonde hair.

"I'm sorry," I blurted out. "I know I must sound like an idiot. You probably don't hear this stuff."

The man chortled, "You'd be surprised."

He had one leg out of the booth. If the pinball machine illuminated his face, I could not see it. Only the turned-up collar of his army parka and a few more whorls of hair. "One other thing…"

I thought he would simply ignore me or even drop the envelope back on the table. In his business, question-asking customers were a liability. But, no, he hesitated and, without turning, spoke. "He won't feel any pain, if that's what you're wondering."

"I wouldn't mind it if he did."

With that, the man named Ray drifted out of the pinball light and disappeared into the murk of the bar. But I remained seated for hours. No matter, the bar never closed and its tender—if there was one—never noticed. A pitcher of beer would have been cherished, and a succession of tequila shots, but the last of my cash had gone into that envelope. There was nothing to do but wait out the night and the morning.

During that time, I thought again about the devastation my enemy had caused me. The bankruptcy, the wife who left because of it, the kids I no longer see. The death of my reputation in a town too small to disappear in. I can't even walk down the street without wanting to hide my face.

* * * * *

If the sun rose outside the bar, if people went to work, took their coffee breaks, I could not tell. Still lurking in the last of the booths, steeped in stench and the pinball's strobe, I sat and counted the bells. Ten, eleven, the corner clock struck. And then, finally, noon.

Only then do I pick myself up from the bench. More numb than nervous now. I feel ready, I feel relieved. Justice and revenge are near.

No need to rush, I tell myself. In fifteen minutes, I can easily walk those few blocks. Exiting the bar, squinting into the midday glare, I say out loud, "Just look innocent," and flip on my deerstalker hat.

The Secret of 16/B

Varda wiped her forehead with the back of a wrist and reached for the Number 6 scraper. Even under the black, non-reflecting net, the newly risen sun spiked the temperature to unbearable. Especially in section 16/B, located at the epicenter of the site, far from the sparse eucalyptus trees that shaded its perimeters. Heat was an inescapable discomfort of her profession, along with back and shoulder pains, chaffed knees, dust-inhalation, and snakes. Only here, at Azaria, lurked entirely unusual hazards. Curses, imprecations, and the occasional stone tossed high over the "Danger: Excavation" signs to penetrate the net and smack some defenseless archaeologist.

Bertolt, her colleague from Freiberg, had already been rushed to Hadassah Hospital with an oozing head wound and a possible concussion. Later, there had been talk of postponing the entire expedition. The government reportedly met in an emergency session to discuss the crisis, and the Foreign Ministry set up a special task force to deal with its diplomatic fallout. Only the press rejoiced in the controversy inflamed by those probing the earth for remnants of villagers who lived two thousand years ago, while their descendants shouted maledictions and punched the air with their fists. The Ultra-Orthodox Jews protested the desecration of their ancestors' bones and Palestinian Arabs demonstrated against an attempt—so they saw it—to stake an Israeli claim to their land.

Varda, never a political person, an atheist, understood little of it. She felt nothing, not even fear. Only the slight gratification of seeing two peoples so opposed at present united in protecting the past.

The police assured the team that they would not let the rabble get within rock-chucking distance of their work, and for the past two days, at least, the worst that had happened to Varda was a bee sting. She'd even stopped hearing the Arabic and Yiddish swears, and again focused on the gentle rasp of her scraper.

This was her favorite tool, reserved for the lowermost layers. Meters beneath the topsoil with its detritus of plastic bags and soda cans. Under the strata of machine gun bullets and musket balls, the Turkish pipes and Mamluk pottery. Down, down, to the bedrock of what the aerial photos had indicated was buried beneath these flinty Judean Hills. A mid-sized farming community, complete with modest dwellings and workshops, and ritual baths—the tell-tale sign of an ancient Jewish community destroyed, most likely, by the Romans.

And sure enough, here, at maximum depth, she found the crust of that trauma. Ash and bitumen, a jigsaw of shards scattered as if by sword-tip. That is where she began, around the shattered amphorae, scraping. Number 6, reminiscent of a dentist's implement with its textured grip and its hooked, stainless steel tip sharp enough to cut human skin, could shift bits of soot aside without disturbing what lay underneath.

That, Varda knew, could be anything. Coins in near-mint condition, utensils, perhaps even parchments—anything that a simple man might hide at the last moment before fleeing. Anything a believing man— and these Jews believed—could retrieve once the Roman millstone had smashed over them.

So she scraped, much as she had for the past three decades of her career, burrowing particle by particle, through centuries, seasons, and days. Wearing a pair of old gardening gloves, with army-issue knee pads and her head concealed in a floppy kayaking hat, she bent over a square slightly larger than her face, pausing only to exchange the scraper for a makeup brush that whisked aside the loosened filaments. Methodically, she worked, diligently and patiently, aware that the slightest mis-movement could ruin a discovery.

She scraped and brushed and wondered for a moment what anybody might find, two thousand years from now, excavating her life.

Not much. An ambitious student with limited time for social matters, much less a family. Nothing resulted from a short marriage in her twenties—another archaeology student, a sweet boy but unserious, today a businessman with a wife and three kids. There was, in fact, a child, or rather the beginnings of one, but the timing, just before her thesis presentation, was all wrong. Nothing unearthable remained.

She brushed and noticed the emergence of a rectangular shape. A small table, maybe, or kneading board. Not wooden or stone but baked clay—an oven? She scraped again, resisting the urge to gouge quicker. She strove to focus but found herself, once again, boring back to more recent years. That time when, in a fit she barely understood at the time and now could only recall incredulously, she attempted single motherhood. But that, too, failed—some vague ovarian deficiency— and she returned to work, telling herself that it was all for the better. Otherwise, she might not have been here, at the Azaria site, slowly revealing this relic.

An oven, indeed. Here were the fired tiles that intensified the heat. Here was the lid for inserting the dough, the eyehole for watching it rise. Protocol called for informing the head of the international team, a distinguished professor from Chicago, and documenting the find. Photographs would be taken, measurements made. But for once, Varda hesitated.

Her wrist again trolled her forehead. A fly made her upper lip twitch. From nearby sections came the rasp of other tools and, more distantly, the shouts. Without thinking, she put aside the Number 6 scraper and bit the fingers of one glove.

The hand that emerged was the hand of a much older woman— leathern, nails clipped and unpolished. This, too, was a tool. She inserted in into the oven's opening and flexed her fingers inside. They touched something. Hard yet not heavy and with a human form she could already feel through her calluses. Pinching delicately, she extracted it.

She blew on its surface—how unprofessional!—and shook off the dust. A statuette. Though smaller than her palm, Varda instantly made out its abnormally enlarged breasts and hips, its sex intimated with a V. A fertility goddess, Bona Dea, probably, or Aphrodite. Crudely crafted, as one might expect in the provinces, but nevertheless irrefutably pagan. Outrageously pagan here, in a village of believers in the one God with no face who prohibited the slightest human likeness. Hidden in an oven so that not only the Romans would not find it, but neither would her own people.

Her. Why did she assume the owner was a woman? Because, she reasoned, who else would conceal this most invidious of sins in an oven? Where else might a man's hand never wander? And the figurine—rustic, pathetic, a testament to the despair of one whose prayers remained unanswered. So despairing, Varda surmised, that she was unable to smash the idol even as the enemy approached.

Varda glanced over her shoulders at her teammates, each confined to a section, bent and scraping. She glanced up at the plastic net that diced the sun into razor-edged spangles. Then, with a licked finger, she wet the statue's face.

From under the dust, peeking through millennia, a smile emerged. Half-impish, half-empathetic. A god on my side, Varda thought. The deity dedicated to voluptuous youth and fertility, that nevertheless shared her regret. That grinned at the middle-aged woman with arthritic knees and rounded shoulders and the hands of a day laborer who, despite her sacrifices, would never head her own dig.

All that could change now. Easily, sprinkling dirt around the antiquity and returning it to the oven, she could summon the Chicago professor and indicate she may have found something. The others would gather, hunching around her section as the photographer pushed through. The oven would be revealed and then, with the leader's permission, she might be able to reach inside and remove its contents. Cheers would ring out from the international team and the press would headline, "First Century Jews Worshiped Sex Goddess!" The protesters, Ultra-Orthodox and Arab, would lay down their stones and vanish. Nobody fights over pagans.

But she would remain with her find. She could almost imagine the controversies it would stir, the academic articles devoted to it, and ultimately the special exhibit in which, glass-encased and coned in dramatic lighting, tourists would line up to view. Who knew, during the next excavating season, she might even be granted a dig.

Or not. Protocol called for the team leader to get all the credit. Varda might merit a footnote, at best, if he were generous. She pondered this as a commotion arose on the northernmost flank of the site. No doubt some volunteer chancing on a coin or another of her colleagues struck on the head. More shouts, interspersed with police whistles. She pulled the glove back over her hand, tugged it down with her teeth, and laid the statue on her palm.

It smiled at her as it once smiled at another woman who, childless and aging, appealed to other powers. A woman who, with the crunch of hobnailed soles approaching, concealed her secret in the one place neither her husband nor her neighbors would ever look, where even the war-fires could not singe it. She sealed the lid and—so Varda imagined—covered the oven with dirt. Only then did she join the others in escaping the village, over the scraggly hills into exile.

Varda retrieved the Number 6. Held firmly, at precisely the angle she was taught, it could mend as well as scrape. It could restore the embers to their traumatic state, inter the lid and seal the eyehole, leaving barely a fold. With a hand as expert as it appeared ungainly, she blanketed the oven with ash. Then, rising, slapping her knees, she marked the section with a flag. This meant that 16/B was thoroughly cleared and that—according to Azaria's protocol—need never be excavated again.

Beautiful Bivouac

On a distant ridge, an artillery shell exploded in a plume of phosphorous.

"Beautiful," one of the soldiers—Marciano, he thought—remarked.

Arkus snarled, "No, it isn't. It's disgusting." His judgment was clearly political rather than aesthetic and touched off a round of drowsy observations that for a moment divided the unit into those for and against the war—or all wars in general.

Better to talk about that than Miller's death that morning. His half-head angled toward the sky, his thoughts, dreams, memories piled pink in the dirt. Better than to try to recall Bardugo the day before. And so, beauty.

He came down on the beautiful side, at least with shellfire. The twirling and sometimes entwining blossoms reminded him of bougainvillea or a bouquet of Queen Anne's lace. But he said nothing. Indeed, on all the issues already raised around the bivouac—the weather, the lack of fresh socks, speculations about when they'd move out and to where—he remained silent. Instead he stood there, just outside the huddled circle, awkwardly cradling his gun.

Awkward was the operative word for him and not only because of his inability to become one, as his officers urged, with his weapon. Even before the army, he never fit in. The kid who kept to himself in the classroom and who hid most evenings in his room.

Perhaps the army would change all that, he once told himself. What with so much marching rather than socializing, discipline instead of charm. But the military only accentuated his otherness. Not one of the boys, he was now not among the men who sat and chatted so effortlessly, their rifles laid crosswise across their laps.

The impromptu campfire they'd lit from empty ammo crates cast molten light on the soldiers' faces, filling their creases with gold. These faces, too, seemed beautiful to him—manly and saintly and strangely immortal. But that, too, set him apart. His own face was a frightened child's.

He'd seen it earlier that day during the fighting. Briefly, in a shard of window that somehow survived the blasts, he'd met his own reflection. There, sweating beneath an oversized helmet, was the most terrified expression he'd ever seen. He felt sorry for its owner. But then Sergeant Ramon ordered him to move his ass, and he moved, mindless with fear.

An animal fear, the fear of an insect scurrying from a boot. This, alone, redeemed battle. For those endless minutes under fire, no other thoughts existed. No stink of shit and cordite coiling from his uniform, no body parts littering the street. Crouching for cover, he forgot the women beyond his equal, the father he could never please. His lack of professional success, his loneliness—what, with people he'd never met trying to kill him, could be less pressing?

But all of his inadequacies returned to beset him the moment his unit regrouped. In the night, hanging back from the others, he was once again the outcast, the one who, despite his uniform and standard armaments, remained different.

Another shell erupted in the distance, just as the report of the first one thumped past them. The sound always reminded him of oil drums barreling down stairs. A fighter jet lacerated the horizon. Bullets traced ellipses in the dark.

Marciano said, "It's art, I tell you," and Arkus spit, "Art, my ass. It's garbage."

And still he thought, "Beautiful," without saying the word. "All of it. All of you. Beautiful."

Cigarettes were passed around and a can of something which once was turkey. They ate and they puffed, their eyes like illuminated craters.

No one bothered to sleep. Dawn would break soon anyway. Another day which for some of them might be the last.

He stepped further back as the men rose to their feet, shouldered their guns, and palmed their helmets. Over the ridge, the sun appeared, a fresh wound. Armored engines grumbled and roared. Soon they'll be shooting at me, he thought with a sense of both dread and relief. Time to cower again, in the comforting solitude of fear.

An Agent of
Unit Forty

Ignoring the "Please spare the grass" sign, the students crossed the quad. They huddled and jostled, laughing some of them. All hung back from their professor.

"What are you afraid of?" one of them chided another, an athletic blonde, who insisted they keep distant. "He's going to call you counterfactual?"

"He needs his space," the sophomore explained and held out her arms so that none of her classmates could pass. "Besides…"

A snicker from the rear of the pack. "Besides, what, he won't stare at your boobs?"

"Besides," she huffs, "he could slit your throat. You know what he did before this."

By "this" she meant the selective college and its faux-gothic buildings, the gardens, the quads' awakening green. "This" included the professor's reputation as the world's foremost expert on World War I, his Pulitzer and Bancroft, his lecture halls invariably packed. The suits precision-made in Paris, the shoes hand-tooled. All that and emerald eyes, swells of salt-and-pepper hair, and a gymnast's physique preserved well into middle age—a handsomeness bordering on beauty.

Out of earshot of the students behind him, Professor Morris did not actually hear their conversation, but he imagined it. Such talk was going on all around campus. Ever since his secret was revealed. Asked by an undergraduate reporter for a reaction to the revisionist historians who declared war on his work, he grunted, "I know how we would've handled them in the unit."

The unit? The news ricocheted around school and hit a local newspaper before finally penetrating the national media. On route, the Unit acquired a capital "U" as well as a number, Forty. That was the office which, according to Morris's writings, broke the German code during World War I. But unidentified sources now spoke of new missions. Black ops, espionage, and liquidations—all too classified to record. And Professor Morris had been a member, perhaps under a pseudonym, but certainly in a younger life, explaining a gap in his resume between Amherst and Yale.

The story churned up waves of speculation, admiration from some quarters and from others, disgust. In the faculty club, colleagues treated him with renewed deference or reinvigorated spite, avoiding eye-contact over the salad bar. Administrators pointed out his office to visiting donors and janitors stopped mopping when he passed. But among the students, especially, the reaction was marked. To them, he was no longer Professor Morris, academic superstar and author of too many publications to list, but Benjamin Morris, an agent of Unit Forty.

Throughout, Morris said nothing. No confirmation or denial— indeed, no sign that anything had changed except for a subtle uptick in his rakishness, a predatory glint in his gaze. Even his detractors, those upstart lecturers who viewed the Great War not as the miscalculation of generals, but as a clash of market forces exacerbated by gender and race, suddenly seemed restrained. It was one thing to dismiss a colleague as reactionary, another when that colleague could garrote you.

The situation delighted Morris. To think, a single comment to a college newspaper and his career—even his life—veered in a brighter direction. There was no downside, he felt, just as long as he kept his mouth shut about the Unit and fended off further questions with a peremptory, "Sorry, can't go there." And he did for several months while the articles about him multiplied, along with invitations to TV talk shows, all declined. The curiosity would subside soon, he figured, an oblique chapter in a linear but illustrious life.

Morris erred. An inverse relationship emerged between his silence on Unit Forty and the tales spiraling around it. Suddenly, those same anonymous sources were describing a hit job in Serbia, the elimination of a long-sought war criminal holed up in a mountain retreat. Forty got him there, in his bed, the trigger pulled by a black-clad gunman whose face, behind the balaclava, was Morris's. Then there was Damascus. Abu Yusuf, the head of an international terrorist ring responsible for bombings in eighteen cities across five continents. Dozens had died, and so, ultimately, did Abu Yusuf, while gazing into the eye of a silencer leveled by—who else?—the future Professor Morris.

Nevertheless, he kept mum. By the end of spring semester, the rumors had spun out of his or anybody's control. In class, he felt, the students were no longer listening to him but either whispering to each other or staring in fearful wonder.

"It is a fact that the Germans' first offensive failed not because of the Schlieffen Plan, because the plan was not implemented. A fact," Morris stressed, his voice rising to reclaim attention. "A fact. And it was not the result of industrialists on both sides vying for profits and white male hierarchies competing over turf while denying women the vote."

He spoke or, rather, shouted, his words rebounding around a seemingly empty hall. Until he spotted him in the back row. A young man, from Morris's perspective, but not young enough to be enrolled; shabby, not in the studied student way, but earnestly, his hair unkempt and his terrycloth tie mis-knotted. He, alone, was scribbling. Not surprisingly, after the others left, this man remained and introduced himself as a journalist.

From his podium, leaning over his lectern, Morris squinted. "I told the press many times. No comment."

"You know what they say in my business," the man, still jotting, replied. "No comment is also a comment."

"So be it," Morris pronounced and punctuated his response with a snap of his Dunhill briefcase. Yet, as he left the building, the journalist trailed behind him, puffing to keep up.

"I'm pursuing a different line, Professor Morris," he panted. "I'm not interested in your undercover service. On the contrary, I'm interested in why you made it up."

Morris ignored him, picking up his pace while cutting across a quad. But the man went on: "Like, what would a man like you—renowned scholar, heartthrob—need it for? Glory? *More* glory?"

On the unborn grass, Morris turned suddenly and confronted the journalist. Outdoors, he made an even sorrier sight. His collars curled, jacket ratty, mustard stains on his sleeves and sweat demarking his hairline. A nerd, is what his students would call him, Morris concluded, a twerp.

"Listen, Mr…"

"Hassenfeld. Ezra."

As if offered garbage, Morris sneered at the extended card, just long enough to glimpse the logo. It belonged to a once-radical now highbrow magazine renowned for defrocking bigwigs. His lower belly clenched.

"I gave you my statement, Mr. Hassenfeld, and I have nothing more to say. Only that if you keep stalking me, I'll have to call security."

But Hassenfeld merely shrugged. "Call anybody you want. Free country. I just thought you'd want to give your side of things before I start digging. It won't be deep."

Morris squinted at him, half-threateningly. "Meaning?"

"Meaning, you aren't the CIA, Professor Morris, and it won't be hard finding the holes in your story. You're not even Unit Forty, which I doubt even exists."

Morris drew himself up, peering down his nose at this waif who probably regarded news as those revisionist twits viewed scholarship, not as the procession of truths but a hodgepodge of opinions. "We don't pretend to write history," they taunted him. "We write *our* history."

"Do you know what Unit Forty stands for, Hassenfeld?" he found himself asking.

The investigator shook his head. "Do *you*?"

"Forty, in Roman numerals, is XL. And we excel at getting rid of our enemies. Including those who snoop too close."

Morris watched, angered and dismayed, as Hassenfeld carefully inscribed this quote into his notebook. Then, with a snort, he stomped toward his office, crushing sprouts.

He waited until the elevator reached the top floor of Altier Tower, and he entered his office with its panoramic views of campus. Only then, plunging into his chair, did Morris allow himself to groan. An on-line check of Ezra Hassenfeld's credentials left him groaning still and pounding his cherrywood desk. Along his walls, the honorary degrees and framed distinctions rattled. Books stood in clothbound judgment. All that and more would now be lost—worse, marshalled against him—and because of what, a single wisecrack? The desperate situation called for a drastic recourse. He hated taking it, but realized the choice was sealed.

Later that afternoon, Morris slipped out of the tower, avoided the quads, and escaped through some unused playing fields. Scurrying to the rim of a modest neighborhood, he kept to the backyards. Many faculty members lived there and, though unlikely to be spotted at this hour, he took no chances. Creeping up to a porch and rapping on its screen door, he hissed, "Allison." Louder, he hammered, "Allison, goddamn it!"

"I'm not sure I should let you in," Allison remarked, stepping out. "They say you're a trained assassin."

He pressed against the mesh, reducing his face—and his ex-wife's—to pixels. "Cut the shit, Allison, please. This is no time."

"No time, indeed," she said, releasing the lock and helping him into the house.

Morris squinted for signs of the new husband. Only when assured that Stephen was still at his practice did the professor collapse into the nearest chair. Allison brought him a tumbler of scotch along with an indulgent smile and the question, "What the fuck were you thinking?"

"Thinking? Who the hell was thinking?" Already he was sounding defensive, though he didn't have to, not with Allison. His second wife, the only one who understood him, painfully so. "How am I going to get out of this?"

She pulled up a seat next to him, her wineglass separating their knees. A long-bodied woman, horse-faced but endearing, dressed much as she did as his graduate student, in a sweatshirt and jeans. Graying hair still braided, oversized eyes that often said more than she spoke.

"You want the truth, don't you?" Morris plugged at his drink. "You want me to make an announcement."

Those eyes now laughed at him. "It's your only option."

"And be ridiculed by my entire field—the entire country? Besides…" Forlornly, he studied his glass. "It's too late. A journalist is after me. An *investigative* journalist. Annoying little turd, he rankled me, and I told him…"

"Told him what, Ben?"

The professor pouted. "That Unit Forty meant excel and that we'd excel in getting rid of him."

"I'm missing something…"

"Roman Numerals? Excel? Never mind. I just wanted him gone."

A silent interlude followed, during which Morris peered around the living room that used to be his and for an instant wished it was. He scarcely noticed Allison's wineglass knocking his kneecap or heard her urging, "A simple statement, one line. Say it was an innocent mistake, a practical joke gone wrong. Say you're sorry."

"You're right, of course. As always." Morris emptied the last of the Scotch, drawing strength. "I'll do it tomorrow. No, right now."

He pushed himself up from the chair and let Allison escort him to the porch. She, in turn, permitted him to peck her cheek while she posed a final question, "Why?"

"Why what?"

"Why, when you have all the fame you'll ever need—awards, accolades, women? Just to get back at your critics?"

It was the same question that Hassenfeld had asked him, only Allison's could never be dodged. "Those dimwits?" he replied with an imperiousness she knew well. "They aren't even *worth* a lie."

"I see. It's never enough for you, Benjamin. You have to be the great historian *and* the secret agent." Allison's eyes lit up. "Brilliant professor *and* a spy."

He didn't answer her but hurried back across the playing fields to his office. There, he drafted a terse release and read it aloud to his library. He read it again, hoping the indignity would subside, and stashed it away in a drawer. Why apologize when he'd yet to be publicly accused, he asked himself, when the entire affair might vanish? He would never see that mud-chucking Hassenfeld again or even hear his name.

And his judgment seemed sound for the next few days as spring aroused the campus. The crocuses were out, together with the young women who, shedding boots and sweaters, blossomed. This was his favorite moment of the year, when any desire seemed fulfillable. Whistling, he light-footed along the path worn diagonally across the quad and strode into his brimming lecture hall. There, without pause, he lunged into his nemeses' arguments.

"Yes, yes, colonial troops took part in some of the biggest battles. Tirailleurs, Sénégalais, Gurkhas—they were all there. But so were Canadians, Anzacs, and Boers. That's why we call it a *World* War. But to say that and then conclude that the war was all about race and racism is nothing short of moronic."

He was soaring now, and the students were once again taking notes. All but one. Seated not in the rear which the professor had scanned earlier on but in the front, where he went for a long while unnoticed, Hassenfeld. Catching sight of him finally, Morris coughed and lost his thrust. He rambled on about colonials at the Somme, straining to regain some focus, until the class adjourned. The students sauntered out while the journalist casually remained.

"I don't know about them," he said, referring to the undergrads, "but I believe you. The war wasn't about color. It was about lies."

Ignoring him, Morris shut his briefcase and tried a leisurely exit. A single word sufficed to stop him.

"Matala."

He pivoted to find Hassenfeld still in his seat but fanning himself with a photograph.

"Matala?"

"The caves, Professor Morris. On Crete. Of course, you remember." He held the photo up to the light which, though scant, showed a scraggly, long-haired youth smoking a joint. "It's where you spent the time between your BA and graduate work. In the caves, playing music, getting stoned, getting laid hopefully. Not eliminating enemies. Not operating behind dangerous lines. In Matala, having fun."

With two hands, Morris held his briefcase before him. "And what if that was my cover?"

"A good one, maybe, but for what? You see, I snooped around Washington a bit, contacted some friends in sensitive places, and guess what? No Unit Forty. Nothing about excel." ·

"So say you."

"So will say my magazine in its very next edition." Hassenfeld reached into his shoddy jacket for a notepad and pen. Now he was ready to write. "Your last chance, professor. Care to comment?"

"No," Morris spat out before retreating. "*That* is my comment."

Back in his office, he ground his forehead into the desk. His name, his life's work, would be devastated. The charlatans would rejoice. He couldn't face them or the shame of resignation. For hours he sat, racked by indecision. But then it struck him. As simply, as incontrovertibly, as any fact he knew.

Morris reached into his drawer and extracted the apology. He read it once more, folded it neatly, and ripped it into quarters. Then, on stationary emblazoned with his title and chair, he penned a new note. Shorter. Immune to interpretation.

He left the letter face up on his desk and moved toward the window. Opening it, he let the late spring breeze tussle his hair. The night was clear, the stars beaconing, Gothic spires, lamplights twinkling on campus. He would lose all this, either through a frantic leap or prolonged humiliation. Both options made him shake. Then again, he reasoned, he would still have his looks, his publications, his prizes. No scandal could strip him of those. He thought of Allison and his other wives and of the women yet to come. And of the idiots who'd dominate the field in his absence, desecrating history with myths.

Minutes passed and Morris remained at the window, deliberating. He was dithering still when the intruder stepped through his door. The professor barely had time to turn, much less protest. Only his face writhed with recognition as his feet lifted off the floor.

The intruder backed away from the window, glanced down at the desk, and perused the letter approvingly. Then, with a gloved hand, he reached within his jacket pocket and produced an encoded phone.

"It's over, sir," he said, waited for a response, then added, "No worry. It'll look like he did it himself."

He quietly backed out of the office. "Unit Forty? Excel? An unlucky guess, maybe, we don't know sir," he continued while shutting the door behind him. "Probably never will."

Ten stories below, students inspected the crumpled mass blocking their shortcut across the quad.

"The good news, sir, is," the man posing as Ezra Hassenfeld said in the hallway, above the echo of screams, "neither will anybody else."

The House on
Kittatinny Lake

The story was about an insecure woman in an abusive marriage who one day meets a man who tells her that she's perfect. She's more than perfect, he assures her—goddess-like. Leaving her husband, the woman moves in with this man who replaces her self-doubt with a self-love so unassailable that she begins to think she's too good for him. She abandons this husband for someone better-looking and rich but who, after time, again persuades her that she's worthless. So the cycle spins and, with it, this woman. Around and around until she dies, marred and marvelous and alone.

Another story starts with a young man, the square-jawed heroic type, climbing the cliffs of Dingle. The wind lashes his auburn hair and waves smash against the gnarled Irish coast that dares stand up to the Atlantic. Athlete, a straight-A student, the man stands strong against the elements. He believes he was born to greatness but to what greatness, exactly, he's uncertain. This is why he wanders, searching, hungering, for himself. "Fate is what you travel to," is his logo, and he shouts it into the gale. "But destiny comes to you."

* * * * *

Pamela leans back on her desk and chews the end of her pencil. The ideas she's jotted on her yellow legal pad look, on rereading, yellow and legal.

Again, she stiffens with the fear that her best writing—*any* writing—is behind her. The days when she could scribble off the top of her head and riff on for pages, when reviewers referred to her as "one of *our* best," feel distant. The pencils that she habitually chews while writing—a ten-pencil story was once standard—remain stacked in a jar, like some rare, pollarded plant.

Instead, she stares out of her office window at Kittatinny's banks below. Named for the Native Americans who once fished it, the lake is, in fact, an elongated pond too small for vacation boats. Which is one of the reasons Pamela settled here. The other reason—the real one—is a dream she once had of a white, antebellum two-story with black shutters, its reflection shimmering on water. The image was both comforting and wistful. It stayed with her for days until miraculously, on a rural leg of a book tour, she chanced on the real thing. At once, she made an outrageous offer. The house, the lakeside, the dream—became hers.

Here she can live out her life after Maxwell's death, in celebrated solitude. Readers still made pilgrimages to her, a succession of old ladies who remembered her from book clubs and wide-eyed students who'd discovered her on syllabi. Through her editor or the station agent in town, paid to phone when strangers asked directions to the house, Pamela can control the flow. She touches up her fine dishevelment and, in a whiff of silken scarfs, glides to the door with a face both startled and imperious.

Yet even those visits have dwindled of late, leaving her more than enough time to write or, failing that, to gaze at Kittatinny. She adores the way it wears the seasons—luscious green in spring and summer, confetti-colored patches in the fall—mirroring the trees along its shores. Winter, though, is her favorite. Those months, when the waters freeze and are hidden by snow, make her feel that she and the lake share secrets.

Now it is March, no foliage, no ice, and the lake looks like a moldy soap dish. Days pass without the phone, much less the doorbell ringing, and the pencils sit unchewed. Such times she finds herself dwelling on Maxwell or, at least, the early Maxwell. The scruffy, lustful writer with the voice that sounded scoured with borax. He lived hard, he said, meaning he drank and smoked until his body surrendered, and lived wantonly, helping himself to whatever and whoever he desired.

And he desired Pamela. Many men did back then. Though box-shaped now, Pamela was once what they called stacked—ample of bosom, broad of hips, a model for fertility goddesses. Her features were handsome, fleshy, feral. All that and she could write, her stories compared to symphonies or expansive canvases of art. No genre could contain her. Nor could any man and certainly not Larry, the delicate soul she married right after his graduation from dental school. Larry, who financed her writing habit until she was famous enough to deceive him with a succession of lovers and to leave him, finally, for Maxwell.

How could she have resisted him? He wrote the way he made love, furiously, with vengeance. War stories, detective stories, noire stuff. Cigarette stubs like crimped exclamation points piling up in his ashtray. For hours, while pretending to write herself, Pamela would watch him pounding a keyboard as if it were his enemy's face. That was Maxwell at his fiercest and most irresistible. And how could she not have foreseen the later Maxwell, looking like a Thanksgiving Day balloon, post-parade, deflated and tied down with tubes?

She thought of him and wondered if there wasn't a story. A young man who is angry about nothing in particular, just angry, and sees life as an adversary to be pummeled. An artist angry because he is a great artist who can never be great enough. Mulling over the idea, Pamela selects a pencil from the jar and inserts the blunt end between her teeth. Outside the old white house with black shutters, the world and the lake are gray. Inside, though, the legal pad and the bits of pencil paint that stick to her lips are yellow. Colors could be coaxed from the page.

But no sooner has she started writing than a knock sounds on the front door. A knock? Can't she see the bell, Pamela grouses. And why hasn't the station agent called? Irritably, she gets up from her desk and plods downstairs, adjusting her hair and scarves. "Yes?" she asks, haughtily surprised, as the door swings open not to a book club nanny or a giggly undergraduate but to a tidily-dressed man in his early-thirties. At first, she doesn't recognize him, or rather refuses to, but realizes ignorance isn't optional. "Yes," she says to Roger, for that is his name. Yes, not a question but a sigh.

He enters and looks around, nodding slightly at objects that might be familiar.

"Please," she says, "a cup of tea?" as she always does with visitors, but this is not one of her readers. In fact, Pamela would bet that he's uninterested in her work and doesn't enjoy fiction.

Roger ignores the offer and removes his coat. Cold clings to its shoulders as she takes it from him and hangs it on a peg. When she turns, he is already positioned in her living room and glancing over the awards aligned on the mantel, the framed bestseller lists.

Pamela steps toward him, then halts. "It's good to see you," she says, and the words are as flat and bleak as the lake. He does not answer but sits in the armchair that's traditionally hers when entertaining. Struggling to maintain stature, but still sheepishly, she takes a place on the couch.

"You look well," she says, as if she would know if he didn't. Yet he does look like his father at his age—hair, chin, even his teeth receding. As if his entire being were recoiling from some threat. "You sure no tea?" she asks him instead of "why have you come here?" But it's the second, unuttered, question he answers.

"I'm divorcing Melanie."

"Oh," she gasps, though more out of relief than sorrow. Pamela could never have guessed her name.

"Trust issues."

"I see…" Of course, she doesn't, not yet. What does catch her eye is the resemblance. The same features that were sensual on her face suggest, on his, weakness. And he has his father's tenuous build.

"My trust in her. My trust in myself."

"Um-hmm." Her head rocks in understanding but in truth she's clueless. All Pamela knows is that this will somehow come back to her. Already she's braced for recrimination. Already she's preparing to defend herself, recalling how Roger was a baby when she left and was raised by Larry's second wife. That marriage also ended in divorce, Pamela later heard, but how was that her fault? How could this breakup with Melanie—that was her name, right?—be remotely attributed to her?

She readies to say all of this, but merely replies, "I'm sorry to hear that."

"Sorry? Really?" Roger's eyes, unlike the rest of his retreating face, seem to lunge at her. "My father never recovered."

"But...he remarried."

"Remarried but never healed. Did you know that he cheated on Mom?" Roger crosses his legs and cups a knee in his hands. Subtly, in the armchair, he rocks. "And when I asked him why, do you know what he said?" He doesn't wait for an answer. "He said that he did it to her before she could do it to him. Because he couldn't survive another betrayal. Crazy, isn't it?"

No crazier than abandoning a kindly dentist and his infant son for a self-destructive egoist. Pamela declaims, "We all have our scars."

Again, he glares at her. Is he, sitting cross-legged in his navy crew-neck and corduroys, her scar? The child whose custody she at first fought for and then conceded, whom she visited regularly for a while, then infrequently, and then never—all before he was old enough to remember. By that time, he had a more caring mother, she'd told herself, and she needed to devote herself to art. To Maxwell. Better that Roger lived his own life—so the justification went—and grew into manhood free of anger.

Still, he could lace into her, she fears, become violent perhaps with no one around the lake to hear. But instead he merely shrugs. "Scars, indeed."

"But what does this have to do with Mel...your divorce?"

Roger chuckles acidly. "Trust. Distrust. I was jealous of every man she talked to, even her oldest friends. And suspicious. Every time she was out of the house, not within eyesight, I imagined her in bed, in various positions, with many partners. I drove myself insane. I drove *her* insane."

"And this is somehow connected with me?" The question, for Pamela, is half-serious. To pin his irrational envy on her is truly deranged, she concludes. She never even knew her son, much less influenced his behavior. But then came the other half. She never *wanted* to know him—in fact, forced herself to forget him, which was easy enough with Maxwell sucking up her air. Still, there were moments when she'd be clipping the hedges, perhaps, or proofreading a text, when the thought of her son intruded. It would give her pause and often make her wonder what he was doing just then, what he looked like, how he was managing in the world. But those instances would pass. Roger was a reality, like faltering book sales, like death, that dwelling on only caused pain.

"I know you'd like to think it wasn't." Roger is responding, but to what, she no longer remembers. "But it turns out there is such a thing as original sin. Turns out that the sins of the mother are visited through the tenth generation, maybe the hundredth." He says this with his knee still slung in his palms, as if he's talking statistics. "You leave Dad. Dad leaves Mom. Melanie and I leave each other."

Oh, that—now Pamela recalls. "Is it an apology you want? I can't. I *won't*." She struggles to sound kindly. "We are who we are."

"Indeed," Roger says. He liked that word. "I didn't come here for an apology. I came to ask you a question."

Pamela's eyebrows rise.

"Was it worth it?"

"It?"

"Your decision. I've followed your career—I shouldn't've but I couldn't help myself. It's successes and now. I saw how you lived your life as if you were writing it. And I wanted to know, looking back from this last chapter, was it worth it?"

Hand to her breast, Pamela exhales, "Why, of course." Her hand sweeps the trophied mantel, the artwork on the walls, the bay window with the leaden lake behind. "All of this is because of that decision—that and sweat. All of this and much more."

Roger nods. "Good. I needed to hear that. It might surprise you, but expressions of regret would've been worse."

They chat for a while longer. Seems Roger followed his father's path into dentistry but has yet to become a father himself. "The curse ends with me," he smiles. Pamela mentions some stories she's finishing, the fans that persistently show up. Less than an hour passes and already he is on his feet, a small man, she notices, on whose shoulders she can lay—rather than hook—his coat.

"Call you a cab?"

"No need. I drove."

Ah-hah, she thinks. Hence no heads-up from the station agent.

"Well, drive safely," she begins and almost adds, "and please visit again," but doesn't. Nor does he offer.

At the door, he hesitates and turns. Pamela tenses, fearing he wants to kiss her goodbye. But he only twitches a finger on his lower lip. A second passes before she mutters, "Oh," and scrapes beneath her mouth. A chip of yellow paint comes off on her fingernail. "Chewing pencils," she says, expertly rolling her eyes. "Horrible habit."

She lets him out and admits the cold, which leaves her shivering long after the door is closed. An engine growls, gravel crunches, and then there is silence. Her breath drums in the hallway as she plods up her office stairs. The chair creaks beneath her weight. She thinks of Maxwell or tries to think of him, while trying not to think of Larry. But what she wants most of all—desperately—is a story. Stories, alone, are her life, and they are what make it livable.

Pamela stares out of the window at the barren trees veined across Kittatinny's surface. How about this one, she ponders. The professor whose great-great grandfather is executed for petty theft. Traumatized, humiliated, his son becomes a revolutionary, blaming society for his father's crime. He, too, is killed, cut down by a barrage of militia fire. But he leaves an orphaned son who grows up hating his radical father and becomes, instead, a reactionary. A dictator who rules with blood-drenched hands. A car bomb ends his reign, but not before he sires yet another son who, in defiance of his forebears, joins the priesthood. But, alas, the chastity vows prove too draconian for him and the result is yet another offspring—the professor, his life now jeopardized by semi-auto-biographical works that provoke a rival's grudge.

Pamela scribbles on her pad. She scribbles and selects a pencil for chewing. The past may be sepia but the present's yellow. The house is whitewashed, and the lake is gray. The world is any color we choose.

The Boys' Room

Half-bounding, half-plodding up the stairs, he wasn't sure he would make it. A cascade of kids slowed his ascent while the din of slamming lockers and the second period bell befuddled his calculation of the route. Why had he put off going until after algebra, he berated himself; why was he always procrastinating? And about this, of all things. Grunting as he clutched the handrail, he hoisted himself onto the floor. The classrooms were already sealed and the hallways silent as he staggered the few remaining feet. Then, stifling a cry, he shoulder-butted into the nearest lavatory and pitched toward the furthest stall.

The eruption was monumental, record-breaking perhaps, but at least he'd gotten his pants down. With a thunderous gurgle, his innards emptied. Only now he could sigh, relishing the relief and his own pungent solitude.

He studied the metal walls and their key-etched graffiti. The highlight was always a hotdog-shaped object pumping into what looked like a human eye standing on its duct. Beneath it was scratched "Kitty Morgan"—a girl probably long graduated—"is a hore." Yet, to his puzzlement, the hotdog and the eye were gone, along with Kitty Morgan. In their place were a nicely rendered image of a pitcher of flowers and another of a cat frolicking on its back.

He didn't dwell on the mystery but merely shrugged and reached for the toilet paper. Reached and plumbed, but the aluminum dispenser was empty. "Shit," he muttered, and was old enough to appreciate the irony. He also knew there was no choice but to hitch up his underwear as high as he dared and waddle into the adjacent stall. Halfway into this delicate maneuver, though, he heard the bathroom door squealing open and sneakers padding on the tiles.

"Shit," he gasped again, but not out loud. The picture of him with his belt around his ankles and his thing hanging out would be all over the seventh grade, he knew, and well before lunchtime. So, instead, he sat again and prepared to wait it out. The signal would be the urinal's gush.

But there was no gush, only a high-pitched whine, "I cannot believe this zit."

Another voice, equally shrill, counseled, "Leave it alone. You'll only make it worse."

"Bad enough the zit, worse with that asshole De Vingo. You believe the way he hit on me?"

"A dickhead, that's what he is. A teeny-weeny little dick."

He glanced at the walls. The paint, he now registered, was no longer army brown but an overly-cheery pink. The cat, the flowers, delicately rendered. And, come to think of it, he didn't remember there even *being* urinals. The realization made him feel as if he had to go all over again and, at the same time, throw up.

The first voice giggled, "He's teenier than your pinky, I heard." And both of them snorted, "What? Is it in me? I can't feel a thing."

He thought of Andy DeVingo. The Horse, they called him. The way he strutted around the showers after gym, showing off his pubes. He glanced down at his lap which had yet to sprout a single strand. If the Horse was teeny, what, then, was he?

And what did they mean by feeling it? He struggled to understand, shuddered at the possibility that he did.

"And Gerry Franks. He swings both ways, you know."

He tried to place the voices. They sounded vaguely like Linda and Stacey, two of his quietest classmates. Always taking the desks furthest from the teacher, never hanging out in the halls, avoiding the popular kids' lunch tables. Linda and Stacey, who dressed in plaid skirts and pants that were never jeans, according to the code. The one with a ponytail, the other with bangs and braids. The girls he sometimes glimpsed and watched, wanting, as they chewed their pens.

"I heard that, too. Both ways."

For a second, he imagined the pimply, bespectacled Gerry Franks seated on a swing and pumping his legs in the air. Then, one of the girls snorted, "Ewww."

"Yeah, somebody's dumping in here."

"More like somebody died."

He cringed. He pictured them peeking under the stall and catching sight of his loafers or climbing up on the next-door toilet, looking down and howling. Silently as possible, he brought his knees upward and hugged them with both his arms.

"Whoever you are in there," Stacey or Linda called out, "lay off the garlic bread."

"Whoever you are in there, forget about ever getting laid."

More chortles, followed by the slap of tender hands high-fiving. "And if we find out who you are, we'll turn you over to DeVingo," one of them warned, and the other added, "No, to Gerry Franks." And they giggled.

He said nothing, of course, tried not to breathe. Fear and confusion careened in his head. How long would they stay there, he fretted? What if one of them wanted to pee?

The hiss of water in the sink. "Crap. We'd better get back."

"At least there's Mister Margolis."

"Oh my god, Mister Margolis. I would *so* do him."

"He could so do me."

A collective grunt, "Mister Margolis."

The crunch of paper towels sounded musical.

"Christ, I have to go and sit next to that Reeseman kid. Douchebag."

"Talk about douchebags, I've got Schletter."

He sunk his face into the wedge between his knees. God, he prayed, don't let them say anything about me. But they said nothing, which seemed like a miracle but was also strangely disappointing.

The lid to the trash bin opened and clanged. Sneakered feet skipped across the tiles. "Pee-eww," a voice shot back at him as the bathroom door opened to the ghostly murmurs of the hall. "Pee-eww," someone seconded as the door swung shut.

Their snickers, though, kept rattling around the porcelain fixtures. He sat there listening, scarcely moving, hurt and perplexed. Curled up in his stall, he was suddenly aware of his ignorance of the world. A cruel and deceiving world, to tell from Linda and Stacey. Mysterious and threatening.

The bell would ring soon, sending countless kids stampeding through the halls. Pouring into the bathrooms, too. He could not stay there another minute. He had to move. Drag up his pants, wash his hands, and emerge, an underclassman, into school.

Live in Studio

"Zoom in to head," said the voice in his ear, and he focused the camera on Jennifer's face. Not the best call, he thought. The new weather woman looked pretty enough from this three-yard distance but close-ups showed the pockmarks that must have tormented her as a teenager and that not even foundation could hide. Not a good call, but then again, he wasn't the producer, merely a cameraman on a local station. Unionized, seasoned, professional, and bored into a decades-long stupor.

He wasn't always this way. As a much younger man, a hard-drinking and who-gives-a-shit man, he dreamed of becoming a photographer. Not a wedding and family portrait photographer who lines up customers like bowling pins and imagines smashing them. No, he would be a photographer of the wild—human and animal—the chronicler of life's cruelty and passions. At the precise moment the jaguar locked his teeth into a tapir's neck, when a mother learned of her soldier son's death or a street bum won the lottery, he would be there, clicking. The prizes would pile up, the announcements for exhibitions. Photographers would stand in line to take *his* picture.

But, as it happened, he was too hard-drinking, too don't-give-a-shit, and, other than preserving details of some girlfriend's body, his Nikon remained shuttered. A buddy of a buddy got him an apprenticeship as a TV cameraman, and the rest was a blur of bouffanty hairdos and enameled teeth. He'd seen all the fads—the Asian anchor women, the Latinos and the Blacks—and watched the average viewer's age inch past sixty. His own hair had thinned and whitened, his belly bulged so ludicrously that, looking down, he could read his own t-shirts. And meanwhile no jaguars, no gold star mothers or bums transformed into millionaires. No photographers, certainly, waiting to immortalize him. Only this morning's forecast brought to some early-rising pensioners by Jennifer whatever-her-fake-name was. Jennifer the generically pretty. Jennifer the scarred.

"A high-pressure front is moving into our region from the West," he heard her say through his headphones, and wondered who in the hell knew what a high-pressure front was or even cared. "We can expect some mighty unstable weather." The fear of instability, he momentarily hoped, would detract the audience's attention from the craters on Jennifer's cheeks. He might have felt sorry for her, the rookie struggling to overcome handicaps, the kid just trying to make her way out of backwater TV and into the Big Time. But he'd seen too many Jennifers come and go, ruthlessly pushing others off the set. The closest he'd ever gotten to a jungle.

And this Jennifer had ejected the closest thing he had to a friend, Walter. Weatherman Walt, he called himself, and so did everyone, never bothering to learn his last name. A man his contemporary with the same early dreams eroded by fate and alcohol. Or so he heard more than once at the Tory Corner over cigarettes and nightcaps. Got to the point where he could scarcely distinguish Weatherman Walt's story from his own.

Plump, balding broadcasters were all the rage once, their ruddy faces glowing through the makeup as they rattled on about golf tips and rain. But that fad, too, had passed, to be replaced by homecoming blondes like Jennifer. Which was why he hesitated, befuddled, when his camera caught a sliver of Walt entering the frame.

Jennifer saw him as well, maybe even faster than he did, for she stopped in mid-forecast and gasped. She had little time for much else. Girth notwithstanding, Walt could move. He barreled onto the riser and shoved her away from the blue screen.

"Sorry, girlie," Walt said, calmly enough, though his expression looked molten. "And sorry, folks, to interrupt your broadcast." His eyes were wet fire.

"What's he doing here?" He heard the producer shouting into his microphone. "Somebody, get him off the set!"

The noise made him wince, but no more. His only job was to keep the camera operating and focused, and that he did as Weatherman Walt addressed the lens.

"Thirty years I gave to this shithole," he cried. "Thirty fuckin' years. And then one day, wham, fuck you, you're gone!"

Walt was sounding much like he did at the Tory Corner, after midnight, on his fifth round. Only there was an edginess to his tone, a rage. Still, the old forecaster kept his gaze fixed on the black disc that televised him throughout the Tri-state area.

"So I just wanted you to know that you did this! All of you. You in the studio and you in your tidy little homes watching. You!"

Walt repeated that "you" several times, each one louder, as if he were hyperventilating. The last one sounded like a scream and rounded his mouth into an almost-perfect O into which he inserted a gun barrel.

"Stop him! Somebody stop him!" He heard roaring in his headphones and maybe outside them as well. Yet he didn't move, didn't pan back or away. Later, he was unsure if he joined the chorus of "no" and "please don't" and "for God's sake." But whether silent or not, he never lunged for the set. He never left his camera but instead remained with his eyes pressing the viewer while Walt's finger did likewise on the trigger.

The shot nearly burst his eardrums. He may even have blacked out for an instant, as the next thing he saw was a squid-shaped splash of red and grey dripping down the blue screen. A patch of smoke, not unlike the animated cloud they often posted for rainfall, hovered over the set, and the studio reeked of burnt fuse box. People everywhere were running and flailing their hands. Only Walter the Weatherman lay motionless, his head on the line of duct tape that once showed him where to stand.

"How could you?" were the first words he could make out, and he turned to confront Jennifer. Her face no longer pretty but contorted beneath splotches of blood that mixed with the pancake. "You were the closest to him and you just stood there." She screamed at him, "You animal!"

He listened to her holler but said nothing. He was shaking, he realized, but not only from shock. These were also the jitters he might have felt long ago up close and capturing that jaguar on film. Within seconds—right now, probably—the image of Walter's eyes widening blankly as the bullet blasted out the back of his skull would be flashing far beyond the three states. And he, the unflappable professional, would finally be asked, "just how did you keep your cool?"

Crime Scene

Long after the door closed, she stood in her apartment and wished she could rope it off. Bright yellow tape wrapped around the bathroom and, of course, the bed, but also the living room and kitchen. All of them crime scenes.

Victim and detective, eyewitness and accessory—she was all those and more: forensic expert. The bristles in the sink where she made him shave because his stubble chafed her. The toilet seat raised to reveal orangey streaks on the rim where he always missed. The mangled sheets and pummeled pillows. Everywhere, the evidence. His presence made palpable now by his utter absence, and by her own complicity.

As if in the aftermath of some massacre, the proof was inescapable. The sofa's misaligned cushions and the depressions in her fuzzy rug. Even the tabletop with its piles of junk mail now crimped. She stood hugging herself as she surveyed her own home as one who had never set foot in it and could hardly imagine inhabiting it alone.

"Touch nothing," she wanted to tell herself. "Don't tamper." Yet she found herself peeking under chairs and behind her dresser, hoping to chance on some mislaid button or cufflink. Then she opened the refrigerator and saw it. The cream cheese tub with its lid ajar and the deep groove gouged in its contents. "For chrissakes," she remembered chiding him, pretending to be angry when she really wanted to sigh, awed by the humming light on his nakedness. "You might want to use a spoon..."

she began but never finished as his finger brought the dollop of cheese to his mouth.

Now that finger remained, a perfect cast, prints and all. She held up the tub and examined it, checked for the expiration date and wondered how long—a month, at most—she could preserve that impression. Tightly, she replaced the lid and vowed not to open it again for hours at least and not more than twice daily.

In the middle of her apartment that would never be entirely hers again, she peered sleuth-like but shivered like a survivor. She sized up the scene and analyzed the data. Exhibits A and B, damning DNA in abundance. And the residue that could not be tagged or jarred: their mongrel smells, the gasps that lingered.

He was gone but had left too much behind him. Precious lover, sloppy perp, leaving a trail that led unmistakably out the door. At that, too, she stared and wondered if its handle retained his warmth.

Outside, in the hallway, she imagined, the yellow tape would stretch, winding into the elevator and through the lobby to flounce in the pre-dawn breeze. Not only her apartment, she realized, but her whole building and the city beyond would remain off-limits. Without him, the world itself was a crime scene.

The Reenactor

How much chicken soup can one man eat, I ask myself as the waiter shoves me yet another bowl. "Be thankful," Wojchiech, my boss, snaps at me. "At the factory, they're spooning out swill. And besides, you have to stay in character. It's why we pay you twelve hundred a month."

In character, yes, I remind myself as I pause with my face hovering over the bowl. My eyes close, my lips flutter and emit some guttural grunts. That is the way they used to pray, I was instructed, before and after meals. So I pray, and I push back my sidelocks—*payos* I'm told to call them—and lift my wooden spoon. Only then, just before the first sip, do I catch my gauzy reflection in the broth. Behind the matzo balls which, like twin goiters extend from my neck, I see the sidelocks and the unkempt beard, the fur-lined hat I'm supposed to call a *shtreimel*, and the itchy collar of my made-in-China *kaftan*.

"Hurry. Eat," Wojchiech growls. "A group's due any minute."

I slurp, I dribble—that's in character, too—and scoop out dollops of matzo balls which once tasted sugary to me but now go down like sawdust. When there's time, and when Wojchiech's not looking, the waiter will sneak me a kishke or a knish or two. And I'm grateful, though a knish could make anyone gag. What I really want is a fresh-fried kielbasa or pork knuckle washed down with white sausage soup. What I really need, as I hear the bus pulling up and gulp down the last of the balls, is a brimming glass of wódka.

Times are tough in our village, I know, and work's hard to find. Not as lucky as me, others stand in line for government doles or deal in black market cigarettes. But all I have to do is wear these freaky clothes, the fake beard and wig, and memorize a bunch of bullshit. I just have to wait outside the L'Chaim Restaurant and Lounge for the tourists to come down off the bus. Then I dance a bit, bouncing from heel to heel on my clunky boots, with my hands flapping above my heard, and chirp "ay yai yai" and "bim boim bim boim." I pass out menus and pose for selfies.

You see, the secret of this town, its only advantage, is Jews. Not real Jews, dead Jews. Thousands of them. Half of the town once, they say, before the war. Dentists, teachers, doctors, butchers—all the good jobs they had. The good apartments, too. In this neighborhood, especially, they lived, with their kishke and kasha and klezmer music blasting all day. At least that's what the tourists think. Filing off the buses into L'Chaim and other traps like the Mazal Tov Inn and the Altshul Museum. I don't know. Maybe it was different. Maybe it was like today with people going around minding their own business, bringing up kids, fucking and cheating on their wives, doing their damnedest to get by. Just people. Life.

But all that ended when Germans came—Szkops, we called them back then—and crowded the Jews into a few alleyways. They walled them in and shot anyone trying to escape. Where the Zabka market is now. A plaque shows the spot, though nobody but the tourists notice. The plaque says that the Jews froze and starved in those alleys for a year or so until one winter night the Szkops marched them out of town, straight down Kościuszko Boulevard and past the Jewish graveyard where, as kids, my gang used to squat with our backs to the stones with their fading Jew letters, gab, and smoke weed.

A few minutes' walk from there is this little forest—it's still there—with nice trees and soft earth. A big hole had been dug, so all the guys with guns had to do was line the Jews up and, one by one, shoot them in the back of the head. They fell, row after neat row, until the hole was filled and covered up. A plaque hangs there as well, where the hole was. The tourists leave flowers and flags.

These newest tourists have only cameras in their hands and handkerchiefs for tapping their eyes. Which means they must have already visited the little forest. Which means the last thing they're thinking about is our borscht and kreplach special, complete with watered-down schnapps. This is where I come in. My job is to get them toasting l'Chaim to one another, to life or to hell with it or whatever, at fifty zlotys a shot.

"What are you waiting for?" Wojchiech hisses. "Get your ass moving."

I make some more of those prayer-like snorts and wipe my mouth with my kaftan. Smooth out my phony beard and tuck strands of blonde hair under my *shtreimel*. Rising, my hands twisting above my head, I look pretty much like the people in the paintings on L'Chaim's walls. Men dressed just like I am, their *payos* flailing as they dance around this scrolled-up thing. The paintings are everywhere—even over the urinals—along with pictures of candles and bread and silver cups. Jew-y things. Maybe the tourists know what they are, but I'll be damned. I've never even met a Jew.

Some of the tourists might be Jews, but they sure don't dress like one. Americans, mostly, in their windbreakers and sneakers, their visored caps with all sorts of crap written on them, they peer at me from behind their cameras and smartphones and click photos of me bobbing up and down, ay aying and bim boiming and doling out menus. "Sholom Aleichem!" I bark at them. And "Es gezunterheyt!" Whatever that means. And slowly, most of them anyway, begin to smile. Some of them even want to eat, even though the food's shitty and the prices downright criminal. All of which makes Wojchiech happy.

My life meanwhile's a mess. No steady job, no future. No money, which means no girl, and no hope of ever getting out of this shithole. Just smoking weed with the same kids who aren't kids anymore but grownup losers like me, doing odd jobs, dressing up like zhids. Nothing like the people who used to live in this neighborhood—the dentists and the teachers and whatnot—who had real lives, real futures, until the Szkops came and marched them down Kościuszko to the forest.

The tourists today are really buying into my routine. They stand in line to take selfies with me. The tables are full, and the chicken soup is flowing. Wojchiech is practically gleaming, reaching now behind the bar for the wódka bottle that he tips into a coffee mug and plugs.

So it goes throughout the day and late into the evening. One tourist bus after another. More borscht, more schnapps, and Wojchiech getting happier and happier, slapping my back and toasting me with his mug "L'Chaim!" One could almost think that what happened to those Jews was this town's only break.

It's nearly midnight when the last of the tourists stagger out for their hotel. The waiter's long gone home and Wojchiech's slumped down in a chair with his mug, a half-eaten knish, and his cheek on the table in front of him. The klezmer tape's been turned off and the only sound comes from a clock with strange Jew letters instead of numbers on its face. Bim Boim Bim Boim, it ticks.

This is the moment I wait for. To sneak behind the bar and see what's left—no more schnapps or wódka but a half-empty bottle of Slivovitz that should do the trick. I swig it deeply and swig again as I slip out of L'Chaim and steal past the Mazal Tov Inn. The smack of my clunky boots echo in the courtyard of the Altshul Museum and then go silent as the cobblestones underfoot turn to pavement. Soon I'm on Kościuszko Boulevard, empty of traffic at this hour, with nobody around to screw up their eyes or make catcalls at some drunk in a Chinese-made robe and ridiculous fur-lined hat. The Zabka Market is closed for the night. But its yellow neon sign remains flickering, illuminating now and then the plaque that only the tourists ever notice.

Kościuszko ends at a crumbling brick wall behind which stands the graveyard. Not really stands but slants this way and that, the tombstones like crooked teeth. Still, guzzling, I make my way through the most distant rows were the stones are no more than stubbles.

The silence is so complete that I can almost imagine the Szkops cursing and shouting, the howl of their dogs, and the shuffle of the Jews too weak to plead or even cry. And from somewhere up ahead, strange, too-sharp pops.

Then, suddenly, the forest. Into a chilly mist I stumble, drunk enough now to slip and break my neck, sidestepping the trees that seem to rise up ghost-like in front of me. I try to think, imagine what it'd be like to be somebody, not some underpaid clown in a cheap tourist joint, but a man with a family, a profession, with dignity. Maybe it's the Slivovitz, but I try to picture myself with a life worth losing, a life that somebody—even tourists—might remember.

Surprisingly, since I can't see a meter in front of me, I find myself standing at the hole. The earth is sunken here and surrounded by a knee-high fence. I climb over it, trying not to stomp on the flags and flowers strewn on the ground or trip over the plaque in the center. But the booze has rubbered my knees. I fall to them and then, finishing off the Slivovitz and chucking the bottle, I let myself lie flat.

Face-down in the spongy grass, I can feel the fog penetrating my kaftan, wafting up under the shtreimel. I wait like that for who knows how long, wrapped in earth and darkness. Waiting for what—a pop, a bang to the back of my head?—or for the guttural noises I'm supposed to make each day the sun comes up. The grunt of morning prayers.

Prodigal Son

He didn't appear shocked or even surprised to see him seated on the stone. Flummoxed was more like it, or piqued. As though he lacked the patience, if not the time, for such meetings.

"Why now? Why here?" he asked.

"You've got a likelier place?" the older man replied as he often did, with a question. He, too, was not astonished, even though it was early afternoon and the weather pleasant. Even though he could no longer remember how many days he'd sat there ruminating alone. "And why haven't you ever met me?"

The younger one shrugged. "This may come as a revelation to you, but I have other things to do."

"A revelation and how."

"So," the son said, kicking the turf toward his father's heels. "To what do I owe the honor?"

"Owe? Are there debts where you come from? Credits?"

The son removed his baseball cap. He always wore a baseball cap, and in the traditional way, visor-forward. A denim work shirt, half-laced construction boots, and jeans. "Well, yes, there is a ledger of sorts. An accounting."

"How then's my tally?"

The son scrutinized his father. "Again, I don't want to shatter illusions here, but it's not you who's getting tallied." He scowled, "And that stone's not for you."

Now it was the father's turn to shrug, but in a toddler's way, defiant. "Here or anywhere, this stone's always with me. It's there, under my head, when I go to sleep at night, and in the morning, it's inside my chest." He tapped both sides of the tablet. "Sitting on it, at least, brings me peace."

"Bullshit," the son spit into the lawn. "You get nothing here but dirty shoes and a sore butt. Enough already. Go home to Mom."

The gray-haired gentleman in the sports jacket and khaki slacks looked slighted. "Mom divorced me years ago." He stared into the grass. "Blamed me, I guess."

"Like it's all about you," the young man sighed, despairing not only of his parents' pettiness but the pettiness of people in general. "You think it's easy being the source of that much grief?"

The father looked distant. "I guess we were all new at it."

The son's expression changed from peevish to pitying. "I know," he muttered. "It took some getting used to."

"You at least did," the father's attention returned. "I wanted to tear the sky apart."

"And me the earth."

"I found myself hating that big fat oak tree. I found myself hating the big fat oak tree that planted its seed right there, by that hairpin turn in the road. I hated all oak trees, going back to creation."

"And I hated the rocks that yielded the metals," the young man admitted. "I hated the metals that were forged into bumpers, engines, grills."

"I suppose we hated God. At least that we can agree on," the father nearly smiled. He began extending his hand to shake, but retracted it.

"I suppose we hated," the son paused as if to swallow. "Love."

"No," the father demurred. "We mustn't hate love. We can only hate the anguish losing it causes."

The young man grimaced. "Offering one means risking the other."

"Indeed," the gentleman said and conceded, "But what choice do we really have?"

The two remained silent for a moment, the one still seated, the other loitering nearby. "You're such a good boy," the aging man finally said. "Smart. Not school smart, maybe, and rebellious. But look how wise you've become. And strong. Growing up, you were always needing new clothes."

Wistfully, the son chuckled, "I outgrew them."

"You outgrew life."

"Don't we all? In time."

"I suppose I should hate time as well," the father went on. "The time that turns unbearable pain into sustaining pain. That compresses a vast absence into a presence that never leaves you."

"In one form or another."

"Time that grinds trees and rocks, love and anguish, into this, stone and turf. And then, nothing."

"Into *everything*." The chuckle became a laugh. "Don't you get that, Dad?"

With gratefulness, with hope, the father beamed at his son. But his expression darkened as the young man started to turn.

"Don't leave me," he found himself begging. "Not yet."

"Don't leave *me*," the son insisted, though they both knew the request was unnecessary. Still, he added, "Ever."

"Never."

"Never. Good."

Tucking his shirttails into his jeans, pivoting on his boots, the teenager who should have been forty went back to sounding business-like. A father to his old man. "As I said, I've got things to do. Now go home. Clean yourself up and find something softer to sit on."

The father obediently nodded and rose. He brushed off his slacks and buffed one loafer on the other. Then, aware suddenly of the stillness, he froze. How could he have forgotten to say thank you? Why didn't he set another date?

He might have continued berating himself, but his anger was soon calmed by that persistent, immaterial, presence. "Ever," he said out loud, as if someone were listening. "Never," he whispered as he bent to touch the stone, caressing the letters he still wished spelled his own name and not his son's.

Good Table

The sketch on the whiteboard—circles, arrows, and stars—might have described a complex football play or the flow of corporate information. But it merely represented seating.

"The national chairman was up here with the security advisor," Matteo said, a marker clenched between his teeth. Though no artist, he had accurately recreated the layout of a fundraiser to which they had contributed richly, only to find themselves in the back of the hall. "The director sat here, right next to the chief of staff. And we..." He removed the marker and pointed at the bottom of the board. "We were with the Schwartzes and the Dudleys, way down there."

"The Schwartzes, for chrissakes," his wife, Adrianna, huffed. "The Dudleys!"

"The Dudleys, I know," Matteo scowled. He fidgeted with the crested ring on his pinkie. "We just have to think strategically. We just have to...."

He paused while movers set down a large cardboard crate in their salon. It contained one of the handmade dining pieces imported from Sweden. Elsewhere in their Tudor revival home, workmen were screwing in wrought-iron sconces and candelabra. The walls would be eggshell.

"Get this place up and running," Adrianna completed his sentence.

"I know. I know."

They gazed at their buffet—temporary, store-bought—and the magazines shingling it. *Washington Nights. Dupont Circles. D.C. Diplomats.*

Capitol Games. Each contained glittery photos of balls and receptions. Only the most illustrious events made these pages, and the most glamorous guests. But whereas in New York or Los Angeles, where fame could be measured in hedge funds and Oscars, here the sole metric was power. Or at least the appearance of it.

"That," Adrianna stated while drumming a lacquered fingertip on the journals. "That is where we've got to be."

Matteo nodded resignedly. "And to get good table, we've got to give it."

Giving it, though, required more than sconces and candelabra. The truly influential could attend at most two or three galas per week, while the city boasted dozens. Choosing the right ones was a matter of brute calculation, often conducted by senior staffers and secretaries. Each day, thousands of invitations went out—from embassies, Federal agencies, lobbies, charities, and museums—the vast bulk of them in vain. Receiving the right invites while getting yours accepted remained the key. And behind the lock lay power.

But Matteo and Adrianna Hallaby—a.k.a. Devereux and Bethune— could not even find the door. Four months in Washington and they had yet to be seen at any prestigious function or even a minor ambassadorial residence. And those dinners they did attend relegated them to the rearmost seats, alongside mid-level Treasury officials and the editors of local rags. Yet the task, they knew, required patience, and the pluck to stay in the fight. Hence, the house in lavish Kalorama, the Swedish imports, the candelabra. Still, while he world's finest table could be purchased, they knew, its diners had to be coaxed.

But why dine with the Hallabys? True, they made a striking couple. He, slim and as delicately handsome as some inbred Sardinian count, and she a nearly natural redhead with the figure of Marilyn Monroe. Comfortable with any congregation, changing religions almost as frequently as first names, they voted for both parties and hailed from virtually everywhere. And money they amassed through lucrative marriages and shares in Russian gas. But they still lacked that quintessential plus. Neither had served as secretary, or even deputy assistant undersecretary of anything, neither were Members of Congress, present, ex, or future or were related to the highly placed. Judges, generals, syndicated columnists, or commentators on cable TV—they could claim to be none. No, Adrianna and Matteo possessed only one advantage: their single-minded drive to hobnob.

Their objective was also unique. While Washington always attracted gold-diggers—the right connections could light up the shadiest deals—riches were not their goal. Elbows, rather, should be rubbed for rubbing's sake, they believed, the way the Himalayas rose to be climbed. And just as mountaineers scaled first lesser, then greater heights, so, too, would they plant the Hallaby flag on ever-elevated peaks.

"Once the right people see who's having dinner with us," Adrianna always said, "even righter people will want to."

A week later, the house was girded for hospitality. Adrianna prepared the flower arrangements and supervised the menu, while Matteo perused the registers. The invitations, emblazoned with an equestrian herald, went out by first-class mail. A month was the appropriate heads-up time, but twenty days passed and not one senator or even an assemblyman responded. The sole RSVPs came from third-tier choices selected from the protocol lists of previous administrations.

Later, over the dirty plates and wine pools that stained their new Swedish wood, Adrianna lamented, "We should have canceled."

She wore a lacy fit-and-flare dress, short enough to show off her knees, and an aquamarine choker that further elongated her neck. Adrianna listened rigorously to the guests on either side of her and spoke in her most mousse-smooth tone. Matteo, too, was refined, almost painfully. And still the evening flopped. Oh, the conversation was lively enough, but who cared about sports or politics or even the weather when those babbling about them were nobodies?

"No," insisted Matteo as he retrieved one of her cast-off shoes from the floor. "No, we have to learn from our missteps and move on." Though usually the more complacent of the pair, he was also the more even-keeled. "We," he announced, leveling a stiletto heel at her heart, "are getting a gun."

The weapon, when it arrived, scarcely looked lethal. A small, plain woman of sixty-some years, gray-haired, tartan-skirted, bloused and buttoned. Behind that blunt exterior, though, lay one of Washington's most incisive planners. "Miss Billington, are we glad to see *you*," Matteo greeted her at the door.

"Not Miss, Ms. or Mrs.," she corrected him, "Just Billington," while marching inside and glancing censoriously around. "I see we need to work."

Work began with dispensing with the Hallabys' postmodern canvases and replacing them with colonial portraits and landscapes of the Hudson River School. Wrought iron was out, pewter in, as medieval gave way to Early American. Next, came the sartorial tweaks. A Patek Philippe would be Matteo's watch, never a Rolex, and the pinkie ring was jettisoned, along with Adrianna's choker. Meals were themed, not eaten. Drinks poured generously but never consumed by the hosts, who were to remain at all times sober. Along with imparting these truths to the Hallabys, Billington lectured them on the musts.

"The Opera Ball, the Ballet Ball, the Meridian, anyone who's nothing is there," she explained. "The White House Correspondents' Dinner, you'd have to axe-murder somebody *not* to get invited. It's for the snootier events—the Gridiron Club roast, the Alfalfa Club—that you'll need sponsors. And sponsors aren't found, they're cultivated."

And cultivating first meant mapping. Scribbling on her tiptoes across Matteo's whiteboard, Billington sketched out not only who was who but, more saliently, who *knew* who. These could be courted through intimate soirees with notables and leaks to the gossip columns. An image or two of the Hallabys chatting with, say, a special prosecutor, cast into the ethersphere, would also prove efficacious. "The idea is to pick your target and then attack it from multiple directions," Billington attested. A stubby finger hammered the highlighted names. "Aim straight and kill."

The path to those tables was circuitous, but, Billington assured them, navigable. It began with what she called the "Disease Sprees," the Leukemia Ball and the Multiple Sclerosis Gala, admittance to which was tax-deductible. But getting *in* was merely preliminary to getting *where,* and Billington had already set her sights on the dais. And then came looking at *how.* Here, Matteo, a man, was useless. Tuxes were tuxes whether worn by royalty or a corpse. A woman's body, though, could be jeweled and gowned, pursed and muffed and gloved. In social climbing, a woman's body was the rope.

Billington spent hours scouring patterns for Adrianna's gowns, and assuring through dogged research that nobody else had worn them. Accessorizing, the advisor proclaimed, was an art form. They decided on styles that accentuated her curves, with neck and back lines that not only plunged, they plummeted. The colors—scarlet, teal, chartreuse—brought out her complexion, and sapphires advertised her eyes. As for the material, Billington would hear only of satin, sleek and unembellished. "Sequins," she said, "are for hacks."

"My God, you look like…" Matteo gulped as Adrianna sashayed down their staircase. "Like…"

"Like the cover of this," Billington waved one of Washington's glitziest weeklies.

And so she did, with a distinguished Matteo posing beside her. The caption, secured through networking debts forgiven its editor, read: "Meet D.C.'s Most Sought-After Couple!" The article listed some of the charities to which the Hallabys were devoted and the black-tie events they graced. Most importantly, the text hinted at some political clout, clandestine but effectively swung.

The results were seismic. Recipients of the Hallabys' next invitation vied with each other to RSVP. The meal, timed with Easter, emphasized rebirth—many eggs and baby vegetables—and arrangements of daffodils and crocuses. As instructed, Adrianna and Matteo barely touched their food, much less their drink, and instead focused on the guests. These were seated with the precision of eye surgery so that no matter which way they leaned—right, left, forward—the hosts looked directly into the face of a Majority Leader or, at the very least, a Whip. The conversation was pertinent but uncontroversial. Between the main course and dessert, Matteo tapped on his wine glass and rose for a toast. "To the President of the United States who we all agree, irrespective of party, is the leader of the free world. And to my wife, Adrianna, the sublime hostess of *this* party, and the leader of *my* world." Twenty stems held by high-ranking Executive and Legislative hands were raised to a chorus of "Here, here."

By the end of the ball season, the Hallabys' delectable image—his beef bourguignon to her strawberries and cream—was everywhere. Even *The Washington Post*, that gray disdainer of socialites, ran a profile. Most of it was fictional, fed to the wide-eyed reporter by Billington. Beyond their popularity, she somehow let slip, the couple also wielded untold influence, their opinions sought in places too towering to name.

The upshot was more invitations, more front-page spreads. From Billington, the Hallabys learned the technique of the drop-in, how to arrive with great fanfare at one event, march in and shake the valuable hands and quietly depart for another; how to change from cocktail to formal dress, black tie to white and back to business casual in a single, overbooked night. They grew accustomed to emerging from some fete only to be blinded by camera flashes. They smiled and waved, beamed and strutted into their chauffeured Continental.

Driving away, still blinking the blue spots from their vision, they failed to glimpse another car, similarly black but downscale, following them.

In fact, they saw nothing but the ultimate prize. Attaining it, though, seemed remoter than ever. Having reached a respectable crest, the Hallabys plateaued. Another gala season unfolded—the themes were autumnal, Adrianna's shoulders coddled in fur—but the one invitation they longed for remained unreceived.

"I've taken you as high as I could," Billington said. "You should be satisfied."

Matteo exchanged shrugs with his wife, as if "satisfied" were not among their words. "We paid you a fortune," Adrianna reminded her. "We expected to get to the top."

Now it was Billington's turn to shrug. "Money, flattery, baloney—it can only get you so far."

"So far? So far! The paparazzi love us. We're the darlings of the diplomatic corps. Hell, the papers think we run the place!" Matteo realized he was shouting.

Still, Billington remained calm. "You want to get higher, there's only one way."

"What event do we have to attend?" From her colonial rocker, Adrianna slung. "What cause do we give?"

"Not what but to who," Billington answered. "And not give, beg."

The Hallabys were ready to grovel. They dressed the part—striped tie, slacks, and jacket for him, and for her, a demure agora outfit. The driver let them off short of the door of a modest house in the Woodley section of Washington where a housekeeper in jeans let them in. They followed her into a den with a toasty fire and a Christmas tree as yet untrimmed—unexceptionable except for the walls, every inch of which was covered with autographed photos. Supreme Justices, prime ministers, network anchors, the Pope. The Hallabys' eyes darted from image to image, envious and awed. A second passed before they realized that the person posing with each of the grandees was occupying the armchair in front of them.

"We've heard so much about you," Matteo stammered.

The woman, whose social résumé began with the Truman administration, stroked the Persian cat in her lap and chortled. "I hope not too much."

Adrianna rushed to explain their predicament, but the woman held up a tremulous hand and smiled at them through strata of rouge. "I know who you are, or rather what. And I know why you've come. Why they all do."

Her name was Harriet Bravermann and she resembled a brown plastic Buddha left out in the sun too long. Rolls of spotted skin, wisps of once-chestnut hair, but with an impish, inextinguishable glint. The price of her services, the Hallabys were told, was patience. They were to wait while she toured them through every frame on her Me Wall, relating an anecdote about each. "That Henry," she laughed after one vignette, and "Oh, John Paul."

Adrianna and Matteo, cradling tea mugs, listened raptly, unsure whether Harriet would help. Not until she completed a surprisingly ribald account of accompanying a king on a road race with Elvis did she finally pause and grin.

"Well?" Matteo hazarded after several moments' silence.

"I think," the old woman cackled, more to the cat than to them. "I think I can be of assistance."

The Hallabys contained themselves until they were clear of the house and almost out of Woodley Park. Only then did they cheer and high-five and hug. They now had Harriet Bravermann on their side, not merely a gun but a cannon.

But they also had that old black four-door behind them, following at a pre-prescribed distance. Inside were two men, both of them shabbier than their car, but just as fixed on the Continental. And they, too, were armed.

Yet the Hallabys never noticed them as, with Harriet Bravermann pushing discreetly from behind, they bounded from one alpine event to the next. Up through the Cabinet, they ascended, to the senior counsels and visiting heads of state. With springtime near and the snow melting, there remained only one more white-crowned mount, stately with porticos.

Then, one sparkling June day, the invitation arrived. The faces of Thomas Jefferson and other Founders watched from the eggshell walls as Adrianna and her husband waltzed around the living room and into the parlor. Crystal jingled against pewter. Serious work resumed soon, though, as she weighed her wardrobe and he brushed up on the news. It was not enough just to stand on the pinnacle, they concluded, they had to stand there with style.

And this was the pinnacle: an intimate dinner in the Lincoln Room on the night of July 4th. The Hallabys' driver took the long way, crawling up Connecticut, while tourists swarmed toward the Washington Memorial to watch the celebrations. An hour of savoring passed before the Continental finally pulled up to 1600 Pennsylvania. The beat-up black car rolled to a stop thirty yards behind it with killed lights.

The evening exceeded their fantasies. The president could not have been more interested in Matteo's views on tax reform, leaning sideways to catch his words, and the First Lady could not get over Adrianna's chiffon A-line and the Mikimoto pearl necklace which, she claimed, belonged to her great-great grandmother. They, too, discussed policy, from international trade to minorities' rights. The other guests, among them two Nobel Prize winners, a former NFL quarterback, and a bipartisan selection of lawmakers, held forth. The silver shimmered, the candles revolved. Lincoln looked down pensively from the wall.

The Hallabys were the last to leave and the only guests to be personally escorted to the door. Afterward, the President and his wife lingered in the hallway, marveling. "I understand they have some pretty powerful ears, too," he said, and she added, "Yes, and now they have ours."

The trek down a mountain is often harder than the climb, and the Hallabys resisted the urge to sprint. They strolled arm-in-arm along the winding drive to the visitors' gate.

"You did it," Matteo said, still hesitant to raise his voice.

Adrianna had no problem announcing, "We did!"

"I'm so proud of us."

"Darling, me too."

They saluted the guards as they held open the gates. The night was glistening, the air, electric.

"Where do we go now?"

"What?"

Fireworks were bursting over the capital, practically above their heads. Confetti colors rippled across the marble façades and explosions reverberated around the columns. The Hallabys could hardly hear one another.

"What did you say?"

"I said, where do we go from here?"

"Where? I'll tell you where…"

But he never finished the answer. Nearby tourists thought the booms and flashes came from the display. None lowered their gazes long enough to see the dented black car speeding away. Nobody noticed—not that it would have mattered—the pair of riddled bodies on the curb.

News of the Hallabys' elimination stunned Washington. Embassies, charities, cultural institutions, all expressed the profoundest shock. The White House, too, put out a statement. Matteo and Adrianna were, the President said, "generous philanthropists, committed civic servants, and great Americans." He swore to track down their assassins, who were purported to be either Mexican drug dealers or Iranian spies or both. Their identities remained unknown but not so their motives. The Hallabys died, so the wisdom held, because they knew too much and moved in ultra-sensitive circles.

All of D.C. lamented, but few attended the funeral. Apart from a clergyman of indeterminate faith and pall bearers paid for by the estate, almost no one was on hand to mourn. Only Billington, with Harriet Bravermann leaning heavily on her arm, stayed for the first part of the service but left before the caskets were lowered.

"They gave good table," Billington rued with the graves behind her.

"Yes," Harriet agreed, "and they got it."

A Cure for Suburban Boredom

Outside of the convenience store, I watch the digital clock on my dashboard and wait for it to read 11:45. That is the time I chose—quite arbitrarily—to act.

Occasionally, my stare wanders to other objects. The store itself, which seems to float in gelatin, and its feeble customer stream. Working people, from the look of them: Caterpillar caps, indifferently fitting jeans, dreadlocks, a determination to tattoo every inch of skin. They enter and exit grimly with their cigarettes and six-packs, many wolfing down doughnuts. The clock, the store, the customers, and, once in a while, the tawny oilcloth roll on the seat next to me catches my eye. Only then I admit why I'm here.

Such moments, in fact, are my only wakeful ones. The rest are spent dreamily appearing as the company man, the family man, the man who could be counted on never to do anything undependable. A life that bores me so comprehensively that I cannot imagine how it fails to put others to sleep. And yet, that very sameness brings me distinction, whether from my wife, our children, colleagues at work, or the people we reflexively label friends. A good man, a principled man, they call me. A pillar of the community, if community is indeed what he had.

What he possesses, really, is this one secret self. The one that could never be suspected. And the self that, just minutes before 11:45, whispers to me the truth about who and what I am.

And what I am, what I live for, is frisson. The jacked-up state that infuses the dashboard dials, the spattered windshield, even the asphalt outside, with life. The sense that what I am about to do—what I've done before but never dared to think I'd repeat—is somehow preventable while at the same time, I know it isn't. This is the moment when everything else, from reading the morning paper to commuting and drifting through my day, becomes fiction. This, now, with only a few moments to go, is reality. This and the oilcloth carefully folded on the seat next to me.

Will I get caught? No chance! And, yes, of course I will. Those mutually exclusive, mutually inevitable scenarios—what sharper source of thrill and horror? Nothing, not rock climbing or hang gliding or deep-sea diving, competes. No booze, no drug. And nothing, I admit while pulling on the mask, leaves me more exposed. And though it's nearly midnight, I've never been more awake.

The clock says 11:43 and I imagine the numbers branded on my cheek. My knuckles, gnarled around the steering wheel, seem so white now, I half-fear they'll attract attention. Another customer, obese and wobbling buoy-like, waddles out of the glass doors with a family-sized bag of popcorn. I count his tormented steps. I count my breaths, shortening.

A digit flips. Seconds race to keep pace with my heartbeats. But ultimately there is no alarm, no buzz or even a tremor. Merely a faint crack of joints as one hand unfurls and stretches toward the oilcloth.

The other hand finds the door handle and lifts it, slowly, releasing my true self into the night. Ready to be wicked and inexplicable. Preparing, as I stride toward the light, to be.

Skirmish on
Chickamaw Ridge

Fog thick as hay bundles hid the tree line. One could barely see the trunks, much less the vines and undergrowth. From inside the forest came the squawk of chickadees, croaking frogs, and countless insects clicking. But, through the mist and the din, other noises emerged. The suck of boots in swamp mud, the clang of steel on tin. And one more sound: darrump, darrump, like some urgently repetitive message. And then the forms, slowly assuming dimension, gradually coalescing into a tattered line of men. Weather-worn but determined, they formed at the edge of the field.

"Company halt!" an officer shouted, and the marching ceased.

Dressed in butternut and grey with an assortment of hats—hardees and kepis—and with their Springfields still shouldered, they stood facing a row of cross-picket fences and a stirring patch of meadow.

"Present arms!" the officer continued. "Fix bayonets!"

From belts and scabbards, a hundred blades flickered in the fresh morning's sun.

"Prepare to advance! On my command, double-time, march!"

And they marched, weapons leveled, through the knee-high pasture. Drums thumping, Stars and Bars fluttering overhead, they neared the fences and began to pick up their pace.

"Steady men! Steady!"

"Steady men. Steady," a different officer ordered, but almost in a whisper, on the opposite side of the fence. As the tip of the flags and the first of enemy's sword-tips quivered over the rise, other muzzles lowered.

This officer and his men wore blue, though, and their uniforms were braided and crisp. Their flags, with stripes instead of bars, snapped defiantly over the formation.

So the two forces converged, ineluctably, on this field as they did on innumerable and often nameless fields in this ferocious war between brothers. And here, as in so many clashes, real brothers actually fought. Wilfred, in line with the rebels, assaulted his little sibling Jeb, standing his ground as a Yank. Fifty paces were all that remained before they shot at one another to kill.

And they were ready to kill, to maim first then murder, without hesitation or mercy. Mutually hostile since childhood, Wilfred resented Jeb's better looks, his quicker brain, his way with finances and women. One woman in particular, the love of Wilfred's youth, now called Jeb husband. Jeb, in turn, accused Wilfred of cheating their father—long deceased—out of all his lands and savings, of altering his will to make him, the firstborn, his heir.

To say that they hated one another was to admit the inadequacy of the verb. They lived on opposite fringes of the town, belonged to irreconcilable churches, campaigned for candidates ready to duel, and spat at the uttering of their nemesis' name. Their sole agreement, implicitly reached, was that the east side of Main Street belonged to Wilfred and the west to Jeb, so that the two could not randomly meet.

Such men did not need a war to battle. Without grapeshot and Minié balls, each could have torn his brother's innards out with his fingernails. And so, when the time came to pick sides, the two chose the one most likely to put the other in his sights.

Indeed, as the opposing lines converged, the brothers began their search. It would not be difficult. In addition to his slower mind, the older man was ungainly, wide at the mid-section, and in no shape to keep up with fleet-footed recruits. His spectacles glittered in the thickening light. The younger man similarly stood out. Flamboyant even in civilian clothes, Jeb in uniform preened himself with golden epaulettes and a bright purple plume in his hatband. Rarely in this war did enemies so savage make themselves such discernible targets.

"Steady, men. Hold your fire," urged the Union commander as first the heads and then the torsos of the Confederates came into view. With his thumb, Jeb cocked the hammer on his carbine. Huffing, struggling to keep up, Wilfred did the same. Yet, no sooner did he finish anchoring his weapon's stock in his armpit than he saw, just beyond the fence, the flash of an officer's saber followed by a blazing fusillade.

"Fire!" the order reverberated, but from which of the lines no one could tell. Irrespective, men began falling. Slapping their foreheads as if in afterthought, clutching their bellies and chests, they screamed and folded. Once hit by a Minié ball, their chances for survival were few. A spinning projectile of hot, hollow lead, a massive .58 caliber, the Minié shattered bones and splattered organs. There was little left for a surgeon to sew. But none of today's wounded would ever see a surgeon. The meadow depressed with bodies.

And still the fighting raged. Swiftly, mechanically, the soldiers spread their boots at right angles and planted a wooden butt between them. They reached into cases and rucksacks and fished for a paper cartridge, ripped off a corner with their teeth, and poured the contents down the barrel. Unsheathing ramrods, they ran the charges through and then they raised their rifles to hip-level. Pulled back hammers and crowned the nipples with a percussion cap priming their weapons. Only then, did they carefully take aim and, with a beckoning movement, close a finger on the trigger.

The blast bruised their shoulders. The smoke blinded and nearly choked them, and their mouths ran black with powder. Still, a well-drilled soldier could get off three or more shots every minute, and both Jeb and Wilfred were exceptionally drilled. Each fired multiple rounds and were down to their last, very special, cartridge.

By then, both lines were depleted, with those standing drenched beneath their woolen uniforms as the sun ascended to noon. Small arms rattled, less intensely now, and the drums only wearily beat. A cannon blasted a cauliflower of smoke. Wilfred and Jeb placed one another in their crosshairs, held their breaths, and shot.

The killing would persist until every last man lay prone and unshifting in the grass—or so it seemed. But, suddenly, a voice came down from on high. An otherworldly voice—a woman's—that might have begged her sons to cease this fratricide and reduce their muskets into mantelpieces. But, instead, the voice, accompanied by an ear-spitting electric screech, announced, "Let's all give a huge round of applause for our boys!"

Another crackle, not of sparks on powder this time but of a thousand palms on palms. Whistles and cheering, too. And, as if in some messianic vision, one by one, the fallen rose. They wiped the dirt from their pants and tunics, picked up their kepis, and hoisted their replica guns. Once again, the men approached the cross-picket fence but individually now, with no care for lines, and with hands rather than bayonets extended. Slapping dusty shoulders, they waded through the pasture toward the banner proclaiming "Chickamaw Ridge" and an array of refreshment tables.

Children hugged their father's knees, grandfathers posed for family photos, and the townspeople continued to applaud. Holly brought her husband a hotdog and a beer. "Best battle ever," she laughed. "For a moment there, I thought this time the South would win."

He laughed too, a little nervously at first but soon with his usual bravura. "No way. Johnny Reb ain't never getting past me. Ever again."

"But honey," Holly said, half-disconcerted, "I think you've been wounded."

She pointed at a glistening stain spreading down her husband's pants. But he just snickered. "It's just water, silly. My canteen must've spilled."

He held up the tin flask—an original, purchased on eBay—to show her. Only Holly didn't smile. She didn't sweep off his plumed hat as she usually did after the annual re-enactment, twirl his epaulettes and whisper, "Let's go home, hero, and get some real action." Rather, her violet lips parted, and her lovely sunburnt face blanched. In the dead center of the flask was a jagged hole just the width, she knew, of a Minié ball.

"Jeb…," she began, only to be interrupted by a scream.

One of the event's volunteers, a retired nurse, was cleaning up the field and chanced upon Wilfred. Sprawled face-up with his paunch barely concealed by the blades of grass, his glasses refracted the sun. He might have been resting—the battle was a bit much for a man of his condition—except for his hardened expression of hate. Except for the hole, much like the one in Jeb's canteen, in his forehead.

Penitence

"One spring night, David roamed his palace, and, from the roof, he saw a beautiful woman bathing. 'Find out who that woman is,' the king ordered one of his servants. Her name was Bathsheba, and, turns out, she was the wife of David's own general, Uriah. But that didn't stop the king. He had Bathsheba brought to his bed."

I always adored watching my husband preach. From the front pew where I sat with our sons, Timothy and Luke, I looked up at him as teenaged girls once ogled Elvis. Though Nathan was anything but flashy. Earthy's more like it, and compassionate. Especially compassionate, with a power to bring peace to the most tormented hearts.

And many hearts were anguished. Throughout the country, yes, but disproportionately, it seemed, in our church. First there was women's ordination, then gay marriage and gay clergy. Matters that went unuttered in my childhood were suddenly discussed in Sunday School. Those once branded sinners became, just by "coming out," heroes.

From his pulpit, Nathan went on. "When David found out that Bathsheba was pregnant, he sent Uriah back to battle, in the front lines where he was sure to be killed. And he was."

The congregation gasped, as if hearing this Old Testament tale for the first time. But everybody of course knew the story, and the gasp was their usual response to Nathan's sermons—quiet, learned, intense. From his unadorned pulpit, in his dove-grey vestment and its small, crimson cross, he looked out at us with an expression of rapt sincerity, of empathy for every soul.

That is the reason why, while controversies splintered other communities, ours flourished. Other mainline churches stood empty—the First Presbyterian down the road was recently sold to a bank—but our pews were packed. No, we weren't born-agains. We studied Bibles, not thumped them, spoke in no tongues other than Midwestern English. Yet people flocked to us. To the Reverend Nathan Philpot who, with a soft but principled hand, anchored this church on a rock.

"Bathsheba gave birth to a boy, who quickly fell ill," my husband continued. Through round, tortoise-shell glasses, he peered through the shafts of church-light the color of my old hymnal. He looked out over the congregants, above our sons and me, in search of Vivian Roberts.

I knew that because I knew my husband. Typical of him to reach out to a parishioner in need. Poor Vivian Roberts, whose own spouse of thirty years recently left her for a much younger woman—his secretary, according to reports. Vivian, who, after services, waited at the back of the line so that Nathan could take her hands in his and ask about her wellbeing, about the state of her children, and about whether he could be of any help. "May the Lord give you strength," he blessed her.

Here's another reason why I loved our church. While others bent God to their own preferences, remade Him in their own mortal image, we stood stalwart. Not every human weakness was sanctified, not every deviation affirmed. Adulterer, philanderer—there is no good word for a man who violates his vows. Betrayal still means disbelief, according to the Reverend Dr. Philpot. Infidelity breeds infidels.

Each Sunday after receiving Nathan's blessing, Vivian Roberts would be surrounded on the lawn. Person after kind-hearted person approached and hugged her, invited her for brunch. I embraced her, too. Plain, buck-toothed Vivian, in a worsted dress that her mother probably wore, reveled in the solace. Visibly, she glowed.

"King David prayed for that baby," preached Nathan Philpot. "He wept and fasted for days. In the end, though, his prayers went unanswered. The infant's death, he understood, was God's punishment for faithlessness. For his iniquity. Poor, broken David."

The congregation grew hushed, ashamed for the ancient Israelite but moved by Nathan's sympathy for him. For even sinners deserve our mercy, he always said, and to be welcomed back to the fold. Yet Vivian Robert's ex was not welcomed. Whatever-his-name-was never dared to soil our sacred space, not since his transgression, and even if he did, certainly he'd be shunned.

Nathan paused to remove and wipe his glasses, revealing the full gentleness of his eyes, stained-glass blue and backlit. His lifted a glass of water and sipped. I couldn't help but notice his fingers, long and delicate yet steadfast—a scholar's fingers, a saint's. Those same fingers swept sandy strands from his forehead and then spread out firmly on the pulpit.

"The Lord in his infinite grace forgave David. He forgave Bathsheba, too. And the two of them went on to wed and have another son, Solomon, author of the Song of Songs and Ecclesiastes, the wisest king of all."

I glanced over at our sons. Timothy had his father's tender manner, his pale but luminous complexion, and his caring for all things alive. Abandoned chicks, stray kittens, and puppies—Lord, the creatures I'd find under his bed. And Luke, studious Luke, knew Scripture better than any of us. God willing, he will make an inspiring pastor.

Back then, the two teenaged boys were, like me, content just to admire their father. And I was proud of them as well, the products of that early time in our marriage when I stared at Nathan with more urgent feelings. Those times passed, though. Quoting Corinthians, Nathan explained why we must no longer indulge. Our purpose on earth is to gain redemption not approval, he reminded me, to seek, however painfully, the truth.

"King Solomon who never once cheated on his wife because, friends, he had a thousand of them!"

The congregation laughed, uneasily at first and then uproariously. Their minister's razor-sharp humor, another reason for the church's popularity, could slice them at any moment. I laughed, too, and clapped my hands with delight. I was clapping still when Nathan's voice changed suddenly, grew whispery and still.

"Solomon who, according to Matthew chapter 1, verse 6, was the direct forefather of our Lord, Jesus Christ."

Someone somewhere shouted "Amen!" A visitor from another church, I supposed, where they do such things.

But Nathan just smiled and repeated, "Amen, indeed, for when asked whether a woman caught in adultery should be put to death, Jesus says, 'may he who is without guilt cast the first stone.'"

He stopped again and removed his glasses, not to clean them this time but to lay them flat on the pulpit. He stared at the half-emptied glass of water but left it unsipped. His point, I think, was meant for Vivian Roberts or, rather, for Vivian's ex. Yet then his gaze rose above the heads of his wife and children and beyond where Vivian usually sat. It fixed on the church's farthest reaches, on a person I imagined recoiling there.

"I come here today to lay down a stone. A stone that I have carried all my life but which I can no longer bear. Before you, my brothers and sisters in Christ, I place that rock."

The congregation, even the church itself, went silent, so much so that I thought I heard its old foundations creak. No one understood what the Reverend Philpot was talking about or what that rock could be. My feelings were also confused. Anxiety mixed with curiosity and fear as I awaited my husband's next words.

"When growing up in a little farming town and, later, at seminary, there were words that the boys used to joke about. Fairy, fag, queer. My worst nightmare was that someday those same words would be flung at me. Hell, with all of its fires and agonies, was preferable, I believed.

"But today, finally, I am putting that nightmare to rest. Today, from this pulpit in this, our hallowed church, I am declaring that I can no longer lead a double life. I can no longer lie. Seeking redemption, I must publicly confess that I, your pastor, am gay."

Nathan, still squinting at the rear of the church, nodded at someone and smiled. Then he gazed down at us. "My family will always remain my family," he said, "cherished and beloved. I'm sorry if I've caused you any embarrassment or pain. My only hope is that you can find it in your hearts to accept me as I now confess myself to be." Benevolently, he beamed at the congregation. "Forgive me, all, of you, if, by coming out in this way, I have let you down or caused you distress. Have faith in the Lord and have mercy, I beg you, on me."

No one stirred. No one even breathed, it felt. The organ which, at the end of sermons, traditionally thundered "A Mighty Fortress is Our God," stood mute. In the church-light, even the dust-motes hung motionless.

Later, I tried to remember who among the worshipers—Carl Wathney, perhaps—was the first to stand up in his pew. Who was the first to stride solemnly up to the pulpit? Soon, though, everyone ascended, even Luke and Timothy, beguiled.

They surrounded Nathan and locked him in their arms. They stroked his robe, his hair, his hands, and shed real tears of acceptance. The organ erupted into Bach.

Only I remained seated. Alone, uncomforted, clutching the old hymnal to my throat. No one approached to salve my humiliation, to commiserate with a woman betrayed. Vivian Roberts walked past me without notice. She embraced my husband, praised his courage, and wished him the Lord's strength.

The World of
Antonia Flechette

There were women who abhorred looking at themselves in the mirror each day, but she wasn't one of them. From the morning's first long study to the casual glances thereafter, the reflection deeply pleased and often elated her. The stately straight nose slightly cleft at the tip, and the cheeks that peeled away from it like Alpine saddles. The whorls of mahogany hair whisked aside by a back-wave of sculptured nails. The sapphire eyes, the slender neck often likened to a swan's. But the clincher, she knew, was the mouth, red and pulpy as tropical fruit. That was the beauty that her audiences adored and desperate lovers craved. And it kept the paparazzi trailing her, like the pair in the street below.

Dexterously, she applied her makeup. The base that she didn't need but that her agent claimed muted flashbulbs. The liner and mascara in which the jewels of her pupils were set. The lips needed nothing but a dab of Vaseline. That alone sufficed to raise sighs as she passed, striding in her sequined Givenchy to the ball, in the mauve Brenton hat that shadowed all but her mouth. Posing for photographs, stretching out fingers to her fans, she laughed and twirled La Pelegrina pearls that Enrico had bought her in Venice.

"Povero Enrico," she thought, one pallid hand on the wheel of his Spitfire and the other ineffectually pumping his lighter as they meandered the Amalfi Coast. Her laugher whisked off by the sea gusts that buoyed her hair behind the convertible. Poor Enrico, said to be Europe's hottest director, with his ivory cigarette holder and shoulders draped in sharkskin, that ridiculous pencil moustache and fedora. A competent-enough lovemaker when he wasn't in love but hopelessly self-conscious once he was. And how couldn't he be, favored to look at, to touch, and, when the whim induced her, to possess that daydream of millions, the idol, Antonia Flechette?

For Enrico knew that he was merely the latest in a procession of men, stunning, savvy, and rich, fated to be followed by others. A single dot on a lovers' line rumored to include Stony McClean, swashbuckling stuntman both on and off set, and Jesse Calhoun, who'd shot more Injuns in Hollywood than all the real cowboys on the range. Oil moguls, bankers, and underworld figures, a Latin American president or two—all stepped up for their fleeting turn and, even if heartbroken, left grateful. For just to be briefly in the bed of the starlet slated to surpass Hepburn and Monroe, to lay their head on breasts that billowingly defied all lingerie, and to inhale the ambrosia of her sheets, was invariably blessing enough.

Detaching herself from the mirror momentarily, she peered out of the windows and down at the street. Her palm waved gracefully, side-to-side, in the manner of Monaco's princess. The paparazzi hoisted their cameras. Little better than guttersnipes, their sole hope was to get a shot of Antonia as she appeared in those matinee posters, in a tattered dress exposing a thigh and her head thrust back in passion. Or a glittery profile such as often appeared in *Vogue* or *Look* or one of those tell-all rags. But scant chance of snapping that, Antonia knew, through the twin tablet-shaped windows. At best they'd catch a chin or jawline, framed within the Ten Commandments.

It wasn't always like this, Antonia recalled as she dabbled *Joy* by Patou on her throat. A miracle, in fact, that it ever could happen at all, remembering the ramshackle house she grew up in, the drug-peddling brothers, her mother a shipwreck in a bottle. Yet it was the daughter, Henrietta, who was the curse of the Arowitcz family, the disgrace, at least according to her father.

An air force man, a sergeant in charge of bombs, he frequently pummeled her. Not drunk, just kickass mean and furious at the luckless life Henrietta mirrored. No beauty, then, but beauty's opposite: barrel-chested, plump, with formless features that seemed stuck to her face like mudballs. And defenseless against the blows he landed on her, the open hand or uncinched belt doubled into a strop that raised bright red streaks across her backside. She screamed, she howled, but no one heard her—not her brothers out pushing dope or her mother well into her second fifth. "Daddy," she begged him, "Daddy," she asked, "why?" But the answer was always identical. Another slap, a few more strappings, his face a contorted welt.

Her only relief was the movies. A double feature for fifty cents, an afternoon spent far from pain in the company of Kim Novak and Eva Marie Saint. Or, for a dime, the latest issues of *Confidential* and *Photoplay* to be pored over in her room, devoured, until the pounding on the door resumed. Until the bomb sergeant burst in and once again unleashed.

Finally, she decided to flee. In her hand-me-down housedress, with little more than a toothbrush in her pocket, she snuck out of that house one late summer night and vanished—so she imagined it—with the fireflies. The rest was a story of rebirth, excruciating as all births are, but also triumphant. The ruthless dieting, the laboring on her wardrobe and posture. She waitressed and cooked, modeled and bit-acted, as well as other odd-jobs never to be mentioned, but made enough money to remake herself. And then the break, a supporting role in a Roman extravaganza with the legendary Robert Sitwell as Caesar. The film put her name on every marquee and all the critics' lips, her body in Sitwell's bedroom. The studios took numbers to sign her.

But Antonia did not like to think back to that and did her best to keep it her secret. As far as her fans were concerned, she was born to the Flechettes of Canada, renowned for their sable furs, raised in Manhattan but at home in the Marais, in Belgravia and the Riviera as well. She was always as she saw herself in the mirror today—crystal-eyed, juicy-mouthed, a confection, a dream, a goddess peeled off the screen and worshipped.

A final glimpse. Pinching the lapels of her serge Nina Ricci jacket, retrieving her matching Gucci bag, Antonia smiled at herself and preened. Enrico would be waiting for her, chain-smoking in his Triumph and worried that she wouldn't show up, that she'd left him for another director or heartthrob. That's the way she liked to preserve them, uncertain, watching and longing as she leapt carefree across the gilded stones of her life.

Perhaps she would keep him idling still while she posed for the two paparazzi. Why not give them the break even a deadbeat deserved? She waved again through the twin windows and turned on the gem-studded heels that made her already-majestic legs look monumental. That's when the juggernaut struck.

"Holy shit," one of the sewer workers hollered.

The second, chest-deep in a manhole, sounded louder. "Jesus fuckin' Christ! Did you see that?"

She hadn't, clearly. The cement truck struck her full-on, without the faintest chance of survival. Now she lay in the middle of the street, in a torn, faded housedress, a frumpy old lady with steel wool for hair and a face no less disfigured by death.

A cell phone lit up the hole. "I'm calling 911. See if she's got any ID."

Searching her pockets produced a card from some outpatient service. "Too much blood, I can't read it," the worker complained. "Henrietta, something."

"Then see what she's pointing at. Up there."

The dead woman was indeed pointing, smiling open-mawed at the top floor of a nearby tenement. Identical to all the others on the block except for a strange pair of windows. Vaguely bullet-shaped, sepulchral, the panes were thickly dusted. Still, squinting, the worker thought he saw something—a shadow, a ghost—but only for an instant. "My imagination," he said out loud to the rising acclaim of sirens.

The Curio Cabinet

My cell phone rings on Monday night at 9:30, right as I'm admiring my collection. Scowling, I close the curio cabinet and turn down the recording of *Macbeth*—to my mind, Verdi's best. The dispatcher, when I answer, briefly describes the victim and provides me with an address.

Grabbing my jacket—it's already chilly outside—I head for the door. But, typically, Punchau, my Inca Orchid, runs barking after me. I pause to rustle the chestnut crest of hair between her ears and assure her, with some confidence, that papa will be back soon. Only then do I hustle out the door and down three flights of dimly lit stairs to the granite front steps and the cobbled street in Inwood.

The working-class neighborhood's quiet this time of night. Dominican music faintly throbs. A whiff of that weird Cuban Chinese food. I get into the unmarked car and turn west from Staff Street onto Dyckman, past Fort Tryon and onto the Hudson Parkway. Lights flashing, I head south.

Not far, to 103rd and Broadway, just above a bodega and the subway stop. Three precinct vehicles are already parked there, and the area's taped off. A pair of plainclothesmen loiter outside. One greets me, "Hey, Birdman, how's flying?" insolently using my nickname. Another laughs, "Great tan you got there. Been fishing?"

"No," I reply, "basking in your fucking light," and push by them. Up two stories and into one of those Upper West Side apartments—long, narrow corridor leading to closet-like rooms—that used to be called a tenement and now rents for more than my pay. I haven't even reached the scene and I can already smell it. Death. Sudden, brutal death.

And, sure enough, fixed in the forensic lights, frozen in the photographer's flashes, the body. The coroner updates me but shouldn't waste his breath. I can see it all for myself. Plump woman in her late forties, early fifties, stripped and pushed face-down onto the dining room floor. Perhaps violated—the autopsy will tell—but unquestionably stabbed multiple times in the back, neck, and buttocks. She lies with her face to the side and her arms flailed outward, making blood-angels.

"Some job, huh Birdman?" a fat, balding detective sighs while he chews. He holds out a handful of peanuts. "Hungry?" he asks and nearly makes me leap.

"Very funny, Desabbato," I gasp. "You know where to shove those nuts."

Other detectives scour the apartment, gathering filaments with tweezers and depositing them into sealed plastic bags. But the chances they'll find anything are nil. This makes six homicides in our district in the last year alone, all of them unsolved and seemingly unrelated. Different victims, surroundings, modes of murder—except for one similarity. There's no DNA evidence, no finger or footprints, no threads or even a random human hair. No sign, even, of forced entry. The perpetrator's too cautious, and too familiar with police work. Though I'm probably the only one on the force to admit it, the killer we're after is serial.

I look at my watch—10:14—and pull on elastic gloves. I don't bother with the body and the dingy furniture around it, but instead slip into the kitchen. There's a wooden knife rack on the counter and I pull out the biggest blade. Sure enough, bloody. I bag the weapon, pass it to a sergeant, and move on to the refrigerator.

One can learn a lot from a refrigerator. Whether the victim was a vegetarian, for example, or an alcoholic. But the interior doesn't interest me as much as the exterior which, thanks to magnets, tells me volumes.

That's how I discover the dead woman's name, Freida Adams, and her occasional need for chiropody. There's a monthly staff meeting where

Freida worked, in the social services division of St. John's Cathedral, and a charity bake sale in the park. Not many Adams's sending Aunt Freida Christmas cards or family photos, though, and she apparently traveled alone. And Freida liked to travel. To Charleston and Sedona, Hialeah and New Orleans. Each destination has its own magnet, many shaped like the state or island, each enameled with coconut trees and beaches, racehorses and jazz bands. Freida prided herself on those magnets, arranging them on the freezer door in a rectangle so neat I could clearly see that one of them—vaguely fist-shaped—was missing.

Back in the dining room, Desabbato is taking another woman's statement. Her sobbing, actually, for it appears that she knows the victim from work. Through stringy gray strands plastered to her face, she wails about Freida, her tender soul and heart, and basically ignores the detective. That's where I step in.

"Miss?"

"Kesselring."

"Can you tell me, Miss Kesselring"—I offer her a tissue—"did Freida Adams recently go on vacation?"

Through the strings, she looks up at me and blows, a pale woman with splotchy cheeks. "*Vacation?*"

She glares at me as if I'm insane, but my nod tells her otherwise.

"A cruise, maybe? Somewhere, say, exotic?"

Ms. Kesselring glances around the room. Her eyes land on the body just as it's being bagged. "Yes. Yes, Freida went away in August," she slobbers. "But nowhere exotic."

I nod again.

"She went to Maine."

Within a minute, Ms. Kesselring is showing me Facebook pictures of Freida's trip. Among these is one shot of the deceased posing in front of a white clapboard building—The Bristol Bay Restaurant and Inn—and another standing next to a twenty-foot statue of a lobster. Turns out there aren't many such monuments, even in Maine, and that the lobster is something of a landmark. It belongs to the otherwise undistinguished Hathaway Lodgings located further up the coast.

I hand Ms. Kesselring a second tissue, thank her, and check my watch. Twelve thirty-five Tuesday morning, it says. So far, I'm precisely on time.

Still, it's hard for me to wait all night at the station, filing reports, faking interest in the autopsy report, trying to look busy. At 9:15, I make the first of several calls to local law enforcement officials in Maine. I identify myself and ask them to stop by the two hotels and question the proprietors. I'm interested if, during the late Freida Adams's stay, any other single guests were registered and, if so, what were their names and addresses.

Bless those small-town cops, they're always eager to help. By 11:00 a.m., I have the first of my answers. Turns out that both establishments hosted single male visitors during the time in question. A Robert J. Egret and one Timothy Smew. When it comes to false identities, you don't have to be Sherlock Holmes. These practically scream at me, since both of them are types of waterfowl. Still, the coincidence doesn't help me much, since the contact information they gave to the proprietors was also made-up. Less than fifteen hours into my investigation, I feel stonewalled.

But then, when I least expect it, a break. I suppose you couldn't call him a concierge, but the young man at the desk of one of the places where Freida stayed provides a description of Smew. Thirty-five, more or less, medium height, with thinning brown hair and—this he was specific about—a moustache like the kind men once wore in the movies. A pencil moustache, I guessed. Also, the young man took a liking to the kind of car Smew drove, a copper Kia Sportage. He happened to notice that it had New York plates and—the real tip-off—a rental sticker.

This is where the process gets boring. Assuming the man calling himself Smew did not reside in Buffalo, I access the data banks of rent-a-cars in the Greater Metropolitan area. They keep lists of vehicles rented according to date, mileage, and make. The search is disappointingly swift.

At 4:47, I'm at Cheap Car Rental—no kidding, that's the name—in Washington Heights. Luck sticks with me and the Sportage in question is still sitting in the lot. Seems nobody else likes copper.

Flashing my badge, the Dominican guy on duty rushes to open the doors. Even Cheap cleans its cars after they're returned, and this one's been thoroughly vacuumed. Well, not thoroughly. Gloves on, my hands probe the places nozzles can't reach: deep under the seat cushions, in the cracks beside the console, behind the pedals. The last spot's where I find it. A receipt which I see, holding it up to the last autumn light, comes from a pharmacy.

And not just any pharmacy, but one located right down the street. Not much challenge here either. The young Indian woman behind the counter can't look it up faster. The receipt's for the purchase of an epinephrine autoinjector. Well, I think, even a master makes mistakes. The prescription yields the customer's info.

There is little sense waiting, certainly not to call it in. The distance is a matter of blocks. At 5:53, I turn down Dyckman Street onto Staff, and park in front of a granite-faced building typical of the neighborhood. The list of names next to the buzzer tells me the man called Segal lives in 3E. Seated on the top of the steps, a dark-skinned kid eats from a container of Cuban Chinese and taps his feet to distant Reggaeton. He smiles and lets me inside.

I haven't slept in more than two days, but the clock is rushing and so's the adrenaline. Three landings later, hardly winded, I'm standing outside his door. Pushing back my jacket to expose the butt of my Sig Sauer—I like doing that—I knock and knock again. The third time, though, the door swings inward. And instantly I'm attacked.

Not so much attacked as assaulted. Paws on my chest, dripping tongue lapping my neck. It doesn't take much to subdue the animal, though, just a rustle of the crest between her ears. Relaxing, I take off my jacket and put on Act 2 of *Macbeth*, the part when Banco foresees his own assassination. "Come dal ciel precipita," he sings, "O, how the darkness falls from heaven." And I open the curio cabinet.

Displayed inside are six pieces of evidence. An EpiPen, a ticket stub from a Verdi Extravaganza, a chestnut hair from a rare Peruvian dog—these are the latest entries. Over each item hangs an index card inscribed with a time. Two days, nine hours, and sixteen minutes. Four days, one hour, thirty-seven minutes. And so on.

Reaching into my pocket, I produce a small metallic object. Reminiscent of a fist, it features a glittery lighthouse, a moose and several pelicans and, of course, a lobster. "Visit Scenic Maine!" it shouts. Placing the magnet on the shelf, I examine my watch. Eleven hours and fifty-eight minutes. A new record. Yet I can't decide whether to celebrate or cry.

Some people play solitaire and others challenge themselves at chess. I remember this as I close the curio cabinet and see my adversary's reflection—the thinning brown hair, the Clark Gable moustache—in the glass. Your win is my loss, I want to both congratulate and condemn him. My success is your downfall. And only the dead stay dead.

Nuevo Mundo

July 25, Anno Domini 1536

The rigging creaks like hangmen's ropes, and the beat of the sails recalls the thud of bodies cut down. More than eight months at sea, six adrift in these doldrums, our ship, *Delfina*, is lost. And we are alone. Shortly after provisioning at Tenerife, the waves rose in monstrous claws that snatched our three sister ships—two caravels and a carrack—along with their provender, armaments, and two hundred men, and dragged them under. Since then, we have wandered in this endless, windless ocean. Once we longed for bullion, silver, and slaves. Now all we yearn for is life.

Yet that yearning is unlikely to be filled. Our compliment of fifty hands is sliced to twenty—scarcely enough to man the three masts—and the larder yawns empty. Each day we consign at least one poor soul to the depths and watch, almost enviously, his descent. Father Rodrigo, his white hair and beard ghostly against his cassock's blackness, still recites the Requiem Aeternam. But his prayers are needed more by the survivors, condemned to slower, unspeakable deaths. Only our admiral, Miguel Bueno de Mesquita, remains hopeful. Day and night, he stands at the forecastle, his doublet stuffed with cordage to disguise his own emaciation. Shielding his eyes from the ruthless sun, he peers westward. But, alas, all he sees is the West. Shimmering. Blinding. Empty.

JULY 28, ANNO DOMINI 1536

I, Luis de los Rios y Guitierrez, serve as the admiral's page. The riches of the Indies also fired my mind, but so, too, did the thought of finding my mentor, the famous Captain Lope Acuña. When barely able to dress myself, I was apprenticed to him by my father, and from Captain Acuña I learned all that a man needs to cross oceans. Yet, when the King commanded him to explore the farthest shores, to plant there our Catholic faith and enrich its Earthly Ruler, the captain ordered me ashore. "Grow up," he scolded even as I wept. "Great seamen must first become men."

Those were the last words I heard from him. Four years passed and no letters, much less treasure, returned. But grow I did and strong enough to wield a sword in our Savior's name. Like many squires, I listened raptly to the tales of New Spain and Peru, of Cortés, de Soto, and Pizarro, of the small bands of conquistadors vanquishing vast savage armies. I ached to join those bringing civilization to a bestial world. I dreamed of El Dorado. But most of all I dwelled on Captain Acuña, who was more of a father to me than my own. A locket with his likeness—balding yet comely, battle scars cleaving his beard—dangled from my neck even as I boarded the *Delfina*.

The voyage was to replicate that of Acuña and perhaps reveal his fate. But our paramount quest was discovery. New lands, new missions, and mines to fill the kingdom's coffers. To enlighten the natives, we carry the fruit of our science—astrolabes and clocks—as well as the harquebuses and cannons, powder and shot, to subdue them.

All that is a miserable memory. After the storm, after months without easterlies or landfall, nothing remains but the specter of death by starvation or worse. Sailors often tell of crews left floundering and bereft of food who devoured, ultimately, one another. One captain, it was said, after feasting on the last of his men, mounted the masthead and, with a wheel-lock in his mouth, fed his brains to the fishes. This truly is the evilest of crimes, the undoing of all that we stand and sail for. Instead of saving savages, we become them. Our souls sink not into seas, but hellfire.

AUGUST 1, ANNO DOMINI 1536

Along with the locket of Acuña, I now wear around my neck the keys to the magazine. My eyes cautiously follow the crew—Moors and Morannos escaping torture and the stake, desperados fleeing the gallows. My fear is not of mutiny, for which few of them retain muscle. Deranged by hunger, though, they might eat the gunpowder, rendering our firearms useless. Already, they have sickened drinking bilge water. Not far is the lure of human flesh.

Before succumbing to that urge, I will follow that captain's example. My blade will pass over such veins that, when severed, will deprive me of life but assure me peace eternal. No doubt Acuña did the same, if lost in these latitudes.

With one hand on the locket, the other on my hilt, I keep watch over the deck. Behind me, Admiral Bueno de Mesquita is still peering. With his arm looped around a hawser for support, he gazes and gazes West.

AUGUST 4

Land!

I was just completing my watch, fighting to keep on my feet and not faint in front of the men, when Curiel, our helmsman, shouted. A stunted, one-eyed Converso, Curiel was nevertheless deft with a rudder and his surviving eye keener than any pair. Excitedly on his dwarfish feet, he pointed toward the horizon. The clouds, though low and thick, seemed to part for him, and then he spied it. Barely containing my only exuberance, I stood behind Bueno de Mesquita as he inquired whether Curiel had reverted to his old Jewish falsehoods. Desperate minds can cruelly deceive, the admiral warned. But no, I found myself crying aloud, it's real. Not only land but trees. And not only trees but, gathering curiously on the shore as we hoved, people.

The admiral selected the ten men best able to stand and ordered them to arm. My chest nearly buckled under my breastplate, my arms and legs sagged beneath their greaves. My helmet felt like a hundredweight. Even this ledger of leather-bound vellum, once insubstantial, proved leaden.

With great exertion, we managed to lower the dinghy, to rappel ourselves inside, and row. Curiel manned the tiller as Bueno de Mesquita stood braced in the bow with Father Rodrigo, cross and missal in hand, fast behind. When the keel scraped sand, the admiral and the priest managed to hoist themselves over the gunwale, and I followed them, sword drawn. The three of us waded toward the natives.

They were mostly naked, as expected, their delicate parts covered by tight, brightly colored cloths. But their skin, rather than brown, was of a flaxen cast, as was their hair. A comely race, lithe and well-proportioned. And curious. Rather than dispersing at the mere glint of our armor, they congregated around us only to sneer and step back, as if from some noxious odor.

The admiral raised his blade and declared, "In the name of Our Lord Jesus Christ and of His Highness…" only to collapse to his knees. Father Rodrigo uttered something in Latin before presently doing the same. Only I was left with the white of the sand, the blue sky and sea, swirling around my eyes and my body sloping backward, listless, into the arms of one of the tribe.

AUGUST 11

How shall I begin to describe the wonders we have witnessed in this land? How, if I had not experienced them with sound mind and Christian heart, might I relate miracles performed for us and the mercies bestowed on our souls? I do not know if El Dorado indeed exists, but if it does, it resembles this, a city not of gold but of magic.

From the beach, the natives bore us a league or so to their capital. No moat or battlements—no defenses whatsoever, only hard-tarred roads and bridges made of burnished steel, and structures higher than the tallest castle, tablet-shaped and constructed entirely of glass. Across the ground and throughout the air whirred the most marvelous machines and at speeds many times the swiftest stallion's. There are, in fact, no horses to be seen, nor carts or litters. No sails for harnessing wind. Only engines of ingenious design and unfathomable reservoirs of power.

In one such vehicle we were borne, the admiral, the priest, and I, and escorted into a chamber of soothing light and refreshing air, both from indeterminate sources. Natives, men and women, pressed fantastic tools to our eyes, tongues, and chests. Bags of liquid, conducted through hose and needles, streamed into our arms. They stripped and washed us with aromatic ointments, dispersed with our rancid vestments and draped us in white linen robes.

One of the conquistador's first tasks is to train native translators, but our hosts relieved us of this toil. We conversed and a machine the size of a hand transformed our well-mannered words into their babble and their babble into our mother tongue. We made it clear that not only the three of us, but also the remainder of the crew were in urgent need of salvation. With smiles and pacific gestures, they assured us that all of our men would be supremely cared-for, treated and feasted like kings.

We, too, when bodily able, partook of strangely textured juices and meat of a delicacy unknown to my palate. In a short while, Miguel Bueno de Mesquita looked once again like the vigorous admiral I served and even Father Rodrigo regained his ruddiness.

Recovered, we were led into an even larger hall, to be greeted by the tribal elders. Unlike those on the beach, clothed in what I now understood to be raiment for bathing, these savages were cloaked in jackets of dark material and pantaloons not unlike a peasant's, with white shirts beneath and bandanas of florid silk knotted around their necks. One of them stepped forward and, with a half-bow, presented himself. His name, translated by that hand-sized machine, was El Líder.

More or less the admiral's age, El Líder was significantly taller, broader-limbed, and robust. From a face as regal as any in Christendom, his white teeth blazed, and his blue eyes glinted like Dutch porcelain. His hair was a rolling, golden sea. He took each of our hands in both of his and bade us ardent welcome. We returned his courtesies and assured him of our sovereign's mercy.

AUGUST 15

Mere quill and ink cannot convey all that we have seen and experienced. From the portraits on the wall in which the images both move and speak to the fireless ovens and the staircases that rise while climbers stand motionless—all defy lettering, even language. Our hosts do not even need ledgers to record events but merely press little buttons. Words appear on a bright surface before them, perfectly formed.

We have so much to learn from these aboriginals, and so much to take home. The admiral is especially impressed. He speaks endlessly of the advantages these blessings can bring to our own people, easing their pains and relieving their hunger, entertaining them. So exhilarated is he that he barely hears Rodrigo's grumbling about the absence of priests in this land, or even churches.

My mind also whirls in astonishment. Often, I merely sit in my cabana, a simple room with two windows that look out at the dinghy, still beached and attracting the natives' curiosity, and at the unmanned *Delfina* off-shore. I rarely notice them, though. My attention rather fixes on the floors that reflect my likeness and the water that runs, both cold and hot, without pumping. I sit in a bath of glistening spume or turn the dials that bring forth music of all manners and loudness, or that stoke and extinguish the light.

The lack of priests is the least of my thoughts, along with the paucity of churches. Not once did I question the whereabouts of Curiel and our crew. And while Bueno de Mesquita dreams of returning home with our discoveries, I fantasize about taking one of the native girls I saw on the beach, bronzed with clean-shaven legs and a nose like a miniature prow, of forgoing fortunes in wilder climes and remaining in this Eden forever.

September 5

Once again and perhaps for the last time, penmanship fails me. This ledger is inadequate to contain the chronicle I must inscribe and its pages too diaphanous for its burden.

So busy had I been for the previous fortnight, so preoccupied learning everything I could about this enchanted New World, that I lost all interest in the ledger. It remained in my room, gathering motes, alongside my sword, which the tribesmen were kind enough to return to me. I had no use for either the log or the rapier or for the Old World they represented. A world of ceaseless wars, famines, and the auto-da-fé. Here, by contrast, men lived in peace and plenty, and accepted one another not for the God they did or did not worship, but for the humanity we commonly enjoy.

To Father Rodrigo's rage and then anguish, I missed Mass one day and then two, and finally stopped attending altogether. I felt cleansed of any sins to confess, other than my dwindling devotion to Acuña. The captain who had, through his rigorous instruction, taught me all that was needed to bring me here, who fathered me without ever once meeting my mother, was receding from my mind. I ceased gazing at the locket still centered on my chest and contemplated removing it entirely.

Then, last night, to celebrate the first month's anniversary of our landing, El Líder invited us to a feast. All of the tribal elders were gathered, arrayed in black frocks not unlike those worn by noblemen back home, but hatless. Black sashes, like sideways hourglasses, adorned their necks. The three of us—the admiral, the priest, and I—remained robed in white linen, which could have made us feel uncouth. But the setting was so grand, with enough silver in the candlesticks and the cutlery to stir any conquistador's heart, that we all but forgot our apparel. Bounteous mounds of food were laid before us—exotic fruits, savory legumes, and that meat of such singular tenderness.

Raising a glass, El Líder toasted to the admiral and expressed his delight in hosting him. Bueno de Mesquita returned the honor, with blandishments usually reserved for court, while Father Rodrigo looked on sourly. Other salutations followed, and many spirits were imbibed. Too many, for, in short, I felt in need of a privy.

Exiting the chamber, I entered a long hallway where, I learned, the natives keep their latrines. These, too, were dazzling, a luxuriance of mirrors and fountains and tiles to rival Alhambra's. Closing my robe, relieved, I turned to rejoin the festivities, only to come face to swarthy face with Curiel, our helmsman.

Winking his only eye, he rose on his undersized feet and whispered at length into my ear. His words, more than any tales of El Dorado, astounded me. "No tarrying, then," I rasped back at him, quietly as possible, but my words resounded like cannon fire. "We must alert the admiral."

Back toward the main chamber we ran, I in my robe and Curiel in the gray pantaloons and threadbare shirt of prisoners, both of us barefoot. We arrived and peeked through the same door I had exited. Too late. The next scene will remain furrowed in my mind—and my ghastliest dreams—until Reckoning.

El Líder, laughing, leaned toward the admiral as if to impart some secret. But instead of speaking, he fixed his teeth deep into the explorer's throat, and tore it out with one gnash. Blood spurted furiously across the tablecloth and other finery and with such copiousness that I could hope my commander had expired instantly, without suffering. For pain was presently inflicted, lavishly, ravenously, as the other natives pounced on the admiral and gouged his eyes, his heart, and viscera. They ripped and, with whatever tissue or organ their fists detached, stuffed their gore-dripping mouths.

Father Rodrigo attempted to scream, or perhaps to pray, but not before he, too, was set upon. Disrobed, dismembered, the priest was devoured before our eyes. And our eyes had seen enough. If shocked into inaction, Curiel awakened me with a slap of his gnarled hand on my cheek. Lacking shoes, our departure went for a few moments unnoted, but then I heard harder footsteps—the natives'—nearing ours. I motioned him to follow me through yet another door, not another latrine, but into some kind of stateroom.

Throne-like chairs lined the walls and an incalculable number of books. Plush rugs, soft on our soles, bedecked the parquet and a fire crackled in the hearth. We waited while the footfalls passed down the hallway outside and fled beyond earshot. Only then did I notice the stone mantel and above it, stuffed and mounted, a human head. I looked at it and with frozen eyes it stared back. The balding pate, the beard-defying scars—there was no need to consult the locket, I recognized him at once. Acuña.

How many seconds passed before I responded to Curiel's tugs on my sleeve? Suddenly, we were running again, this time out through a fence with pickets just wide enough for us, but not our pursuers, to squeeze through. Then we dashed toward the dingy. Most reluctantly, Curiel allowed me to stop in my cabana and retrieve the ledger and sword. Of the former, the helmsman cared nothing, but he praised his Maker—Yahweh or Christ—for the blade. This I used to dispatch a brace of savages who were still gawking at our craft which we then heaved into the surf. Scurrying inside, we each took up an oar and plied with all our souls' might.

Of all I learned as a guest in that land, I never gleaned its name. And I thanked God for that, for otherwise it would relentlessly haunt me. I was grateful, too, not to have witnessed the torment of the crew who, once greeted and fed, were swiftly reduced to slavery, assembling pieces of alien machines that floated past them as they labored. They worked until no longer capable and then were condemned to the tribesmen's table.

So Curiel informed me as we rowed past the *Delfina*, its anchor too heavy for the two of us to raise. Past the reefs and the breakers we plied, out into the ocean, where a chance current might carry us to one of our American colonies or some other civilized post. We rowed until dawn, without food or water, and scarcely enough ink to conclude this entry.

APRIL 19, ANNO DOMINI 1540

To the Capitán General at Veracruz, greetings,

Along with the shipment of two hundred weight of iron ingots, forty powder barrels, and assorted African slaves who were watered at my Mission, I am pleased to enclose this ledger. It came to me by way of a native fisherman who claims to have found it aboard a dinghy.

The boat contained the skeletons of its two navigators, one of whom, according to the savage, looked deformed. The other was clutching the ledger. The inscriptions inside, though scarcely legible, are outlandish. One can only assume that, except for the name *Delfina*, a royal carrack that indeed went missing some years ago, the tale told within is the work of a depleted mind. I would not be surprised to learn that the name Luis de los Rios y Guitierrez appears nowhere in our records, nor does that of Lope Acuña.

For your distraction, I will relate that the sword of the self-same skeleton lay crosswise across his wrists and from his ribcage dangled a rusted locket. The portrait inside had long washed away, though one could assume it depicted Santiago, our patron saint, or some other sacred image.

Such are the sacrifices of our quest. May these mariners' souls, along with our enlightened efforts, be blessed.

Alien Report

Entering the galaxy via the trans-axymortic portal, we considered pausing on a bluish-gray planet which, according to our records, supports peculiar strains of existence. In preparation for a possible descent, we queried Bina, which illuminated us as follows:

"Over the course of four billion of its stellar orbits, the planet spawned roughly 14 million species. These began with prokaryotic to photosynthetic organisms and progressed into aquatic and land-based life. Of the latter, the most complex, adaptable, and largely sentient species is 605431.

"Nocturnally supine and diurnally erect, 605431 first appeared very late in the planet's span but quickly rose to dominance. Originally dwellers in metamorphic cavities and, later, in habitats constructed from easily procured materials, 605431 soon concentrated in colonies. These grew increasingly dense and were often led by the least capable specimens. The close-knit associations that once provided for mutual help and defense were replaced by isolation and vulnerability. This process is known to 605431 as evolution.

"Like all of the planet's life-forms, 605431 must respire the bluish-gray atmosphere. The species eats many of its fellow creatures but feeds and shelters others. Food is introduced through an aperture which is also used for communication. Two additional holes serve to eject unused nutrients in maligned form. Through much of its history, masses of 605431 succumbed to a scarcity of sustenance. Yet many now suffer from excess.

"Unique among the planet's life forms, past and present, 605431 is gratuitously violent. The species fights not only for food and space but also for shiny metals. It fights for pleasure and pride. Colonies, meanwhile, strive to conquer one another. The conflicts can be justified by the different sounds used to describe the same object, by mode of colonial rule or, simply, the need for self-acclaim. Combatants battle under a colored square of cloth for which they will both kill and die. Though the organs inside 605431 are identical, the membrane containing them are variously shaded. Such diversity, however superficial, also causes strife.

"Yet no violence spills more of 605431's liquids than that spurred by belief. And belief not in laws, number systems, and similar abstractions, but in the most hypothetical notion of all. Though almost none of the specimens claim to have seen it, most believe that they and their planet were created by a Great Force. But disagreements over the words, desires, and even the name of this Force spark the fiercest clashes. Citing that name, bands of 605431 can treat others even worse than the creatures they slaughter.

"Still, existence for 605431 is not entirely belligerent. Specimens are divided into two iterations which may be mutually attracted. Magnetism is expressed by attaching the apertures used for mastication and communication. This linking can, when most intense, lead to the insertion of a segment of one iteration into a second's receptacles. The action also enables 605431 to reproduce. The products usually experience a sense of affinity to their producers as well as to their co-products. The creation of this impulse is widely ascribed to the Great Force.

"But even this benign drive can be transformed into a source of discord. The iterations, though reciprocally drawn, are frequently at odds. While usually pleasurable, the insertion process can also cause anxiety, pain, and even conflict. Producers, products, and co-products compete, at times to the death. The presumed predilection of the Great Source for one band of 605431 can mean total annihilation for another.

"Strangest of all is the 605431 concept of 'I.' Though possessed with a potent—relative to its planet—ability to garner information, the species seems unable to grasp the oneness of its surroundings, much less the universe. Instead, it condenses reality into the most miniscule compartments for which we have no counterpart, but which translates remotely into 'me.' More inexplicable still is the result of this condensation which 605431 calls loneliness. It is the cause of a persistent anguish that can lead certain specimens to self-destruct."

Bina's illumination complete, we considered the following: while not toxic or inordinately hazardous, the planet's bluish-gray atmosphere and manifold organisms do not present us with any insurmountable challenge. But 605431 necessitates entirely different calculations. Its savage nature, determination to inflict harm whether for parcels of land or pieces of fabric, its rivalries, jealousies, and vicious beliefs and, above all, its impenetrable focus on self, render it unsuitable for even the briefest visitation. The species, we determined, was simply too alien. Accordingly, we altered course, re-entered the portal, and left this galaxy behind.

The Perfect Couple

How did two of the world's loneliest people ever meet? Where else but in a hotel bar where Lionel fled to escape the photographers and Ruth to deaden her thoughts. He had just finished interviewing for a magazine dedicated to prettiness—big on glossies, lean on text—and she lecturing at a nearby college where the faculty walked out exhausted. Both sought refuge in the bar where, over beer nuts and pretzels, they found each other, the genius and the heartthrob.

What was the mutual attraction? The fact that Ruth only glanced at him once, sideways, before gazing back into her drink? That Lionel asked her what time it was rather than what time itself was, and seemed thoroughly satisfied with the answer? No, it was the recognition of the singular knowledge they shared. That perfection, whether of body or mind, is lonesome.

For Ruth it began in infancy. Able to add before she could walk, to tie together complex sentences, and read her own diaper box, she'd completed elementary school by kindergarten and entered university at twelve. She memorized Shakespeare and saw through Bach's exactitude to the foaming madness behind. Her parents, though both professors, long failed to keep up with her, as did a succession of tutors and deans. The rest—string theorists, slam poets—vied for her attention, but not so boys her age. Plain, loamy eyed and haired, with a figure little advanced past puberty, Ruth was scarcely an object of lust. Girls, too, kept their distance, for how to discuss the wildest shoes or sneak a cigarette with a person who doodled in Sanskrit? Well into adulthood, ideas were her only companions, a rarefied circle of equations and verse that none would approach much less penetrate.

For Lionel, too, loneliness came with birth. The doctor, the nurses, he later heard, stepped back as he emerged and even his mother shrunk from cradling him, so stunning was his face. His hands and fingers, too—indeed, every part of him, as if especially selected from a catalogue of features. But while exquisiteness in most attracts admirers, the sight of Lionel scattered them. As if they were looking at a godhead, forbidden and potentially fatal. Gawkers, then, kept a distance, or cowered behind cameras. Occasionally, he glimpsed the sadness of women beholding what they could never possess, or the resentment of men confronted with their own mortality. But mostly Lionel saw fear. Of the dimpled chest and chin, ringlets the colors of precious metals and eyes a Caribbean blue—fear of a beauty that defied natural boundaries and threatened to upend the world.

Which was why Lionel shocked himself by being the first one to speak. "Is it really that bad?" he asked, referring to the way Ruth glowered at her glass, as if at a wellspring of faults.

She replied to her gin. "Did you know that algorithms have attitudes? That conchoids often talk back?" He didn't, clearly, but Ruth asked another question, "Did you know that all of Chaucer can be reduced to co-signs?"

Lionel crunched on a nut. "No kidding," was all he said before posing some questions of his own. "Have you ever heard of mirrors that were peeked into and melted?" Gravely, he sighed. "Did you know that looks from the drop-dead gorgeous can, in fact, kill?"

Ruth laughed her immeasurable-IQ laugh—three chortles in exactly the same key. "By your accounts, I should be dead already."

"And by yours," he guffawed, "I'm just a stack of numbers."

They giggled and clinked, toasted and sighed, as the liquor poured and confessions flowed about lives lived within a head and just beneath the surface. They exchanged tales of nights dreaming of what it'd be like to be a normal person—not stupid, perhaps, or ugly, but moderately smart and attractive and surrounded with real friends who liked them for who they were and not for their epidermis or cerebellum. Hours passed in that hotel bar, while Ruth admitted that she didn't know beauty except for physics, and Lionel confessed to failing math. Bowls of beer nuts emptied and by closing time, the two of them, the Einstein and Adonis, were matched.

Theirs was a low-key romance, totally removed from the public. Entire days were spent in bed, lovemaking at times, but mostly just clutching. As if Ruth wanted only to let Lionel inside her skull, to allow him to linger there and not be afraid of its contents. Similarly, he wanted to lead her to a heart identical to everyone else's, his gut and liver, too. Embraced, they experienced a sensation unlike any they'd ever known. For once, deliriously, neither was ever alone.

That is, as long as they stayed indoors. Outside, though, the reporters gathered for a scoop. Like a pair of royalty or rock stars, Ruth and Lionel were the source of endless fascination—and guesswork. What would their children be like? Brilliant and hideous? Half-witted and handsome? Articles often cited the eminent author who, when invited by a diva to make a baby "with your brains and my figure," famously quipped, "yes, madam, but what if it's the other way around?"

Ruth and Lionel ignored the chatter and focused solely on their love. But the laws of attraction and motion prevailed and, less than a year after that portentous night in the bar, Ruth was already expecting. Now it was their turn to ask, or rather pray. "Let her look like you and have all of my mental capacity," he wished, while his wife laughed in monotone. "May he be blessed with inner beauty and outer grit." She rubbed her vertex parabola. "May he never know solitude."

Nine months later, alas, the medical staff again went rigid and even Ruth hesitated to nurse. The child was flawless. The feet, the nose, even the eyelashes seemed imaginary, conjured from a mythical list. The face could easily adorn a diaper box and the only question was: could she read it?

So Ruth and Lionel asked themselves as anxious weeks passed. Intentionally, the baby's room was decorated like any other, with rainbows on the walls and a menagerie of cuddly dolls. A mobile of the sun and its planets orbited the crib. Still, the parents hung back at the door while little Gaia slept, as though she might suddenly start speaking in Latin.

She didn't, and Lionel and Ruth were relieved. Instead she cooed and cried and pooped just like any newborn, and steadily they bonded with her. They joked about how they would make Gaia fat or dress her shabbily—anything to blunt the sublime. But dazzling she remained well into her fifth month and the morning they found her standing in the crib. In her delectable grip, she stayed the mobile and reordered its orbs. She stopped, though, at the sound of a gasp and smiled. "Look Mommy, Daddy," Gaia exclaimed, at least not in Latin. "Our solar system!"

They gaped at her in wonder. In horror. Here was a child who could grow up to redeem humanity or destroy it. A savior, potentially, or satan. Either way, their daughter was doomed. The world's most perfect person, they knew, Gaia would be its loneliest.

Live in Fame,
Dive in Flames

I n the first three years of World War II, the United States produced more than 200,000 combat aircraft. Thousands crashed in training accidents or vanished flying overseas. And those that did make it into action were frequently shot down on their first missions. On a single raid in 1943, sixty bombers were lost and six hundred airmen killed.

Civilian deaths were massively higher. Not only Germans and Japanese, but hundreds of thousands of Frenchmen, Italians, Austrians, and Czechs were killed—collaterally or intentionally—by allied bombing.

None of this slaughter slowed down the enemy's war effort. On the contrary, it only accelerated.

* * * * *

Chester blew on his balled hands. Though only September, the chill came early to Kansas this year and, pre-dawn, made it feel like late autumn. He blew and rubbed and looked over his shoulder at the headlights sweeping up the runway. Then, he went back to his contraption—tightening a rivet here, there securing a wire—minimizing the chances of failure.

"They're coming, Pop," Scotty informed him.

"I know, son."

"Maybe you can put in a word for me," the young man added as his father, crouched on one knee with a flashlight between his teeth, fidgeted. "My number's coming up next year, you know."

"Pass me that ratchet wrench, will you."

Socking his palm, rocking eagerly on his heels, Scotty addressed the approaching beams. "There's a thousand guys for every pilot spot, I heard. But they could get me in, betcha."

"Betcha," Chester grunted, giving a hex bolt a final torque. Only then did he stand up and slap his hands on his thighs. He stood next to his son who, though lanky like him and tawny-haired, was hatless and at seventeen, taller by a head. They stood just off the end of the runway, the two of them in their pleated pants and waist-length canvas jackets, as a U.S. Army Packard pulled up. Four men stepped out.

Three were in civilian clothes—double-breasted suits and somber ties, wingtips, and fedoras—but the fourth wore the peaked cap and uniform of a full-bird colonel. He was the one who spoke.

"Twenty minutes, that's what you got, McGarry." Armed with a mass-produced military face, his only distinction was the paunch straining his tunic. "These gentlemen are busy."

Chester removed his workman's cap and held it before his chest. Clearing his throat, he said, "Thank you all for coming." Then he turned to his son. "Okay, Arthur."

But the young man did not react. He remained, rather, fixated on the three men on whose lapels he pinned his dreams. Chester frowned at him. This was his only son, named for a grandfather he never met, but who supposedly died broken-hearted and drunk on these plains. The son whose late mother hated that name and so called him just what she wanted and what he, growing up without her, preferred.

"Scotty," his father conceded and finally the boy snapped to.

"Sure, Pop." He bent into the grass and retrieved a kettle-shaped object, transparent with an elongated grip.

"This, gentlemen, is a Super-Emitron," Chester began. "It's an advanced iconoscope with an improved photocathode that captures light and turns it into electron images. It then projects those images onto metallic granules that can be scanned and made to emit the images on a…"

"McGarry," the colonel barked, "cut the voodoo and get on."

Chester clutched his hat to his throat. "Television. The Germans have been experimenting with it for decades. They used it to broadcast the 1936 Olympics."

The colonel scowled. "War's no game, McGarry, and no damned teelee whatever-the-hell-you-call-it." He consulted his watch. "Fifteen minutes."

Rising, the sun regarded itself in the pale, glassy sky. The first rays illuminated the prairie, accentuating each blade. By the Packard, three bright dots, like morning stars, glimmered as the civilians lit up.

"A Super-Emitron can transmit a picture of, say, us, standing off this runway, to anywhere in the world. To Washington, D.C. To England!" Congenitally quiet, Chester nevertheless let himself go. Even his face, so spare it barely contained his sorrows, gleamed. "But here, here!" He snapped his fingers at Scotty, signaling him to lug over the camera.

And lug he had to, despite his youthful strength. Together with its tripod, the camera was an unwieldy monstrosity weighing more than he did.

"It's so big because the Super-Emitron's inside," Chester narrated. "But we can reduce it all, the iconoscope and the camera to something like this." He held his wan hands the width of his sternum. "And put it in the nose of a rocket."

The four men might have reacted to this information but, just at that moment, the air rippled with a deep, droning sound. It seemed to emanate from far down the runway, beyond eyeshot. As if to catch a whiff of wild indigo, the civilians lifted their noses, exposing slight smiles. Chester, somewhat louder, kept talking:

"And once we implant the camera, we can see where the rocket's going." He practically leapt. "We can guide it!"

The colonel glowered at him but the others, if only for a moment, leaned forward. "Guide it?" one of them asked.

"Exactly, Mr..."

"Never mind their names," the colonel cut in. "He's Mister Ford to you. The others, Mister Grumman, Mister Douglas."

"Okay. Yes, guide it, Mister Ford, the way you'd guide a radio signal. Except in this case, your target audience is just that, a target. Your audience is the enemy."

The three civilians appeared dumbfounded. Only the colonel snorted and was again lifting his watch when Chester pre-empted him. "I'll show you."

He limped ten yards to a spot where the sun now revealed a table and a ziggurat of gadgets—dials, buttons, meters, and a dull, bible-sized screen. Chester laid his hat beside the set and started adjusting. His back was to the runway now, but still he talked.

"Each B-17 and B-24 costs you—well, maybe not you but the tax-payer—about $200,000. That's more than most folks around here earn in a lifetime."

The colonel stepped forward, stiff-armed. "Where'd you get those numbers?"

"The Army's Statistic Bureau. It's where I serve," Chester replied and explained how a childhood harvester accident left him 4-F and fit only for desk jobs. "So I see a lot of numbers. For instance, statistically speaking, American airmen cannot survive their required twenty-five missions."

"And what about this"—the colonel gestured dismissively at the table—"crap?"

Chester considered telling him about teaching science before the war, his fascination with optics, the nights tinkering alone in his shed. He wanted to describe his desperate struggle with time, but instead he answered, "This crap is my hobby."

The droning sound, meanwhile, intensified. It reverberated through the ground and up into their soles. The tips of the prairie grass quivered. The minutes, Chester realized, were dwindling. He turned and began "Arth…" but checked himself. "Scotty. If you don't mind."

A second passed before the young man managed to detach himself from the buzz and take up a small cardboard box. He presented it to the colonel and his civilian guests, treating them each to binoculars.

"May I direct your attention to the rise about two hundred feet to our east?" He pointed at a mowed circle surrounding a rocket-like device. Rocket-*like* because, rather than conical, the head was bulky and roughly rectangular, with swept-back wings at its neck. "And then, a football field away, to the south." Chester again pointed and four pairs of binoculars trained on the rusted tractor hull that he and Scotty had hauled with a pick-up.

He nodded at Scotty who produced a matchbox from his pocket and lit the fuse that ran from under the table and burrowed into the grass. "What you're about to see, gentlemen, could change the course of the war." Chester's body stiffened but his eyes lingered on his son. "What you'll see could save uncountable lives."

* * * * *

The water, split by the prow, reminds me of the part in her hair. Everything reminds me of her. The sea smell—salt, sand, hemp—surrounding her. The sweep of her heron-like neck, her skin the white of gull feathers. Marie-Madelène. Her name is whispered by the tide.

Pepe—my father—opens the throttle as our skiff rounds the promontory. He is singing to himself, I see, the words drowned out by the motor, but the tempo kept by the cigarette bouncing in his toothless mouth. He takes no notice of the big guns and barbed wire lining the beaches of Le Portel. He cares nothing about the Germans—*le boche*—nothing even about the war, only about his mussels and how many he can market today. The world can wreck itself—"*Va au diable*," he spits. He seems to me an old man already, indifferent to the same soiled sweater and overalls he wears every day, his stubble, caring only for his nightly dram of calvados and the mussels. *Toujours les moules.* They have fed us since time began, he once told me, and they, alone, matter. Germans, wars, they come and disappear, but mussels always remain.

And Marie-Madelène. We have always been together, she was born two months after me in a house down the street, and together we will always live. There is the lighthouse whose corkscrew ladder we used to climb as children. I blush now remembering how I used to let her go first so that I could peek up her skirt. And there, jutting out in the ocean, the great stone slab of Fort de l'Heurt, home to endless bouts of hide 'n seek and duels with driftwood sticks. She never failed to win, and not because I let her.

The lighthouse, the fort, all have been taken over by the Germans. But I no longer care. We do not play, Marie-Madelène and me, at least not those kind of games. Since turning fifteen, our rollicking has become something else. Where once I could not get her out of my life, today she possesses it. Now everything—the waves, the foam—recalls some part of her. The air itself wafts her brine.

The promontory is behind us, and the Équihen Plage comes into view. Pepe steers the skiff landward, the wind lifting his tattered collars. I, though, stay perched in the prow. The ripples breaking against the gunwales recall my moods the night before when the two of us, Marie-Madelène and I, snuck into a warehouse near the port and there, hidden by the cages, buoys, and nets, embraced and kissed and more. She never removed her plaid skirt with the shoulder braces or even her ankle socks. Nor did my trousers come off. And yet, somehow, thrashing, we fused.

Later, exhilarated, frightened by this power and mystery, I lay, listening to her tell me how we'll have to wait two more years to get married. "Je t'oime," I confessed to her in our Norman dialect, but she only shushed me and explained that her parents would never allow it.

Two years! Could have been two centuries. Who knew where I might be at seventeen—September, 1945!—conscripted into one of the *boche*'s work gangs, probably, half-way to being an old man like Pepe. Or caught in a squall, I might be mussel food.

Death, in truth, was easier to contemplate than those endless two years. How much suffering could I endure, this anguish of seeing her in everything around me? The thump of the hull against the ebbing surf, like the sounds we made in the warehouse, as Pepe guns the outboard toward shore.

They stand like sentries—not soldiers but our *bouchots*. Rope-spiraled stakes are set in the sand and seeded with baby mussels. There, shielded by mesh, they grow and fatten until ready to be pried off, fried, and eaten. This my job, mostly, to select the ripe ones and dislodge them with a three-pronged hand-rake and drop them into big tin buckets half-filled with seawater. Pepe meanwhile lights one butt with the tip of the other, curses, spits, and watches me.

This is the part I hate most. Not because the mussels do not detach easily, even with the rake, and have to be clawed by hand. No, I hate the resemblance between the mussels and her eyes, black-blue and tear-shaped. I hate that the spiral stakes recall the dark braid that falls to the small of her back and which I wrap around my face lying next to her. I hate that from here, on Équihen Plage, I can see across the grassy bluffs to Le Portel and the sloped, coral-colored roof of her house.

Marie-Madelène. I repeat her name to myself with every plop of mussel into the bucket. I sing it to the sea and the sky. I would shout it up and down the Norman coast if the Germans would let me, and even if they wouldn't. Instead I sigh while hauling the harvest to the skiff where my father, hounded by gulls, waits smoking. Her eyes, her braid. The billowing clouds that recall the softness of her body. Her breath in my ear as we lay in the warehouse becomes the buzz of airplanes approaching.

* * * * *

When Negroponte said, "Don't worry, I've got your back," he meant it literally, his buttocks knocking against Tully's throughout the flight. They bumped again, hard, bruising both their coccyges just as the bombardier announced ten minutes to target. Not that anybody needed updating. A pair of 109s had already probed the squadron's perimeter, picking off stragglers. With three of its four engines sputtering, the first of the Fortresses fell.

Tully watched it drop from his waist gunner's window and waited to count the chutes. Four bloomed. It was the *Apache Squaw,* and he knew all ten men aboard. But he had no time to mourn. "Nine o'clock! Nine o'clock!" The tail gunner cried into the radio and shook the plane with his twin .50 calibers.

Tully bolted his own Browning, crouched as low as he could in his steel helmet and 24-pound flak jacket, peering through the ball and ring sights at the slipstream hissing outside. His face was frozen—frostbitten, again, probably—and his fingers numb, even the thumbs on the trigger. What did they expect at forty below, he wondered? What did they expect with the sweat of lower altitudes freezing behind his knees and his oxygen mask rank with the spam and powdered eggs he wolfed down after briefing? The smell, almost aromatic but still acrid, of airplane fuel. Tully needed to pee, he wanted to puke. He longed to be back in Chelveston.

Not the town, which resembled any other in central England, with its mossy churches and overpriced pubs, cold and fog-girded, but for the girl, Beryl Nicholls. Supple body cloaked in flannel, a woolen beret battening her hair, back home she would have passed for a child. Yet though three years younger than Tully, at sixteen she knew far more. Maybe it came from living near the RAF base, but she knew how to kiss him, nibbling his lips and tongue, and where to guide his hand. And she promised far more than that—everything—after his twenty-first mission.

He ached to be back at the Enlisted Men's Club. There the gunners, sergeants all, drank, and the pilots and other officers sometimes stopped by to bullshit. Beer bottles clinking. Laughter like ack-ack piercing the smoke. Anything to conceal their terror from one another but above all from themselves.

Here was his crew of the Wildcat Wendy, as they dubbed it, a scantily-clad pinup wooing on its nose. Simpson and Wazowski, Rice, Cunnigham and Sokolov, Torentelli and Smith—natives of places Tully mostly never heard of, from scarcely imaginable lives, bonded by a war utterly inconceivable to them as kids. Still, he loved them all—more, he often felt, than he did his own family back in Edison, New Jersey.

And most of all he loved Negroponte. "Blackbridge," he sometimes called him, or simply "the Greek." A hulk of a man, destined like his father for the docks of Stockton. Tully's age, but somehow, he, too, seemed older. Wiser. Able to listen to his friend when he confessed his fear of being trapped in a cigar tube 22,000 feet over the earth while hundreds of strangers shot at it. Only to him could Tully admit that he had never known a woman and dreaded dying before he could.

Negroponte who, as the other waist gunner, worked directly opposite him on an aluminum walkway barely wide enough for one man, much less two in thick winter overalls, hunched with their butts sticking out and swerving as they fired. And each time they smacked, Tully, a bantam, got the worst of it. Which was why at the end of each mission, the Greek would turn with a big-toothed smile that lifted his earphones and swiveled his chin like a ball turret. "I got your back, Tully boy," Negroponte winked. "All over mine."

But Negroponte wasn't winking anymore, not smiling either, but jolting hard into Tully's spine as the plane lurched side to side, struggling to stay in formation. More screams on the radio, more bursts from the tail, and the bombardier cursing, "Fuck this cloud cover, I can't see shit."

Someone suggested, "Then just drop our sticks and get out of here," or rather begged. But the cockpit urged steadiness. Six more minutes to target.

Wildcat Wendy bounced and pitched, and Tully barely kept hold of his gun, much less fired it. Yet somehow Negroponte managed. He got a bead on something and peppered the air. Empty cartridges rattled across the walkway, further tripping Tully. He only gained his balance once, long enough to blast at a shadow zipping past his window—a Messerschmitt, he hoped, and not a fellow bomber.

Another B-17 disintegrated but slowly. Sliced in half by a nosediving 109, the bomber broke midway through its fuselage. Its wings folded and snapped. Through the clouds it drilled, flaming. No chutes.

"Three minutes to target."

"Fuck the target!" someone shrieked, but the cockpit ordered everyone to shut up.

Negroponte, meanwhile, was firing and then wasn't. The plane, blind-sided, jerked horizontally before righting itself and allowing Tully to stand. His vision cleared and discerned just to the right of his window a yard-long gash spurting light. Viscous liquid dripped from the frame in front of him and he thought, "Shit, the hydraulic line's broke." With landing gear stuck, they might have to bail or worse, belly-land. "Beryl Nicholls," he said to himself and pictured her skirt and beret.

"One minute. Bomb bay open."

"Hold on, everybody. Hold on."

"Just drop the fucking bombs."

And then, all at once, quiet. The 109s vanished, the firing stopped, and only the engines thrummed. Tully watched as the liquid froze but not before he dabbed it with a finger and saw a color not hydraulic brown.

"Here it comes, boys, get…" a voice began warning but was cut off by a deafening smack. The first of the flak bursts snapped not far from his window and reeled him backward. The formation had entered "the box," the section of sky nearest the target and studded with anti-aircraft batteries, their shells set to burst at 22,000 feet. Ragged black nimbuses with angry red cores, they dotted the sky, missing most of the planes, but then, one after another, igniting three of them.

"Greek! Greek!" Tully wailed. Enemy fighters he could cope with, but not the flak. He felt like a pheasant flying over a field of hunters with their 12-gauges raised and firing.

"Twenty seconds to target."

Another burst and Tully could see the number two starboard engine trailing smoke.

"We're hit!"

"Five seconds. Hold on."

"Get us out of here!"

"Blackbridge," Tully sobbed and reached behind him for his friend's hulking back but felt only emptiness.

"Bombs away."

Relieved of 5,000 lb. payload, Wildcat Wendy rose slightly and cruised. Tully turned to find Negroponte sitting on the floor, leaning against the fuselage and smiling. Above that smile, though, his head was gone.

The whine of bombs descending became Tully's scream, but then both were muted by a boom and a fist of fire unfurling from the cockpit.

"No! No!"

Tully groped for the sack with his parachute but could not find it in the smoke. No matter: his body was too burnt to bail. Pinned by the ammunition belt, his gun and its pintle, he found himself glaring upward as the B-17 unwound. The September sun was suddenly in his face and sucking out the contents of the plane: radios, aid kits, fuse boxes, electrically-heated boots. Last to fly were a flannel skirt and woollen beret. They twirled and fluttered out of reach as the young man plummeted toward France.

* * * * *

Resistant to the three-pronged fork, the last of the ripe mussels gives way to my fingernails ripping it from the *bouchot*. It reminds me of how, as dawn penetrated the warehouse, I had to tear myself away from her. The weight of the tin bucket, now nearly filled, is feather-like compared to my heart. Only the hum of engines above grants me hope of some higher redemption. Though never much of a believer, suddenly I am, and I know that God will unite Marie-Madelène and me two years from now, if not sooner.

I drag the bucket to the skiff and expect Pepe to spit as he always does and curse me for not hauling more. But my father is not belittling the bucket or even scowling at me. His bloodshot eyes are squinting rather at Le Portel which is suddenly sparkled by flashes. A second or so passes before the rumbling reaches us. The *boche* are shooting their guns. The clouds are also illuminated here and there, as if by a summer storm.

"*Dieu nous sauve*," Pepe mutters as the droplets descend. That's what it looks like at first, rainfall, though rain does not fall in lines. Rain is not drab and, striking the earth, does not erupt in flames.

I watch as the coral-colored rooftops rise and disintegrate. Cobblestones scatter like pigeons. A fishing boat bobs in mid-air.

For an instant, I consider pushing my Pepe aside and gunning the skiff, but that will take too long. Instead, I drop the bucket, spilling its contents into the sea, and set off running across the promontory.

Through the high grass of the bluffs I tear, howling her name even as the explosions hammer it down my throat. Already I can feel the heat of the fires, smell the burning petrol and meat. The Germans in Fort de l'Heurt, though dowsed by geysers, are still firing, but my village is wrapped in flames.

She lives, I tell myself with each gasp. She lives and will rush to meet me on the bluffs. We will embrace and bless whatever God she wishes and wed once the rubble is cleared.

Above me, one of the bombers corkscrews through the clouds and breaks apart, but I hardly notice. I care only about running and reaching her. The last stretch of grass is littered with debris—a bedstead, a cross, a bicycle, a hoof—that I sidestep before hurling into the blaze.

I cannot see, cannot breathe. Fiery figures thrash past me. Beams and steeples collapse. Screams, cries, sounds made by men or animals. Even if blind, I could always find her street, but her street—any street— no longer exits. So I call out to her. *Marie-Madelène. Marie-Madelène.* Through the fire that reminds me of passions.

My face and hands are scorched, but I feel nothing. Not even when I fall to my knees on the broken glass and shards of masonry and sift through the ash. I will dig and strain, comb and claw, fingers bloody. Forever I will search for the hair like water split by a prow and the spiraled stake of a braid. I will seek, peering through the embers, a pair of mussel-gray eyes.

* * * * *

Like a tiny train puffing through the prairie grass, the lit fuse raced. The colonel and his three civilian guests peered through their binoculars and watched the smoke climb to an eastern rise. Chester, meanwhile, assisted by his son, was already twisting the dials on his table and turning on the screen. It flickered with soapy light.

"A real rocket will be electrically ignited, of course," Chester commented. "Our budget was kind of limited."

None of the observers nodded, perhaps because they could no longer hear. The droning from the far end of the runway grew louder still. But no noise could muffle the crack of fuse and fuel. Curls of flame unraveled across the rise and the hammer-headed rocket wobbled. It tilted one direction and then another and appeared about to collapse, engulfed in its own propulsion. Then, with a shudder, it rose.

Several feet into the air, the fire-spewing rocket hovered. But a secondary explosion sent it soaring so high that sunlight blinded the binoculars. The colonel was about to complain but Chester preceded him with, "Watch the screen."

"Screen, hell," the colonel huffed. "It's empty."

Chester half-turned and grinned. "Watch," he repeated and then enjoyed seeing the four men's faces fall.

On the screen, grainy but identifiable, were three fedoras and a peaked military hat, all seen from above and rapidly looming closer. An instant later, the rocket shrieked over their heads. Everybody except Chester ducked, even Scotty, who hissed at him, "*Dad…*"

"Don't worry, son. I've got it."

Chester twisted furiously and dialed. The rocket swung into a wide arc that led back over the runway and southward toward the prairie.

"Watch!" Chester shouted.

Scotty pointed at the tractor hull a hundred yards away. The binoculars followed his finger, just in time to see the rocket strike the wreck. A bouquet of smoke, flame, and rusty shrapnel blossomed over the grass.

"That, gentlemen," Chester cheered, "that is the end of World War II!"

Yet the civilians on the runway said nothing. Rather, lowering their binoculars, they let the colonel react. "You can't be serious, McGarry. What, with this…this *toy*." Glancing over his shoulder, he smirked at his guests who seemed to smirk in return.

"No, no toy." Chester limped past the colonel and practically lunged at the three men, who reflexively stepped back. "Guided rockets can take out Hitler's bunker," he exhorted them. "Hell, they can take out Hitler. They can take out Tojo, too. No need to invade Europe. No need for Marines to die on no-name islands just to get closer to Japan. We can win the war right from here, in Kansas, and with a fraction of the sums you pour into your planes."

Only now did one of the civilians—Mr. Ford, perhaps—speak. "With all due respect, Mister McGarry, your rocket will take years to develop. But we don't have years. We have a job to do right now." He tugged his fedora definitively. "And we make the tools to do it."

Chester started to respond but was cut off by the drone which, at that moment, became thunderous. The runway darkened, the prairie grass bowed, and colossal motors churned up the sky. The men held their hats and looked up as the B-24s roared over.

The colonel patted his paunch. "Off we go into the wild blue yonder," he sang, laughing, while rejoining the civilians in the Packard. "Live in fame or go down in flame!"

Chester gimped after them. "No, please, listen. It's doable, I know it. You can save millions. Dollars. Lives."

Car doors shut in his face, Chester looked desperately around the runway. "Arthur," he cried to his son, "Scotty. *You* tell them."

But Scotty was not looking at his father or even at the Packard as it sped off. He stood in the grass with his hands in his pockets and stared upward. Wondrously he gazed as the cruciform Liberators, ten men pinned in each, vanished over the horizon.

* * * * *

Sick as it sounded, he welcomed the heat. The city already awash in flames from the British bombing the night before, the firestorm respiring, glowing with each breath. And so hot that, four miles up, you thawed. The only problem was the smell. Just like a Fourth of July barbecue only bitterer. Sinister. He would never forget that smell, he thought, or enjoy another cookout. He might never see another one anyway.

This was only his seventh run and already he teetered on madness. Already, he had seen a bomber in his squadron crash on take-off, its nose stabbed into a ditch. Little fire balls, like tumbleweeds, scurried away from the wreckage and, watching from his cockpit, he remembered thinking how strange that seemed. Until he realized that the weeds had heads and arms.

Then, two sorties ago, he saw an 8,000 lb. bomb dropped by a plane in his formation hit another one directly in front of its tail. The stricken aircraft blew up—nothing, not even tinsel, remained of it. Only viscera splattered on his windshield.

Ten, fifteen, or more men he had breakfasted with those mornings and got shit-faced drunk with the nights before—whose names he could still remember, already long dead.

Only mission seven and the boy who never touched a cigarette back home was up to two packs of Luckies daily. Who never sipped a beer much less heavier alcohol could now not sleep without guzzling both.

Seven down and an unfathomable eighteen to go, and his grip on the throttle and half-circle yoke were far from solid. So were his bowels. He feared showing himself a coward in front of his co-pilot and crew. He feared being hit by flak and falling like that plane, in countless pieces, downward.

For there was only flak now; the enemy was out of Messerschmitts. All those gunners—tail, waist, turret—aboard and nothing to shoot at, nothing to do but wait and pray not to become a statistic. That and make fun of their captain.

"How about a bedtime story, Arty," the radioman riled him, "to keep us all awake?"

He had a reputation for talkativeness around the Officers' Club and for being tight-lipped once aloft. Both from nerves, he knew.

"Something spooky, please. While we sit by the fire." This from the bombardier, to which the navigator added: "No one spins 'em like Arthur."

He was going to tell them to shut the fuck up and stop calling him Arthur. Call him King Kong, because of his height, but never call him Arthur. But when he pressed the microphone to his throat, all he could grumble was, "Cut the chatter. I can see the city ahead—the fires anyway. Any second, we're in the box."

That second was now. The clouds ahead were blemished with black and red. The wall of ack-ack looked impenetrable. Soon the explosions would rock their craft and fling chunks of jagged metal at its fuselage. Some planes would be hit, damaged, downed, while others randomly got through and roasted another town.

He clasped his fingers firmly around the yoke and squeezed his sphincter. While keeping a steady course, he tried to think of safer moments—chasing his gimpy father through the prairie grass, tinkering with him late nights in the shed. He thought of rockets running ribbon-like through their formation, braiding their contrails into garlands. He thought of the longer life he might have lived.

"Hold on, boys," the airman said as the first .88 burst near their wing. "Hold on."

* * * * *

By the last year of World War II, 2.4 million Americans—a third of all those fighting—were serving in the Army Air Force. The cost was $50 billion and nearly 90,000 dead.

Civilian deaths mounted radically—more than a million Germans and Japanese killed by firebombing.

While the Allies continued to rely on air attacks, the Nazis developed the V1 and V2 rocket. Radio-guided, some 14,000 of these missiles inflicted significant damage on their targets and more efficiently—according to a U.S. Army intelligence report—than bombers.

Though it possessed the technical means to make rockets, the U.S. instead invested $2 billion in producing the two atomic bombs that killed an additional 220,000 Japanese.

In total, the United States rolled out 33,000 B-17s and 24s. After the war, almost all were scrapped.

Pray, Prey

Cicadas crackle in the heat of the juniper tree that shades my after-feed nap. Sleep comes effortlessly in this late afternoon hour, numbing my paws as I lick them and yawn. My belly rises and contracts, rumbles and purrs, with meat. The flies are already working over the carcass and soon the vultures will arrive and other scavengers. But I will lie here, dozing, digesting, awakening only to gnaw on the succulent bones of my most recent—and curiously easy—kill.

How different this one was. Other animals try to blend in, furs and feathers mimicking the jungle. They prick up their ears to listen, their snouts to sniff, sensitive to the slightest growl or whiff of my scat. Their eyes scan the underbrush for a subtle shifting of stripes. Registering danger, they will bound away on spindly limbs or, if heavy-hoofed, lower their horns to fight. Once pounced upon, though, their end is predetermined. As they, themselves, seem to know. There is little crying as my claws slice through their hides. No pleading, certainly, as my jaws crush their skulls. Only a solemn resignation that they, too, have joined the cycle of death and consumption which I and my appetite drive.

But not this one. Swathed in a red brighter than the blood that would soak it, indifferent to contrasts and camouflage, it padded along the trail. With a stick, beating the fronds which, nodding, marked its progress. Neither a grunt nor a bark rose from its mouth, but rather this high-pitched warble, part caw, part murmur. Mindless of the jungle.

Impervious to movements and smells. And emitting this mawkish odor—not of fear or even rutting, but of sandalwood and spice.

An unusual animal, to say the least, for even I enjoy a struggle. Even I relish the hunt. But it denied me both. And I might have let it pass, this prey unworthy of the name, singing and swatting fronds. But hunger trumped my contempt. So, I tracked it, slithering through the growth, stalking at a distance that would have sent all other beasts scurrying. Then, catapulting off my hind legs, my body launched into a spine-smashing arc.

But the animal did not flee. Shockingly, it did not even battle. Instead, it merely curled in on itself and squirmed on the ground like a new-born. A scream, louder than a hyena's, rifled the jungle, followed by noises I have never heard. "Mercy, please," the animal kept braying, and something that sounded like "God." Until my canines pierced its skull and filled my mouth with sweet, creamy brains.

A most unsatisfying kill; I was relieved when the whimpering ceased. Then I took my meal. First the fleshy parts behind the rump, that separated with a single bite, and then the mid-section. This was less palatable, perhaps because of the creature's last meal, something leafy and tart. Most organs, though, were tasty enough, and for a long while I dipped by face deeper and deeper into the cavity I chewed. My coat and whiskers reddened.

Finally, only my victim's face remained. Its eyes strained wide, lips stiffened around that last, peculiar sigh. The cheeks, the nose, tongue and brows—these and the bones were the treats that completed my feast in the buzzing shade of the juniper.

A curious creature, indeed. Unafraid yet panicked, vulnerable but bold. Hubris and simple mindedness mixed. And guided by an instinct that it, alone, lived outside the cycle. To eat and be eaten, this is the only equation. Every breathing thing knows it, accepts it, succumbs to it. Everyone, apparently, but this one, for whom that knowledge no longer applies. Who once ambled and warbled and unsettled the leaves and now remains, as do all once-living things, offal.

My Little Whiffle

The corridor reeks of imprisonment. Not a conventional stench, not of unwashed skin and soiled clothing, but of faces unraised to sunlight, of souls perpetually sealed. Mawkish, antiseptic. It always strikes him entering the wing—that and the presence of evil.

It exudes from the cell of the Boonton Butcher, the blood of a dozen children on her hands, and from the bunk of Betsy Rae Hanson, who strangled and chopped up her husband before feeding his entrails to the pigs. Evil, it makes Beecham clutch his pistol butt as he files past the bars, striding toward the final set. There, in a chair afforded him by the guards, campaign hat perched on piped trousers, he sits.

"How's My Little Whiffle doing?" he asks, and from the ball of orange crunched up in the corner emerges the reply, "About as good as anybody, I guess, with three more days to live."

He smiles at her. A knowing, empathetic smile that acknowledges the hopelessness of the circumstances and yet assures her—irrationally—that all will be fine. "I brought you your favorite," he says, reaching into a paper bag. "Ham and cheese."

A chortle. "And I thought my favorite was baloney."

Through the bars, Beecham presses the sandwich. The overhead light—leaden, unblinking—burnishes his badge and his trooper's boots but not the slag of his eyes. The orange ball unravels enough to accept the food. But she stays curled, hair curtaining her face as she chews. Not until she pauses and requests, "Tell me about it again, Beech," does the prisoner finally look up.

The features are unchanged. The same spit of a nose and puckish mouth, the beanball chin that crimps whenever she pouts. But her complexion, once ruddy, has turned ashen, and her flaxen hair, matte. Her eyes are empty cells. "You will tell me, won't you?" She practically begs, "One last time?" and shows him the gap in her teeth.

She whistled through it as a kid whenever she talked, which wasn't often, or rounded the bases, which was. So they called her Whiffle. A wisp of a girl through which winds seemed to pass, flapping the hand-me-downs her body never filled. Whiffle, a weightless ball easily pitched and smacked.

Her real name, not that anybody remembered it, was Emma. But that didn't fit the tomboy who preferred baseball to Barbie dolls and warmed to the company of roughnecks. Not brilliant—never finished ninth grade—but able to distinguish bad from criminal, sinister from the merely wrong. Yet even that skill was beaten out of her by a drunken father who appeared sporadically to do just that, and a mother too addled by Superglue to be one. Whiffle grew, wild and vulnerable, surrounded by semi-siblings either in or on route to jail, doomed by poverty, ignorance, and abuse.

Years on the force, Beecham heard a thousand stories like hers. His own was almost identical. The same rain-pierced trailer rusting on cement blocks, the same thrift store jeans and premature exposure to life. He learned to drive before turning eleven, to hotwire pickups at twelve, and lost his virginity without quite understanding he possessed it. His rap sheet, at sixteen, would have haunted him at thirty if he hadn't skirted the law. If he hadn't grown up to enforce it.

But Beecham was smart, not school smart, but wise in the ways of survival. He early on identified a system made to be sidestepped and exploited. Others might be crushed by it or paralyzed, but he could manipulate it and come out on top which, for him, meant joining the state police. With authority in his badge and punch in his gun belt, he could cash in and leave trash like Whiffle to pay for it.

And Whiffle was born to pay, her purpose in a curt existence utterly shorn of details. For she remembered little of it—thank the H and the rotgut—especially not the night of the murder. Beecham did, though, with a clarity that would beam from the pages of a report that would galvanize the jury. His testimony, the judge revealed, proved critical in reaching the verdict.

"It was raining," Beecham begins. "It was always raining," only to be cut off by a retching sound from the Boonton Butcher's cell, followed by a bray of expletives. Betsy Rae curses her with words that could shame a trailer park, and the guards swear back, warning them both to shut their traps or forfeit their dose of pentobarbital. Beecham resumes, "And the field was mud."

Pale lids descend over his eyes, shuttering for a moment the lusterless blue that serves him as a kind of passport. Flashing it, together with a naturally gleaming smile, enabled him to escape the fixes of his youth and divert the blame to others. "You were out there, though. You and Chaz Lo Duca."

"Raining, you say? Mud?"

The orange ball unfurls. Emerging is a woman who, though puffed by prison fat, remains waif-like. Words still hiss through her teeth. "Chaz?"

"Charlie. Chucky. Lo Duca," he refreshes her. "But we just called him the Duke."

A pinch of lip appears in the gap in her teeth as she chews. On hands and knees, she crawls past the bunk, the sink and the toilet, to press her face to the bars. "Tell me more."

"The Duke. Sole supplier for our park and the others around it. A liar, a cheat, a bastard who'd steal the rags off your back—off your mother's back—if that's all you had for collateral." Without being asked, Beecham describes the man. Five-foot-eight and rangy, scraggly black hair, pitted skin gone yellow. Breath like an open grave. A shame the court photo showed him in his Sunday best, the one Sunday out of hundreds he wasn't dealing.

"But he liked me..."

"Liked you, yeah, like a fisherman likes fish." Beecham's smile turns cynical. "He wanted your money, Whiffle. He wanted your life."

"And you protected me."

She says this and her expression is again that amalgam of adoration and awe that he, several years older and keen to such things, had noticed whenever they were together as kids. Yes, he protected her, kept her from being used too liberally by the other boys, shielding her from her father whenever he showed up, controlling as best he could her passage from pot to the hard stuff. Fed her ham and cheese. To him, alone, she was My Little Whiffle, his sidekick, his charge, if never his lover. No, Beecham had calculated when still in their teens, their connection had to be pure.

"True, true," Beecham lies. Fact was, she defended him, furnishing an elder brother's cover almost as complete as his uniform's. For who would believe that the tow-headed youth who watched out for Whiffle was also preparing her downfall? Who would doubt his version? And who could suspect that he, with those guileless eyes and smile, the badge and the boots, was secretly running the Duke?

"I did my best," he continues with a shake of his buzzcut head. "But then…"

"But then what? It's so hard to remember."

Then she got into debt and the Duke didn't suffer debtors indefinitely. And Beecham couldn't stomach his stealing. It threatened first his reputation in the parks and ultimately his freedom when the pusher, once squeezed, threatened to turn him in. Such drastic situations called for radical remedies, he knew, and he'd been brewing one since childhood.

"Then that night in the field. In rain, the mud."

That's where the Duke did business, with trailer lights glistening in the mist. And there he waited for the payoff from Whiffle, alone, unarmed, an innocent man unsuspectingly meeting a woman who often forgot what month it was, much less the sums she owed.

"You went without a coat, without the cash. Carrying only that ax."

It belonged to her father, for the fires he never got around to lighting. For safety, Beecham gave it to her—"Just in case"—along with an extra fix. The plan was to have her confront the dealer while Beecham watched in the dark, waiting to make the arrest. Or so he told her. "Don't you worry, My Little Whiffle, I got your back."

The prisoner's hand flails the air in front of her face, as if to ward off flies. "And you were…? Remind me, please."

"On the interstate." He says this with a widening of the eyes intended to broadcast blue. "Patrolling."

She nods as if to indicate, "Of course." For the rest of that night is a blank. Nothing shook her memory of it, not even the photograph of the Duke looking much different from the first, with his head and half a torso shredded.

An anonymous phone call brought a local cop to the scene. The rain had removed most of the evidence, the boot prints, the blood. But there was the Duke all divvied up and Whiffle cradling the weapon. She offered no resistance, only a sigh as she submitted to the cuffs, that came out sounding like a whistle.

That was one sound more than she made during the trial. Flaccidly she sat while the prosecution presented its case. This was so compelling that the trial might have ended swiftly if not for Beecham's taking the stand. The tale he spun under oath—of addiction and larceny and blackmail—was commonplace in the parks, he said, and the life of the accused was no different. But while these woes might have moved the jurors to pity, its ultimate benefactor was Beecham. There were other choices in life, he attested, alternative paths, and as evidence cited himself. The comparison he struck, rather than saving the defendant, conclusively established her guilt.

Whiffle, alone, didn't know that. Blurry of thought, bereft of any memory that might link her to the murder, she believed that Beecham still had her back. Her single emotion was gratitude to him, which she showed with a gap-toothed grin even as the sentence was read.

And she is indebted to him still, pressing childlike fingers through the bars. "Thank you."

Even Beecham can be taken aback. "For what?"

"For helping me remember. For making sense of all this."

Betsy Rae howls like a gutted dog while a different stink pervades the row, from the excrement coating her cell. The guards hose it down, cursing and threatening to go light on her potassium chloride. The Boonton Butcher gurgles and spits. Evil congeals around Beecham.

Whiffle continues, "Otherwise, I'd be punished for a crime I can't remember." She grants him one last view of that gap. "Like it was committed by somebody else."

He touches his fingers to hers, clammy with ham and cheese, and wonders if she might yet recall the truth. Whether the chemicals that convey death through her veins can also stimulate memory. Would he, seated among witnesses as he promised, hear the whistle of her final recollection?

"No need to thank me," Beecham says with an affidavit of smile and eyes. "Anything for My Little Whiffle."

The Book of Jakiriah

"Goddammit!" Jakiriah cried, and his agony echoed through canyons. "Goddammit," he hissed while hauling his foot by its ankle upwards toward his butt and, with his free hand, plucking the thorn from his heel. Up to the blazing sun he held the thistle, examining it with one rheumy eye, then ranted, "You! You made this!"

"That," the sky suddenly admitted, "and the carbuncle, the kidney stone, sciatica, and toe fungus. I created them all."

Hearing these words, Jakiriah might have his fallen on his face and prayed. Instead, he waxed indignant. "You make it sound like something good," he spat and flicked the thorn heavenward. "You sound like you're actually proud of it."

"Proud?" The clouds seemed to shrug. "Not proud, just factual. I made everything. Remember, in Genesis, the chaos that preceded creation? Who do you think made the chaos?"

"Then why didn't you make me what I wanted to be?" the man, crusty and unkempt and far more aged-looking than his years, shook a horny fist. "What I was born to be?"

"What makes you think I didn't?"

Jakiriah sneered. "I see now why we're your chosen people—always answering questions with questions." He gathered his rags around him and squatted, the heat of the sand roasting his haunches. To the south he saw the Valley of Zin with its conical peaks like unspun potter's clay, and to the north, the vast plain of Uvdah stretching as far as Azazel in a punishing strop of flint. And to the East there was, well, the East, with its ravenous empires—Persian, Babylonian, Assyrian.

The holy man continued, "Why do I think you let me down, I'll tell you why. I do everything I'm supposed to do—warn about war and exile…"

"It's a timing issue. The Philistines are currently tied up with the Greeks."

"Keep the commandments, study the sacred texts. Not once has a razor touched my head."

"I was meaning to say something," the voice interrupted. "High time for a haircut and a shave."

"I wear sackcloth."

"That's got to itch."

"I eat locusts."

"I'm not even going there."

"And what do I get?" Jakiriah lamented. "One passing mention in the Bible? A book in Prophets? I mean, not even in the *minor* Prophets? What's Habakkuk got that I haven't?"

"A ludicrous name?"

"Well my name's not ludicrous." Protesting, he pounded the bars of his chest. "Jakiriah—Precious of God. My parents gave it to me. Perhaps they were as comical as you are. Maybe they were in on the joke."

The desert grew motionless for a moment; not even the tumbleweeds stirred. The world seemed steeped in introspection. "You know what *is* a joke?" Jakiriah was finally asked. "You folks assign me all sorts of human qualities—compassion, wrath, even jealousy. But there's one characteristic you never give me. You never say I'm funny."

"Let me get this straight," Jakiriah smirked, "you're supposed to have a sense of humor?"

"Ever seen a blobfish?" came his answer. "A platypus?"

As if toward an incomprehensible child, Jakiriah shook his head.

"Take Abraham," the voice continued. "I tell him, bind up Isaac, your beloved son, put him on a bunch of sticks and sacrifice him to me. I say that to him, and the guy actually does it, grabs this poor little boy and nearly slits his throat—would have, too, if I hadn't sent somebody to stop him. Abraham—the Ur Push-Over, I call him—couldn't even take a joke."

"Okay, okay. So you're compassionate, wrathful, jealous, *and* hysterical," Jakiriah tried to run fingers through his long, matted hair. Tried, but failed. "Abraham, at least, so loved you that he was willing to sacrifice his only son for you. That's a lot more than you're willing to do for us."

"Not so fast," cautioned the voice. "Give me seven centuries."

"I haven't got seven days." The mendicant began to stomp his foot but, remembering the thorn, thought better of it. "I've wandered out into this desolation without food, without water, in order to meet you. To pray to you and beseech you."

"And, look, your prayers have been answered."

"Yeah and so where's my revelation?"

"This *is* your revelation."

"That I'm not good enough to make it into the canon? I don't cut it, is that what you're telling me?"

He felt the desert staring at him, the very air taking a breath. Long moments passed before he finally merited a response:

"I'm telling you that whether you're in the Good Book or not isn't the point. Ever hear of Avimelekh?"

"If memory serves. Killed his seventy brothers."

"There you go. And Haggai ben Yuktiel? Heard of him?

"Can't say I have."

"Best man ever to tread Canaan, trust me. But you won't find him in any concordance."

"Why not?" Jakiriah was shouting again, a madman railing against the void.

"Because the Bible is not about who's good enough to be included and who isn't. It's about who can make its readers better people. It's about making you love me so that you can love one another."

"Easy for you to say. You're the world's bestselling author." These words Jakiriah muttered into the cinders, as if no one else could hear them.

"It's about knowing, not renown. About wonder and inspiration and hope."

"But I can do inspiration." Jakiriah puffed up his chest. "Walk in my ways, sayeth the Lord of Hosts, walk in my paths of righteousness." Scrofulous arms flung out toward the canyons. "Virgins of Jerusalem, strike the timbrel and dance, for the day of our deliverance is here!" Those same arms now folded over their owner's ash-encrusted chest, vaunting.

"Nice but derivative," came the comment, sotto voce, followed as if on the wings of some wilderness bird by, "Alas, Jakiriah, you are a not-for-prophet."

The ascetic scratched his scalp hard enough to feel it. "You've lost me…"

"Sorry. Works in a later language."

"You created the thorn," Jakiriah, returning to his original complaint, fumed. "Impetigo, famine, depression, death—you created them all. Can't you at least make a patriarch of me?"

The answer was: silence.

"Can't you justify my suffering? I'll be dust soon, can't you at least leave my name on the lips of men?" In the midst of the desert, alone and unwashed, Jakiriah thrashed. His rags flailed around him unheralded. "Goddammit, will I never be blessed?"

And the answer was barely detectable, a mere titter above the clouds. A lilting beyond the canyons, bitter and keen. Laughter.

Dead of Old Wounds

"What?" Geoffrey gasped, as if gazing at his own distorted reflection. But, instead of a mirror, he was looking into the x-ray the doctor at the hospice held up. And the image he encountered was not of himself but the pelvis of his dying father. "Is that what I think it is?"

"You tell me," the doctor responded, genuinely perplexed. "Did he ever mention anything?"

Geoffrey brought his eyes closer to the film, superimposing them over the bones. "I don't believe this," he mumbled before answering the doctor. "No, not a word." He paused for a moment and pinched the bridge of his nose. "Well, once, a real long time ago—I was a kid—he said something about landing on Normandy."

Now the doctor was really perplexed. "Normandy? Once?"

"He didn't like talking about it," Geoffrey shrugged. "Said he was in the war for all of forty seconds before…"

"Before what?"

"Before," the patient's son studied the floor. "Getting hurt. Wounded, I guess. But he never said how or where."

The doctor's hand, the one he used for bedside reassurances, found Geoffrey's shoulder. "Now we know."

And, then, for several quiet seconds, the two of them stared at Mr. Gorelik's ilium, or hip bone, and at the thumb-sized object embedded in it. Conical at the top, ragged at the tail, it pointed downward toward the coccyx like a rocket aimed at an asteroid. But, in contrast to the rest of the ilium, which was stellar white, the area around the rocket was space-black, indicating infection.

A half-hour of counselling and waiver-signing passed before Geoffrey emerged into the waiting room and the impatient glare of his wife, Helen. "Don't look so sad," she greeted him. "He's ninety-three and going peacefully. You should be thankful."

Geoffrey cut her off, "My father's been shot."

Helen's magazine slapped down on her thighs. "Shot, right. By who? The night nurse?"

He plopped into the plastic seat next to her. "The Germans."

She closed a skeptical eye. "On Normandy Beach," her husband continued. "Dad landed there, you know, during the invasion, and was wounded right away. Shot in the hip, turns out." He gazed blankly at the vending machines, at the gleeful art on the hospice walls. "And the bullet's still in there, they never took it out. That's what's causing the sepsis, the doctor told me. The bullet's moved."

"Jesus," Helen, with the magazine, hammered her knees. "Je-sus."

Two weeks later—eight days after the funeral—the last of the guests finally departed. Geoffrey's brother, Richard, a retired English professor, flew back to Oregon with his new Vietnamese wife and assorted step-kids, and the Gorelik's two children, Amy and Charles, returned to their jobs in the city. The house, a Dutch-style multiplex that felt half-vacant even when crowded, suddenly seemed cavernous.

Geoffrey wandered the halls, trying to remember his father before the dementia set in. He preferred not to dwell on those forty seconds on Normandy, the wound that left that young soldier suffering and rolling in the surf. He focused, rather, on the good-natured man, faithful to the plain, hardworking young woman he married a few years after the war and still mourned decades after her death. Not deep in the edu-cated sense but no lightweight either, a supportive dad even when his son disappointed him. And, though he'd never said anything, Geof-frey let him down. All those years slaving in the furniture business so that his two boys would have the best education, the utmost chance of elevating themselves above the world of inventories and sales. That backing, together with a trust fund set up especially for the purpose, enabled Geoffrey to seek a literary career right after college, to move to a funky neighborhood and befriend other struggling—and similarly subsidized—artists.

There, when drafting his novel in all-night cafes, he met Helen. Vegetarian, feminist, environmentalist, Buddhist—she came with more labels, he quipped, than a formula race car—he liked her earthiness, however studied. He liked that she liked Ted Hughes and Robertson Davies and hated coriander even more than he did. She laughed sardonically and made love with the same commitment she reserved for causes. Most crucially, she believed in him, hugged and consoled him after each rejection letter. She encouraged him, finally, to teach writing at the community college where she worked as a librarian. The arrangement was only temporary, she assured him, until he could establish himself creatively.

But the rejection slips mounted and temporary became years. His mother died, his brother moved out West, and his father showed signs of early-onset dementia. Children came and with them financial demands beyond their parents' salaries. And then there was the incident at the college that cost Geoffrey his job and nearly his marriage as well. Saving it required giving up the dream of writing for a while and moving, repentantly, back home.

This, too, was to have been a limited stint as head of the family business. Yet, much to his discomfort, Geoffrey excelled. Turned out he enjoyed sales, enjoyed making profits even more and lavishing them on Helen. They were a type of offering and Helen, reluctantly at first but then with relish, accepted. Gradually, she admitted that she did not miss her boring library job and artsy lifestyle but preferred her new routine of charity work and daily yoga classes at the club. Not that she ever forgot the pain that Geoffrey had inflicted on her, the shame, or the failure to live up to his earlier promise. But the injury eventually healed, at least superficially. Rushing from soccer games to rallies for municipal issues left her little time to dwell on the scar, much less the inflammation beneath.

The kids, meanwhile, needed music lessons and summer camps and a backyard to play in. Other payments—cars, vacations, landscapers—mounted, and college tuition loomed. Geoffrey abandoned his literary dreams. He focused, rather, on expanding the furniture store into a chain which, after his father's death, locked him in his large, empty house.

The ringtone on Geoffrey's cell phone sent the New World Symphony resounding through the den. He answered and spoke for a while, fielding questions guardedly at first and then with an exuberance that surprised him. When, a half hour later, he hung up, Helen, who was just out of earshot in the kitchen, asked what had excited him so.

"A reporter from the local television station," Geoffrey practically chirped. "It seems I'm famous."

"Famous?" Helen called out over the splash of water on the kale she was washing. "Right."

"No, really. Somehow word of Dad's death got out to the media. They're calling him the last KIA of World War II. The last man killed on Normandy."

Helen smirked. "Your father, Geoffrey, died in a hospice twenty minutes from here. He died of complications from dementia."

"He wouldn't have died from dementia if he wasn't wounded." Geoffrey was adamant—weirdly so, Helen thought. "He wouldn't have died—at least not right then—if not for that bullet."

"And why does that make you famous?"

Geoffrey shook the cell phone, trophy-like, above him. "Because it makes me a war orphan. The reporter said that I might even be entitled to an army pension. No kidding."

"Is that what you want, an army pension?" she asked with a critical shake of the kale. "No, silly. But she did say she wants to interview me."

"She?" Helen, drying her hands on her apron, recalled for a moment the last time he called her silly. "And what's her name, might I ask?"

The phone froze next to Geoffrey's ear. He considered lying for a moment, rejected that option, and tried for nonchalance. After all, years had passed, and the name had grown common enough. "Caitlin," he said.

In truth, before the day she entered his community college office, he had never heard that name before.

"It's Irish," she explained matter-of-factly, then ironically, "It means 'pure.'"

Geoffrey perused her composition. "You're Irish…"

"And Scottish," she answered, "And Cherokee and Welsh." Her voice buoyed in a way that raised his eyes from her paper to her smile, which was vermillion. Behind it shone even white teeth when she laughed, "I'm a mutt."

So much for the assignment. He spent the next hour—other students were waiting in the hallway outside—asking Caitlin about her life. There was much to tell, at least for a nineteen-year-old. She claimed to come from an upscale family able to send her to respectable boarding schools and pricey summer camps. Ballet lessons, horseback riding. Engrossed, he forgot to ask her why a young person so privileged was not attending a better university. It never occurred to him to ask if somewhere in her resplendent story something had gone awry. Instead, he found himself staring at her French-braided hair that was so golden it seemed to suck up the light. Her eyes were ceramic blue, her fingers spindly. An oversized sweater and old plaid skirt could not hide a body that promised to be supple. Vaguely he heard the students outside curse and quit the building.

Which left them to adjourn to a nearby coffee shop, the kind he used to frequent as a writer, dim and aromatic. Now came his turn to tell his tale of novels too avant-garde for the market, the agents who let him down, the editors. He was aware, cupping his cappuccino, of becoming the most pathetic stereotype—the rumpled, balding teacher who could not do and so sought solace in an impressionable undergrad. He was conscious of how recklessly he acted. But Caitlin listened to him the way Helen once did, with compassion and surety. "Don't give up," she urged him while squeezing the back of his hand. "Never give up," and her red-lacquered fingernails nearly broke his skin.

Perhaps it would have ended then if they hadn't gone back to her place, slipping past the junk and curious roommates, to her bedroom.

Maybe it would have ended if he hadn't found there the tragic bliss that always eluded him on the page. He imagined that he could have died in that cheap apartment with its stir fry smell and never return to the decorative pillows and the ruckus of two little children, to Helen.

"And where have you been?" she asked as if addressing Amy or Charles, while placing wet dishes on a rack.

"Nowhere. At work," he lied to her for the very first time and marveled how easy it was.

Helen looked tired. In her household smock she was frumpy, her frizzy hair tied up in a knot. "At work, right," she said with a piercing eye. "Watch yourself, buster. You'll work your way out of a job and a home."

"Helen, please," he forced himself to laugh. "Don't be silly."

Don't be silly. Those words beguiled him over the next few weeks as he made himself sillier with lust, with jealousy over imagined rivals, and with fantasies about his and Caitlin's future. They would run away to New Mexico, join an artists' colony, live off the land, create. Each night, he came home later and later, lied with greater brazenness, and finally failed to come home at all.

And it might have happened—the desertion, the self-destructive spree with a cunning, half-crazed girl—if not for the college shrink. He was the one who noticed that Caitlin had missed two sessions, who called the administration which, in turn, looked into some rumors circulating campus. That he was hauled in and fired on the spot was humiliating enough, but returning home with his effects in a box, climbing the dreary stairs and opening the door to Helen—that was nightmarish.

"Caitlin," she laughed many years later. She practically howled, "Caitlin."

The coincidence of the names was sufficient grounds for cancelling the interview, he told himself and also informed Helen. "Whatever," she shrugged, which was her way of hiding hurt. But the next week brought more phone calls, more inquiries from veterans' groups, history buffs, museum curators, and, most alluringly, book publishers fishing for a contract. What began as an in-studio chat rapidly expanded into a press conference which the hospice—of all places—offered to host.

In the days leading up to the event, Geoffrey barely saw, much less placated, his wife. He hoped that she would see how unfounded her reactions were, and that she could allow him this one last spotlight. Hell, he was practically an old man himself, hairless and plump and no magnet for young women, certainly not television stars. And as for that other, earlier Caitlin, she was probably middle-aged and unrecognizable now, maybe institutionalized.

The waiting room of the hospice had been transformed into a studio, complete with Klieg lights and booms. Geoffrey was made up and brought out to sit in a chair that faced the vending machines that were hidden by nurses and other medical staff members, all standing. The few seats were taken by dignitaries, among them the mayor, a senator, and a former VFW Commander-in-Chief. Geoffrey smiled at them. He waved at the cameras, all the while searching for Helen in the crowd. Then, to a brush of applause, Caitlin came out.

This Caitlin was indeed young, long-legged, and startlingly beautiful—and, Geoffrey noted with relief, Eurasian. She shook his hand and took up the seat opposite him.

"So, tell me, Geoffrey," she began, "How did it feel to find out that your father was shot on D-Day?"

"Well, Caitlin," he responded, at once beaming and squinting into the lights. He told the story as dramatically as he could, emphasizing his father's heroism, his selflessness, and his refusal to surrender to the pain which no doubt plagued him. He talked about the Greatest Generation and how much we, their offspring, owed them. He talked and still he looked for Helen.

In the final segment, the doctor came out with the x-ray. The camera zoomed in and showed the rocket-shaped object lodged in the late Mr. Gorelik's hip. While the audience focused on the image, Geoffrey finally caught sight of Helen, or thought he did, but only for an instant. Then the journalist turned back to him.

"So, in conclusion, Geoffrey, what have you learned from this remarkable experience?"

Geoffrey swallowed hard and appeared to blush. "I've learned that life is one big landing on Normandy Beach. That often we're under fire, but we've got to keep going, keep plowing forward, just like my dad did. And I've learned, Caitlin," he concluded, recalling that possible army pension. "That one can die of very old wounds."

Later, when the regular lights came on, Geoffrey remained for a long time shaking hands with the guests. He received a framed copy of the x-ray and the card of one interested publisher. He chatted and schmoozed until the waiting room was once again empty. Then he was alone, with no sign whatsoever of Helen.

Sir Reginald and the Purple Prince

At last, after ages of struggle, I have him. Holed up at the top of Tottenham Hill, worn out by siege, abandoned by his men, he will soon be compelled to surrender—or worse. Either way, justice will be upheld. Too long has he humiliated me, exposed me to mockery and scorn. From him spread the myths of my inadequacies—my feebleness, my cowardice, my flaws. But no more. Now the world will know of the truth of who is weak and who unconquerable. All will witness the triumph of Sir Reginald over arrogance, over the once proud, but now vanquished, Purple Prince.

Drawing my sword, I salute my steadfast knights. Thomas, though poor of sight and pigeon footed, never once left me, not even after the Mayfair defeat. Not even after the debacles at Crestmont Lane and Pleasantdale—Thomas unflinching at my side. And Harry, who I sometimes call Henry (more fitting for a duke), unyielding behind the shield that nearly conceals his girth, nodding at me in deference. The assault will not be simple, I confess to them, and not without cost. But victory will be ours, finally, I pledge, and the glory long denied us in the realm.

In truth, the realm's respect means less to me than the affection of one of its subjects. Amelia, emerald-eyed and garnet-lipped, her hair the color of daises. Maid Amelia, I refer to her, though never to her face, a mere glimpse of which causes my own to redden. How splendorous it was to see her observing one of our battles and to what valor her presence spurred me. But how crestfallen I was when the offensive failed and Amelia applauded. With a sound like burbling waters, she cheered. More excruciating than being beaten was the sight of those flowery curls draped on his shoulder, as the Purple Prince turned back to me and winked.

The ultimate insult, he hurls it often—on the playing field, where he and his followers invariably prevail, and in matters of the mind, in which he proves equally nimble. In no endeavor does the Prince not excel, and no contest which, winning, he fails to seal with that wink. As if by sword-point, it skewers me.

Dungeon-like tortures, all of them, and yet none so unbearable as the indifference of the Queen. Or perhaps indifference is too gentle a word—more like disbelief. She seems to doubt I'll ever prosper, and to fear for my safety if I try. As if I were to blame for the King's departure, but was nevertheless all that remained. The way she scolds me when returning dusty from the fray or hounds me at the height of battle—that harrowing squawk—makes me wonder whether the Queen is secretly in league with the Prince. A conspiracy to replace me with a worthier heir and lure the King back to the castle.

Beset by such thoughts, I allow myself to tarry, but not for long. Already, I can see the purple tunic peaking over Tottenham's crest and the spokes of an overturned carriage. Now is the time to strike. Sword raised, visor lowered, I shout the order to charge.

We run, we slide, over this much-contested span, the soil slick with recent rains and—one might imagine—the blood of former combatants. Yet we persevere, Thomas and Henry and the army I see myself leading. And predictably the enemy resists, hurling every projectile in reach. One such, ball-shaped, barely misses my head and lands in a mud-burst behind me. But nothing can stop our advance, not even when Thomas stumbles over his own pigeon feet and Henry's weight delays him. Not even when I find myself, all at once, alone at the top of Tottenham.

Or almost alone. From here, the highest point in the realm, I can see Amelia watching below, perched on her royal pink mount, looking anxious. There, too, is the castle and, in an upper portal, the Queen.

She, too, is gazing—or so I assume, for her face is shrouded by the cloud of smoke she blows, on which her crown of curlers floats. There is not much time to do what I must. Kicking away the carriage, the cans and the hubcaps that serve as shields, I stand above my nemesis.

And he quivers worm-like on the ground. Still purple, perhaps, but no longer a prince in my eyes. In Amelia's, I trust, either. He is just a boy, frightened and ashamed and as vulnerable as I once was, but now our roles are reversed, and he kneels exposed to my fury. Or mercy? For a moment, I cannot decide whether to forget all the slights and, instead of my blade, offer him a hand in peace.

I choose the blade. Hoisting it, lifting the glittery visor, I prepare to strike. He shrinks, I lunge, and the wrath of Sir Reginald descends. And it almost cleaves when an ear-splitting shriek arrests it.

"Stop that! Right now! Before somebody gets hurt!" That familiar raven's caw. "You put down that stick, Reggie, and come back home this instant!"

Disgraced, degraded, I cast away my sword and crumble my silvery helmet. "Jesus, Mom," I protest, while the Purple Prince exults. Humbled no more but one again haughty, he leaps to his feet with a laugh that resounds throughout the realm. It's heard, no doubt, by Amelia.

I turn to retreat down Tottenham, head bent, when a surly voice calls out. "Better luck next time, Reggie," the Purple Prince lords over me, blows a bubble, and winks.

Rosen in Paradise

"Hey, ass-wipe, watch where you're going!" was the first thing Mickey Rosen shouted after stepping off the curb and nearly getting swiped by a car. The second, much quieter, was, "What the fuck…?"

The car, he saw, was a Studebaker. Which was weird, but not as weird as people who wasted time refurbishing clunkers. Stranger still was the intersection. No walk or don't walk indicators, not even a "ped xing" sign, only a pole-mounted traffic signal with three metal-hooded lights. And a billboard for a cigarette brand defunct for many decades.

He couldn't see much else, the sun blazing in his eyes, but, through a combination of squinting and saluting, he began to pick out storefronts. Bergaman's Bakery, Moskowitz the Butcher, their windows shimmering under candy-striped awnings. Still blinking, Mickey Rosen staggered into town.

More cars—Hudsons, DeSotos—and businesses, hobby and soda shops, Herman's Radio Repairs. A portly policeman with a leather shoulder strap and necktie touched a baton to his cap. A gaggle of kids, ten years old at most, in jeans and t-shirts, some crowned with Jughead caps, scurried by. Girls in bright jumpers played jacks. From the office of the local daily, perhaps, the clack and ding of typewriters.

It all looked familiar. Similar scenes proliferated his novels, much to his critics' distress. "Enough, already," they cried, "You're the country's leading writer, our nation's most poignant voice, why the constant nostalgia? Why this myth of the past?"

How could he explain to them that the world he grew up in was a metaphor for all that was lost—the simplicity, the good. The world he longed to return to but spent his entire artistic life destroying. Beginning with his scantily-masked memoirs, the ones that lampooned his hardworking parents as lowbrows and his brother Seth as a wimp. Women were strongboxes just waiting to be jimmied and robbed. But worse was Altholtz, a composite of his Hebrew schoolteachers, the neighborhood's unscrupulous rabbi. More than any of his caricatures, his depiction of Altholtz got him branded an anti-Semite. Rosen the Self-hating Jew.

In time, his judgements softened somewhat, the parents endowed with a humble heroism and his brother with pathos, the victim of a meaningless war. Women were not so much strongboxes anymore as safes with mysterious combinations. Only Altholtz remained unredeemed. He lied to his congregants, fornicated and stole, all the while feigning devotion. But Rosen's readers no longer cared. On the contrary, they now embraced a rabbinical anti-hero as ardently as Rosen craved his old world. And the further away he moved from it, the more perfect it loomed.

He passed through the downtown and into a residential area. Modest two-stories, each with a single-car driveway and carriage-house garage, a patch of diehard grass. Leafy trees—maples or elms—cooled the street. There were people around, Rosen could tell from the zing-zing of bicycle bells and the smack of a sandlot game. A Big Band scratched on a Victrola. Yet he seemed to be walking alone, and back.

For this was not just any street, but *his* street, the scene of his boyhood. On its stone-dappled asphalt, reminiscences were rolled into dramas. Themes revolved, like push mower blades, ponderous yet sharp. Yet from here he dreamed of escaping, of writing and achieving fame. He couldn't get fast enough away.

And he couldn't have soared more meteorically. A best-seller by twenty-five, a symbol of the sexuality and revolt of the age, and of appetites his audiences both recoiled from and fed. Mickey Rosen was a celebrity, feted on campuses and headlined in the gossip columns. His exploits—four marriages abandoned together with a child or two from each, rumors of domestic violence—became legend. But his novels were praised, as anticipated as the reports of his latest subpoena. Yet, whether pilloried or acclaimed, in court or his country estate, his thoughts always returned to this street. Here he regained—on the page, at least—his paradise.

Already he could see his house. He caught the cinnamon whiffs of the lokshen kugel his mother baked on Fridays and heard the cheers of the baseball game his father religiously listened to, devoted to a team that later left him for the coast. Rosen quickened his pace. What would happen, he wondered, if he burst into their kitchen with its Aunt Jemima cookie jars and checkered linoleum floor and bellowed, "Hey, Ma, Pa, I'm home!"

Before he could, though, a trio of girls marched past him on the sidewalk. Seventeen, maybe twenty years old—he'd lost the ability to distinguish—but uniformly pretty in their pleated dresses and saddle shoes, their long pearl necklaces and ponytails. Even he, a man in his eighties, felt aroused. Rosen stepped away, as one would back then, to let them pass, and caught their scent of lavender and mint. And something else, moldy.

The girls strolled by, seemingly unaware of him, then one of them half-turned. He raised a hand in greeting, but the girl hacked up a throat-full of phlegm and unleashed what used to be called a loogie. It landed, dayglo green and quivering, at his feet. Swabbing a wrist across her mouth, smearing it red, the girl skipped back to her friends.

And Rosen, startled, confused, faltered on to his house. His mother was just coming out the front. Less rectangular than he remembered, shapely even in her formless dress. Her hair, though netted, was not steely as he recollected it but copper. In her mitted hands, she carried a baking tray and bore it four houses away to what Rosen recalled was Mr. Friedlander's. Childless, a widower, Mr. Friedlander had always been an object of pity in their home, and of curiosity, a recluse. No wonder his mother, a saint before he satirized her, brought him kugel.

He followed her, keeping a safe distance, to Mr. Friedlander's door which she entered without a key. Through the large bay windows, he saw her glide from the kitchen to the living room where Mr. Friedlander presumably waited on a sofa. His mother's hands were no longer mitted but reaching up, first, to remove the hair net, and then behind, to unzipper her dress. She stood naked as Rosen had never seen her before but with the same smile once reserved for tucking him in.

Rosen gasped. He nearly screamed. Running, he retreated to his own house and up the driveway. A window there afforded a glimpse of the den where his father sat fast by the radio. Only he wasn't listening. Rather, he was knotting a fat rubber band around his forearm and piercing it with a syringe. "No, Dad, don't!" Rosen wanted to holler but his voice felt strangely detached. He saw his father's face, an old man's already, defeated. He watched him swoon as the drug surged through his veins.

Back down the driveway Rosen teetered, but not without noticing another set of windows—the garage's—and another unnerving view. This was of his brother, Seth, lifting weights. Bare-chested and benching hundreds of pounds, his muscles glistening, teeth bared. Barbells and medicine balls studded the floor. He grunted and huffed under the high-gloss gaze of pinups. Not just of starlets in swimsuits but of the heroes of the previous war, commanders of the army that would soon take him and send him off to a less-than-glorious death, crushed by an overturned truck, in Asia. It would be Seth's twenty-fourth birthday, the age at which Rosen portrayed him as a cry-baby, at best, and at worst, a timorous martyr.

He didn't know how long he spied, but eventually Rosen found himself back on the street. The leaves, rustling, cackled at him. A Packard nearly ran him down. The musty smell he first detected on those teenaged girls grew heavier now, permeating the air, almost rancid. He wandered, and the sun sought him out through the foliage, again making it difficult to see. Rosen worried about his pills—had he forgotten them? —and the books he left in the hospice. Didn't he tell them to pack them all before his discharge, his Kafka and his Proust? Did they really believe that the same Mickey Rosen who defied the critics, the disgruntled lovers and their entitled brats, the lawyers, and the holier-than-thous, would have so easily succumbed? Fools, just thinking about them made him chortle, and he did, all the way to the synagogue.

The temple, they called it, the *shul*, or as Rosen preferred, the Altar to High Hypocrisy. That is where people came, most of them only once or twice a year, dressed in their most expensive duds, to mispronounce words they didn't understand, and make a show of atonement. But the misdeeds only multiplied and nowhere more vilely than this so-called sanctuary with its electric memorial flames and faux-plush curtains, the ark concealing both scrolls and secrets. And Altholtz, the outwardly pious and Yiddish-inflected rabbi, sucking up to the rich and browbeating the frail, all for his unholy indulgence. Altholtz, whose real name Rosen forgot but not his unctuousness. In novel after novel, he appeared, a reminder that even an Eden has snakes.

And there was Altholtz, his crooked frame shifting behind the stained glass. He was attending to people, no doubt squeezing them for money or filling them with self-serving ideas. Bending and straightening in a feigned calisthenic of prayer. After passively observing his family, Rosen was no longer willing to play the on-looker. Fuming, he strutted inside.

"Ah," was all that Altholtz said when Rosen confronted him in the chapel. "You certainly took your time."

The rabbi scarcely looked up from what he was doing, tending to the aged in wheelchairs, people visibly sick or mentally impaired, the homeless. Ladling out soup and kasha.

Rosen, with an accusatory finger, barked, "Get your hands off them!"

But Altholtz kept ladling, spoon-feeding a boy no older than ten but hairless. "Perhaps you would like to help," he said, offering the utensil to Rosen.

"Me?"

"Why not?" the rabbi chimed while wiping a colorless chin. "It's never too late. Not even for you."

Rosen was speechless, perhaps for the first time ever, but the rabbi came to his aid. "You're surprised, I know, after all those things you wrote."

"I never imagined. I'm sorry…" Rosen, muttering, felt his body shake.

"Hey, it's not me you need to apologize to. Of all your characters, mine was the most autobiographical."

With that, Altholtz straightened and stared. No hawk-nosed, fat-lipped stereotype but serenely handsome with a wispy beard and fine-tooled features. His eyes, celestially blue, peered straight through the author and beyond. "It's not what we write about people that matters, Mickey, but how we treat them in life." His yarmulke gleamed like a crown. "You remember that, don't you? Life."

He did, suddenly, vaguely. His cries for more morphine, the fading light on the walls. The absence of any mourners. As he never had in all those years, not since his childhood, Rosen understood. That every-one has their paradises, and all of them ultimately lost. Trembling, he accepted the spoon.

"Good," Altholtz pronounced and indicated a pot in which matzoh balls floated liked memories. "There's a lot of work to do and a hell of a lot of time."

The Thirty-Year Rule

K ew in the rain looks preserved in amber. That is the color of the bricks in the village's gingerbread houses, the color of their hydrangeas and primrose, and even the saturated sidewalks. So preciously English, so cloyingly quaint.

Leaving the Victorian rail station, I join a procession of backpacked students and academicians in tweed, all bowed under umbrellas and streaming toward a post-modern monstrosity. It rises, four stories of alabaster and glass reflected in a pond broken only by fountains and the inevitable swans. Ravens would be more appropriate.

Or vultures, for these are the National Archives, the repository of Britain's records going back centuries, and the researchers who pick over the bones. Here, the Elizabethan-minded can peruse the Earl of Essex's love letters to his "Noble and dear lady," or, if more sanguinary, Jack the Ripper's notes to Scotland Yard, penned in his victims' blood. Others hunt for a personal past—an ancestor lost in the Great War or exiled for life to Australia. But a few rummage for something more intimate. Bittersweet, half-recollected, old. Some come in search of themselves.

I am one of the latter, or so I remind myself while filling out the visitors' questionnaires and requesting the relevant file. As a long-time expat, I'd forgotten the British passion for procedure, our obsession with the just so. Yet even this properness has its rewards, and mine shortly appears in the form of a slender brown folder. This, presumably, contains a chapter of history, or at least history as we want it remembered.

A lesson for the uninitiated: no statesman worth his wingtips ever writes the truth. On the contrary, those countless cables sent to and from the Foreign Office are designed as much to convey what didn't happen as what did, while always portraying the author as right. Only a scholar would believe that real events can be reconstructed from telegrams. Footnotes are only for fools.

Folder in hand, I assume my assigned seat at one of the reading room's hexagonal tables. To my right sits a shapely blonde undergraduate, prim in a flannel suit and fishnet stockings, and next to her, a young South Asian man, his white shirt buttoned up to the collar, who one cannot imagine not whispering. A pensioner in a shiny suit trembles opposite me, leafing through what look like government pay stubs. And then, to my left, a pair of fops, Ph.D. students probably, pretty and dressed ever-so-conspicuously down. They earn my brief, wistful smile. I was like them once: cavalier, flirtatious. Now, though, I'm just a bald, portly auntie, in need not of love but of closure. Probing, while I still can, for peace.

But is peace attainable here among the self-justifying telexes, the misleading memoranda, the lies? And what of memory, that other dispatcher of myths? Consider the deception they could pull off, those reports and recollections, combined.

And consider it I do while staring at the folder, labelled FO 145/4871. The covers are bound with a silky ribbon, like an unopened Christmas gift. In line with most enlightened states, Britain observes the thirty-year rule. Three decades must pass before the government discloses its declassified files. Thirty years separate the sealing of FO 145/4871 and today, its disinterment. I am the first to pull on the ribbon's end and unravel it. The first to behold its discolored contents and inhale the stale cold dust of time.

The earliest entry is dated May 20, 1980 and addressed from the Ambassador to the Permanent Under-Secretary. *The warmth has returned to the capital of Darja*, it begins, and so, too, do the falsehoods.

Situated several hundred nautical miles off the coast of Oman and Yemen, relieved neither by breezes nor a single merciful stream, Darja was never warm. It was, rather, molten. Mid-mornings and the sun already blasted its hardscrabble streets, melting its rubbish—tin cans, rotted vegetables, carcasses—into slag. And Darja had no capital, at least not one serrated with skyscrapers or even minarets. Think, rather, nameless alleys winding nowhere and hovels reverting into sand. Think vermin. Think stench. Think the most wretched conditions under which humans might squirm and then blacken your imagination ten-fold.

The warmth has returned to the capital of Darja, the document continues, *along with the zeal of our American friends and Soviet adversaries.* Sir Nigel always had a weakness for hyperbole. "Zeal" scarcely described the interest, at best, shown by other nations in this miniscule island that remained, like a button that somebody popped and forgot, on the floor of the Indian Ocean. Even "interest" was overstated, as Darja appeared on virtually no maps and merited no international attention except for the fact that its bum-shaped coast contained, precisely at the crack, a deep-water port. This, the Royal Navy determined, would provide a handy coaling station for destroyers. But that was a hundred years earlier, when destroyers still steamed on coal.

No, if our allies and foes attached the faintest importance to Darja it was solely because it belonged to Britain. And that, too, was a fluke. Back in 1950, Sultan Abd al-Rahman Qaboos decided he needed a patron. His previous emir, some fattened Arabian sheikh, died or disappeared, leaving the island bankrupt. But then the sultan remembered us. Our empire was just then unravelling, but the poor bugger somehow missed the news. And London never let on. Instead, to much fanfare— an assemblage of goatherds and beggars—we raised the Union Jack and erected a colonial-style embassy. Darja gained the privilege of printing our sovereign's head on all of its coins, should it ever mint any.

Still, the mere prospect of palming the Queen's face was a slap to that of the Soviets. Their diplomats had a Blue Water fleet to consider, a war in Afghanistan and, above all, the fear of being repatriated to Moscow. In Darja, their consulate resembled a car battery that powered three cylinders at most, but all of them churning up unrest. This proved difficult, however, as the bulk of the inhabitants spent much of the day napping. Yet a certain greengrocer and part-time brigand named Razi did hole up in a cave and, brandishing a Kalashnikov, proclaimed the island's independence.

In this direst of crises, the Americans were supposed to stand behind us, and they did. With a butcher's knife. *I have spoken with my U.S. colleague (Coulson), who pledged his country's full cooperation with us in suppressing this Communist-backed revolt*, Sir Nigel apprised. Did he remotely believe this, I wonder, or had he teletyped it chuckling out loud?

In fact, William "Wild Bill" Coulson was a careerist who, much like his British counterpart, wanted nothing more than to quit Darja as soon as mortally possible. In contrast to Nigel Ringwald, though, a slope-shouldered, overwrought man who took to drink several years back when his wife took her life, Coulson was milkshake smooth, lanky in his tan suit and with a grin half-hidden by his moustache. A Tennessee plantation awaited his retirement back home where he would coddle his grandkids and tie flies for catfishing. That estate was built by slaves, but that did not prevent Washington's envoy from lecturing Darjans about the glories of Yankee-style freedom. If he had his "druthers"—Coulson's favorite word—Razi the rebel would've traded in his rusty Kalashnikov for a spanking new M-16.

Countering the Russians' predilection for insurgency and the Americans' (sadly outdated) perception of us imperialists are our primary missions in Darja. That, I thought, and stocking our larder with enough canned beans and gin to last each month. *With this goal in mind, our able staff has labored tirelessly, meeting with local chieftains and educating the public about the benefits of British rule. I have assigned this delicate but crucial task to an individual of apparent stature and diverse talents, our Second Secretary (Crosthwaite).*

I peer around the hexagonal table in case someone heard me snort. The pensioner, though, is still fumbling through ancient affidavits. Miss Flannel Suit and Mr. Subcontinent scrutinize their documents while exchanging the occasional glance. And the dandy doctoral candidates—so I've dubbed them—are busy playing footsie. No one heard me chuckle, not even the ushers who hover over the researchers lest any of them pocket a Cromwellian request for reinforcements or Churchill's shopping list for Scotch.

I chortled because *our able staff* amounted to three local hires. An enervated janitor who pushed a Sisyphean broom, a gardener bitter over having to trim our single row of shrubbery and sporadic patches of grass, and a secretary who industriously pecked at her electric typewriter despite her semi-literacy. But the real kicker was the ambassador's reference to the *stature* and *talents* of Second Secretary Crosthwaite. If not so woeful, it could've made me roar.

The scion of a once-venerable Cumbrian family fallen on hard times and harder liquor, I had few prospects in life. The Crosthwaites had already generated enough scandals to drown Fleet Street in its own ink, my father always told me, and hardly needed another. In earlier times, the first of three sons inherited the estate, the second enlisted in the military, and the third took up the cloth. But we had long lost our lands as well as our faith, and my two older brothers fought only in pubs. And for a young man of my proclivities, who could not get buggered *enough* at school, not especially attractive or clever, there seemed only one sensible route—overseas, via the Foreign Office.

My first assignment, though, to the Falklands, ended in disgrace—or worse for us British, indiscretion. The details, involving a bronzed Gibraltarian, are relevant only in that certain pro-Argentines began accusing me of doing to him what Her Majesty's Government had long done to the archipelago. Hushing up was in order and Whitehall shushed me off to Darja on the other side of the globe, there to serve as a lowly Second Secretary. Pity I wasn't working for the French. For the same offense, the Quai d'Orsay would have made me Ministre Extraordinaire in Rome.

My *apparent stature*, then, related neither to my height nor girth— the latter regrettably superior to the first—rather to that air of English gentry that presumably impresses the natives. My *diverse talents*, on the other hand, hinted at unique insights into Darjan politics, such as they were, not attained by the usual route of hosting local sheikhs on the embassy veranda and sipping the melted crayons they called coffee. No, my secret was to insinuate myself into the population itself and see the world through their inflamed and understandably cynical eyes.

* * * * *

British diplomatic documents, unlike those of other foreign services, leave a wide right margin in which the officials who read them can comment. Though rarely legible, these scribblings typically recommend further review or actions such as "Urgently convey to the PM" or "This calls for a peremptory response." Yet, except for the occasional "ho-hum" and "why, why must I endure this?" our Darja dispatches stayed blank.

I remark on this, silently, while noticing that the South Asian student, contrary to his reticent demeanor, has struck up a conversation with Flannel Lady. The old geezer, meanwhile, has found something that's making him cry. Tears stream down his veined and wine-stained nose and drip onto the crinkly registers. As for the pretty boys, they suddenly seem less interested in teasing one another than, for some reason, taunting me. Winking, simpering, sensing, perhaps, that they possess what this lumpish ex-civil servant will never regain. Truth is, though, I'm beyond derision. My only concern is reading on.

June 15, 1980

To: The Permanent Under-Secretary

From: Embassy, Darja

Local sources have reported to me regarding the recent disquiet. The rebels retain the high ground and insist on ridding the island of all foreign influence. They appear to enjoy significant popular support which is, no doubt, incited by Moscow. The U.S. position remains, nevertheless, unclear. As previously communicated, my American colleague professes full support for Her Majesty's Government's position. Yet evidence exists of efforts to replace our Protectorate with a sovereign nation-state, democratic, and firmly allied with Washington.

I await your instructions.

Sir Nigel Ringwald (Ambassador)

Those *local sources* were, once again, me. Now one might think that a pale, plump Caucasian in sweated khakis might stick out in a developing society such as Darja's. Fact was, though, nobody stuck out because everybody was different. From the descendants of shipwrecked African slaves to disoriented seamen who believed they'd landed in Madagascar, the inhabitants were not merely mixed but jumbled. Indians, Arabs, Sixties' hippies too stoned to reach their ashrams—Darja had them all and they all had nothing. The only thing they were "developing" was glaucoma.

Yet I adored them. Admired their kaleidoscopic ethnicity, their thorough dedication to torpor. Rarely bothering to fan themselves, they were the last to be stoked by the USSR or any other power. A quiet people—calling to prayer, the lone muezzin was routinely pelted with trash—seemingly incapable of hate. Hating required exertion.

But not so love. However listless, the Darjans returned my affection, gossiping with me in their Arabic and Hindi lingo, sharing their spare meals of rice and pulverized hermit crabs. There was love around the driftwood fires where I'd sit listening to their tales of Somalian pirates and Mormon missionaries desperate for anyone to convert. And love atop the rag-stuffed mattress which I often shared with Mutassif.

Sleek, lissome-limbed, his hair a soft black profusion of curls. Not yet nineteen and already the head of his family, the caretaker of innumerable siblings, the provider for his widowed mother who spent much of her day searching for his lucrative match. All of which was why we kept our profile low, though I scarcely minded. It was enough just to look into those eyes like emarche puddles and the teeth, dazzling against mocha skin.

"You are a good man, Allah Istar," he'd smile at me. "Good and fat!"

"And you, Mutassif, are better and thin."

He spooned me some crabby rice and poked me playfully in the gut. "And I shall make you fatter still. Fat enough to sink this island."

I chewed and swallowed and tried not to weep. Imagine the gratitude of a man who, though over thirty, had never really been accepted, much less loved, and without a thought to my rank or station. Without judgment or even pity.

Late afternoons, when the temperature dropped low enough to be measured, we strolled along the dilapidated docks of that deep-water port long forgotten by our navy. The random holiday ship still stopped by, its passengers peering over the rail while lithe African boys dove for pearls. They emerged from the surf, bodies glistening like licorice, and sold their gems for fortunes. We laughed, Mutassif and I, for the island had no pearls, only seeded Japanese fakes. The entire world, outside of our own, was a sham.

In that fuck-it-all spirit, we sometimes followed "Wild Bill" Coulson on his insidious missions around Darja. Why "Wild" I had no idea, perhaps an impetuous moment cheerleading for Princeton, though he did show a penchant for mayhem. Keeping a safe distance—roughly a third of the island—we kept sight of the freckled neck that shone under the brim of his Panama. That was how I witnessed, among the copse of wilted eucalyptus and burnt-out scrub, behind the "Nashionel Park" sign, Coulson liaising with his Soviet counterpart, Kabashkin.

The Russian was half Coulson's size and buoy-shaped, the owner of a single Stalin-grey suit. The two of them conferred in the copse for an hour, at least, the American tossing pebbles at the few birds seeking shade there, Kabashkin studying his shoes. I wondered out loud what in hell's name could two old Cold Warriors be jabbering about in 1980—disco music, defections? But Mutassif merely elbowed me in the flank, as he frequently did, and chided, "Do not be worried so, Allah Istar. There are no secrets in Darja."

And there weren't. Mutassif knew the smuggler who provided vodka to the Russians as well as his brother, a whiskey-runner for the Yanks. They confirmed what I already knew: that both legations were vying for the allegiance of Razi, promising to make him, respectively, premier and president. But the next bit of intelligence shocked me. Seems the superpowers had agreed to fight it out for Darja fair-and-square, once they ousted Great Britain.

I paused only to visit a third brother, our supplier of black-market gin, before hightailing it back to the embassy. There I found Sir Nigel, as usual, alone in his office, shades drawn, a fan revolving ineffectually overhead.

The somberness burst, though, when I smacked the bottle onto his desk and delivered the astonishing news. His Excellency's expressions, alternating between downcast and sour, rarely registered agitation. Merely, staring at my gift as if it was his mother's urn, he muttered, "I must cable this development at once."

"Cable?" I gasped. "Humbly, I submit, sir, we have no time for cables. We must act."

He glowered at me with a face drawn by sorrow and drink, a person who, like me, had spent much of his life hiding a truth—in his case, a Hebrew heritage—and despairing of love. "Act?" he asked absently. "How?"

"By going to see the Sultan. And if that doesn't work..."

As if hauled by a heavy-duty crane, his eyes lifted to mine. "And if that doesn't work?"

"Razi."

The matte teletype paper muted the gravity of its contents. *Pursuant to my previous transmission, I have confirmed the nature of U.S. and Soviet intentions regarding this island's status, I am today making a formal démarche to the monarch.*

Again, I have to suppress a chuckle. Sir Nigel wasn't démarching anywhere except the bottom of that bottle. While he remained in the gin and gloom, his trusted Second Secretary braved the furnace of Darja's streets to reach the palace.

Of course, to the dwellers in sand, an abandoned RAF hanger might indeed appear palatial. This one, moreover, was adorned with several anemic palms and a crescent drive of crushed crab shells. Inside, there were Persian rugs and divans as befitting any minor Oriental despot, and potted plants whose contents were solidly frozen. Yes, frozen, for the one indulgence of Sultan Abd al-Rahman Qaboos II—courtesy of British taxpayers—was an air conditioner that he kept at maximum blast. It made most supplicants shiver in his presence, for they were otherwise under-awed. Physically, constitutionally, Qaboos lived up to his name as the end of a long-outdated train.

"Second Secretary Costhwaite, to what do we owe this honor?" Stretched out on an ottoman that doubled as his throne, the sultan scarcely shifted.

I affected the bow taught me in diplomacy school and cursed myself for forgetting to wear a coat. Not so Qaboos. His arraignment featured winter garb that would have marked him a skier if not for the lavender turban on his head. "A matter of state, Your Highness," I replied through chattering teeth. "We believe that foreign powers are plotting to pry Darja out of Britain's orbit." I did not even own a coat.

Predictably, the sultan grunted. "Pry? Pray with what, a toothpick?"

Though well past middle age, perhaps because of the temperature or lack of it, he remained youthful. A smooth if receding chin, a skeptically creased forehead, and eyelids weighted as if with ice. "You are referring to your colleagues, Kabashkin and Coulson, I assume. From the first I could get weaponry, from the second, free elections. Why be pried by them when you have given me all this." A gloved hand swept across the hanger with its retinue of three sleepy wazirs, bearded and berobed, behind him. "That and this flawless accent."

His English was, in fact, posher than mine, the product of an Eton education long beyond my family's means. So expert were we once at ennobling our subjects' deference.

"Whatever they are offering, Your Highness, I assure you our dominion will more than match."

Another grunt, this one echoed by the wazirs, chorus-like. "And I assure you, Mr. Secretary, we could not care less. Darja wishes only to remain overlooked. The world is kindest to those it forgets."

The soundness of this wisdom might have been debated if my mind hadn't numbed. "I am gladdened by your response, Highness, and will submit it at once to my superiors."

"Do that, Costhwaite, by all means do. And please give my regards to Sir Nigel." With a twirl of his gloved fingers, the sultan signaled his court to snicker. "My *warmest* regards."

Outside, the sun hit me like a homicidal batsman, and I staggered half-concussed through a throng of ragged petitioners until I finally reunited with Mutassif.

"He said…he said," I stammered through lips transformed, in seconds, from frostbitten to fried.

"He could not care less."

"How did you know that?"

With his dark warm hands, Mutassif massaged feeling into mine. "How many times have I told you, Allah Istar," he beamed. "There are no secrets in Darja."

* * * * *

This was news to Sir Nigel, unfortunately, who reacted to it with more than his usual moroseness. "Seems we have no choice."

"Seems, indeed."

He bent behind his desk to the safe which I always assumed contained his emergency stock of Sapphire. How surprised was I to see, when the ambassador returned to his usual stoop, thick bundles of cash that he proceeded to stuff into a canvas bag? "Take this to him, appeal to his self-interest. Hearts and minds will likely follow." And how shocked when he once again dipped down and surfaced with an object that, when placed even gingerly on the desk, thundered. "And in case they don't."

I accepted the bag and uncertainly lifted the pistol.

"And for God's sake be careful with that thing, Costhwaite. It's loaded."

* * * * *

That conversation took place on July 2, the day that Sir Nigel informed the Foreign Office of *high-level representations to the Sultan* and *discreet contacts with irregular elements*. Reading these communiqués, some future researcher might envision an ambassador in tails clicking his heels and a trench-coated agent slipping through shadows. The reality, of course, was far more prosaic: a cheaply-clad diplomat at first freezing and now awash in sweat as he huffed up Darja's only hill.

I, too, was breathing hard at the reading table where the too-cool graduate students mistook my panting for something else and meanly mimicked it. Elsewhere, East and West were defiantly meeting as the Indian boy and Saxon girl lost all interest in their files and solely studied one another. The old man, though no longer crying, flipped angrily through the stubs as if one of them were missing. I understood his frustration over the fudging of facts and memory. Such was the text which spoke of *certain inducements* proffered at *a select location* to the rebel—his name, alone, was true—Razi.

* * * * *

Never much for the playing fields, much less for mountain scaling, I was wheezing halfway to the top. Clutched to my chest, the cash bag, I imagined, kept my heart inside. The revolver, meanwhile, an old Webley that may or may not have had a safety, slipped down the back of my pants. Fear of it hitting the ground and going off was one of the reasons I rejected Mutassif's pleas to come along. That, and the possibility that, however incongruously for Darja, this Razi man was serious.

Just how serious was imparted to me just short of the summit, when the otherwise comatose air suddenly sprung alive. "Bloody hell," I shouted, realizing that a bullet had whizzed by my ear. "Don't shoot!" I begged and begged again in every local dialect. "Don't shoot! I only want to talk!"

"We only want to buy you off," I should have said, but saw soon enough that Razi could not be purchased. He could not even be rented, this former greengrocer who once hawked turnips in the *souq*, and clearly, he did not want to talk.

He stood, rather, at the mouth of the cave, a strapping man not yet thirty, dressed in a white shalwar kameez and a strip of linen wrapped revolutionary-style around his head. His face was as beautiful as Mutassif's yet also ruggedly handsome, unshaven, intelligent, intent. I would have relished staring at it, except for the Kalashnikov still smoking and aimed at my gut.

"I know what you want, Englishman," he began in the usual patois, "and I am not interested."

I tried to straighten my back, struggled not to gasp. "Are you sure? We could call this a first instalment."

The muzzle of his rifle nodded up and down, not in agreement. "Take your money, your evil ways, and leave our nation *now*."

I had heard Darja described in many ways, most of them scatological, but never as a nation. But who was I to argue with an automatic rifle? My only desire was to get off that hill, out of range, and back to Mutassif. "What do you say I just leave this here and you think about it?" I laid the bag on the sand. "There's a lifetime there of turnip-selling."

The muzzle nodded again, "Yes, yes," meaning "No, and I'll blow your brains out."

"Okay. Very well. I'm leaving." I retrieved the bag, frustrated about having to lug it all the way down.

"And Englishman," Razi laughed at me when I turned. "Take the gun out of your backside. You might just shoot off your balls."

* * * * *

The sun had already set by the time I returned to the embassy ,but the sky was pinkish bright. A crowd roiled outside, big, greasy men who were clearly non-Darjans, probably imports from some coast, and carrying torches. And not British torches, either, with batteries, but native torches on fire that they shared with the building. Thirty years later, I read about what was happening inside:

Situation urgent, the cable cried. *Legation under attack, apparently by foreign elements. Position no longer tenable. Recommend Operation Bailout.*

* * * * *

"Bailout…" I mutter audibly enough for one of my tablemates to note, though thankfully none of them does. The Sahib and the Saxon are too deeply engaged with one another, and the Fair Youths have finally lost interest in mocking me. Even the pensioner seems indifferent, his forehead laid flat on a file into which he intermittently snores. The only response comes in my document's margins which, for once, are crammed with notes.

"Bailout, yes, at once," the first reads, followed by, "The PM must be briefed. The First Sea Lord instructed." And finally, "Send in the Royal Marines."

There is no description of what occurred next. Nor could I begin to explain how a jellied pencil-pusher, not known for his pluck, managed to make his way to the rear entrance and reach Sir Nigel's office. Dismal at the best of times, the room was now smoke stuffed, and the ambassador, whose face often recalled a half-burnt funeral candle, sat in a puddle of his own dejection.

"Come, sir, there's no time," I urged him and succeeded in extracting him from behind his desk. There was no need to rescue the staff, all three of whom had fled, or to burn his papers, of importance to no one. The cash would have to remain with me as would the pistol, still wedged between my buttocks. Hugging the bag with one hand and the scruff of Sir Nigel's neck with the other, I led us both out through the flames and the throng.

But not before I noticed, hanging back from the mob, a pair of familiar figures. The two of them, one stick-thin and the other rotund, stood in the shadows like an ominous number 10. Coulson and Kabashkin. The demonstration, the destruction—suddenly, I understood.

Not that there was time to contemplate the deviousness. The first task was to get Sir Nigel to safety, first at Mutassif's, whose mother nursed the traumatized diplomat with an extra scoop of mashed hermit crabs. Later, I stashed the money under the rag-filled mattress and took my superior by the arm to my own humble flat near the port.

"Humble" might be an inappropriate word, conjuring as it does cushy armchairs and low-wattage bulbs. My place was a dump. Four concrete walls, a cot and a kitchenette that I barely used but which afforded a view of any randomly anchoring vessel. Such as the small ship, unmarked yet unmistakably Naval, moored there the next morning.

I didn't ask Sir Nigel about it, though—curled up on the cot, he snored dolefully—until I returned from the *souq*. While shopping for flatbread and coffee, I noticed more than the usual litter of carcasses in the street. Not just cats and vermin this time, but the goats and sheep that Darjans often valued more than blood-relatives. Only when I served my guest his breakfast did I mention the strange sight, and only then did I hear him murmur, "Bailout."

Mistaking the word for a certain brand of whiskey, I apologized for being plum out, and suggested we locate one of the island's two or three phones and communicate our situation. But Sir Nigel merely grumbled again, "Bailout," and rather violently shook his head. That was when I realized that something else was afoot, something perverse.

My first instinct was to rush to Mutassif, but instead of weaving through the usual beggars and goatherds, I found myself face to mask with men in full-body bio-suits. Through megaphones, they were warning—in English!—of some dire bacterial danger, and urging all residents to evacuate at once. Some of the men were spraying the street, others assisting the elderly to depart. Others, still, prodded the majority who were more than content to watch this all half-snoozing until stirred into motion at rifle-point.

In seconds, the unpaved drag of what Sir Nigel once called Darja's capital was a torrent of panicked islanders. The flood was too intense to penetrate—on the contrary, it swept me with it toward the port. The mysterious boat was no longer alone now but accompanied by far larger military transports. A helicopter thwacked overhead. "Mutassif!" I shouted, straining on my toes, but the noise was all-drowning. Brown, black, mulatto faces melded in the heat as they surged toward the transports' ramps. Howling "Mutassif!" I tried to break through the corridor of Royal Marines arrayed, for some reason, in battle gear.

"Sorry, sir. Off-limits," one pumped-up sergeant apologized in a voice which, underscored by his brandished weapon, sounded threatening.

I was about to start arguing with him, was ready to plead, when I again spied that incongruous duo. They were spectating, it seemed, Kabashkin with his Soviet architecture features, and Coulson, all freckles and cream, moustache shielding his smirk.

"Happy are you, Nate?" I accosted him. "Is this what you wanted?"

The Panama hat was already half-pushed up the American's head, but he tipped it up further. "It's a sight to be seen, I do confess," he drawled. "Though another outcome might have been preferred. If I had my druthers."

"If I had my druthers," I lurched at him. "You'd both be on a leaky dhow to Bombay."

And I might have taken a swipe at Coulson, anything to wipe off that sneer, if my name was not just then called.

"Allah Istar! Over here! Allah Istar!"

Mutassif. Between the human flotsam, for a fleeting second, I glimpsed his quiet beauty. Perhaps his mother was with him, too, and his assorted siblings. Perhaps, in the burlap sack he hauled with all his family's belongings, was the bag I'd hidden under the bed.

"Wait for me! I'm coming!"

I rushed toward the line of Marines. "Let me in!"

"Sorry, sir." This time no garnishing the threat.

"Goddamn you…"

I wasn't thinking, not even feeling, and only vaguely aware of reaching under the small of my back. And then, somehow, I found myself pointing that pistol straight at the sergeant's nose. He didn't budge, though, didn't blink. And barely had I yammered, "Let me in or I'll…" when another Marine's rifle butt knocked me senseless on the jaw.

Puking, I awoke on a military hospital ship some hours later, handcuffed to the bed and guarded. Yet, by chatting up the orderlies, I managed to piece together much of what happened. How the entire population of Darja, several thousand souls, had been hauled East and West and deposited on foreign shores. Among the last to leave, I learned were the U.S. and Soviet legations. Once the flotillas were out of range, a massive explosion enveloped the island. The flash could be seen from as far away as Sri Lanka.

I understood that if Britain couldn't keep the island, no one would. Not so much as a last gasp but as the final spit-in-the-world's-eye from a dying empire. Thus ended our thirty-year rule over Darja, with a whimper as well as a bang.

I understood and so did senior officials in Whitehall. A week later, I was back in the Foreign Office, seated in an overstuffed Edwardian chair, surrounded by furnishings pilfered from Delhi and Rangoon, in a high-ceiling office overlooking Buckingham Palace. There, I was informed of my pending resignation from the service as well as the terms of my retirement.

The backstory, it seemed, was complete. The germs that contaminated Darja were anomalous but deadly, the evacuation a humanitarian necessity. As for the bomb, the press obligingly attributed it to Israel, whose leaders were chided by London. Only the internal record remained to be closed and that task—given Sir Nigel's incapacity—fell to me. Write the summary and all charges of insubordination and attempting to shoot a

Royal Marine would be dropped, the deal offered. Write it, and I could fade unremarked into history.

Leaning back into the brocade, rubbing my still-swollen jaw, I contemplated this for a moment. Whether to conclude my public career with pride or turpitude, complicity or honor. I pictured myself in prison, on the one hand, and on the other, a free man unburdened of all but the truth.

* * * * *

The document, the last in FO 145/4871, jiggles slightly in my grip. The date on top, August 25, 1980, remains a kind of anniversary for me, a day of remembrance and regret. Under the antiseptic light of the archive reading room, even the heading seems unholy:

> **To: The Permanent Under-Secretary**
>
> **From: Embassy, Darja**
>
> **Sir,**
>
> **It is my duty to summarize recent events in Darja. Following the outbreak of disease, our Mission effected a temporary relocation of the populace.**

Lies! Lies! I want to scream out. There was no outbreak, no disease, only the deliberate poisoning of flocks. No temporary relocation but a permanent cleansing. Yet still the prevarications unwound.

> **Despite the attack on his office, Ambassador Ringwald remained in complete control, ensuring the suppression of all rebel groups and the orderly return of the Sultan.**

Of course, Ambassador Ringwald was hors de combat, as we say in diplomacy, and in life, totally out of it. Rather than being suppressed, Razi the brigand was hauled off with the others and could conceivably be seen even today selling turnips in Sana'a. Sultan Qaboos was derailed, as it were, and cast into Manchester exile.

Finally, the ultimate fallacy—the whopper:

I have stayed in our Mission preparing for a peaceful transition from Colonial rule to a popular republic happily secured in our Commonwealth.

Never would I see Darja again and nor would anyone else. The few strips of the island not reduced below sea level were rendered indefinitely toxic to all life forms. As for staying in the Mission, that part was true if it referred to the San Francisco neighborhood where I took my little severance pay and opened a kitchen accessories store. There, amidst the French presses and edge grain cutting boards, I still watch the front door and wait, hoping against logic, that Mutassif will enter.

He will not have aged a day—so my fantasy spools—but will have remained as he was, kind-hearted and pristine. My imagination occasionally allows for a proper education, not only for him but for his many brothers and sisters, and an international profession that brings him to the Bay Area. All this was paid for, I daydream, by that single bag of cash. "Allah Istar!" he'll bellow, all teeth and dimples. "Allah Istar, you are still so good and fat!

But then the door opens, the bell rings, and instead of a supple, smiling islander there's some giggly newlyweds waving gift certificates or a rich family's cook searching for a microplane zester. Sometimes, they know my name, though not the real one I left back in Britain. The name I used for the last time to sign this final fakery from Darja.

Be assured, sir, of my highest considerations,

Alistair Crosthwaite (Second Secretary)

* * * * *

The reading room is nearly empty when I look up from the file. The couples—the Asian boy and the English girl, the two randy graduates—have gone off to some pub somewhere and from there quite possibly to bed. For that is the prerogative, or better yet, the imperative, of youth. Only the pensioner remains, awakened now and trembling even harder, his nose an indignant maroon.

"I'll tell you wot it is," he barks at me as if I'd asked. "It's foked. That's what it is. Foked."

He slams his file closed and I slam mine, though careful to retie the ribbon. "Foked," I agree. "Indeed."

Outside, darkness has replaced the rain as Kew's preservative. The Victorian homes are gripped by it, the gardens encaged. Only the moon, embedded in the reflector pool, defies the gloom. But that image is also a fiction—all of it is, the village, the Victorian station. The only reality is the one we file away in our hearts, whether for thirty years or three hundred. Everlastingly, love rules us, and so willingly we submit.

Personal Assistance

Chloe knocked again, brisker this time, with knuckles, and tried to keep the coffee cup still. "Mister Anthony, sir," she began, whispering, then added several decibels to her tone. "Please open up, Mister Anthony. I have your latte."

Behind the luxury suite doors, she could hear an alarm clock buzzing and even the wake-up call. But no other sounds emanated, certainly no movement, and she considered employing her whole fist. She pounded once, twice, gritting her teeth at the sight of the saucer wobbling. "Please, Mister Anthony, get up. You're supposed to be on set in an hour!"

She was about to wallop when an even harsher voice thundered from the end of the hall.

"Stop that, Zoe! Are you insane?"

The young woman turned toward Cheryl—Miss Milgram—with a crosscurrent of emotions. Hurt, anger, but mostly confusion coursed across her face. Not only young, but Afro-Caribbean and pretty, a recent graduate of Yale, she was unaccustomed to being spoken to so tartly. And how was she to respond to this much older person with the sexless hairstyle and doughy pants suit, white but probably uneducated? Disdain? Indignation? The most she could muster was fear.

"But my schedule says ten o'clock wake-up."

She tried to reach into her rear pocket for her cell phone and nearly spilled some coffee.

"Jesus, Zoe," Cheryl snapped and plucked the cup by its handle. "Now get out of here."

Producing an electronic key, Cheryl let herself into the room and slammed the doors behind her. The personal assistant's helper shivered in the hallway alone.

"Not Zoe," she sobbed into the empty saucer. "Chloe."

In a single gulp, Cheryl downed the latte and got to work. The odor choking the room could only be less offensive than the sight awaiting her inside. Vomit, sweat, stale booze, and cheap lubricant, she'd long ago learned to deal with, but she still dreaded pulling back the knotted covers to the cadaverous scene underneath.

Actually, "cadaverous" was insulting to the dead. Few stiffs would exhibit the varicose veins and distended belly, the pallor broken only by capillaries, the pores like termite holes. A forensic identification, she often thought, would be cake compared to recognizing the body which once evoked Michelangelo's David. Summoning Banquo's ghost was easier than slapping one of those wattled cheeks and barking, "Yo, Bogdan, Dobro jutro. Time to get your ass out of bed."

Anthony got his ass up, or at least half of it, by groaning onto his side. The other portion had to be hoisted by Cheryl, by inserting her wrists under his armpits. She balanced his naked torso against hers, indifferent to its jellied coldness, even to the prune-like knob that pleasured numerous starlets—"pleasured" being his word.

Like a half-paralyzed crab, she hauled him into the shower and lowered him onto the tiles. The water rained artic cold at first and then lukewarm, but only because she pitied him.

"But what about her?" he groaned and raised a flaccid wrist.

"Her," she understood, was the woman who supposedly remained in the bed. But there was no woman nor any signs that there had been. Just a few empty minibar items and the syringe which she diligently disposed. "It's okay, honey," Cheryl assured him. "She left you all her love."

"Good. Good," Anthony blubbered as Cheryl with accordioned sleeves shaved and shampooed him. "You're a fine person, Milgram, you know that? Fucking first class. Where did I ever find you?"

Dabbing the lather from his earlobes, she sighed as always, "Under a rock."

Under the worker wanted list was more like it. A bland request for a personal assistant's helper, minimum salary, no experience necessary. The latter stipulation especially appealed to her, just out of Michigan State and newly arrived in Hollywood. The ad said nothing about films, but at twenty-two she already exhibited the gut for opportunity and danger that assured her long-term survival.

The address took her to a production studio much like the ones she'd seen in the movies—dour executives, perky extras, grips and gaffers ambling at unionized rates—and to a trailer emblazoned with a star. There she met Miss Houlihan, reviled on the lot as Mothra, a sour, strident woman of indeterminate age and barbarous disposition.

"You don't do a thing unless I tell you to. Period," she spat at Cheryl. "Even if he asks. *Specifically*, if he asks."

It took another two days before she even found out who "he" was. Two days of ferrying bottles of Mey Eden water and Siberian cedar nuts in Lalique crystal bowls to and from the trailer. Each morning she delivered a latte that was mostly booze and another in the evening almost coffee-less. How many cups had she ferried before finally meeting her employer—accidentally—as he stepped out of his trailer. He breathed triumphantly and yanked up his fly.

"I'm so sorry," Cheryl muttered and wished she had worn makeup that day, if only to cover her blush.

"Hi, there," he chirped from the top of his stairs, three above Cheryl. He thrust his hand down to shake. "Yes, it's me, Robert P. Anthony."

Cheryl fumbled the bottle but managed to pin it between her elbow and flank. She took the star's hand and almost introduced herself before Mothra came screeching at her.

"You! New girl! Get away from there and do your job!"

Their fingers unwound but not before Cheryl accorded him a view down the front of her T-shirt. Her hair was the color of maple candy and her eyes sylvan green. When her lips smiled sweetly, she knew, his would lasciviously respond. These, too, were instincts.

And she needed them, for the average longevity of a personal assistant's helper, she learned, was less than a month. She had to be quick on her feet, responsible but cunning, innocent yet seductive. At twenty-two, in her first Hollywood job, Cheryl already understood that her only option was murder.

* * * * *

Deodorized, combed-over, and girdled, he was ready to be Robert P. Anthony. Getting him into the elevator, though, through the lobby's swarm of autograph hounds and paparazzi, and into the limo without splintering his skull remained her daily ordeal. Yet, Cheryl weathered it as she always did, with grit and a backhand swat capable of dislodging a lens.

"Can't be late," Anthony reminded her as he strode, waving, toward the revolving doors.

Cheryl wanted to curse him for refusing to take the service entrance. Instead, she replied, "No worry, we're right on time," and, in the same breath, shoulder-butted a portly man with a camcorder. "Hey, fatso, that fucking thing's out of here or I'm making it part of your head."

"Can't keep Lilly waiting."

"She'll wait," Cheryl patted the pashmina sleeve of the suit she had crammed him into that morning. "And *you*! Want to taste that Canon?"

The Lilly in waiting was Lillian Drop, Anthony's co-star, a petite brunette whose name, alone, was genuine. The rest was rhinoplasty and silicon, courtesy of a career which, if not meteoric, at least paid the surgeon's bills. In this feature, *Sidebar*, she played a young, ambitious attorney struggling against an equally spry and gamey prosecutor trying to put her client, a wrongly accused ne'er-do-well, behind bars. Anthony portrayed the judge, sage and curmudgeonly. And when not in character, he was insanely in love with Lilly.

Such on-set crushes were common in Cheryl's line of work. A box office draw such as Anthony was almost expected to have his way with the leading lady or at least a supporting actress, a kind of seigniorial right. But technology had all but done in privacy without retarding the old idol's decline. Yet the truth about Lillian, Cheryl knew, was harsher than that. She did not need him. A romp in his trailer or a night feigning bliss was no longer a career enhancer. Professionally speaking, Robert P. Anthony could not help anybody, least of all himself.

Cheryl knew all of that but kept it from him. She could see him debauched and hung over or even strung out, but not hurt. More than caring for what remained of his body, her job was to watch out for his heart. She was its guardian, ruthlessly monitoring who gained entry and who didn't. Preserving the tiny corner that was hers.

* * * * *

When Mothra caught her a second time approaching Anthony's room, she realized there would not be a third. A message on Cheryl's hotel phone asked her to fetch a cold compress for an ankle Anthony had strained during the day's shooting. A comedy, *The Mean Streets of Cleveland* required him to run, and his feet needed nursing.

But she never got out of the elevator. Her boss stood there with arms akimbo, rasping, "What? What in god's-fucking-name do you think you're doing?" She snatched the compress from Cheryl's hands and waited as the doors closed on her scowl.

The choice, for Cheryl, was obvious: leave Cleveland unemployed or access Anthony's room. The deliberation took five minutes, the execution somewhat longer, but even Mothras have to sleep. Still, she took the stairs, which exited near the presidential suite. A single knock sufficed.

How did she feel—sluttish? Cheap? On the contrary, the maneuver flushed her with power. And something unexpected. Though scarcely pleasured, she found herself sliding into love. Not with his physique or his face, majestic even without makeup. No, what sent her slipping, clawing ineffectually to slow her descent, was his soul.

He revealed it that night, a mere glimpse at first, but then the spectacle. It began with the story of his childhood in a tiny Bulgarian enclave in Los Angeles. The mailman father and his mother a sometimes five n' dime store worker, the older brothers and sisters who married as soon as they could and relocated. Bogdan Antonov was a quiet kid, compulsively shy, and apparently not gifted in anything. Not until high school did he discover that girls found him attractive and that, once forced onto stage in the senior play, he could play any part. As long as it wasn't Bogdan.

Escaping that character proved easier than he imagined. It involved getting on a bus the day after his graduation and traveling across town to the studios. From there, the journey from extra to walk-on to star was rapid—too rapid, for he never had the chance to grow up. Though his name was now anglicized and appointed a middle initial, Robert P. Anthony remained Bogdan inside.

The tale unwound over several nights, Scheherazade-like, during which she held him and stroked his hair. A large man, he felt babyish in her lap. He opened up to her and, letting go of herself finally, Cheryl fell.

By the end of the week on location, Mothra was gone, and Cheryl held a new position. She also possessed a life partner, or so she believed while landing at LAX. But the limo left her off at her apartment in Westwood while Anthony rode up to the Hills. By the time she saw him again, on the set of *August Autumn*, he was already bedding his co-star. Cleveland was never again mentioned. Cheryl became Miss Milgram and he reverted to Mr. Anthony, except at those times when he was bespoiled and too drunk to notice the difference. Only then did she call him Bogdan.

* * * * *

Lillian Drop made an enormous show of meeting the "*real* Robert P. Anthony," as if there were numerous fakes, and "in the flesh," as though it were not so abundant. Cheryl looked on saccharinely. She could discern an act, even off-set, and knew that Lilly, as she insisted on being called, had no more interest in her boss than she did in his personal assistant. She could also tell that Anthony was doomed. Along with that predatory expression she remembered from years back, eyeing her from the top of the stairs, she saw a hunger and sorrowful need. Here, Cheryl feared, was a heart too papery to break.

But busted it was, and perhaps fatally, as Lilly showed no sign of reciprocating. His gifts of Richart chocolates and Lady Slipper Orchids went unappreciated, and his dinner invitations ignored. By the second of the two-week shoot, Anthony was drinking alone in his room or sulking in his trailer. He could neither eat nor sleep, only whimper. Cheryl ceased to exist.

And for this she hated Lilly, almost as much as she hated Anthony for loving her. Wandering the lot, Cheryl considered her options. Decades on the job had taught her much, although at an abominable price. Every mirror showed her how much she now resembled Mothra. The same short, worn out hair and indifferent pants suits, the same bitter crimp in her mouth. Her helpers lasted three weeks at most. Yet, while no longer innocent or seductive, she remained more responsible than ever, and more cunning.

That afternoon's break, she kept a watch on Lilly's trailer. A few minutes passed before her hunch materialized. Roger Rimrauld, the casting confection who played the prosecutor in *Sidebar*, made a show of sneaking inside. Not a very convincing performance—Cheryl was in plain view—or perhaps he wanted to be seen. Personal assistants might be invisible, but not so the gossip rags. A magazine cover of Roger's sculpted face with Lilly's reconstructed one was worth another contract, at least, when exhibited next to the cash register.

Cheryl had to hurry. Roger did not look like a long-laster, and Anthony could barely limp. She hustled back to his trailer, just in time to find her newest helper climbing the steps with yet another latte.

"You've got to be joking, Zoe."

"Please, Miss Milgram. Production said Mister Anthony requested it." The young woman visibly trembled, dribbling coffee and booze.

"Production?" Cheryl fumed, "Production! Since when does production tell you what only a personal assistant can? Since when, you dimwit?"

Again, Cheryl wrenched the latte away and snarled, "Bye, Zoe, you're fired."

"I'm Chloe," the ex-helper wailed, but Cheryl was already pushing through the starred door and dusting off Anthony's blazer.

"Quick, straighten yourself up!" she ordered him, pausing only to down the mug. "She's asking for you."

"Who?" Anthony tried to look clueless.

Cheryl angled her head in the direction she came from and jiggled her eyebrows.

"Oh," Anthony shouted, "Oh!" and extended a trembling hand. "Help me."

She helped him as fast as he could be assisted down the three steep stairs and the seemingly infinite stretch of the lot to Lilly's trailer. There, too, Cheryl lifted him from behind by the elbows and gently prodded his butt. Anthony knocked but fortunately not loud enough. Nor did he wait but instead stumbled through the door.

"Oh!" he exclaimed again, much as Cheryl anticipated. "I'm most terribly sorry…"

Peering around him, she could see Lilly on her knees in front of Roger's naked half. All of her surgery could not prevent her face from transforming into a monstrous mask. "Get the fuck out of here!" she hissed at Robert P. Anthony. "Crazy old perv."

* * * * *

She held him for hours that night, lolled him while he bawled. "You're a good woman, Milgram," he finally sniffled. "Where did I ever find you?"

His head rose and fell on her shoulder. "Under that rock."

Later, he reminisced about past performances, his two Oscar nominations, his marriages, and his many affairs. Cheryl never interrupted him, not even when she injected him and waited for the drug to kick in. It did, eventually, but not before Anthony started burbling.

"But there was one I loved more than all the others. More than that slut Lillian, for sure. I loved her but, God help me, I lost her."

"There, there," Cheryl comforted him, caressed his adored, addled head.

"A beautiful, intelligent, young woman. A woman I could tell anything to, all of my secrets. Who could have made me happy. But I lost her, Milgram. I lost her in Cleveland."

Cheryl whispered, "No, Bogdan, you didn't." Rocking him, she sang, "Nani, nani, brate, S'nco se ti prati." A Bulgarian lullaby he taught her once, long ago. "The cradle is swinging Kalina"—so he translated it for her. "Sleep, little brother, sleep."

Noah Simkin, Athlete, Scholar, Renaissance Man, Is Dead

Noah H. Simkin has died, a family spokesman announced. Though well over one hundred years of age, the cause of his passing was uncertain. "He simply fulfilled all of his dreams," said his eldest son, Adam, adding that, "even in death, he was bigger than life."

Such sentiments were widespread among those privileged to know Mr. Simkin. His remarkable rise from challenging, if not humble, origins, his meteoric career, and his renowned compassion for family and friends alike, became legendary. Indeed, a summary of his accomplishments reads like an adventure novel—that, or a guide to impassioned living.

Born to middle-class parents—his father was a podiatrist, his mother, a realtor—and raised in a Long Island suburb, the young Simkin showed little of his later pre-eminence. His grades at the Davison Regional High School were mediocre, at best, and difficulties with concentration severely constricted his horizons. Looking back from his extraordinary adulthood, Mr. Simkin often lamented his early lack of popularity, most painfully with female classmates, and his inability to excel at sports. His sole athletic achievement was serving as manager for the Davison tennis team.

Like a carriage wheel that seems to spin backward or the rowboat oars that merely dip, Noah Simkin appeared to regress or, at best, stay in place. But in fact, he raced into life.

A crafty and original writer, he secured admission to several Ivy League universities, obtaining degrees in anthropology, psychology, and hermeneutics. He applied these disciplines to a ground-breaking study of love. From the sophomore crush to the oceanic ardor for humanity, Mr. Simkin revealed, love is the irreducible emotion, as uniquely human as the smile, potentially more devastating than nature. His volumes on the subject earned him numerous prizes, among them a National Critics Circle Award and a Pulitzer, along with some twenty honorary doctorates.

While attaining literary prominence, Mr. Simkin similarly overcame his physical limitations. From the last-listed player on the junior varsity football squad, he rose to become an all-star running back, setting several collegiate records that stand to this day. After graduation and well into his last decade, Mr. Simkin remained an avid athlete, a scratch golfer and competitive skier. Asked how he managed to outshine so many of his peers, the Professor—so he was genially known—pointed once again to love. "Just tap into it," he remarked, "and you'll always come out a champ."

And at love, too, Mr. Simkin eventually triumphed. Blossoming to over six feet, investing in his musculature, he found himself the object of desires once directed at others. Olivia Fanning who, as captain of the Davison cheerleaders, never once glanced in Mr. Simkin's direction, married him when she was still a community college undergraduate. Together they had four sons and a daughter, all of whom achieved distinction in law and medicine.

Before that, though, Olivia Fanning Simkin died from cancer, leaving her husband bereft. Two years passed before he met Valeri Bartucci, the former Bond girl and advocate for African orphans. Their marriage made the front cover of numerous celebrity magazines, which continued to headline their philanthropic missions as well as their gala appearances until Ms. Bartucci, too, passed away from a rare strain of Zambian malaria.

Still, Mr. Simkin retained his fervor for life. Whether on the links or down the slopes, in classrooms or galas, he remained engaged and thoroughly engaging. His disquisitions on love, and especially his advice to lovers, made him a standard guest on daytime talk shows and a much-sought-after inspirational speaker. Long after his centennial birthday, Noah Haskell Simkin was overwhelmingly deemed a success.

Approached by a reporter several weeks before his death and queried about his favorite reading material, Mr. Simkin recommended obituaries. "I've been reading them since high school," he responded. "Every young person should. Obits are the blueprints for life." Those last six words are now inscribed on the walls of this department, whose writers are woefully underappreciated in journalism.

In addition to his children, Mr. Simkin is survived by thirteen grandchildren and twenty-four great-grandchildren. The family asks that donations be made to the Davison Regional High School which has established a scholarship in his memory and placed a plaque on his locker. Several production companies have expressed an interest in making a film based on Mr. Simkin's story—this according to Adam, the eldest son—though some thought it might prove too implausible.

Noah Simkin pushed back from his desk. He looked wistfully at his bulletin board, at the D letter emblazoned with a tennis racket and the smaller m for manager, and at the photograph of a young woman pumping poms-poms. He sighed at his computer screen with its reflection of a short, plump, rather pimply teenager with eyes that were nevertheless irrepressible. He moved the cursor across the site of his college application and centered it on the Personal Essay box. Then, with a grunt if not a flourish, he clicked on the word, "submit."

Jorge

What could be lonelier, and scarier, than the subway at 6:00 a.m.? Lonely because, apart from some slumbering drunks, George was the only passenger. He was traveling back to the Bronx from the midtown rink where his intermural hockey team practiced pre-dawn. The uptown express raced past local stops of sooty light and plunged into tunnels that seemed to suck the train's power. And scary because he could never forget how, as a child, his father took him to see a horror film in which a monster plucked precisely such a subway off an elevated track and hurled it, riders screaming, onto the street. At nineteen, that memory mixed with the clang and screech into images of giant claws crushing the car like a soda can. The solitude, the fear, made him clutch the hockey stick weapon-like between his knees.

He was clutching still when, short of the Harlem River crossing, the doors opened for two women. Actually, one was a woman and the other a girl, seventeen at most, holding her by the elbow. Hispanic—Guatemalan, Honduran?—with the off-shoulder blouses and red plastic jewelry favored by Latinas of the time. Mother and daughter, George guessed, though they look nothing alike—the first overweight and fat-featured, and the second slim, almost feathery. They sat on the bench opposite his and watched the windows flickering behind him.

So they rumbled for another stop or two, swaying, before George's eyes caught the girl's. They were the shape and color of footballs, black-lashed and mascaraed. Her jet black hair, pulled back and tied—too rigorously for a teenager, he thought—revealed bite-sized ears and fruity lips and a nose tilted upward without exposing a nostril. But it was her skin that most transfixed him. Burnished, coppery, it radiated in the train's chiaroscuro.

George tried not to stare. He focused, instead, on the advertisements for driving lessons and personal injury lawyers. The hockey stick twirled in his hands. Still, his eyes wandered back to her. Her eyes also kept drifting. Given the time and the limited vision field, their glances would inevitably meet. And when they did, it was George who blushed, seeing himself as she must—a gangling, pale, freckled undergrad, in torn Manhattan College sweatgear, a ski cap slapped over his head.

The girl didn't blush, though, or divert her gaze. Instead, she held his, cupped it, he felt, and appraised it. Then, baring a row of tiny white teeth, she smiled. George smiled back, his head hot with embarrassment. He wished he could hide behind his stick.

How long did that smile endure—a second or two probably, though he later measured it in minutes—before the mother intervened? The same elbow that her daughter had cradled now jabbed her side. George also received a threatening look that stung like a slap on his cheek.

They looked away from each other, the two young people, though both sensed the pull. Both knew that their eyes would gravitate and link again, and they did but only fleetingly before the train shrieked to a halt. The doors drummed open, and this time the mother took her daughter's arm and lifted her from the bench. They began to exit, the wide woman and the girl who pranced limberly on platform shoes, her body in tight jeans looking cookie-cut. She stepped out of the train but not before twisting her chin over one bare shoulder and casting a final, rueful, smile.

George sat there stunned, aware that something immense hung in the balance, but unsure exactly what. A few stops remained before his, the Grand Concourse, and getting off now meant missing his first class. Not that it mattered. He was scarcely the studious type, pleased to squeak by with Cs. Nor was he aggressive, not on the ice, not in life, the trajectory of which was set. Marriage to some local Irish girl, work in his father's roofing business, a house with a one-car driveway and a small backyard in Queens. Mets games on the radio, a beer at the end of each day, a son if he were lucky.

The car shivered, meanwhile, the engine revved. Hissing, the doors began to close. In that instant, he thought: I'll never see her again, never learn her name. The mother and daughter were no longer in view, only a barren platform, but that very emptiness filled him. Inflated him, almost against his will, and lifted him off the bench. His hockey stick clattered as it vaulted him toward the doors that he clutched and pried open, just wide enough to squeeze through. To the curses of some unseen conductor, George stumbled out of the train.

Bent over, a muscle snapped in his back, he groaned and managed to straighten himself only to find the two women gaping at him. "I'm sorry, Ma'am," he gasped, limping toward them as the mother pulled her daughter away. "No, please, let me explain. My name is George McDonough. I'm a student. Just a guy. I didn't mea,n to scare you. I just…just…"

The younger one cut in, "Speak slowly. Her English is not that good."

George gulped and nodded. "If it's okay with you, Ma'am," he began again, very slowly indeed.

"She's not deaf. You don't have to shout."

He stopped and swept the cap from his head, exposing an orangey mop. Slowly, softly he said, "I really want to meet your daughter."

The daughter held up a hand to him and turned to her mother, translating. He cursed himself for dropping out of Spanish 101. The only word he caught was "Jorge."

The mother leered at him. "Jorge," she repeated dryly, and George, wringing his cap, echoed her, "Jorge."

"Hola, Jorge!" the girl laughed out loud, and her laughter chimed around the station.

He laughed as well, nervously under the mother's glower, as the girl scribbled on the inside of a wrapper. That was how he gained her number and how he learned her name, Carmen.

* * * * *

She lived in a fourth-floor walk-up on 136th Street in Mott Haven, in a neighborhood alive with peppery smells and music that sounded to him like pots being dropped off balconies. They would meet on the doorstop framed between the brownstones and iron railings where Carmen's mother—he would soon call her Mamá—could monitor them from above. She had three younger sisters and a brother, some, he suspected, from different fathers, and supported by a family of cousins who, however distant, kept one another above poverty. Carmen never felt poor, at least, though she worked after school and weekends at an uncle's bodega in Inwood. He visited her there often, drawn—so he ribbed her—by the crispy tostones she snuck him but really for the chance of stealing into the storage closet where, between the stacks of toilet paper and refried beans, they kissed.

For kisses had to be stolen, at least at first. But how much fun was the theft! Guarded by a mother sworn to spare her the trauma she suffered at that age and observed by a vigilante corps of relatives, Carmen could rarely be alone with him. Inventively, they found not only the storage closet but also a junky-free alleyway and the struggling urban park, behind a stand of plane trees. Propped by one of these, one balmy night, Carmen let him insert his hand beneath her blouse. That first sensation of her breast in his hand—hot, trembling slightly but strangely tenacious—would remain ineffable to him always, long after they became lovers.

That could only happen in his fraternity house, in his room crammed with Mets banners and bruised hockey sticks, where the stale beer smell was hard-baked into the floor. The sex, bumbling at first, became fiery. Most wondrous for him, though, was the sight of her knees which seemed to condense the nut-colored sheen of her face and her spindly fingers with nails painted the same defiant red as her earrings. Her hair, let free, cascaded like black satin down her neck.

Carmen fit in well with his frat brothers, mostly working-class Irish guys like him but with a smattering of Italians, jocks and toughies who nevertheless cowered in front of her. Instead, they teased him for falling so obviously and stupidly in love. They dubbed him Jorge and warned him to treat her right.

He treated her right. Never one for religion, he joined Carmen and her family for Sunday Mass and even made confession. He helped them spruce up the Mott Haven apartment, dumping the detritus of Mamá's boyfriends and clearing a space for the children to play in. He cleaned and she quizzed him—on the names of her uncles and cousins but also on math and history, preparing him for exams. For Carmen had made up her mind.

"This is not for you," she informed him one night, sitting up abruptly in his bed.

"This. You mean what we just did?"

She socked him in the chest. "No, *tonto*, dummy. This frat house. This dead-end life. You're going to give up the beer and the weed, focus on your studies. You're going to be something, McDonough. A lawyer. No tacking shingles like your dad."

He had told her about his father—his father who, after his army service, intended to learn accounting but never finished his degree, blaming it on his mother's pregnancies. He described the roofing trade which, though punishing and hazardous, proved lucrative enough, and how his father drank and smoked in spite.

But talking to her about his father and introducing her remained separate. George McDonough, Sr. was no Mamá, he explained, nor was his mother, who shared her husband's dependence on cigarettes and booze. Hard people, not prone to tolerance. One look at Carmen's coloring was enough, he feared, to bar her from their house. Yet she told him not to worry, that his parents would love her just as she would love them.

"Everything's always negative with you, Jorge," she berated him, tenderly. "Everything will be fine, you'll see." She smiled, showing him not only the tips but the breadth of her dove-white teeth. "Life is so much more incredible than you think."

And it was. His parents, after little more than a moment's befuddlement, practically embraced her. Offered her a drink, which she politely refused, and showed her around their clapboard Rego Park home. Escorting her through the glass patio door to a backyard barely big enough for a picnic table, they fed her and questioned her about her family. They seemed to listen to every word she said—George hardly recognized them—except when it came to their son.

"A lawyer?" they laughed.

But Carmen stood firm. "And not just any lawyer, Mr. and Mrs. McDonough, but a successful lawyer. A respected lawyer. I know Jorge—George. You'll see."

They stopped laughing. And soon they started believing, as he moved out of the frat house and buckled down at school. His grades skyrocketed, propelling him near the top of his class. Carmen, meanwhile, finished high school—so many family members crammed the commencement photo that there was barely room for her boyfriend—and kept working at the bodega, all the while studying for her real estate broker's license. There was a path for them, straight and obstacle-free. They merely had to stroll it.

So they strode up the aisle in the church where Carmen became Carmen McDonough and danced in the modest hall where the guests got plastered on Jameson and Mama Juana. A few days later, as they lay dreaming out loud of someday taking a honeymoon, the acceptance letter arrived from Fordham. There was a money issue, but Carmen said, "No worries, Jorge. We'll both work. We'll get you through," and they did.

He liked the law, its clear, clean dimensions. Torts, contracts—somehow they reminded him of roofing, the elevation, the way each shingle overlapped the next, shielding every inch. He was a diligent, if not brilliant student, proficient enough to be hired by a mid-sized firm out on Long Island.

They moved into a house—no mansion, certainly, but their own real house—and launched into their lives. No one, of course, could resist Carmen's pitch for real estate, and, together with her husband's salary, they more than made do. That Christmas, he unwrapped his gift to find a pacifier, diapers, and a rattle. He kissed her and, for the first time since grade school, he cried.

Deidre, their firstborn, was followed by Rosa, both girls whose complexions clashed with their names. Deidre dark, midnight-haired, and Rosa, cinnamon and cream. Good, fun, adorable girls. Rushing to hug his knees when he returned from the office, they made him feel princely, enchanted almost.

"What have I done to deserve all this?" he frequently asked Carmen.

She still punched him in the chest. "You know the answer, *tonto*. You knew it that morning on the train."

Yes, that morning on the train. He would recall it many times over the next ten years whenever he cared for Harry.

Henry, Enrique, who somehow merged into Harry, became the family's heart. That was because Harry's own heart—so said a doctor with a face as pale as his gown—was congenitally damaged. Procedures were required, therapies, and even then, the chances were few. And yet, beautiful at birth, angelic through childhood, Harry never once complained. He never sobbed as his father did, out of view, into Carmen's arms. "There, there," she'd comfort him. "Where's my brave young Jorge? Harry will get better, you'll see."

Most times Harry indeed acted like the healthy one, bucking up his parents and sisters whenever his condition looked bleak. "Lighten up, folks," he reprimanded them when, at age twelve, he was hospitalized for a month. "I'm the sick one around here, remember?" Perhaps it was because he never appeared ill—on the contrary, he had his father's freckles and his mother's glinting eyes. His heart, though, impish and indomitable, was all Carmen's. Even weak, it seemed to beat for them all.

"Why don't you chuck it out already?" Harry once suggested, referring to the tricycle that remained in the backyard, the only place he'd been allowed to ride it. But his father refused. As if it had become a talisman, as sacred as a Virgin statue, the tricycle stayed throughout rain and snowstorms, a reminder of the suffering Harry endured and his grit to overcome it.

That single-mindedness hauled him through high school and into college at Georgetown. An honors student, handsome, easy-going, Harry was enormously popular—the president of this, chairman of that—and prized by women. They wanted him, even when warned of his limitations. Vacations, those handicaps kept him at home where Carmen could dote on him and his father could silently fret. Only once, did they get called down to see him, in the second semester of his junior year which, according to the surgeon at Georgetown Hospital, would likely be his last.

They raced from Long Island, so heedlessly that Carmen had to chastise him, "*Tonto*, you'll get us all killed!" Still, they reached the hospital safely and learned from the surgeon that Harry, already unconscious, would have to be operated on at once. The situation was desperate, yet there was this new protocol involving a piece of somebody else's son's heart. A one-out-of-ten shot, the surgeon reckoned.

They stroked Harry's hair, kissed his forehead, and watched as he was wheeled into prep. As usual, it was he who cried and Carmen who stayed implacable. "No, Jorge. None of that now. Harry needs us strong."

So he acted strong when all he really wanted was to weep and beg the God his wife so staunchly believed in. He wanted to grasp her hand and feel it girding his and to look at her, her body now as plump as her mother's once was, and its features blunted, but with the same enameled eyes, the skin still lustrous.

"What would I have been without you?" he found himself asking her. "I was all alone. Frightened of riding subways." For an instant he became that kid again, indifferent, reticent, hiding behind a hockey stick. "But then you came and gave me everything. A life, a family. You gave me Harry."

She shook her head and the harsh light of the waiting room silver-streaked her hair. "No, Jorge," she said. "You gave all that to yourself. It was your decision. Without it, we wouldn't have anything. No Deidre. No Rosa. We wouldn't have Harry."

Four hours passed, six. Dawn was peeking through some blinds when the doors to the ward swung open. The two of them stood while the surgeon emerged and untied his mask. The face behind it was worn but his expression nevertheless beamed. Carmen, with a cry, hugged her husband.

* * * * *

He can almost imagine that cry still over the roar of the game—Mets versus Cardinals—on the radio. His truck turns down Queens Boulevard toward 63rd Drive and pulls onto a side street lined with clapboard houses. Parking in its single driveway, he kills the engine and smokes a cigarette while listening to the top of the eighth. But then the inning ends, and he has no choice. Exiting, he finds the front knob left unlocked, though he's told her a dozen times not to.

The house is quiet inside, but he knows he's not alone. A soap opera's arguing somewhere in the den and the air tangs with smoke. Another odor—gin, maybe, or bourbon—also lingers. On rubberized boots that pad his steps, he sneaks into the kitchen and helps himself to a beer. Then, sipping, he crosses to the patio door.

The sun's blazing in the backyard where the grass has long expired. Patches cower under lawn chairs and embrace a rusted tricycle. It's been there for years but he refuses to throw it out or even to trim around it. Wincing into the heat, he stands for a moment, motionless, over the bike.

"Are you home?" a slurry voice calls out from the den. "Is that you, George?"

He pauses, as if to ponder his answer.

"George?"

He glances down at the tricycle and then at the name stitched over his pocket. His voice decrescendos. "Yeah, it's me."

With a last bitter swig of his beer, he retreats from the yard and begins to shut the door. But then she appears to him, just as she always does. In jeans and platform shoes, red plastic earrings, her hair pulled back from a face far too radiant to forget.

"Jorge," she whispers and pivots away. "Jorge." Glancing over one of her bared shoulders, she smiles at him sadly as she did that morning so many years ago, while her mother led her off the platform and George just sat there and watched. He couldn't move, couldn't leap onto the alternate path—at the conceivable love—proffered him. Rather, self-deprecatingly, he returned her smile and remained hunkering behind his stick.

The glass door closes like those on the subway that clattered and screeched as it bore him, lonely and scared, to his life.

Aniksht

In the forest, the butterflies look like flakes of folding sunlight. I love the forest. Its trees are birch, with bark that reminds me of the zebras I once saw in a book. The birds, cowering in the branches, call out warnings as I pass. Why fear me, I want to ask them, an eleven-year-old who wishes not you nor anybody harm? Who wants only to escape from the town where everything is darkness and noise and to wander in the forest with its shavings of light, its birches and birds, where my shoes sink silently in the moss?

My town, Anyksciai—Aniksht, in Yiddish—is the biggest, they say, outside of Vilna. But I have never been to Vilna. For all people know, I never venture beyond our house near the main square and the state school down the street and the *shul* where, Sabbaths, my mother still insists on taking me. One of her hands drags mine while the other pushes the pram of my baby brother, Emmanuel. We go alone, my mother's head held high above the tide of our neighbors' whispering that rises as we pass. In the women's section, we pray—actually, she prays, with eyes closed tightly and her fingers in fists on the *siddur*. "God is near to all who call upon Him," she chants. "To all who call upon Him in truth." But I do not call upon him. I do not like the truth.

The truth is with my father, at home in the salon where he smokes and reads the papers, smokes and reads his books. Not prayer books but stories translated from other languages, mostly, about war and evil and love. Especially love. Though he tries to hide them behind the broom closet, I have found those books and read them, or at least tried to. The words are difficult but the tales—of virtue lost, hearts and promises broken—even harder. "Go," he sneers at my mother as she leaves the house for *shul*. "Go and delude yourself—and them," meaning Emmanuel and me. "This," he says and drums a red leather cover. "*This* is my truth."

But I know it isn't. Or at least not all of it. The truth which all the people of Aniksht seem to know, and my mother struggles to forget, is that my father is a man of secrets. He is an accomplished man, one of the town's four lawyers with an office right on the main square. There, he fills out forms and makes petitions for anyone—workers, teachers, farmers unable to write their own names. He is ruthless, I've heard people say, but skilled. He wins most all his cases. But not only his mind is sharp but also his clothing, cut in the latest double-breasted fashion and from the finest imported cloth. With his thin, fine-featured face, his eyes so light a brown they are often mistaken for blue, the pencil moustache, the pomaded hair parted on the right third of his scalp, he could easily star in movies.

Nobody would guess that my father was the son of an impoverished Talmud student, a reader of mystical books and the writer of even more fabulous ones. He lived in a village not far from here, a cluster of wooden shacks with basements where the people used to hide from the Cossacks. The *shul* was of wood as well, little more than a barn. Orphaned after his birth, my father hated that village, and as soon as he could, he moved here, to Aniksht. He hated everything that drove his own father mad and left his mother to die.

So Dovid Leib Gryn became Darius Leibas Girenas, attorney at law, a devoted secularist and intellectual. Fluent in five languages, only one of which, Yiddish, he hesitates to speak. When not calming clients or arguing their claims in court, he busies himself with the news of the day. Russians, Germans, kicking us back and forth like footballs, Britain asleep in the stands. He reads and curses, reads and sighs, and when my mother takes Emmanuel and me to *shul,* he waits for the clatter of the pram to fade.

Only then does my father put down his paper and close up all of his books. Only then does he sneak out the back door and cross the yards, ducking behind steepled wells and stinky outhouses until he reaches the part of town where our people don't live, where my mother tells me never to play. The church bells clang in spiky silver towers, warning us away. But my father doesn't hesitate. Instead, he enters another house. Hers. And then he stays for several hours while my mother closes her eyes and prays. He closes his eyes as well and forgets all about the crazy mystics, the Russians and the Germans and the world. There, finally, my father finds peace.

How do I know all this? From the forest, of course. It knows how to impart secrets and how to keep them as well. It is a wizard of sorts, ancient and wise, a confidante, a friend. Located less than an hour's walk from town, the forest is easily reachable even by a speck of a girl like me. Easy, when my mother thinks I'm out playing, to slip away to. I suppose I should be afraid, ambling alone in the woods, but somehow I'm just the opposite, sheltered. On the contrary, it's home that I fear.

Home is where, if not for Emmanuel's crying, I can hear my mother weeping in her bedroom. Home is where my father sleeps separately, leaves early for work and returns long after I'm asleep, or at least pretend to be. In fact, I lay listening to my parent's arguing, exchanging words of hate. And other words as well—of anxiety about the future, about whether, despite their anger, they could reunite long enough to take the family far away from Aniksht. To Palestine or even the United States. Anywhere safe. Such times it's all I can do to keep from leaping out from under my covers and shouting, "We don't have to go far! Just down the road—to the forest!"

But I say nothing, at least not to them. Why can't they love each other, I ask the trees? Why can't we just live our lives without worry and threat, quietly in Aniksht? And the forest replies: look.

I don't want to, but I have no choice. The forest only gives me a moment's warning and they almost discover me. Instead, I hide behind a birch—I'm that skinny—and observe them. My father and Mrs. Vilkas, the butcher's wife. A tall, high-cheeked woman, with golden hair braided peasant-style and eyes the color of knife blades. I see my father pulling her by the hand, running as fast as they can without tripping over fallen branches, and then stopping, panting, with her back against a tree, and there my father kisses her.

Fury, embarrassment, disgust—how can I describe the sensations? At that moment, watching my father's hands press Mrs. Vilkas' breasts, I see it all. The Sabbaths when my father sneaks off while we're in *shul* and her husband is busy cleaving pigs' heads. I see the two of them, handsome and vital, and then my mother, formlessly gray, her features as drab as her dresses. I can feel their passion and feel her pain but also a kind of power. As if the forest were inside me, suddenly. The treetops nodding approval and the birds singing in praise. The silent applause of butterflies.

But the quiet is broken by thunder. Giant planes roar overhead, blocking the sluices of light. My father and Mrs. Vilkas look up at the sky and then at one another, exchange troubled faces, and hurry back to town. I remain scrunched behind the birch, though, skinny still but enormous with knowledge.

It's times like this that I picture myself as Dalia, who we learned about in the state school where my father sends me. Dalia, the pagan goddess of fate, and Perkunas, the thunder god, their terrible faces carved into wood. So different from the God my mother prays to. The invisible God who she says inhabits not only our yellow concrete *shul* but the entire world. I listen to her, but I cannot agree. God may be in Aniksht, perhaps even in our house, but not out here, in the forest. Here, I am Dalia, empress of my own fate, and the thunder is my husband.

I am a strange little girl, I know. No friends, really, a loner in school. But I'd rather be strange in a town where hatred is normal. And I prefer to feel normal in the forest soothed by the scent of birch mulch and surrounded by zebra-like bark.

I come here more and more as things grow worse at home. Not only between my parents but between our people and the town. Foreigners come and go, come and stay, and soon we are confined inside. My mother cannot pray, and my father cannot sneak through the backyards to Mrs. Vilkas'. Only I manage to escape. Nobody notices the plain skinny girl scurrying across the main square and tiptoeing past my father's shuttered office.

From there, keeping off the roads where the soldiers travel, I cross the wheat fields and enter the burnt-out village where my father's family used to live. Here, in basements, they once hid from the Cossacks—so my father told me. And here, his mother died shortly after giving birth to him. The *shul* still stands but boarded up, and I'm half-inclined to peek inside, to see where my grandfather went crazy. But instead I keep running. Just beyond the village, the forest lies.

Safely within, I wander for hours thinking, why not just stay? With little need for food and now, in summertime, for shelter, I could make my own home out of bark. No arguments, no dangers, only me and the butterflies and the birds. I truly could become like Dalia, deciding how and where to live. And never fear the thunder.

Nor would I fear the clacking sound, like angrily snapped branches, echoing through the trees. I follow the noise, crouching behind trunks, until I see them. A few soldiers but many townspeople. Workers, teachers, illiterate farmers—people my father helped, but also the butcher, Mr. Vilkas. They are shoving my people up to the edge of a big ditch, pressing what look like sticks to their backs and watching them fall inside. They fall and then I hear that clacking. They fall and a mist remains, blue and bloody red, colors unknown to the forest.

How long do I watch—hours? Too afraid to move, too knowing. So it's hardly surprising when I see my father and mother, side-by-side, my mother clutching Emmanuel, pushed up to the lip of the ditch. There is no more arguing, no more crying—even Emmanuel is still—no books or prayers, God or truth. They just stand there for an endless second, my mother pale and my father looking insulted, both of them gazing into the forest as if in search of hope. In search of me. And though I so want to, I cannot run to them, cannot join and hug them.

They fall, finally, and others take their place. The soldiers are quiet, work-like, but the townspeople are excited. Drinking, swearing, laughing. Their cheers drown out the screams. I know that I will hear them always, even in the deepest silence. Or especially. I know that I will always see the red and the blue and smell that stench, like ammonia, tainting the mulch.

The afternoon is ending. Shadows fall across the treetops and filter down to the pit. I've never been in the forest at night but the thought of it somehow comforts me. I have been crying for so long, stifling my sobs with a forearm. The soldiers, the townspeople are gone. I am alone. The bark turns black, the birds are silent. My shoes soundlessly sink into moss. I flee deeper into the forest, as if into a loving embrace. The butterflies, their wings damp with darkness, wave goodbye.

* * * * *

The stalks of wheat, like grateful subjects, bow to her as she runs. Her hair streaming behind her, honeyed, her taffeta gown aglow. Azure eyed, pixie nosed and chinned. In the summer light, burnt around the edges, she is framed and gilded. And she laughs, roaring with each bound, as I chase her. Uselessly, for I know she's impossible to catch. No matter. It's enough just to follow in her sweet stream, the scent of lavender from her bath, the creams of her skin, intoxicating me. An occasional glimpse of ear or a naked raised heel as blinding as any revelation. So she runs, and I stumble after her. Goddess and mortal, worshipped and smitten, dream and relentless reality.

Yet, miraculously, the distance shrivels. My hand—ink-stained, bony— reaches out for hers and nearly glances it. "Malki," I cry, "my queen," and the church bells in the distant town sing out to her from sharpened silver spires. "Malki," I lunge, tripping over an undone lace in my hand-me-down shoes, swimming in clothes my body can no longer fill. But all she does is giggle. Running still, weightless, toward the village and the wooden houses that seem to float atop the wheat. At any moment I feel she will fling her arms airward and soar. And I will be left land-bound, gazing up and gasping, her near-touch enough to scorch my fingers.

The wind shrieks through the worm-eaten slats of the *shul* where Mendel writes by candlelight. Night times such as this, when he's supposed to be studying Gemara, he can scribble for hours, until either his ink or his candle runs out. At which points he writes still, in his mind, stroking his beard and *payos*. Only when the hour is so late the entire shtetl is sleeping, does he groan to his feet and stretch. Behind the Torah ark, safe in the darkness and dust, he hides the manuscript. Then, clutching his coat shreds and donning a threadbare shtreimel, he stumbles out into the drizzle. Into vapors of cowsheds and death.

He trundles down a muck-paved alley, past sighs and wheezes seeping through doors. At the end, he turns into a narrower lane yet, feeling his way along splintered walls and fences, counting the steps. A rodent scurries across his shoes. Finally, Mendel senses the hinge and lifts it. Familiar smells—grease, borax, tallow—envelope him.

"*Iz das dir,*" comes a flimsy voice from the bed.

"*Yo, es is mir,*" he replies. "*Zikher in shtub.*" Safe at home.

In the shadows, a thicker shadow, convex, rising and falling. Mendel pats it as he sits on the side of the bed and then reaches for her forehead. He can see it glistening, even at night, and knows that her fever rages.

"*Vos azoy shpet?*" Why does he have to study so late, she wants to know. More of a cry than a question, and she weeps it often alone. Of course, he has answers. Most frequently: that is what *Ribonu shel HaOlam,* the Universal Sovereign, wants from him, what *Hakoidesh Baruch Hu,* the Holy One of Blessed Name, expects. Other times, especially when he is also sick, the response is more candid.

"What else *can* I do?" Mendel is not a carpenter, not proficient in any trade, a businessman certainly not. All he can do is read the sacred texts or at least appear to. What he can really do, though only secretly, is write stories. Stories! As if he could feed a family with them, provide a roof that didn't leak or even kindling for a fire. The editor of *Kol Mevaser* rejected them, explaining in a terse note that the author's prose, "though vivid," was "too fantastical, too disconnected from real shtetl life." From which life, he wanted to know. This one, with its illness and poverty, its fears and filth? Did anybody truly want to read about that, much less write about it?

"*Kenen makhn ir epes?*" He offers to make her tea, but Rayna shakes her head. She only wants to sleep and guard this baby, the only one she's taken to term. How he will pay for it, he has no idea, with the few kopecks he receives from the *kollel.* But Rayna, plain, warted, skin-and-bones Rayna, never asks for anything for herself. Never demands that he get a real job, that he give up the stories that she somehow knows he writes but never once mentions. A child—that is the least he could give her. An infant to dote on and protect.

Mendel undresses and puts on a nightshirt, blows on the oven's embers but merely worries the ash. Lying next to Rayna but not too close—she needs her heat—he tries to drift off. His eyes shut but his mind's as open as a wheat field in summer. It's warm inside his head and the sun is dazzling.

* * * * *

Kite-like, heron-like, she flies. Over the rooftops with their challah braids of smoke. Over the sheds where horned heads rise in awe. Some of them will be summoned, goats and cows joining her in a graceful swirl over the village.

You see, Malki when she wills can make anything weightless. The sky is her kingdom and there she holds sway. A peasant can fly if she wishes him to, a fiddler. Only I am left to wince upward, shielding my sight with hands almost too feeble to lift. It's enough just to witness her, to behold her home-spun glory.

"Queen Malki, I swear fidelity to you!" I shout and my words, at least, take flight. "I swear devotion and wonder and love!" But laughter is again my only answer. Indulgent laughter, such as a mother's for an unruly child or an eagle's for the wingless.

"Malki," I wail and flap arms as frail as bird bones, plumed with rags but incapable of lifting. Is it enough for me, I ask, just to watch and idolize? Can I survive by adoring below?

* * * * *

A monstrous rapping on the door shakes the entire house. "*Gey aroyse!?*" somebody hollers in Yiddish and then, to underline the danger, in Hebrew, "*Hahuzah!*" Half or wholly asleep, he's uncertain, but summer has been ousted by desolate winter in the golden wheat field by the tatters of their bed.

"Rayna," Mendel shakes her. "Rayna, get up. I think we're under attack."

It's his wife who's still dreaming and probably of Cossacks as she matter-of-factly repeats, "Yes, attack." Still not quite awake, she allows him to throw a shawl across her shoulders and to help her onto swollen feet. Then, Mendel leads her, barefoot, across the earthen floor and out into ice-tipped rain. Over the wind, he hears other cries of *"gey aroyse"* and *"hahuza,"* more pounding of doors. There is screaming and praying but also a different sound—distant but rapidly closing in. Hooves.

"Geshvind!" Their neighbor, Lilienblum, urges them to hurry. A flour merchant, rich, he would probably ignore them if not for Rayna's state. Abandoning a pregnant woman brings on the Evil Eye, they say. So Lilienblum leads them through a kitchen lit by kerosene and into a pantry fat with provisions, back to a half-hidden iron door. *"Geyn. Geyn,"* he orders them, holding a lamp over the steps.

They descend into a basement which, though frosty, is drier than the air outside. The mustiness is less offensive than the shtetl's usual stench, and even the darkness is somehow comforting. The basement is made of brick, with stylish arches. "Who but Jews would decorate a shelter?" Mendel thinks.

Long minutes pass. Mendel holds Rayna and Rayna cradles her stomach. Lilienblum's family, his big-boned wife and overstuffed kids, are with them, too, insulating. They share some biscuits—his first bite, Mendel remembers, in days. He saves all the food for Rayna. The mood is relaxed, almost familial, but then, "Sha!" somebody hisses. The thud of horseshoes on frozen mud, clanging spurs and stirrups, thunders overhead.

Shots blast out, a scream, and someone starting to chant, *"Shma Yisroel Adonoy Eloheinu..."* but not finishing. Lilienblum waits a full hour, long after the storm passes, before hazarding up the stairs. He returns, clay-faced, and informs them quietly. The Cossacks are gone.

Outside, the village is shrouded in smoke. Cows, chickens, children wail. People stumble past, seemingly asleep. Mendel helps Rayna across the frozen ruts, holding her head to his neck so that she won't see the rivulets of blood. Though many houses have been burned, theirs is untouched, perhaps because it resembles a privy. He guides her inside and tucks her back into bed.

"Vau geystu?" she asks, though she already knows the answer. He'll return to the *shul*, to studying, because that's what *Hakoidesh Baruch Hu* wants. Rayna nods in understanding but her dull eyes beg: what about me?

Mendel pets her forehead—still feverish—and assures her that everything will be fine. She will give them a son, he knows, and they will call him Dovid. A royal name for a future king, a special boy who will raise us all out of misery.

He blows on the embers again, retrieves his shtreimel, and steps out into a bone-colored dawn. There are fewer screams now, only whimpering, and the murmurs of *Kaddish* for the dead. He does not pause, though, to offer condolences. He can't. Mendel Gryn doesn't belong to this shtetl, this wretchedness, this death. He belongs in a radiant sky, with Malki.

* * * * *

In backward figure-eights, Malki orbits the village. Animals, musicians, menorahs all hover in her wake. The moon is out now, a milky orb, but its rays—no less than the sun's—illuminate her.

I no longer call out to her, no longer flap my arms. It's enough just to behold her, I realize. Dayenu. Enough merely to revere her from earth. So I watch and marvel, yet my yearning refuses to ebb. Though penniless and hungry, ragged and unkempt, I still have the strength to long. A need more basic than food, than shelter. Love. I crave it and cannot live without hers.

It's hopeless, I know. Hopelessly splendorous. But then, suddenly, Malki drifts off-course. Sailing away from the village, not toward the town but the other direction—toward the forest. There, between the birches, the simplest man might aspire to godliness. Even the most heart-shattered lover might yet become beloved.

Out of the wheat field, through the broad lanes and light-filled plazas of the village I scamper, with one eye still on the clouds. The forest is only a short distance away. Within, I will chase her, woo and seduce her. Straining above the birdsong, my voice will peal with passion.

* * * * *

How many days did he remain locked in the *shul*, how many nights? Not locked in the literal sense—not with chains or bolts—but kept inside by an irresistible force. Not God, or at least not the God of the musty tractate of *Evel Rabbati* opened on his table. It instructs him on the proper means for burying and mourning a man who commits suicide, for mourning one killed by non-Jews. Mendel pretends to study it, especially before prayer hours when many others enter the *shul*. But other times, alone, his candle is reserved for holier texts—those inscribed by his heart.

He does not eat and not only because he lacks food. Matters of this world mean less to him now. Even Rayna lying feverish in their bed, even their unborn child, Dovid, have waned in significance. It is only his hankering, anguished need to write. In those sacred moments, quill in hand, he is no longer of this place. He is no longer Mendel Gryn but a spirit unleashed in the woods.

From tree to tree she scuttles, their black-and-white bark like ermine fur caping her shoulders, her head crowned with butterflies. Nevertheless, I follow her. No longer a pauper but a strapping man of boundless vitality. I close in on her, fingertips brushing her hem...

* * * * *

Perhaps because he is writing or because of the wind howling through the rotted boards, Mendel does not hear the shouts. Cries of *"gey aroyse"* and *"hahuza"* penetrate the *shul* but not his mind, which is deep in a mystical forest. He does not hear the whips and reins, the pleas for mercy, and the crushing of hooves. Instead, he writes, *"One leap, two at most, and I will have her."*

Only when shots and screams resound outside the *shul* does Mendel at last stagger out, but too late. He senses a shadow but otherwise cannot make out the mounted Cossack looming over him. Discerns the sparks flying from torched houses and hears the hiss of the blade. The first blow, cleaving his shtreimel, sends him reeling, and the second lays him down in the mud. There he remains, in the blood and the cow muck, breathing once, twice...

And then, I embrace her. She laughs and laughingly succumbs. In the forest, united, we dance, we fly. Treetops tickle us deliriously. Malki, I burble. Malki, I sob. Malki, for eternity, is mine.

* * * * *

Lately, when not greeting activists or debating his critics on TV, Dudu dwelt on his quirks. Did anybody notice them, he worried, and when did they start? It took time, but he finally recalled that the gray Oxford shoes, triple knotted, were favored by his sixth-grade teacher. His need to always keep his refrigerator full stemmed from a stepfather who survived the 1948 siege of Jerusalem—so he claimed—chewing leather. But the source of his sneezing routine eluded him. Not until one day, in the middle of defending a controversial pension bill, did the memory revisit him of his mother looking down as he wiped his nose and declaring, "That's not good."

The realization that yet another of his characteristics originated with his mother only added to Dudu's distress. It seemed that that there was no facet of his life, public or private, in which she failed to have a hand, if not other appendages as well. Because of her, a firebrand opponent of virtually all the State's founders, he had entered politics, and because of her he walked with his shoulder-blades crimped against the knives that might at any time cleave them. And because of her, Dudu believed, he never fully experienced love. Even today, when he wheeled her from the home to his office, she'd pause at the photos of the long-dead legislators on his wall, raise a crooked finger and cackle, "That one and that one. And oooh, that one."

Dudu had never found love and soon he, too, would be one of those yellowed portraits. This led him from obsessing about his habits to contemplating mortality. Though already a grandfather, he was a healthful one, energetic, handsome in a rough-hewn way. The ghosts of muscles still visited his body, as did the curls that once adorned his scalp. Women of a certain generation found him attractive, and even the occasional twenty-something. Yet there was no dissembling the ripples around his neck, the descending corners of his eyelids. Like his mother, he, too, would eventually reside at the home.

The idea was to keep the mind preoccupied, he concluded, not to think about death. But that understanding also emanated from his mother. For who had known death more intimately than she did, and who had spent more years forgetting it?

Dudu fretted and Dudu forgot. Throughout, he could point to many accomplishments—the mass of admirers and haters that are the measure of any successful politician, children from a scattering of marriages. But he also had problems, serious problems, and if there was anything Dudu Yarkoni lacked more than love it was the time to address them.

"That's not good," he thought to himself—uniquely without sneezing—when he entered his office and found Steinbesser waiting. A bland, dwarfish, middle-aged man in oversized suits that invariably covered his thumbs, the spokesman never showed up suddenly unless something terrible happened. And in Dudu's life of late, the terrible had become commonplace.

"Sit," Steinbesser said and held out a chair, even as Dudu grumbled, "What now? What?"

"Brace yourself. Tomorrow's papers are running the story of a woman who's accusing you of verbal abuse. They're calling her 'Y.'"

"Are they insane? I don't even know any Y." Dudu was no longer sitting.

"Y is a rather popular women's initial," Steinbesser explained, not helpfully. "Yael, Yemima, Yehudit. I seem to recall a Yocheved."

"Stop it!" Against a wall, Dudu hurled the miniature pennant—a gift of his childhood scouting troop—that always flew from his desk. "There is no Y and there was no abuse, verbal or otherwise."

Steinbesser was unimpressed. "Tell that to the media," he counselled. "Tell that to the journalists who, this week alone, have you being investigated by two separate commissions. Tell that to the editors who headlined your remark about reducing preschool subsidies."

"I was totally misquoted."

"Tell that to the mothers."

Steinbesser poured him a glass of water, a sure sign that the situation was serious. "For starters, we'll issue a denial."

"I've got the photo-op with the paratroopers today, tonight's flight to Lithuania. I'll have to cancel." Dudu said this to the glass but, like the glass, Steinbesser was not listening.

"I'll talk to Channels 1 and 2," he rattled off instead. "With all the dailies, the radio shows."

But then, abruptly, Dudu's reaction changed. From panic and despondency, he grew calm, almost dispassionate. This was another quirk: to panic over the trivial—the slightly-off bank statement, the shirt that returned wrinkled from the cleaners—but grapple unflappably with crises. Another kink, another gift from his mother.

"Confirm the photo-op and the flight," he ordered Steinbesser. "And check tomorrow's schedule." He was already stomping out of the door, striding the way he once, long ago as an infantry officer, barreled out of his tent. "Before boarding that plane, I've got to stop at the home."

Now Steinbesser seemed nonplussed. "But where are you going?"

"Where else?" The answer echoed in the hallway. "South."

* * * * *

From his penthouse office in the middle of the country's center, Dudu drove to the periphery. In a state so small, one didn't have to travel days to reach the boondocks, more like hours. Within minutes, the skyscrapers were replaced with tenements and the tenements by shanties. Camels threatened the highway. Soon, there was only desert and scrub and then, anomalously, a klatch of apartment blocks tilting inward as if to gossip.

Dudu found the address, 21 Mounters of the Gallows Street, and parked the car. The entrance to the building was garbage-strewn and picketed by cats. Graffiti advertised excitement on the fourth floor, but Dudu climbed to the fifth. There, after rapping on a mock-oaken door, he found himself in a luxuriously appointed living room and in the presence—debonair, deadly—of Arnon Rothenberg.

He did not rise from his armchair or offer Dudu a seat in the empty one opposite him. He merely said, "I see you got my message," and then, snapping at the rangy henchmen loitering nearby, "coffee."

"This has got to stop, Arnon. Enough." A full head taller than his host, and twice his bulk, Dudu nevertheless felt vulnerable addressing him. "What else do you want from me?"

Arnon shrugged. He might have been asked about the temperature outside, which was rarely less than sizzling. "Really?"

"And so the investigations. The misquotes. And now this? Y?"

Another shrug, followed by a self-congratulatory smirk. Manicured fingernails combed through sculpted hair. He was a pretty man, delicately featured. Such refinement, Arnon knew, when combined with ruthlessness, was unnerving.

"We had a deal."

But Dudu was not unnerved, more like allayed. The moment he'd long dreaded had arrived and yet here he was, still standing.

"You mean, all I have to do is make that call?"

A henchman handed Dudu a demitasse. He was too smart not to accept it and sip. Arnon, meanwhile, waved his cellphone in the air. "Just one."

Just one, but it would set into motion a series of irreversible events. Not only would Y and the alleged investigations disappear but so also would certain zoning restrictions, various bureaucratic barriers, and customs duties. Someday, maybe, there would be questions asked or maybe not. Such were the vagaries of politics. Dudu dialed.

* * * * *

Later, in his car, steeped in nausea and relief, Dudu again thought about his life. Perhaps along with his mother's intensity he'd inherited her father's hauteur, his predilection for dubious affairs. Or maybe he was more like the great-grandfather his mother once told him about, the half-mad Talmud student who lived in a shtetl near the town where she grew up. Who hid from pogroms in basements and wrote hallucinogenic stories in the synagogue where he was supposed to be studying. Twenty minutes passed before Dudu remembered the photo-op. Glancing at his watch, folding his shirtsleeves inward, he sped out of town.

The paratrooper base was also located in the desert, not far from where he, himself, had trained. Only back then, the soldiers sweated in tents, ate C rations, and shat and showered outdoors. Now, though, recruits slept in air-conditioned dorms with bathrooms. Mess halls supplied hot, balanced meals. Back then, the commanders were all males but today many of them were women, like Dalia.

"Don't you think that's a little bit smarmy?" Dudu had questioned Steinbesser when he came up with the photo-op idea.

"You mean for a politician to exploit the fact that his daughter is a drill sergeant in the paratroopers? Smarmy?" the spokesman replied. "You bet."

And yet, passing through the gates, Dudu already cringed at the sight of the reporters and the base commanders turned out to greet him. Stiffly, he nodded through the tour of the high-tech lecture rooms and the virtual target ranges. The lunch they served him could have fed a squad in his day. At last came the time for the shoot. A VIP Humvee whisked him out to a training field where Dalia and her troops were waiting.

"Hey," he merely said, emerging, and "Hey," equally awkward, came her response. Beneath her camouflage paint, he could detect her creamy cheeks. The strands that escaped her floppy hat where flaxen, her eyes, Mediterranean blue. It surprised him just how much she looked like one of his ex-wives and how difficult it was remembering which one. Still, seeing her battle-geared, with an assault rifle slung around her neck and a row of nervous troops behind her, delighted him.

"You could have asked me, you know," she hissed.

"I know, Dalia. I'm sorry."

"Shhh." She motioned with her chin behind her. "I'm Commander Yarkoni to them."

"Commander, of course…"

"Good. Now let's get this over with."

They posed, first Dudu with his daughter, and then the two of them with the entire platoon. He debated which expression to use, the hard-baked ex-colonel's or the pride-filled father's? He compromised with a grin, but then struggled to look at the camera. His eyes kept drifting toward her, to them, so youthful and pure. Armed angels. Had he once been like them, he wondered, before the wars, before politics?

He sensed that the army had not changed that much after all. The same heat, same smell of hot oil on hot metal and the dusty whiff of fatigues. Gunshots popping in the distance. Only he was different. Turning to Dalia, he wanted to tell her that, wanted to apologize for being such a terrible parent and for not quite remembering who her mother was. He wanted to whisper I love you but all that came out was, "Shalom."

"Shalom," she repeated and turned to bark at her men.

* * * * *

Baking in the kiln of his car, Dudu turned northeast. The desert gave way to fields and the fields yielded to mountains. The skeletons of armored vehicles destroyed in war littered the shoulders. The State was much like him, he thought. So many different landscapes, so many of them scarred.

Once inside the capital, the people changed as well. The thugs and soldiers replaced by religious men in shtreimels and frocks and wigged women pushing carriages. A shtetl carved from stone. He steered a route too convoluted for navigation systems and exited in a leafy neighborhood of identical four-story buildings. This was where he had grown up, where he played and kissed his first girl and came home from the army on furloughs. And here, not far from her home was the facility in which his mother now stayed and could still make his life unbearable.

The staff was deferential when he entered. They called him sir and complimented his last debate on television. Your mother must be very proud, they said.

"You blew it," his mother greeted him. "That clown made a clown out of you."

She sat slouched in her wheelchair, the once-disarming beauty reduced to a stack of wattles, age spots, and spleen.

"How do you feel today, Mom?" He angled her into a corner where the window admitted some sun. Its light accentuated her eyes, the only part of her unaltered. Her penetrating, punishing eyes.

"Better if I didn't have to watch my only son make a fool of himself in public."

In fact, she had another son, Itamar, who moved to Phoenix right out of high school and whom she'd rarely heard from since. Dudu never begrudged his departure. Their mother was too vast a burden—the weight of a woman who, as an eleven-year-old, saw her entire family murdered. Who fled into the forest and eventually met up with Koppel and his fighters, becoming the youngest partisan ever. Though more than twice her age, Koppel married her after the war and then widowed her with two babies. She remarried and divorced several times, rapidly. "He couldn't have reached Koppel's ankles," she explained with each breakup. "Koppel could have pissed on him sitting."

A coarse woman, his mother, custom-fit for politics. A legislator who opted always for the Opposition, who thrived on disdain for power; she remained a loner but a redoubtable one. Logically, he would follow in her path but proceeded to tread it differently, with behind-the-scenes deals and favors for his lackeys, with Arnon Rothenberg.

"I went to visit Dalia today," he said, changing the subject. "On the base."

The incisive eyes for once looked lucent. "Ah, Dalia, my favorite. What's her name's daughter."

Dudu gulped. "Yeah, what's her name's."

"Dalia, the goddess of fate. My god," she added. "Wife of the thunder god, Perkunas."

Dudu nodded. He didn't want to let on that he had never heard of any of these gods, of thunder or otherwise, and that Dalia was the Hebrew word for olive branch. He knew better than to argue with his mother who, alone, called him by his real name, David, in memory of her father.

"We took a photograph. Together with her troops."

The concertina of wrinkles in his mother's face contracted. "Sounds smarmy," she said.

Dudu shrugged. He'd long given up trying to win an argument with her. Perhaps he'd never actually tried. "It was good seeing her again, just before my flight."

"Flight? Where to now? Don't you know, David, the people want you here. Here. Not drinking schnapps with some Nazi."

"No schnapps, Mom, no Nazis. I'm signing a trade treaty."

"Trade treaty my ass. With who? Micronesia?"

Dudu inhaled deeply, dreading her response. The room, he noticed, smelled of bleach. "Lithuania."

"Worse than the Nazis," she snorted. Her skin, the color and texture of tissues, crinkled. "Worse than scum. I know."

"I know you know, Mom. But all that was a very long time ago. The country's different, the people. They're some of our best friends."

"They were our best friends, too. Our neighbors. Our lovers. And they butchered us."

"How's the food been?" he asked out of nowhere, despairing. "Any improvement?"

But his mother would not be derailed. "You're not like your father. You're not even like my father. You're more like his. Fooling everybody into thinking he was some kind of scholar when all he did all night was write nonsense—fairy-tales and bullshit—that he hid behind the ark. They found them after he was killed by a Cossack. Crazy stuff. The rabbi had them burnt."

With an effort, Dudu could have understood her meaning but he was too tired to press. He needed to get back to the office, to confirm with Steinbesser the total disappearance of Y from tomorrow's newspapers, to pack his bag, and to head for the airport.

"That's it, Mom, I've got to go."

"Go. Go. Have a schnapps with your Lithuanian Nazis. Raise a toast to me."

He tapped the back of her hand, all gristle and veins. "You be well, mother."

Turning to the door, feeling it coming on, he might have sprinted and released it outside. Fit as he was, though, Dudu could not pull it off. Right there in his mother's room, loudly and wretchedly, he sneezed.

From the corner by the window, with the contemptuous care he knew from earliest childhood, came the pronouncement, "That can't be good."

Lithuania's Trade Minister could not have been happier. He shook Dudu's hand and posed with him over the freshly inked treaty. A gaggle of photographers, Steinbesser among them, eternalized the event. That image, and not that of Y with her face blacked out, would grace the next day's news. Dudu had survived, politically at least, and at a price, but wasn't that always the case with life? One got by with what's at hand, whether guns or wits or influence.

Adjourning to the minister's office, clinking glasses in a toast, Dudu began to unwind. There was no Opposition here, no needling activists, and certainly no mother to harangue him. He only had to remember to call the capital Vilnius rather than Vilna, the city's name in Yiddish.

"To Vilnius!" Dudu exclaimed and downed another vodka.

The beefy minister, red-faced and sweaty, gleamed. "To friendship!"

To friendship indeed. Dudu had rarely met such cordial people, brimming with warmth. Hard to imagine them turning on his people and massacring them. He actually mentioned this—blame it on the alcohol—and was surprised by the minister's response.

"You are from here?"

"Well, not me, personally," Dudu blushed. "My parents."

"Yarkoni?"

"It's the Hebrew version of Gryn, my mother's maiden name. She went back to it after her first husband—my father—died."

"And where was she from?"

Dudu wasn't sure if the minister was interrogating him or not, probing for holes in his story, or simply being inquisitive. Either way, he was embarrassed to say he didn't know.

"Anik something. I think...."

"Anik?" the minister refilled Dudu's glass. "Anykciai?"

"That's it! That's it!" At least he thought that was it.

"But you must go, then," the minister laughed. "It's our best resort, with skiing and spas. Just over an hour from here. My driver will take you."

Dudu wasn't certain—the press could claim he was using public money for pleasure—and told as much to Steinbesser.

"Crap," was the spokesman's retort. "The public loves root-searching. And seeing where your family was shot."

So they travelled, Dudu, Steinbesser, and a septuagenarian driver whose only English words were "go" and "stop." The topography, flat and undistinguished, was broken only by ramshackle villages. The ghosts of shtetls hovered between them. Eighty minutes out, just as the minister estimated, two silver spires came into view and then some roof-tops. "Anyksciai."

The town, too, was nondescript. Shops, restaurants, vaguely Euro-pean with a hint of Slav. No spas, no ski slopes, only drab, squat houses, many with privies out back and steeple-covered wells. Not until they reached the town square did Dudu stop to ponder what connection, if any, he had to this place. He recalled his mother mentioning that her father, a lawyer, had his office on the square, and that the synagogue she and her mother attended was not that far away. And indeed, at the end of a nearby street named Sinagoga, was a yellow-plastered building that had once held worshippers but now only bread, freshly baked on the premises.

Yet still he felt nothing, no sense of connection or the remotest nostalgia. A former soldier, the father of soldiers, an elected official wielding power, he was Dudu Yarkoni, not David Gryn. He did not share this with Steinbesser, though, even as he posed in front of the synagogue-cum-bakery. He settled for his grin again and then told the driver "go."

And they went, but not far. A kilometer or so out of town, while gliding past some tired wheat fields, Dudu noticed something. A farm-house with what looked like a boarded-up barn. "Stop," he ordered the driver and indicated where to turn. Steinbesser chuckled, "Let me guess, a photo with chickens. Great for the farmers' lobby."

Dudu remained silent, though. He emerged from the car and sol-emnly approached the barn. The planks were rotten, the locks rusted solid. Through any of the myriad of cracks he could peer inside but all he saw was ash. It didn't matter. Without being told, without understand-ing quite how he knew, he was sure what this structure was and who had dwelt in it. He saw the dreams filtering through the broken shingles and sailing over them.

He was still pawing the splintered wood, increasingly annoying Stein-besser, when the property's owner appeared. In filthy overalls, unshaven, and with fewer teeth than notions of what this stranger was doing in his yard, he glowered. But the driver explained something to him, and a twenty Euro note from Dudu further clarified the issue. He just wanted a look in the house.

The room was spare. Crucifixes, mock antique clocks, a rustic table set with fruit. Dudu looked around and pointed toward the floor. The owner, perplexed, shook his head. So did Steinbesser and the driver. Dudu pointed again, more emphatically, and this time succeeded. The owner opened a grate set into a bare wall and led them, flashlight in hand, down crudely etched steps, into a miasma of dust motes and mold.

The wan beam swept across a brick wall decorated—incongruously—with arches. Dudu gazed at them, inhaling the soot. Internalizing the past. Somehow, he had come from here, emerged and survived while others hadn't. Yet he still carried the madness and the pain. He plodded on, searching for something he could not begin to define.

Only when exiting the house, squinting into a smudgy sun, did Dudu receive a hint. Not far from where the shtetl stood, a tree line beckoned. In rows of royal black and white, they waited. And steadily, sleepily, he approached them.

"There's no time for this, Dudu!" Steinbesser shouted. "We're due back at the airport in an hour!"

But Dudu kept striding. He did not stop to tie his Oxfords or worry about empty refrigerators. No sneeze triggered horrid predictions. Rather, he fled deeper and deeper into the forest. Moss muffled his footsteps. His spokesman's hollers could no longer be heard. Singing birds lured him inward. Butterflies, like the hands of luminous children, beckoned. "Come," they called to him, "come."

Primus inter Pares

The "oohs" Connie was used to from visitors this age, followed by the almost sensual "ahhs." In fact, she depended on them, as an actress might as the curtain rose on her, act one. She could feed off the enthusiasm during the less stirring parts of the tour—the china sets, for example, hardly riveting for ten-year-olds, and the ceremonial silver. But the starburst of banners, the sword-gifts from Arabian kings, and, of course, the sweeping staircase that even children see in movies—all brought out the gasps. The "oohs" and "ahhs" were expected, but not the glass-pinged clang that Connie in all her years guiding had never heard.

"What?" she asked the class without meaning to, such was her shock. And yet they expressed no surprise whatsoever, but merely rolled their eyes and lifted their chins, motioning behind them.

On heel-tips, she peered over the rims of neatly plaited and prod-uct-ed hair toward the back of the hall, near the paintings of native peoples now extinct. There, indeed, lingered a single student. A girl, slight and ponytailed, had managed to tip over a bronze of a rifleman presumably taking aim at those natives. Its weight alone was enough to crack the display case of arrowheads beneath.

"You…" she began and a girl in the front, in a nice pleated skirt and pumps, whispered "Kayla." The buttoned-up boys mouthed it, too. "Kayla."

"Kayla!" Connie shouted, and the shrillness of her own voice, echo-ing in that hallowed space, shocked her. But Kayla seemed unperturbed.

Instead, with a strength even greater than that needed to upend the piece, she righted it and set the rifleman back to shooting. Then, slapping her hands on the butt of her jeans, pivoting on her sneakers, she turned toward Connie with a look of studied innocence.

"Ooh," she exclaimed and shrugged. "Ahh?"

Straightening her powder blue dress, patting a platinum coif, Connie continued the tour. In view of the disturbance, she thought it best to skip the library—books no longer interested the young—and proceed to the gallery. Here, at least, there were stories to tell. Lessons that every citizen, above all children, must learn.

"He was a fine leader," Connie began at the foot of one of the giant portraits. She mentioned the man's name, cautiously, though there was little danger than any of them would recognize it, not even from the schools and airports from which it had been erased. "Did much for poor people, for the environment. But..."

Like flowers to sunlight, the entire class leaned forward. "But he had some personal problems—weaknesses, we might say—both here and before his election, that simply wouldn't do. Unfortunately, he had to resign."

She angled toward the next canvas and almost managed to speak when a snarky voice cut in. "What weaknesses?"

Connie paused and glared. Kayla, of course, her hands in fists and her mouth implacably scrunched. A dark girl—South Asian, possibly, or Black—tomboyish and clearly stamped with trouble.

"And if he was so good at things, why did he have to quit?"

Connie's own complexion ran pale to buttery, but she suddenly felt it redden. "Because, Kayla—it is, Kayla, isn't it?—we must expect more from our leaders. We must be able to look up to them."

Kayla closed a skeptical eye, but Connie decided to ignore her. "And this," she declared, "was the very first woman to hold this office." The students gaped. The woman was indeed impressive—firm-faced but sensitive, intelligent and proud. Not only the girls, but also the boys in the group might see as her someone to emulate.

"And she earned it. Fighting for equal rights, defending the victims of hatred." She pointed to a medallion mounted on the woman's wall. "Does anyone know what this is?"

Kayla raised her hand, still clenched, but Connie called on the pin-afored girl in front, pigtails bouncing. "Yes, Miss…"

"Ivy, ma'am, and that's the Nobel Prize."

"Right you are, Ivy. And she won it for ending a very destructive war." She pointed at the name emblazoned at the bottom of the frame, confident that no one would recognize it. "How sad it was when she had to leave."

"Weakness?" That same caustic tone.

Connie scowled. "Not weakness. Strength. She had too much of it, you see. Too much power. People were frightened."

"Well maybe the people were weak," Kayla insisted in a tone that reverberated around the gallery. A chevroned guard took notice. "Maybe the people should've quit."

"Oh, Kayla, please…" The girl in the pigtails whimpered, and the boy next to her, in chinos and a V-neck agreed. "You're ruining it for everybody."

"Shut up, Tom. Shut up, Ivy," Kayla snapped back. Her arms made an X over her t-shirt.

"Where," Connie quietly grumbled, "where is their teacher?" Probably off catching a smoke outside or, more likely, in one of the capital's bars. Fortunately, such influences were dying off, the tour guide consoled herself, and this new generation was growing up unmarred. Well-mannered and pure and largely thanks to the example set here. A leader at last that folks could look up to, a role-model with an impeccable future, installed with an immaculate past.

She continued, "Unlike this one, the worst." The students looked flummoxed, and Connie realized that they hadn't been privy to her thoughts. "I'd tell you his name, but you'd have to wash out your ears," she joked but the bewildered expressions remained. But not on Kayla. Glaring now, teeth gritted, and hands plumbed in her pockets, she was clearly geared up to spar.

"This one, how should I say, dipped into the till." The line usually evoked a shudder in audiences, but this time passed unremarked. Connie tried again, "He stole, kids. From the rich and the poor, he stole, day and night. From you and me." This, finally, left the students breathless, flattened hands pressed to their hearts, mouths open fish-like.

"How did you know?"

She hadn't asked for questions, yet here was Kayla raising one and Connie debated whether or not to answer. But she didn't have to. "You didn't," the wispy girl went on. "You never do. You just had to say so, and that's enough to get rid of him."

Now the docent was baffled, her pop-eyed, limp-lipped expression contrasting with the placid smile of the man in the painting, an inkling of sadness in his gaze. He seemed to know what was waiting for him— for them all.

Connie prepared to respond, though unsure of what would come out, a patient reprimand or a rant. She hated smart-alecks like Kayla, thinking they were better than the rest, placing themselves above. Her druthers were to ban them from the capital altogether, perhaps even from the country. People like Kayla had caused the crisis to begin with and had opposed its flawless solution.

She was going to say all that, calmly perhaps, but another's words stopped her.

"Good morning, everyone! And what a perfect morning it is!"

Connie's jaw widened to a gawp even as she came to attention. The chevroned guard went stiff. The children merely stared. There was no need for introductions—the chiseled features, the hair still sandy and slightly salted at the temples. No photograph, though, could prepare them for the size of the man, so tall and broad-shouldered as he loomed imposingly over the group, or for the eyes. Deep-set and glimmering, they appeared not only to see but to evaluate, to take in and store.

"Enjoying our little rogues' gallery? You…" He turned to a clean-cut boy in the front row, "Tom? And you…" The pigtails levitated. "Ivy?"

"Yes, sir," they simultaneously chimed.

"It's their best tour ever," Connie gushed in. "They couldn't be happier."

The monumental head nodded, but gravely. "For everyone, of course." His eyes found the back of the hall. "Except for Kayla."

She responded with arms akimbo. A long-lashed girl with tapered cheeks and lips naturally carmine, she scrunched her face into an obstinate mask.

"Except for Kayla who should be careful about what she watches on the internet. The treasonous lies she reads online." His smile was as flat and dry as the paintings, as lifeless as the native peoples. "Kayla, who doesn't know why this country is great."

With this, his neck extended—a full foot high, perhaps—and those all-knowing eyes went blank. But only for a moment before they filled with images of fighter jets, undulating wheat fields, mountains, lakes, and sky. Finally, there was the flag rippling while the national anthem boomed. Always a favorite with the visitors, kids especially, just as the founders had planned.

"Ooh," the pupils murmured—Connie, too. "Ahh."

Kayla, alone, stayed silent. Her smirk was defiant, her glowering fierce. A girl who would never be anything but difficult, destined for a womanhood of dissent. Framed between the portraits, she posed, sneakers planted, head thrown back, ready to defend her foibles.

The Blind Man

Accursed is he who leads a blind man astray on the road

—DEUTERONOMY 27:18

Autumns, Adam walked home at sunset. Leaving the office at precisely 6:30, he kept a brisk pace throughout the one-mile hike, much of it uphill. It was good exercise, he reasoned, and a good opportunity to clear his head after a day of often stultifying work. This season, especially, he enjoyed the burnt-orange horizons, the balm of dying leaves. The colors, the scents, could lure him into a trance-like state that ended only at the intersection into his neighborhood. That is when Adam saw him.

It was not the first time. On several occasions recently the same blind man stood at the junction. About Adam's age, neatly dressed in a windbreaker, he waited, tapping the curb with his cane. The compassionate type, Adam considered assisting him across the busy street, but hesitated. The pedestrian signal beeped loudly on green and the crosswalk was clearly lit. And, anyway, for the blind man, wasn't it always night?

So Adam paused while the blind man tapped, his face pitched forward as if to peer through his blackened glasses. But then, inexplicably, he stepped off straight into oncoming headlights. Geometry and physics careened through Adam's mind, calculating that walker and car would collide in less than a second. Without thinking, he leapt. Abandoning his briefcase mid-flight, he spread his arms and collapsed them again around the man's surprisingly slender shoulders. The full body thrust sent the two of them tumbling onto the opposite sidewalk. A whoosh of wheels brushed the seats of their pants.

"Are you alright?" Adam gasped, already blushing from the praise sure to be showered. Instead, with the flail of his free arm, the blind man shoved him away.

"Who the hell do you think you are?" The white aluminum stick, rapier-like, jiggled at Adam's belly. "Did I ask for your help? You think I can't cross a fucking street?"

Adam mumbled an apology, turned, and fled into his neighborhood. He felt, at first, embarrassed, caught out for being a do-gooder when no good needed doing. Later, just before reaching his house, the shame turned to fury. "Ingrate," he inwardly growled. "I should have just let him die." But, by the time he started climbing his stairs, the ire and discomfiture had melded into confusion. It was obvious on his face as his wife, Iris, immediately said to him, "*Now* what with Teitelbaum?"

He scowled at the mention of his boss, but only momentarily. And he would have been happy to join their three kids at the dinner table and talk about anything—rap music—rather than relate the incident that left him so flummoxed. Yet such secrets could never be hidden from Iris. Out of their children's earshot, he told her.

"What did you expect," she upbraided him kindly. "You humiliated him."

"I *saved* him!"

Iris, finished seasoning the vegetables, wiped her hand on a dishcloth. "Maybe. Maybe not. But if you did, then what does it matter what he said?" That same hand both touched and slapped his cheek. "Stop taking everything so seriously."

Still, he remained sullen at the table. The children—Dina, Naomi, and Tom, pre-teens with four years between them—jabbered for a while before noticing. "What's got into Dad?" Iris, accustomed to answering for him, explained.

"What an asshole," Tom sneered and was immediately chastened. "Not *Dad*, Mom, the blind man."

Dina recalled, "Dad likes rescuing people. The old lady and the flood. It made the papers."

"And the dog from the fire," Naomi, the youngest, added, unsure if the hero was in fact her father or a cartoon she'd seen on TV.

Nobody corrected her, though, or had time, for Iris was ladling the main course and thinking out loud, "unless…he didn't want to be rescued."

Mid-ladle, she realized that her family was gawking at her. "I mean, being blind is hard," she shrugged, "Maybe he wanted to get hit…"

"Ewww," the children responded, remarkably in tune. Only Adam remained silent, not eating. He saw his kids' freckles and their tussled strawberry hair. That was Iris's color when he met her, now brown and graying. He saw Iris, still heart-faced but fuller beneath the neck, ever nurturing. He should feel thankful, Adam thought, he had his family, he had his life. He, at least, could see.

The next day at work, while struggling with a rush job from Teitelbaum, Adam experienced a chill. Inclined to the hypochondriac, he immediately concluded he was coming down with something. He'd tossed most of the night, hounded by fractured dreams linked by car beams bearing down. He also had a headache. Rifling through the mess in a bottom drawer, he exhumed an old aspirin bottle and, before opening it, glanced at the date.

This was a habit he'd cultivated over the years without ever considering its source. But today, perhaps because of the dust encrusting the cap, he paused and remembered a similar container years ago. The shape was different—not cylindrical but vaguely humanoid with sloping shoulders, and pink rather than white. Adam looked different as well. Thinner, longer-haired, and with a look not of numb resignation but of intense naïveté, of recklessness.

* * * * *

That was the hankering he showed when she opened the first of the crates and showed him row after row of those bottles. "Aspirin," he said and instantly felt stupid. Any idiot could see it was aspirin.

"Ah," Taji laughed. "But these are not just *any* aspirin." She held a vial up to the grimy light and pointed at its label. "These are *expired* aspirin."

So clueless was he at this age that she had to explain expiration dates to him and the fact that these tens of thousands of perfectly good medicines were, financially if not pharmaceutically, worthless. "And that, my sweet Adam, is where we come in."

Where they came in, Taji continued, though she'd been through this with him several times before, was in delivering the crates to a certain Akram she knew not far from the northern border. From there, they passed into a series of stealthy hands that stamped the contents with new labels and updated dates, destined for foreign shelves.

"But that's illegal," Adam muttered, more with frisson than fear.

Taji chortled. "Illegal there, maybe. Not here. Here it's only"—she winced as if inserting something painful—"naughty."

They had met at a reflexology class, the kind taken by people with expendable time and uncertain futures. Partnered, they massaged each other's feet, pressing him into unchartered emotions. Adam blushed at the ungainliness of his toes but was aroused by the delicacy of hers. The softest rub sent her thighs shivering. A graduate of a select college, he had never spoken to someone like her. Head shaved from temple to nape with a sandy profusion on top. A brow, a nostril pierced, and arms not merely tattooed but festooned, hinting at hidden murals. Her name was Taji—"From the Taj Mahal. My mother hitchhiked there"—and she was beautiful in an unexceptional way. Little pink mouth, puckish nose, her eyes feldspar-speckled. A body vacuum-packed into jeans.

After class, they went to one of those billiards-and-darts bars he'd only seen in movies and sat for hours chugging. Adam, never a talker, did the listening and there was much to hear. Successive fathers, a mother who lived in a converted bus until she was too obese to climb in. Schools she went to, schools she dropped out of, jobs from bartender to apple picker. And lovers. A prodigious number of them, to hear her tell it. Football players, gangsters, a scientist and a saxophonist—Adam lost count. But, strangely, he enjoyed it. He could not imagine a life more different from his, so linear and uneventful. "To Adam, the first man on earth," Taji toasted him. "And I can be your Eve."

Sex with her was more like wrestling than lovemaking and often left him bruised. His ego, too, took a beating, from her suggestions, which were more like demands, for satisfying her. Yet she taught him much, got him drinking and smoking and listening to music that sounded like a prison revolt. And, of course, he loved her, a moth-to-flame thing that he knew would scorch him but left him wanting to burn. He yearned to be like her—defiant, indulgent—and to follow her every order.

That longing led him to a dimly lit apartment empty except for the crates. It was all so easy, Taji explained. Just load up his car—Adam came with wheels—and drive up north to Akram. "Give him the pills, take his cash, and go. Think you can handle that, Rambo?" she teased him. Adam nodded. He knew better than to ask where the aspirin had come from, better than to ask if this shipment would be the last.

Instead, he loaded, and he drove, knuckles serrating the wheel. Taji smoked and went on about best-forgotten nights in Kathmandu and somehow the hours passed. Too soon, he felt, they reached the grove that served as their rendezvous and the break in the fence where Akram waited.

He was nothing like Adam pictured him. No muscle-braided thug with shades and a shaved head but a diminutive farmer of scant teeth and fewer words. Far stronger than he appeared, he hoisted the crates and tossed them into the back of a tractor-hauled cart. Taji received an envelope. That was it—no thank yous, not even a goodbye. They got back into the car and headed, giddy, back south.

That night there were shots on the house and sex, violent even by Taji's standards. Still, Adam couldn't sleep. He lay next her to seemingly unbreathing body and studied the walls. He fought to come to grips with what he'd become—into what he'd let her make him—and to decide whether he liked it. Part of him was thrilled but another part horrified, titillated and scared. Yet all these thoughts converged into the single realization that, yes, this could be him.

That awareness crystallized with each excursion, each payment and the inebriated evenings squandering it. Adam acquired an earring and, with Taji's assistance, picked out a death's head tattoo. She even reserved him a date at the parlor the day after their next delivery. This one would be different, though. Adam understood that the minute she pried open one of the crates. Instead of pink plastic, he saw shimmering in the single bulb something long, gray, and oiled. The mere sight of the guns must have made him gasp because the next second Taji was socking him in the arm and telling him what a man he was. They were ready for this, she assured him. They deserved so much more from life.

About this time, through a friend of a friend, Adam met Iris. She was the anti-Taji: hardworking, traditional. She wore her strawberry hair in plaits and preferred cargo pants to jeans. Her skin was unadorned, her eyes, earthy. He looked at her suddenly like a castaway spying land. Though accustomed to rescuing others—a cat from a tree, the boy pinned under his tricycle—Adam now admitted that he was in need of saving.

And Iris saved him. "Can't you see that she's using you, Adam?" she railed at him the moment he confessed. "Can't you see the wreck you're making of your life?"

Iris was adamant in her instructions. He was never to see Taji again or even answer her phone calls. Iris invited him to move in with her—a roommate had just left—and lay low for a while. Cut his hair, get a regular job. Saddened, relieved, Adam obeyed.

The housing arrangement proved permanent. Days passed, weeks, yet Taji never called. Years later, Adam still wondered why. Perhaps she was in prison or overseas or even dead. Or maybe she simply knew. From the beginning she probably sensed that he was not cut out for a life beyond the edge, a life of thrills and hazards unseen. Not cut out for her.

So, the marriage with Iris. So, the house in the quiet neighborhood with Dina, Naomi, and Tom, and the family evenings around the dinner table. So, Teitelbaum and the aspirins Adam frequently downed. He took two now and settled back in his desk. His headache would pass in a little while. It almost always did.

Yet this one continued to nag him throughout the afternoon and right up until quitting time. Autumn was segueing into winter and the streets were already dark when Adam put on his coat and began his homeward trek. Spurred by the pain behind his eyes, he strode faster than usual and didn't even pause at the intersections. Except for the last one, and only because the blind man was there again, his cane like a metronome on the curb.

Adam stood next to him, so near that he could smell antiseptic—a blind man's smell, he figured. And the blind man must have felt Adam there was well, for his cane stopped tapping. Instead, without waiting for the beep on green, he stepped off into the traffic.

Adam began to move. Then he didn't. Then he did. Back and forth he shimmied on the sidewalk, as the blind man marched into the beams. Clutching his briefcase, he watched. Adam, with horror and anger and awe.

What's a Parent to Do?

S eated at a half-circle wooden table fitted into a kitchen niche, under a faux-Tiffany lamp that turned their faces calico, they fretted. Silent at first, hands folded on a surface scored with nicks, many of which they, themselves, had made with misused forks and horseplay. They stared at knitted fingers, at the walls that had seen so many family dramas, though nothing quite like this, and finally at one another.

"We could stop her, you know." Hilary whispered, as if her voice would carry. But the old house was good at compartmentalizing sounds, as they both knew. How many times, as kids, had they fooled around in this kitchen, and as teenagers on the living room sofa, without alerting anyone upstairs?

"She can't hear us," William reminded her. "Especially not with that music."

Hilary groaned, "That music..."

William nodded and sucked in a corner of his mouth, signifying agreement. The gesture might also suggest that he remembered what it was to be wild and devil-may-care, but they both knew that he didn't. Bug-eyed and butt-jawed, he was never popular in school, never went out on hot dates or got in trouble. Not like Hilary who, with a primal handsomeness, played muse to high school poets. Yet neither of them ever behaved so brazenly, with such scandalous delight, as this.

"But we can't stop her," William continued. "That's just the point."

Hilary glared at him, clasping at strands of conversation. Her fingernail deepened a nick. "Those jeans she wears, those skirts."

"Nothing to the imagination."

"Eww. Don't make me think…"

An antique clock measured their beats of silence. It echoed out of the kitchen and into the living room with its dark, brocaded furniture. There, over a mantel, hung a portrait of an elderly man, his expression as steely as his hair. A memorial candle flickered beneath. This was the altar that Hilary and William passed each night in judgment, and every time they failed.

"Maybe some outside counseling?" The bug-eyes brightened. "An intervention!"

Above them, through the kitchen ceiling, music thrumped, a hair dryer wailed. Next, they knew, came the makeup—mascara and rouge over strata of base—enough to please an undertaker. At least that's what Hilary told her, only to receive that same sucked-in lip—a hereditary expression, but in her mouth it snickered, "so what?"

"It happened so fast," Hilary said, but to her knuckles, ignoring William's ideas.

Still, he responded, "*Too* fast."

They both recalled the retiring person they loved, yet never excessively, simply because she never demanded it. She never demanded much of anything, content to be precisely what she seemed—dutiful, unprepossessing, demure. That is until death intervened. One grave closed and another sprung open, and up she arose—in William and Hilary's eyes—monstrous.

"Some limits, then." William was back to advice. "Otherwise she'll be out all night."

"Drinking. Cavorting. And…Eww!"

"Eleven o'clock curfew. Okay, twelve. But not a minute more. We've got to be responsible."

Hilary groaned again, surrendering to a sigh. "Or realistic. She's too old to be told what to do and we're too old-fashioned." Metallic eyes watered as she gazed out of the kitchen and into the living room with its icon. "And after all those years of being good, she only wants to have fun."

Another nod, another retracted lip. She was right, of course. William suddenly felt ancient. But not for long. The dryer-wail ceased and was soon replaced by heel-clacks descending the stairs. They looked up from the table and gasped.

"What do you think?" she said, turning on a spike and showing more flesh than either had seen in years, and even then only in bathing suits. The hair was a color unknown to nature. "It's called Kinky Pink, in case you were wondering."

They weren't. Their minds, in fact, were as blank as their faces as a headlight blazed through the transom windows, violating the living room and its shrine.

"Oops, I've got to jump," she giggled in a tone cheerier than any they remembered. "He hates waiting, that Irving."

Hilary and William gawked at each other. Their expressions asked, "Irving?" But before they could inquire, in a diaphanous cloud and thunderclap of heels, she was gone. Only her parting remark remained.

"Go home, you two," she'd laughed as she hurried through the living room to the foyer. "Go be with your families. Be happy. Live!"

The slamming door shook the table where the two siblings sat speechless, watching their mother depart. It shivered the light on their faces. Over the mantel, the portrait sagged. The candle nearly blew out.

Slave to Power

My ears can scarcely distinguish the thump of waves from the thunder of cannons and the relentless pounding of drums. The sunlight on the water dances with the reflection of helmets and shields. Cheers from the crowd mingle with the prisoners' howls. Only the smells will diverge. Soon, the tang of sea will shrink from the stench of blood and the other putrescence that dependably gush from the impaled.

I, Mehmed Pasha, the *vali* of this entire province, command this ceremony. For this is a festival like any other. A time of gathering, of showing devotion, and even delight, but always within the confines of order. For like the sea and its constant waves, like the sun and all other heavenly spheres, so, too, is our state governed by Allah, blessed be He, who determines our lives from the first drop of sperm to the final exhalation. Who rules with a wise and punishing will through His chosen power on earth.

I am that power. So says the crop with three horse-hair lanyards I slap into my palm, the curled golden slippers adorning my feet, and the gleaming white turban that, cloud-like, envelops my head. My mouth speaks the fate of countless subjects, the marching of soldiers like the hundred mustered here holding back the crowd, and the sailing of the war-galleys rolling behind the surf. I am the power, and yet I am powerless. With all my jewels and concubines and dominion over life and death, I am lower than any of these filthy peasants pushing for a glimpse of the condemned. I am their slave.

Another burst of cannon fire, a further rumble of drums. Three infidels, rags barely covering their uncircumcised parts, are hauled into the square. The clink of the chains on their arms and legs echo the gulls' screeching overhead. The three have been beaten, but not so severely that they will swiftly succumb to the sentence. Blinded in one eye only and their tongues cut in half so that they can still see what is happening to them and vainly babble for mercy.

Here, in my heart, compassion and cruelty merge. Freedom and bondage as well. Soldiers grip the prisoners' limbs, lift them and force them onto their backs. At just such moments, strangely, an image recurs to me. Of a village long ago and in a mountainous place, its horizon emblazoned with crosses. Other soldiers grabbing my spindly arms and legs and dragging me, wailing, from a woman whose cries sounded deep and animal-like. I, too, was beaten, but not so ruthlessly as to not survive the journey. Blindfolded and bound but with my ears open to the smack of cartwheels on the palace flagstones and the call to prayer that I instantly mistook for a curse. And for the first word—*Devshirme*—of the language I would learn for endless hours each day until finally forgetting my own. *Devshirme*, the Collecting.

That, too, is part of the order. The tithe of Christian boys gathered each year and consigned to the state. The strong ones designated as soldiers; the bright ones educated as scribes. And the special ones, those as nimble with a sword as they were with numbers, able to command and judge with no sentiment or interests other than the state's, were destined to be pashas. Trained in the arts, in religion and its sciences, and in all our noblest ways. Instilled with the duty to wage holy war against the Frank and to devote their lives—if ordered, sacrifice them—to our Sultan.

A slave-run state, a divinely ordained state, in rhythm with the sea and the movement of spheres and the dictates of His will. And that will demands that the pashas never marry, never father male heirs who might threaten the Sultan's dynasty. Never enter the harem over which the eunuchs keep vigilant guard. Pashas and eunuchs, the first without pasts and the second without futures—on these twin pillars rests our state.

Our loving and ruthless state, which rewards its subjects' loyalty with booty in wartime and food during famines; which guards the roads against brigands and elevates believers over infidels. And chastises rebels as only those who revolt against the order must, with the long, whetted stake.

The soldiers spread each prisoner's legs and insert a spike between them. At that moment, always, the crowd goes silent. The sea and the gulls, seemingly, as well. The infidels look to their heaven, but there is no hope. No more than when I was torn from that memory village and the crosses scoring its sky. Now, though, I look elsewhere. To the palace and the marble domed window near its tower. There, through the lattice-work, over the rim of her veil, I can see her eyes studying me. Worshipping me and waiting. Samira, whose name means Cool Summer Breeze but whose eyes flare like stoked coals. Stolen from the Sultan's harem, after her eunuch guard was first bribed then garroted. And now here she waits. In my palace, in my *vali*, and bearing my son.

Another soldier, burly and specially trained for the task, appears with a mallet. He approaches the first prisoner, raises the hammer over the blunt end of the stake, and awaits the signal. Here is the power, the order entrusted to me by Allah, achieved by my inbred skills as by my cunning and brutality. Here is the moment when all—the sea, the spheres, the palace's turrets and minarets—meld. The white turban rises and falls, almost imperceptibly, and the mallet strikes.

The crowd erupts, so uproariously that I cannot hear the prisoner's screams. For with that first blow, they all scream. Their single eyes roll and half-tongues flail. Only later, as the spike rips upward through a prisoner's innards, through his belly and chest, do the responses differ. Some will yowl and others whimper, their heads thrashing and pounding the flagstones. Others still will pray. All will be astonished at the thought, if not the agony, of the thick wooden pole skewering them from anus to collarbone, and the death that awaits all too patiently for days, while children gawk at them and ravens circle above.

My thoughts, though, are with Samira. While my eyes observe the ritual, my heart lifts through the lattices to hers and the son slumbering beneath it. From the first drop of sperm, Allah determines, to our lives' last breath. And, this, too, has been foretold.

Or so I must believe. I must believe that this order, like the embroidery on Samira's gown, is sewn from a single thread. Unraveled, a single stitch can dissolve the whole. So the cord that binds my heir to her womb will, once cut, begin the unlacing. The Sultan will fall, and all will declare my dynasty. With soldiers and galleys and lands stretching eastward from the sea. I will bear his title, his slippers and turban. My pashas will all be slaves. And I, at last, will be free.

The mallet's work is almost finished. Yet another soldier steps forward with a knife and slices neatly on the back of each prisoner's neck. There, with one last tap, the stake emerges from the skin. The single eyes strain vainly to watch it, the bright pinewood picket sprouting improbably from the nape. But as the stakes are raised and planted facing west, toward Frankdom, all they see are waves. They hear the cannons, the crowd, and the drums, drowning out their own unintelligible cries. A muezzin reminds them that our God is greater than theirs. The seagulls shriek.

I see and hear it all. From under my turban, with the three-tailed crop rapping my palm, I, Mehmed Pasha, watch dispassionately and wait for the stakes to be secured. Only then, when the drums and cannons grow silent and the crowd begins to thin, do I smell it. As if in the hollows scooped by receding waves, arising from the brine, the smell of blood and putrefaction. The stink of death and human illusions. The reek of slaves, perhaps, who dream of becoming masters.

The Widow's Hero

Shuffling down the aisle, they are heart-warming. She, Alma, holds onto the cart while he braces her back with one arm. Though roughly the same age, she is frailer, her steps less certain, shoulders stooped. Marrick, by contrast, still stands erect. His head, unlike hers, doesn't tremble.

"We need peeled tomatoes," Alma says, and Marrick replies in a mock-military style, "Peeled tomatoes it is!" and reaches for a can from the shelf. These days he does all the reaching.

"And peas. We're low on peas."

"Can't have us low on peas, now, can we?"

Shoppers float through the supermarket ether. A toddler howls, hooked around his mother's calves. A voice on high announces a special on chicken parts and a brand name detergent.

"Artichokes!" Alma gasps. Two fists cover her heart. "Let's get some and I'll make your favorite sauce. I know how much you love artichokes."

Marrick smiles at her. In fact, he hates artichokes. But he has always loved Alma. Even now, with her once-abundant walnut hair reduced to colorless straws, a mottled mask in place of the face that first enchanted him, he worships her. Her mind, too, has largely vanished. A mind so powerful that students and faculty alike called it The Machine, capable of memorizing entire lawbooks. An engine that drove her from classroom to courtroom and to lecture halls the world over. And that kept her excelling while raising a baby alone, after her husband's death.

*   *   *   *   *

His first name was Rami and his last became "The Hero of Post 29." That was the title of a popular song dedicated to him and the movie based on the song. Children's books, annual marathons, even a national math contest—all celebrated his valor. For a nation reeling from an irredeemable war, Rami supplied hope.

He was a reserve officer in command of Post 29, a fortress facing enemy lines. With the attack, Rami ordered his men to their firing positions and fought beside them as one after the other fell. Blinded by sunlight, they shot, through geysers of iron and sand, at the massing shadows. Grenades dropped into the trenches, but still Rami stood. His features, as ruggedly forged as the farm tools he left at home, never quivered. Radioing in, "Post 29 about to be overrun. Long live our nation," his voiced remained calm. Drilled through by a sniper's bullet, his last breath escaping through his chest, Rami asked the medic to tell his wife that he loved her, that she must someday remarry, and that she must never give up on life.

The origins of this account were choppy, pieced together from the few soldiers taken prisoner and another who had played dead. Other, less lionizing, reports had Rami cursing like a madman at the generals for abandoning him and the soldiers who begged him to surrender. They were relieved when he finally was hit. "Fuck you," he gasped at the medic who struggled to plug his wound. "Fuck you *and* your mother."

Such stories were confined to the radical media, though, while the legend of Rami congealed. The song followed, and the film, with tales of the hero's life. A sickle in one hand and a slide rule in the other, a pioneer of the land and linear algebra. And then there was Alma. Waiting stoically for word from the front, bolstering others whose husbands were also away fighting. Wondering if the life inside her would ever know a father.

Contrary to fable, news that her husband had "fallen"—as if he'd tripped over a rake—shattered her. She scarcely remembered the birth of her daughter, Maya, much less the pregnancy before. She locked herself indoors, alternately crying and screaming, unbearably missing Rami but also furious at him for preferring heroism over her. Secretly, she believed in the less valiant narrative, the one with the Rami who swore and lost his temper, not so much brave as stubborn. That was the man who she loved and somewhere always would, she confessed early in her relationship with Marrick.

He understood. Or at least believed he did, initially. Not being intimidated by his predecessor made him feel manly. And the raw emotions that Rami still invoked in Alma rendered her more irresistible in his eyes, a vulnerability behind the grit. For Alma was no grieving homebody by the time Marrick met her, but a firebrand attorney already redoubtable in court.

The state had targeted his firm, a manufacturer of computer frames, for some regulatory infraction. Marrick would have gladly paid the fine— profits easily absorbed it—and moved on, but his lawyers demanded an appeal. The hearing was more a form of entertainment for him and, for a new immigrant to the country, a way of showing he belonged. The last thing he expected to see was a fervid prosecutor with hair piled on her head, dressed in black but with an alabaster face that was both implacable and frail. The last thing that he, a bachelor in his mid-forties, anticipated was the urge to introduce himself to this woman, congratulate her on her victory over him, and invite her out to lunch.

"You should know, I come with baggage," Alma warned him as their salads arrived. The tale of Post 29 followed, and she wielded it as if to ward him off. She must have done so frequently, Marrick reckoned, and successfully. After all, what man would want to share a bed with a myth? That was when he convinced himself that he could accept that part of Alma was reserved for Rami, just as long as the rest of her was his.

For Marrick also had guts. Growing up an egg-headed kid in a tough neighborhood, bespectacled, slight, he learned to use his fists even when the bullies' were bigger. It took nerve to pick up after college and move overseas to a place where wars broke out regularly, but which also lent opportunities to newcomers. Conquering the strange language, the brusque culture and cutthroat competition, he prospered. His life became his business, leaving him little time or taste for relationships. The women he dated were too feckless, he felt, and boring. But then he met Alma.

The way she stabbed at her lettuce that day at lunch, the undainty revolutions of her chews—here, Marrick thought, was a woman of strength and intellect. At last, a woman worthy of him.

But did he merit her? The question rankled him when first entering her office, where Rami's black-and-white army photograph dominated the diplomas on her wall. He asked himself again when accompanying her to Memorial Day events where children recited elegies to the Hero of Post 29. People were staring at him, he sensed, wondering how this owlish man with glasses and an accent could ever be Rami's replacement. And he, too, began to doubt.

Inscribed within him now was the image of Rami fast at the ramparts, invincible. And here he was, a man who never served in the military, who knew nothing of farming and whose math skills barely sufficed to balance books. If proud of Alma in public, alone with her he debated whether he could ever match up.

And yet he stayed with her. For all his insecurities, he refused to give in to what he knew were irrational thoughts. The mere notion of defeat offended him. And, irrespective of her past, Marrick loved Alma.

Such devotion overwhelmed the widow's resistance, reawakening a passion she long believed lost. Soon they were a couple, complete with tiny kindnesses and the occasional bicker. When not abroad for business, Marrick moved in with her. He even won over her daughter.

An introverted girl, Maya was bright like her mother but with her father's flinty looks. His self-righteousness, too. Twelve at the time she met Marrick, she treated him to two years of spite. Maya could shuffle past him at the breakfast table, extract a drink from the refrigerator and shuffle back, without so much as a nod. She could criticize him to Alma, in the third person, in his presence. Refusing to attend those interminable ceremonies, she nevertheless resented him for escorting her mother. Maya, it seemed, was determined to despise him and to prevent any man—especially Marrick—from sharing her mother's life.

But then came the awkwardness, the zits and the slow-sprouting breasts and the jeering of schoolmates whose bodies appeared preformed for adulthood. Hearing her sobs behind her door, Marrick did what he never dared and simply stepped in. More—he sat at the edge of

Maya's bed, held her hand, and listened. He promised her that her life would be joyous and that, in the interim, she should ignore those—his word—assholes. The next day, he waited outside of school and scowled off potential tormenters.

Yet mere empathy could not account for Marrick's victory over Maya. Nor could the support that he lent her as she grew into a handsome young woman and the college tuitions he paid. Rather, affection came with the realization, gradual and unspoken, that the two of them shared a house haunted by the same ghost and the only woman who could see it.

* * * * *

"For you, my queen!" Marrick proclaims, loud enough for Alma as well as passing shoppers to hear. With a slight bow, he presents her with scepter-shaped artichokes which she accepts and lays in the cart.

"My knight," Alma swoons, fists again clasped over her heart. "I'll make them just the way you like, with lots of butter and garlic. No more of you coming home from the army and grousing 'where are my artichokes?'"

"No more. I promise."

He steers down the dry goods aisle, selecting the pastas and grains she swears are urgently needed. Their cart brims with items that they will never eat and which Marrick, in cahoots with the grocer, later returns.

Another elderly couple passes them, their cart a common walker, and appear to recognize them. Marrick is used to that, even now, years after the Incident. Or perhaps they only place him, whose face, more than Alma's, was everywhere.

With a slight pressure, he ushers her forward into the cereals, boxes of which she selects.

"You need your strength," Alma reminds him.

"And so do you."

"How is a man supposed to fight without his strength? How can you defend me?"

"How," Marrick asks as he turns them toward checkout, "could I not?"

* * * * *

An otherwise ordinary day at the office ended when Marrick came home to find Alma and Maya huddled in the study, crying. Together with his wife and his adopted daughter, they formed a close-knit family. Maya became a pediatrician and married an endocrinologist, together raising two tireless children. And Alma was named a judge. Respected by the system, feared by those who flaunted it, she was widely expected to rise to the Supreme Court and even perhaps preside over it. Marrick's business continued to flourish, affording them an insulated lifestyle and an upscale house in the suburbs. Rami's photo faded on the wall but not in the public's—or Marrick's—memory.

But now, suddenly, these tears. And their cause, he learned, was not one but a succession of crises. The first was the near-total hearing loss of one of Maya's patients, brought on by any one of several infections, some of them resistant to treatment. Still, the parents sued. The second and more grievous plight was Alma's—an allegation that she incentivized her legal friends to have the case dismissed. So a single misfortune in Maya's clinic erupted into a national scandal. The entire system was rigged, critics raged, and the press ran with the charge.

"None of it's true!" Alma wept and Maya embraced her. But Marrick just stood there wordless. "You believe me, don't you?"

Of course, he did. He was just shocked to see Alma sob. "We won't let these bastards get to us," he finally declared. "We won't give an inch."

Not yielding proved more harrowing, though, as the issue refused to recede. Rather, it escalated into an anti-corruption campaign with Alma as its bullseye. Rami was also evoked, but as a symptom of society's decline. The Hero of Post 29 would be mortified, columnists surmised, by his widow's dishonesty. Not only had she sullied justice but also her late husband's legacy by marrying a disreputable businessman, and a foreigner to boot.

"I think I should step down."

"Never."

"Say what they want to about me," she whimpered, "but about you—I can't bear it."

Marrick turned a paperweight in his hands. He planted it on the desk with a thud. "I can," he said. "We all can."

But could they? The most agonizing blow had yet to be dealt—not to Alma or Marrick or even Maya, but to Rami. Digging into the archives, reporters unearthed the alternative version of Post 29, complete with its raving commander. And worse. An eyewitness emerged who attested that the record was exactly backward. Instead of exhorting his men to stand firm, Rami pleaded with them to surrender. Under withering enemy fire, at gunpoint, they ordered their officer to fight.

None of the battle's survivors could corroborate this claim, but the media didn't care. Nor did it matter that the veteran had been institutionalized for trauma, was a vagrant and a sometimes thief. Yet the libel devastated Alma, more than the accusations of graft. While she might somehow defend herself, who would stand up for Rami?

That question never occurred to Marrick. For a moment, it seemed that he could be freed from Post 29 and the burden of its myth. But garbage was dumped on their doorstep and their windows smeared with graffiti. Then, one night, a mob roiled on their front lawn and demanded to confront the judge.

"The police will be here any minute," Alma wailed. "You don't have to do this!" She tore at his coat-sleeves as he punched his arms through them.

"Don't I?" he said, absently at first before insisting, "Nobody can violate my house. Nobody can threaten you." Ripping the sleeve from Alma's grip, Marrick barged outside.

In the sudden darkness, he could feel rather than see the crowd and heard some drunken sneers. Still, he drew himself up, calibrated his tone, and stated, "This is private property. Get out, all of you. Now."

The response was laughter and catcalls of "Property brought with bribes!"

"Liars. She's never been anything but straight."

Louder laughter now, and boos. "The authorities are on their way," Marrick responded, adding as he turned back to the door. "Leave while you can."

But the protesters remained, and one of them taunted, "Go, crawl back into your little hole. We know that your wife likes cowards."

Marrick stopped. His cheeks seethed ember-like. Swiveling on a heel, he hollered, "How dare you?" He lunged at the demonstrators who reflexively stepped back. "How dare you disrespect a man who gave everything for this country. For you!"

"Cowards, you and your wife," someone bellowed, and the rest of them took up the chant, "Cowards! Cowards! Cowards!"

A substance hit Marrick's chin and hung there dripping. But he did not flinch or waiver. He stood at attention until the police cars arrived with sirens trumpeting and lights that draped him in blue.

The charges against Alma were ultimately dropped and her judicial reputation restored. Yet the publicity quashed her chances for a Supreme Court appointment, much less to serve as the chief. Alma retired but still offered legal advice. The young attorneys who visited her office gazed respectfully at her diplomas but failed to recognize the young soldier in the yellowed photograph. Only Marrick, when chancing in with her cup of tea, was half-inclined to tell them.

* * * * *

"We forgot green onions," Alma worries as her husband loads groceries on the checkout belt. "To sprinkle on your artichoke sauce. I want it to be just perfect."

"But it is perfect," he assures her. "It always is."

"I'm afraid you'll leave me again. Leave and not come home."

As if to still it, he touches her trembling cheek.

"I'll never leave you. Ever," he says.

In his mid-eighties, Marrick is hale and mentally sharp, still foreign enough to wear a tie to the supermarket. But Alma is vanishing. She needs constant assistance, even for the simplest tasks. He reveres her bravery in the face of dementia and loves her even more.

"Such a gentleman," the cashier says to them. A heavily-accented woman, cheaply dressed, she is clearly an immigrant.

"A *famous* gentleman," Alma replies. "I'm sure you've heard of him."

The woman shrugs. She holds up a can and mentions to Marrick, "These are on sale, you know. Two for one."

He almost winks at her, as if she were in on the secret, but merely responds, "One will do. Thanks."

Alma goes on. "Everyone's heard of him. His name is…is…"

Now Marrick does wink, and the woman, wise if uneducated, understands.

"Of course, I've heard of him, who hasn't?" she chimes while ringing up the artichokes. "Your husband's a hero."

Made to Order

"Don't leave me."

"You know I don't miss appointments."

"Just this one time."

"This *is* one time."

"Everything's just like you instructed. The flowers, the seating."

"And your suit. Go with the gray. Solid blue tie, no stripes. And for God's sakes, get a haircut. Can't have you looking like a street person. Most important..."

"I know. No crying."

"Dignity, Roman, remember."

"I do, but..."

"No buts."

"I can't live without you."

"No," she said, her last words before the rattle. "You won't."

Not only the flowers and the seating but also the prayers were scrupulously planned. So too, was the widower's composure during his eulogy. Even the day, cloudless with a spanking autumn edge, seemed pre-arranged, the mourners quipped. "That was Marci," someone whispered but loud enough for everyone to hear. "Made to order."

And Roman was created to obey. Smart, even talented in his youth, but directionless and slovenly, it took a wife like Marci to mold him into a hyper-focused professional, clean-shaven, and suave. Marci, petite and sardonic Marci, with hair so black it sucked in sunlight and ruthlessly bunned to expose a face with features like woodworking tools, sharp and exactingly practical. Clothes fit tight and never a shade lighter than shale. No sooner had they met when it was clear who would give the orders in their relationship and who would fulfil them forthwith, who could see what was best for them both and who could to achieve it simply by following commands.

Not that he didn't love her, but love is a composite of many emotions, desires, jealousies, and doubts, and yes, also of needs. And Roman needed Marci. Needed her not only to tell him what to wear but how to interact with the world, to hold himself in ways that broadcast self-worth and attracted the right kind of attention. He needed her to be the Roman he always suspected he was but without a clue how to become him. His love for her was also an adoration of himself, or at least the accomplished man Marci fashioned.

That love was reciprocated, the need entirely mutual. For Marci, a jockey in search of a horse, he was the foal she could break, train, groom, and bridle. The thoroughbred that she, alone, could stroke and mount, spurring him across the finish. The races, she believed, were endless.

Until she received the prognosis. "Poor boy," was Marci's first reaction. "How will you survive?"

Roman didn't know. His anguish over Marci's fate was often overshadowed by fears for his own. Life without her would be worthless—worse, unbearable. Prodding was unnecessary when he pledged never to look at another woman, ever. He even purchased the plot next to hers.

"I'll always be there, right by your side."

"Promise?"

"With all my heart."

"Good," Marci, possessive even on her deathbed, croaked, "And I'll hold you to it."

She didn't have to. In the months after the funeral, it was Roman who acted dead. Sure, he still dressed himself each morning, but in mismatched suits and ties, sometimes shaved, and shuffled to an office to pass the hours insensibly. He returned to an apartment once painstakingly clean but now chaotic, with dishes stacked in the kitchen sink and junk mail on every surface. He drank two beers and watched as many hours of television, indifferent to the channels, before falling into a sleep tussled by dreams of Marci excoriating him for all he'd forgotten, for destroying her life's greatest work.

Weekends, rather than going out with his remaining friends or even taking in a movie alone, Roman visited the gravesite. Fresh bouquets replaced the ones barely wilted; winter weeds were clipped. With a meticulousness that would have impressed her, he scraped the ice from the stone. "Come!" he imagined the inscription barking at him, "Join me!" as he laid his head on the frosted grass, on the spot where her heart might've been.

Springtime merely renewed his torment, and while the rest of the world thawed, Roman's resolve solidified. He would put an end to it, right there in the cemetery, stretching out next to her and fulfilling his final pledge. Lacking a gun, he tried it with a razor only to falter, bleeding and berating himself. Without her, he couldn't even do this.

One such Sunday, after yet another failed attempt at reunion, he staggered out to his car and drove sobbing through the surrounding neighborhoods, straight through stop signs and intersections. Unfortunately, there was no policeman around to arrest him before he bumped into a smaller, much older car—or it hit him, Roman wasn't sure—and snapped into consciousness.

"Jesus, I'm sorry!" he burst from his vehicle shouting.

But "No, I'm sorry," the other driver interrupted, "I'm such a ditz," and broke into tears.

Roman was flummoxed, wondering what Marci would've done. "Look, lady, it's nothing. Hardly a scratch." He reached for his wallet and held out some bills. "This should more than cover it."

But she wouldn't take the money, wouldn't stop bawling. Roman tried to comfort her and even patted her wrist while slowly realizing that the woman was young, blonde, dressed in breezy linen, and pretty. The sensation was strange, confusing, unseemly, this attraction. Without thinking, he stammered, "Then at least let me take you to lunch." Which was shocking enough, but not as unnerving as her reply.

Smiling, suddenly, with teeth as white and aligned as cemetery's stones, she murmured, "I know a quiet place nearby."

While he barely touched his sandwich, she virtually inhaled hers, a big-haired woman, feline-eyed, fleshy. So unlike Marci, the gamine. And as talkative as she was taciturn, within this single meal he heard about her failed attempts at acting, designing, and running a home delivery service, about multiple relationships that came to naught, and successive trips to Hawaii. At some point—he couldn't remember which—he learned her name, Olivia, her address, and phone number, and how delighted she'd be to go out with him that Saturday night. "You pick the place," she said. "I'm terrible at making decisions."

Marci, of course, had always chosen where they'd go out and when, and it surprised Roman to discover that he was capable as well. Also astonishing was his ability to select the right clothes for the evening and to spruce himself up on his own. Any guilt he felt about violating his pledge was quelled by a denial of the date's significance, a temporary escape from his gloom. He would never see Olivia again, he assured himself, not even kiss her goodnight.

Yet there he was, several hours and three martinis later, in his apartment which he had whimsically thought to straighten up that evening, on bedsheets changed for the first time in weeks, making love. Not only making it but determining how, which positions and what order, duration and recurrence. No less surprising was his request—more like an insistence—that she see him again the following Saturday, and every one after that, with sporadic liaisons between. Summer began and Roman could no longer deceive himself. He and Olivia were coupled.

Co-joined was a better word, and by a bond he'd never experienced. He gave her a makeover, replacing her gossamer with pant suits and bobbing her cumulus of hair. He instructed her to cut down on sweets and improve her grammar, to stop nibbling her thumbnails, and try her hand at realty. Every "tell me how" and "you make up my mind" he relished, realizing, after years of being ridden, the joy of being in the saddle. Of creating and dominating a mate.

"I'm a totally new woman," Olivia announced to the mirror and to Roman's reflection behind her. "How did you do that?"

"Well, I had a good teacher."

Learning into the mirror, "The best," she agreed, and applied the lipstick he preferred.

Come September, Roman was ready to end his widowerhood. Not that his memories of Marci had faded, but they had mellowed from ominous to warm. In place of remorse for abandoning her for Olivia was a balmy gratitude for teaching him the art of control. Without it, he could never have continued living, much less found another love. Rather than damn his decision—so he inwardly averred—the dead woman would've approved.

Which is why he brought Olivia to the cemetery, to introduce her as he felt he must and formally end his grief. The day was crisp, a tint of fall in the trees. Olivia was dressed as he instructed her, in an alpaca wrap coat and pumps, her hair respectfully veiled. Roman led the way, in his solid gray suit and tie, through the rows to the site where the last of the bouquets had long turned to crusts.

"She would have liked you," Roman began.

"I suppose you're right, dear. As always."

"Picked you out personally, if possible."

Oliva clapped white gloves. "And intuitive."

"Yet somehow I believed that she wanted me here, lying beside her, rather than standing with you."

"No…"

"I even tried it several times—the day we met—but didn't have the courage."

"I can't picture it. Show me, please."

He did, mindless for a moment of his clothes, kneeling onto the empty plot and then straightening his back and legs. "Just like this," he said, feeling the dankness penetrate his skin and the unkempt grass on his throat. Gazing up into a cloudless sky which in the next instant filled with Olivia.

She reached into a fancy handbag that Roman didn't recognize and produced the pistol he never imagined she owned. "Just as you instructed," she said, but not to him. Then, lifting her veil, the woman he called Olivia took aim.

Later, after placing the gun in Roman's hand, she reopened the bag she'd bought with Marci's advance and extracted a set of keys. Pulling off her gloves, she strode through the rows and out to the parking lot. Waiting there was the sportscar that she would now pay off with the balance. Leather interior, carbon finish, made to order.

The Cookie Jar

Three women flung off their coats and tottered in glittering heels as the black BMW approached. Their breath made gray clouds in the darkness and their skin contracted in the sudden cold, yet the expressions they flashed through the lowering window were sultry. "Hiya, babe. What's you up for?"

They chattered their offers, singular and combined, only to turn away cursing. Scampering back to the curb, they collected their coats and spat, "He wants you."

The magenta-haired woman, the only one to remain shivering on the pavement, glared at them through clasped lapels of fake fur.

"He's not waiting on you all night."

She could have bet on it, but instead she just nodded and walked through them. The passenger door opened as she rounded the sports car and climbed in. The engine revved and the other women watched as its rear lights glowed cinder-like, winked, and faded.

"Jesus, what's that stuff you're wearing," the driver asked with an angry sniff.

Her face still buried in the fur, the woman shrugged. "Stuff."

"I mean, is it supposed to make a smell or hide one?"

"Both."

His own car had a resinous scent that seemed to emanate from the glove compartment or perhaps from his hair, slicked-back and dark. His cashmere jacket was the same color, as were his turtleneck and slacks. His complexion, compared to hers, was swarthy.

"Not here," he said when she reached into her coat for a cigarette. "We'll be home soon. You can clean up, eat, get some rest."

"You know what I need." She spoke to the windshield. A pale, dull-eyed face stared back.

"You do what you want, just as long as Regina doesn't see it, and the kids."

"The kids…"

"The whole back of the house is yours. No one will bother you there. Only one condition: no strangers."

By which he meant customers. She huddled inside her coat. "As Mom always said, good girls *never* talk to strangers."

A half-hour later, an electronic gate swung open to a crescent drive-way lined with shrubbery and hidden cameras. Another code unlocked the front door. Large, abstract sculptures loomed over them in the foyer, and vividly splattered canvases. She shielded her eyes from the halogen lamps and tried to shuffle, her heels clacking like gunshots.

He led her into the kitchen with an island as large, she thought, as her rented room. The sinks, the appliances—everything looked industrial. Hard to imagine that food actually emerged from this place—more like auto parts. Except for the ceramic jar.

Half-hidden behind a stainless-steel toaster, the jar nevertheless stood out with its octagonal design and tapered lid. Emblazoned with a clown dancing merrily with balloons in blue, green, and red, it recalled a time when those colors felt warm and clowns were not yet creepy. Its icing-like lacquer embraced, rather than reflected, the light.

The jar caught their gaze for a moment, before the woman whose co-workers called Zeena but was really named Ruth, sighed, "ah."

"The kids never touch it," Paul replied. "They think it's for teabags."

"Teabags," she chortled, and pinched the little green pine tree sprouting from the lid. Lifting, Ruth effected a gasp and plucked out a sparkling cookie.

"They're ninety percent sugar," Paul explained. "Just the way you like."

"Just the way I *need*." Ruth smiled, and took a bitter bite.

Later, after her bath, she would find silk pajamas laid out on her bed and, in the morning, a closet-full of designer clothes just her size. Ruth padded to breakfast—lunch really—looking almost refreshed and allowed the cook to dole her pancakes that she doused with syrup. And then, throughout the afternoon when Paul was at work and Regina out with her friends, the children still at school, she would visit the jar.

She could empty it within an afternoon. Though she indeed needed its contents, Ruth cherished the jar itself, as though it held far more. Another life, a different world, the past.

The next day, invariably, the jar would be filled again. She ate and slept, ate and slept, holding out for as long as she could. Knowing that there would be cookies and, should those run out, the one thing she needed more. On that she could depend on her brother.

* * * * *

And he could rely on her, too, once. Back when she was the darling of her class, their parents' favorite. Their den looked like a gallery of her prizes. Boys lined up to date her and peers vied with each other to call her friend. The sort of person who, if not so charismatic, could be easily hated. But in addition to her gifts, Ruthie was kind, especially to her younger brother.

For kindness was demanded by Paul. Otherwise, he was untouchable. Plagued by dyslexia and other disabilities, fat and socially inept, he was the family embarrassment. A dark-skinned dud compared to his sister, blonde and brilliant. He, alone, occupied his room, where the world seemed pleased to keep him. Only Ruthie took him out.

To the parties that whirled around her and the high school dramas in which she starred, Ruthie always brought Paul. People would wonder why a young woman so beautiful and admired would chain herself to this repulsive child. Yet she not only tolerated him, she virtually showed him off. As if to say, "Here is my brother, can you believe how compassionate I am?" Another badge of merit.

So their relationship remained for years, with Paul playing leper to her saint. But then, in a remarkably short time, their positions reversed.

At sixteen, Paul shed his flab and determined to overcome his handicaps. He learned the keys of human interaction and gradually became popular. He returned to his room only to sleep at night, when not out with girlfriends or on skiing trips or visiting the campuses of which Paul would soon have his pick.

But Ruthie turned the other way. In college she discovered that the edifice she constructed was unsustainable. Under its weight she swayed at first, teetered, then crashed. By the time she dropped out and reappeared on the streets, she was no longer beautiful nor even blonde, and her dates lasted only minutes. Everything had changed except for her need for Paul, which was deeper than ever. A badge still, perhaps, but of shame.

* * * * *

In the intervals when Regina was napping and the kids attending after-school clubs, Ruth could slip into the kitchen and gorge. The cookie jar remained in the same place, tucked beside the toaster. The tri-color balloons delighted her, and the clown's half-circle laugh tickled. Or taunted. How could she not remember, while pinching that little pine tree, her mother singing to her, "Here's an extra one for you, for being so special," and then slapping Paul's hand away. Probably that's why he kept it, she figured, to remind him as well. Why he kept *her* and saw to her needs—to show that he, too, could be kind and cruel.

Paul understood that, or least had inklings, while pausing at his desk in the firm. He would lean back in his Eames chair and think about Regina, his pretty Brazilian wife, warm and dark in their bed. He would think about the children, deliciously chocolate-colored, growing up neither spectacular nor ostracized, but smart, fun, and centered. But mostly he would think of Ruth.

"C'mon, let me enroll you again," he recalled exhorting her in the kitchen, as her hands thrust trembling into the jar. "It's the best in the country, they say. I have connections."

She nodded her head and swallowed. Sugar glinted on her lips. "Enough, Paul. Just leave it. Those things never work."

"It could, this time. I spoke with the doctors…" He was urging her, he realized, but not desperately. And he lied about the doctors. "Just give me the word."

Through ravenous chomps she replied, "Just give me another dozen of these, will you?"

He'd given her the dozen, and the dozen after that. But in the end, he knew, the cookies would not be enough. The jar would be empty and so would Ruth's room.

True to his routine, Paul waited several nights before once again racing out to the corners where his sister was known to work.

"No, no Zeena here," one of the women, pressing her painted face through the BMW's window, swore. "But I'll do you better than Zeena and five bucks off."

That was the response, and the offer, at every curb. Paul was beginning to panic, or at least thought he should. He remembered something Ruth once told him, in another of their conversations by the jar. "The past is a drug, little brother. Get yourself clean while you can."

Finally, he sped to the nearest precinct and submitted a lost person's request. It did not have to be processed. A woman meeting that description had been found only hours before in an alley not far from headquarters.

Not yet tagged or undressed, she lay sheeted on the gurney. Exposed to the coarse light, she looked much as she had as a teenager, fine-featured and bright. Not even her wine-stained hair or hollowed cheeks could hide that. Paul made the identification and considered crying. But he merely motioned for the coroner to cover her up again.

"Hold it," he snapped without thinking. "Hold it," he said and, unable to stop himself, wailed. He wept uncontrollably, more inconsolably than any time as a child, as he pried her not-yet-stiffened fingers. He howled at the sight of that little, cold hand coated with crumbs and sugar.

The Innkeeper's Daughter

Welcome home! Hear the cedarwood sing as you cross the porch with its rockers, its wrought iron tables, and swing. Smell the lush country air outside and, within, the hints of camphor as the screen door sighs wistfully behind you. Here are the earthenware mugs your grandmother may have served cocoa in, the mantel clock noisily ticking the wrong time. The rag rugs and the wainscoting, the damask wallpaper, crochet and brocade. The music box that opens to tutued dancers pirouetting to Brahms. And mounted beside old farm implements, the same tennis racket you learned on and, crisscrossed, your first pair of skis. Welcome to the past you wished you remembered, to a time both precious and clean. Welcome to the inn where you can be the self you yearn to long for, and where, if only for a night, you're safe.

* * * * *

"Welcome!" Harvey bellows, more boisterously than loud, as if the guests were long unseen cousins. "Welcome," he strides in his baggy khaki trousers, his brush denim button-down, and crepe-soled loafers, the tousled gray hair and moustache made famous by a children's television host back when. "Let me take your bags," he offers, though his doctor recommended against it, not with the sciatica and the discs already herniated from lifting. But Harvey can't desist, especially with new arrivals. For here the fantasy begins. And nothing, certainly not an arthritic, browbeaten innkeeper, must spoil it. He smiles, rather, eyes twinkling behind his half-moon reading glasses, wrinkles rippling his face, as the guests check in to their childhoods.

For that is what a country inn is about, Harvey knows. Not merely a bed and a bathtub, a breakfast service and drinks, but a shelter from a world long inured to hospitality, a world of instant needs and ever-swifter gratifications, grimly embedded in the now. An inn is about nostalgia, that yearning for the simple and the quaint. Not a mid-point in anyone's journey, but the destination, the way not forward, but back.

"Please, let me show you to your room," Harvey says, leading the newcomers down dark, narrow hallways lined with creaking floorboards and hunting scenes. A pudgy man, he might have to squeeze by Janine, his wife, who alone takes up much of the passage. She, too, smiles, albeit apologetically—an expression virtually tattooed—and bows slightly with chapeled hands. "So glad to see you," she chimes.

A skeleton key opens the door to a room that seems time-frozen, preserved especially for this guest. The oaken four-poster with its Shaker quilts and pillows, the Chippendale vanity, ornamental rabbit ears on the HD TV. There is a selection of teas with Scottish biscuits, a cut-glass bowl of treats. Wine and beer in a minibar discretely wedged beneath the credenza—"Jot down what you take, we trust you," Harvey winks. He reaches under the tasseled lampshade and turns the room sepia. "Voila," he announces, "home."

But, "voila," he thinks, "hell." For while the inn can be paradise for tourists, for the keeper it's agony. Bedsheets streaked with every human effluvium, toilets clogged, and on top of all that the complaints. The water not hot enough, the bedsprings too twangy, the breakfast bacon that could be crispier, saltier, more copious. The endless griping outdone solely by the unrelieved need to listen. At the dining table or in the den where the overnighters wear on about their lives, their poor dead husbands and trips to the Jersey shore, their third cocker spaniels, their retirement plans and transplants, Harvey has to sit with knee-pinioned elbows and chin laden hands, his face a fabrication of interest. Doggedly, he fights the urge to doze off or, better yet, scream. Instead, "So sorry for your loss," he mutters, and "How marvelous," with an eye on that pounding, off-kilter, clock.

Occasionally, Janine will appear with her cauterized smile and ask if anyone wants tea or "something spicier." Though now formless in stretchy polyester, with doughy features and hair like aluminum shavings, she was once the siren who seduced him to this lair. After meeting him at the rock festival, pert in her peasant top and jeans, after accompanying him to the stock exchange, to the hedge funds and equity firms, and later, when all had failed and the jeans and blouse wilted into pantsuits, it was Janine who suggested, "Let's go somewhere distant. Unspoiled. Let's find a big old Victorian house with gables and maybe a turret." And Janine who fantasized, "The two of us, we'll open an inn!"

At first the idea enchanted him. He saw himself hosting glamorous people, voyagers from around the world. He imagined making friends with individuals like him who had striven and taken knocks and, in the process, acquired knowledge about life and the wisdom of sharing it. He did not envision himself forearms-deep in the decorative spittoon some drunken guest took for genuine or on his knees scrubbing takeout chop suey from the tiles. Hopeless with hammers and saws, hazardous around electricity, Harvey was consigned to greeting and registering, entertaining, and mopping up puke. He cooked and he dusted, ironed linen and scoured out mud. The inn is his punishment, Harvey realizes, but for what crime he cannot recall. Where people may check out but never the proprietor, the keeper of his own lacquered jail.

His only reprieve, the sole respite from geniality, is his daughter, Meredith. Inn-raised and bred, she is accustomed to the comings and goings of strangers. She helps in the kitchen, pitches in with the wash, working every vacation when she's home from her college up north. Meredith, who, as an only child, might have grown up spoiled but in fact became grateful and kind—at least to her father, whom she unabashedly adores. As if she knows the strains the inn places on him, the unrelieved burden of being nice. She hates to see him abased by complainers, spat upon and shrinking. "I don't know why you put up with it," she reproaches him. "In your place, I'd murder them."

But Harvey merely gawks at her—in wonder at the fair, chest-nut-haired beauty that he and Janine somehow produced, but also in awe. The perfect combination of femininity and power, muscular yet petite, she's the handy one around the house, as adept with shears as she is with axes. On the fields where Harvey has watched her play lacrosse, she cradles the ball maternally while mercilessly inflicting body checks. A mystery, Meredith is, and a blessing for her father, his lone redemp-tion from the inn.

And a seasoned staffer in a bright sleeveless summer dress and pumps, echoing her father's welcomes as the latest arrival stomps in. Not your average traveler, she can see, neither carefree nor rumpled, but scrupu-lously prim in khaki slacks and a navy-blue blazer. Slender, tanned, his hair hewed into a crust-colored disc parted just off the middle. Mere-dith studies him, a handsome man with angular features, eyes an arma-ment gray, and already she senses trouble. Before she can investigate, though, Harvey huffs into the den. He is carrying the man's suitcases, the old-fashioned leather-bound kind, one in each hand.

"Here, let me take those," she offers, but Harvey recoils, insisting, "No problem, Merri; they're light."

They are, in fact, empty, or nearly so. Meredith can tell from the ease with which her father balances them and the absence of pain on his face. She says nothing, though, but opens the register book and offers the lodger a pen. His signature is curiously legible.

"Great, Mister Roswell D. Frye," Harvey trumpets, "Let me show you your room."

He lets him, begrudgingly, but not before glancing around the den with a sneer. He lifts from the rack one of those earthenware mugs and sniffs its insides, peers into the unlit fireplace, and fiddles with an eight-track player—all with the same disgust.

"Is something wrong, Mister Frye? Something not to your liking?" Harvey is all pusillanimity again, and Meredith looks on, cringing.

"No, nothing. What could be wrong?" The visitor states, rather than asks, with a display of too-white teeth. He motions to Harvey to lead.

They enter the hallway, the man sandwiched between the innkeeper and his daughter, and their combined weight makes the floorboards shriek. "Horrendous," the visitor grumbles, and "barbarous," at the sight of the fox hunt prints, and finally, "You must be joking…"

Janine is blocking their path. Even turned sideways, her unconstrained bulk looks impassable. "So glad to see you," she gasps as the three grunt by, her smile unaltered by the footfalls on her toes or the jam of leather suitcases into her belly. At last, they reach the room.

Though the best in the house, this, too, is not to the visitor's liking. Punching it, he pronounces the mattress "mushy," and the lamplights, switched on and off, "weak." There's dust on the thumb he draws across a windowsill and mold on the porcelain beneath the sink. The chamber pot's potpourri smells stale.

"We'll fix everything, Mister Frye, right away," Harvey assures him and then, beseechingly, to Meredith, "Won't we?"

"Of course," his daughter usually says, but not today. Perhaps because this is the last weekend before she heads back to school, the final stretch of a summer crammed with faultfinders such as Frye. A summer in which her resentment of them nears the boiling point, as does her passion for defending her dad. "At once," Meredith could be expected to add, and yet she stays silent. Her eyes, Tiffany blue and set far apart, shark-like, are wincing. A muscle in her bare upper arm throbs.

It twitches that afternoon during complimentary tea in the den. Other guests are present—a retired pharmacist and his wife from someplace Midwestern, a classics professor on sabbatical, and a honeymoon couple joined at the thigh on the ottoman—and there is Frye. All praise Janine's cinnamon cakes and toast her with homemade lemonade while he grouses over the paucity of mixing spoons and a shortage of Sweet'n Low. "And will someone get rid of that clock?" Meredith looks on, livid, as her mother smiles and Harvey bustles back and forth from the kitchen. His hair is a maelstrom, his moustache a flag of surrender.

"The patron is king," Harvey reminds her when he locates her in the basement, fuming in front of her workbench. This is where she hides when aggravated by boys or boarders. In the dim light and cobwebs, she hacks and chisels away.

"And what's that make you? A peasant?"

"A servant." Harvey's eyes lower to his half-moon glasses. "And a humble one at that." They rise, but with a look not of pride but of impotence. "The inn, Merri," he whispers, as if his wife might hear him upstairs. "It's all I've got."

Her wide-set eyes are now deer-like. "Really, Daddy?" Meredith asks, hoisting a pneumatic drill. "All?"

That night, when she should've been out in her beat-up Civic, working the bars with townie friends, Meredith sits alone in her room, intense at her desk, surfing. So, at last, she finds it. "Fit to be Fryed," the site is jokingly called, though the content is anything but droll. Seems Roswell D.—for Douchebag, she decides—is in the business of visiting inns, posing as a guest, when in reality he's a hitman, taking aim at the unsuspected keepers and killing them. That was the fate of Irma and Pete's Country Retreat in Ashville, the Whaling Wall of Brattleboro, and Sedona's Last Resort. All rated X for execrable, their accommodations described as disgusting, their owners, boors. All of them consequently closed.

In the glare of her computer screen, Meredith sees her own face redden. Her eyes are once again fierce. Right then she vows to stop this itinerant assassin and send him and his two empty suitcases packing. With that muscle in her upper arm pulsing, she swears to defend the inn which is as much her father's castle as his cell.

The next morning, early in the breakfast room, he's at it again. The pancakes are too soggy, the orange juice lacks pulp. Janine beams and apologizes. Harvey runs with freshened plates and doilies to replace the soiled ones. And still the grievances gush: the coffee's anemic, the hash brown potatoes undercooked. The other guests look on with displeasure—not at Frye but at the owners who cannot please him. Meredith, in a splattered apron, sees it all and bristles. A spatula quivers in her hand.

Later, in the den, she tries to lure him away from the house, far from her parents, with brochures of local sites. But Frye is indifferent to stalagmites and bored by haunted mansions. The farm down the road might indeed have belonged to a famous writer, but the blogger never heard of her. The only interest he displays is in Meredith's eyes, which in the morning light turn Wedgewood, and in the lissome figure beneath her dress. That and, afforded by a bay window, a glimpse of Harvey laboring in the yard.

He's out there still late that afternoon, weeding the azaleas and dredging the fountain with its statue of Xenia, the peeing hospitality god. And that's where Frye finds him. While Meredith at the window watches, he berates her father for everything wrong in his house. The overgrown trellises, the gazebo desperate for paint. From the siding he dislodges an imbricated shingle and holds it under her father's nose. Harvey inhales and sighs in a way that makes his moustache droop and his tired shoulders sag, withered by the weight of courtesy.

"Enough," Meredith declares, silently, as she extracts a pewter tray from the vitrine cabinet. She fills it with a slice of her mother's Huckleberry pie and a decanter of rosé, the country's finest. She exits the kitchen and crosses the den, pausing to inspect herself in the mirror. Gazing from its gilded frame is the very image of a hostess, unflappably sweet and servile, a lady of the house, replete with fork and knife. She examines them both for polish and sharpness as the clock on the mantel strikes twelve.

Down the dark hallway she advances, gingerly in her pumps. Past the scenes of hound dogs dismembering foxes, for once not running into her mother before she reaches his door. Perhaps it's the squealing boards but, before she can knock, a snarly voice commands her, "Come in."

He's seated at the credenza, legs astride the minibar, computer glowing atop. Turning as she enters, Frye snorts, "What took you?"

She lays down the tray as he brushes his slacks and combs his lozenge of hair. One buckled shoe balances on a suitcase and rocks it imperiously.

"I brought you a snack," Meredith informs him, needlessly, "I thought…"

"You thought you could bribe me."

Meredith glowers at him and Frye smirks in return. Leaning back in his chair, he laughs, "Thought maybe a piece of your mom's shitty baking and a swig of your country swill would change what I'm going to write about this flophouse. It," he grins, "and its ridiculously incompetent keeper."

Such words might paralyze one of the townies, but Meredith's weathered worse on the field. "What *will* it take?"

Frye's already on his feet, striding toward her, eyes fixed like gun muzzles. But the innkeeper's daughter doesn't flinch. Merely, she touches her fingers to his chest, murmuring, "Not here."

"Where, then?"

"Where no one will hear us. Downstairs. In the basement."

* * * * *

Goodbye! Drive Safely! You hear as you exit the sighing screen door and cross the gentle chorus of the porch. You have slept the sleep of yesterday and awakened to sunlight spread icing-like on the sheets. Eaten meals slathered with syrup and buttermilk without a thought of your waist or heart, strolled the garden in the afternoon heat but never once raised a sweat. You found it all—the cloisonné, the macramé, and the lace—together with that rarest of artifacts called peace. All this you received at the inn, delivered with deference and grace, and if the price seemed initially prohibitive, in retrospect it seemed almost free. Goodbye and come and see us again soon! The words flutter across the lawn, weightless as dandelion puffs, as the weekend guests trundle back to their cars, back to their lives, and the oppressive truths of the present.

From the rocker where he rests his back, sore from handling luggage, Harvey waves as the last of the weekenders depart. Now there is only Meredith. She has already embraced her mother, still smiling garishly through tears, and hugged and kissed her dad. Made him promise not to work too hard or take the customers' bellyaching so seriously. "The patron is king," he reminds her, but his daughter just giggles and dries off his moustache with her cheek.

And then she is also gone. Marching to her Civic with a lacrosse bag slung over one shoulder and a backpack over the other, and in each hand a suitcase which she won't let anybody touch. Old-fashioned leather-bound valises, their heft makes her arm muscles bulge. Harvey watches as she lifts them into the trunk. Through his fogged, half-moon glasses, he thinks he sees something leak. An antique embroidery of blood.

The Betsybob

Dogwood leaves nod with falling dewdrops, the fern fronds, too. The forest appears to be motioning its approval—or reproach— as the low-lying branches part. A dim, humid morning alive with bug buzz, the undergrowth stirring with efts. Mist like a fabric unraveling. Dried twigs crackle, switches hiss until the thicket gives way to a clearing. Scattered boulders and stumps, and at the far end, a knoll. Inside, there's a cave of sorts or a grotto, its entrance curtained by vines. But even then, a presence emerges, an energy and a song. And light. Clarified beams that pierce the ivy and turn the moss incandescent, but then, once unveiled, explode. Blinding, searing, redeeming. The light that reveals all secrets, promising to fulfil any wish.

* * * * *

Flinching awake in her chair, squinting and shielding her eyes, Randy mutters, "No."

"Sorry," the night nurse assures her. "Routine check." She turns a switch and the room again darkens. "If you're having trouble sleeping, I can give you something…"

"No. No, it's okay." The hand that had been saluting now fluttered, shooing the RN away.

"Alright, then," she says, merely one of many shadows, "goodnight," and exits the sterilized room.

Randy groans to her feet. Approaches the bed with its tubes and monitors, blinking like the controls of some alien ship. And lying there, resting after celestial flight, hairless and gray, the visitor from the planet Cancer. The creature who is also her son.

She feels his forehead. Clammy and hot all at once, a single vein pulsing beneath her fingers. Onion-skinned eyelids flitting. Emaciated, his features are thrown into relief, the deep-set eyes, the blunt-tipped nose, the mouth that obstinately remains fleshy. His father's face, not that she entirely remembers it. A man she met in a bar and then in her bed for a fitful week eleven years earlier, but who then vanished without ever knowing the life he left inside her. Randy did not follow him, never tried to track him down. It wasn't her way, a woman unaccustomed to asking. Believing it best to accept whatever the world gave her, convinced that she deserved little more, fearful of receiving less.

So it was with her son. The child she didn't dream of, much less demand, but who seemed nothing short of miraculous. T.J., she called him, as though unwilling to waste time on his name, knowing he wouldn't wait for it as he ran around and out of her apartment. Restless, rambunctious, he both frazzled and astonished his teachers, their report cards reading like tributes. Any day he might return with either a gold-starred math test or an eye swollen from some spat, but Randy hardly cared. To her, T.J. was the gift she wouldn't have dreamed of, a wish she never made come true. Catching him as he burst through the door, she kissed his beaded forehead and nested her face in his curls. "T.J.," she sighed, inhaling his bubble-gum breath. "T.J.," short for the love a universe might not contain.

Strange, then, the way he murmured "Mom" at the dinner table and pointed to his scoop of potatoes. There, on the crown beside a dollop of butter, was a bright red dot. Then another, on the lambchop, and several stippling his plate.

"Nothing, hon, a nosebleed." But there was no stopping the flow, no explaining the pallor, the bruises, and the weight loss. No preventing the doctor from pronouncing the word that made that very same universe shatter.

And now in the night she stands over him, the patient who never complains, the darling of doctors and nurses, who snorts "Jesus, Mom," every time she cries. Who, even in sleep, reminds her that there is more to lose than life itself and that she is helpless to save it.

It's then that she remembers the dream. Or the memory—she's not sure which—only that it recurred to her for a reason. Somehow, she knew it would, was yearning for it. The scrunch of mulch and the rich scent of duff. The clearing and the knoll. And the light, most desperately the light. There, in the antiseptic ward, by the glow of her son's vital signs, she decides to act on the impulse she's had now for weeks. Stepping out into the corridor, cupping her phone so the medical staff won't overhear, she makes three improbable calls.

* * * * *

The first forces her to distance the phone from her ear. Hooting, applause, a whistle or two, followed by Marla's laugh, part honk, part thunderclap. She's backstage at a comedy club, about to go on, but can't ignore the name on her cell.

"Randy! Sweetie! *Whaaat?*"

Another of Marla's signatures, that *whaaat*. Depending on the tone, it could mean "how are you?" or "is this for real?" or "holy shit." In this case, though, it stands for "why is my camp friend from a zillion years ago suddenly calling?"

She tells her, trying to sound serious as she shouts.

"Jessie. Sweetie. That really sucks."

She imagines Marla bulging out of that too-tight, too-short outfit she wears when performing, an essential prop in an act about the fat frizzy redhead trying to get laid, about sagging breasts and desiccated vaginas, her fans alternatively tantalized and repelled. Randy has seen her on cable TV and might have been disgusted if not for the memory of Marla going into sixth grade, overweight and outrageous. Marla, who could never be surprised by anything, no matter how weird, responding as she now does to Randy's request with another ear-splitting laugh. Another "whaaat?" this time meaning "are you nuts?"

Randy admits, "Yeah, I know," then explains how all the therapies have failed and that this is her final option. "It happened, Marl. You saw it. We all did. And now we have to go back."

"We?"

"I don't think I can find my way alone. It might not appear just to me."

"And why exactly?"

"The wish. I didn't make one..." The silliness of this, once spoken, embarrasses her. Randy considers hanging up but instead breaks out sobbing. "Don't make me beg!"

Weeping is the last thing a stand-up needs to hear right before going up, yet it somehow triggers a laugh. "Hey, I'm the one, sweetie, who begs."

On stage, Marla's name is announced and instantly the audience erupts. The phone again flies from Randy's ear but not so far that she can't hear Marla's final *whaaat*. "Don't be an idiot," this one says. "Of course, I'll come."

The next call, made mid-morning in a time zone only one hour behind, catches Jane in the sanctuary. Here, too, there is background noise, but a different kind, softer, sacred. A children's choir, tremulous voices singing a prayer of some kind, to the tune of Scarborough Fair. Normally, Jane lets nothing interfere with her duties, certainly not an incessantly vibrating phone. But the name on the screen tells her that this interruption is justified. Though she hasn't spoken with Randy for some time, her attention sapped by professional and personal demands, social media has kept her informed. Laying her guitar on the nearest pew, she steps to the rear of the hall, away from the singing, and summons her tone of condolence.

"I am so sorry..."

"Hold on, Jane, nobody's died," Randy stammers, resisting the urge to add "yet."

"Thank God."

"And nobody might if you help."

Unlike with Marla, there is no need to explain Randy's reasoning—or lack of it. Jane already inhabits the world of faith, dwelt in it even as a teenager, as infused with spirituality as others were with hormones. The only one of their foursome to actually say the Sabbath prayers and attend the voluntary services, to succor the weak and befriend the unpopular, and to try to understand what she, Randy, was going through that summer. An infinitely caring soul, Jane's, but encased in an inadequate body. Even now, Randy imagines her swamped in her robes, a wispy woman bowed by the weight of her skullcap, fragile-featured and wan. And yet, she totally expects Jane to say yes to her proposal, even to coordinate the trip. What she doesn't anticipate is the cracking voice in her ear, that all but mutes the canticle.

"I'm going through some stuff in my life just now. Difficult stuff."

Randy's reaction, too, is surprising. "I am going through difficult *stuff*," she snaps. "My son's *stuff* is difficult."

"I understand, of course."

Understanding, Randy knows, is the first step to conceding, to acknowledging that a person of her piety cannot ignore the prayers of a half-crazed mother, the pleas of her old Willowbrook friend. That a believer in mana from heaven or the parting of the Red Sea cannot doubt the power of one little marvel in the woods. Randy knows that, without saying so, Jane has already agreed, even as the singing stops and another voice intrudes. Some woman reminding her, "the children are waiting for you, Rabbi Jane," with cloying petulance. "*Our* children."

A twang of strings escapes the phone as Jane accepts the outstretched guitar. "Coming, love. Sorry," she apologizes but not to Randy. To her she whispers, "Just tell me when," before clicking off. "I'll be there."

That leaves Danielle. Who should have been her first call, seeing as she was always the leader, the captain of their team in color war, the fastest runner, swimmer, thinker. Convince Danielle and the others would have followed willingly, just as they did as children. But Danielle was no longer sleeping in a bunk next to them or plotting their course through the trees. Her cabins are now first-class and her planning fiscal. The head of a multi-national firm, she sits in an office high above the city surveying its forest of skyscrapers, handily navigating through.

Reaching her at that altitude proves exasperating, though. It means wading through pools of secretaries and administrative assistants, all of them asking who she is and why she needs to speak to the president. And how should Randy answer? Tell them that their boss is needed for a reunion with three of her friends, searching for the vision they glimpsed only once but that changed their lives forever? That the life of a boy exactly the same age they were back then might very well depend on it?

Instead, "Just want to reconnect," Randy lies. "Five minutes, no more."

Finally, she hears her name on the phone. Broken into two even syllables, each one pronounced like a sentence. "How are you?" she inquires and then, when told, says, "Dreadful."

"Oh, my God, no!" would be the reply of a fellow mother, but Danielle's never had kids. Unlike Marla, twice-divorced, and Jane with her longtime wife and their adopted Dominican daughters, Danielle had no time for marriage and easily intimidated men. Most emotions she keeps at a distance—as much an asset in the corporate world as in relationships susceptible to loss. Rather, she stands aloof as she did on the cover of a waiting room magazine Randy once saw, in a custom-made suit and clipped bronze coiffure and an expression both imperious and knowing. A hard, handsome woman with a face devoid of curves, only angles, jagged as broken glass.

For that reason, though, Danielle is the least likely to agree. Even Randy finds it difficult to picture her plying through the woods today in jeans and sneakers, leading them as she once did with aplomb. Not unexpectedly, she hears, "I can't be away from the firm."

Unlike with Marla, there is no sense of empathy to appeal to, none of Jane's mystical bent. But there is another route. "*You* be firm," Randy assuages her, "Show them who's the boss."

"I *am* the boss," Danielle declares, seemingly to herself, before coming back to Randy. "Besides, that camp was knocked down ages ago. The forest probably, too."

"And if it wasn't?" Randy persists, "We need you to guide us again." Subtly, her *I* has morphed into *we*. "We can't do it without you."

"No, you couldn't..."

Someone enters Danielle's office, a secretary or junior exec. She's wanted in the boardroom, he says. Not a request. "Send me the info," she rasps to Randy. "I'll schedule it."

The line goes dead but for minutes she remains at the nurse's station, stunned. Randy has won something but she's unsure what. An irrational hike through non-existent woods to a cave most likely mythic? To recreate a moment perhaps produced by their prepubescent imaginations, that probably never happened at all?

Orderlies whisk by and downcast visitors shuffle, but Randy's still staring at her phone. At the screen with its photo of T.J., healthy and beaming in his baseball cap. His smile, alone, suffices to remind her why she's doing this. And superimposed over her son's image is her own, shockingly haggard, and behind that, yet another. A palimpsest of an eleven-year-old confused and frightened by the harshness of the world and yet open to the possibility of wonder. Who gazes out across the years and imparts the secret words that not even Randy dared utter. With a finger to her lips and the wink of one innocent eye, the young girl whispers, "the Betsybob."

* * * * *

There were many secret words that summer. "Puke fest" for the bowls of Sloppy Joes served every Wednesday night for dinner and "Gold-digger" for the girl in their bunk fond of nose-picking. "Dartboard," described their sadly-acned counselor while the captious unit head was "Godzilla." Willowbrook's owner, Samantha Shapira, the gauntly elegant Auntie Sam who first interviewed them in her mid-town apartment and now oversaw them from the camp's highest hill, was simply "God."

This was their fourth summer together and their last, though they could not have known the financial crisis the camp was in or their lives' divergent paths. Rather, they existed in the present, as unaware of the date as they were of the dangers, reveling in a friendship that had no origin they remembered—no common interests or hobbies—only that they were and always would be a team.

An anomalous team comprised of the reticent, reflective Jane, and Marla, a wisecracking butterball. At its head, Danielle, long-limbed and flaxen-braided, giraffe and gazelle-like in height and speed. And Randy. Like the others, born into a well-to-do home with maids and piano lessons, vacations on capes and ski slopes, but a home that was breaking up. Her father had moved out, leaving her mother in the company of bottles and their daughter alone fearing that the tiniest mis-move, the merest slip, could collapse the remains of her world.

So she was happy just to tag along, silently for the most part, to witness and keep their secrets. Not yet interested in boys, these focused mainly on nicknames and pranks—short-sheeting bunks and rearranging footlockers—and disseminating rumors both comical and cruel. In impermeable circles, they giggled, they snickered and shared. Girlish in a way that girls can be just before they become women. And feeling inestimably special.

Randy needed that feeling just then, the summer of her worthlessness, and never questioned Danielle when she proposed even the most devious schemes. Even when she told them about the cave.

"It's in the woods. Not too deep. Near the dining hall, there's a trail…" Danielle's features, even back then, were razor-like, lacerating the air as she spoke. Her sky-blue eyes seemed to darken. "We follow it, far, but we can't be afraid 'cause at the end of it there's a place with no trees, only this cave, and inside the cave…"

Marla was already bouncing on her pudgy feet and Jane, if incredulous, was too in love with Danielle to question her. Randy merely listened, feeling both privileged and afraid but saying nothing, nodding as Danielle spoke.

"Inside the cave is…the counselors' hideout! Empty beer cars, dirty pictures, maybe even some drugs. We find it," Danielle declared, "and we will be queens of Willowbrook!"

Stridently, braces flashing, Marla laughed, and Jane nervously chortled. Randy imagined herself crowned. But when could they do this, how, what with every minute taken up with activities and Auntie Sam observing them from her porch, with a cigarette in one hand and in the other, reportedly, binoculars? "No problem," Danielle assured them. "I've got it all planned."

They'd get up the next morning and go through the usual routine—breakfast, flag-raising, inspection—until first period. Then, slipping away from whatever they were doing, archery or crafts, and rendezvousing behind the dining hall, they could hurry to the cave, peep inside, and be back in time for lunch.

Marla might have objected—first period, drama, was her favorite—and Jane hated to skip guitar lessons, but Danielle's decision was made. And Randy was only too thrilled to miss swim class, the pond water icy and metallic-tasting. She wouldn't have to wear the bathing suit that displayed her body in all its formlessness, lusterless hair plastered around a face she, herself, judged nondescript. In the forest, rather, she'd be feather-like, as graceful and shimmering as the fairies her father used to tell her about, nighttimes while putting her to bed.

And like all of Danielle's schemes, this one began auspiciously. Each managed to sneak off undetected and meet up at the rear of the dining hall, between the concrete loading dock and cast-iron boilers. From there they embarked. Four girls—lithe and blubbery, diminutive and professedly bland—in their yellow Willowbrook t-shirts and shorts, filed through a break in the woods.

The trail was not well-trodden. Brambles crisscrossed it, prickling their knees, and sumac that would later inflame their ankles. Mosquitos whined, the deadwood shifted, and for seconds all of them, even Danielle, pictured getting lost, with no trace of them ever found. But forebodings faded the deeper they penetrated the bush. The sun, sluicing through the treetops, backlit the butterflies and bejeweled a single web. Breezes applauded in the leaves. Dripping with dew, the foliage waved them inward.

But an hour passed, or so they felt, and they could no longer hear the camp's shouts and whistles, only their sneakers' crackle. The trail all but disappeared. "Maybe there is no cave," Marla hazarded, airing the other two's thoughts. "Maybe we should turn back."

But Danielle, supple arms folded, dug in. "It's here, I know it. Just keep quiet," she insisted. "Follow me."

They followed until the trees converged around them and the day grew unnaturally still. Yet Danielle keep thrashing, snapping off branches as she plunged. The others stumbled after her, panicky, when suddenly they heard her bellow, "Eureka!"

The clearing they entered was perfectly round, as if deliberately carved from the wild. As though the forest, itself, had recoiled—out of reverence, perhaps, or fear. Once inside the circle, though, they felt a strange sensation, half-tingle, half-kiss, on their skin, and a dizzying intensity of air. Then they heard the music. A high-pitched hum, neither electronic nor human. Angelic.

"There!" Danielle announced. "It's coming from there."

She was pointing at a knoll rising from the clearing's center, a heap of rock slightly taller than their heads and ivy-draped. This was it, the home of the cave and its many dirty secrets, the beer cans and cigarette butts. They'd found it! Giddily, they broke into a run, slaloming around half-buried boulders and tree stumps, only to stop abruptly. Shooting through the vines were rays of light so cylindrical they almost looked solid and brighter than any flash.

Marla exclaimed, "Whaaat?" and the rest of them gasped. But Danielle pressed on. She thrust her hands between the creepers and pulled them apart as a blast of light sent her reeling. They all did, hands thrust over their faces, with hollers of "Jesus!" and "holy shit!"

But, as in darkness, their eyes grew accustomed to the blaze. They stood, blinking but otherwise frozen, before a mossy opening smaller than a cave—a grotto, though they would not yet know the word—and inside, a being. That was the only way to describe it, an entity, a presence, for while vaguely flame-shaped with a cowl-like taper at the top, it had no body to speak of, only luminance. And no face except for darker patches, like sunspots, where the eyes could have been, and a translucent line for a mouth. Even those patches seemed to gleam at them. The line curved upward in a smile.

Randy shuttered and Jane audibly prayed. Marla started chuckling, anxiously, until Danielle told them all to calm down. "I think it wants us to do something."

In unison, "Like what?" they replied.

"I don't know. Make a wish."

"In that case," Marla chimed. "I want to be famous!" and Jane mumbled something about love.

"Rich!" Danielle announced and then turned and glared at Randy. They all did, but all she could do was shrug.

What could she possibly wish for? That her father would come back home, that her mother abandon her bottles, that they would make up and be a family again? No, she couldn't ask for that, not out loud in front of her friends.

"Come on, Randy. Wish!"

She shrugged again and ogled the being in the cave. It seemed to be glimmering right at her. That's when she remembered the pony. The frisky Shetland she'd always wanted, that would follow her around and nuzzle her, rubbing its velvety nose on her neck. That she would ride, clutching its silvery mane, across beaches and fields of tulips. The pony she fantasized about as a younger child and now ached for. The dappled pony of joy.

"Don't be like that, Ran-*dy*..."

But she was too old to wish for a pony, and too young to ask for peace. Randy said nothing and finally Danielle gave up.

"None of us speaks a word of this. Ever," she commanded, and three heads dutifully shook. "It's our secret. Only ours. For life."

Already she was about-facing, about to head back to the forest. But her best friends dallied for a moment, glazed in unalloyed light.

"But what do we call it?" Marla wondered.

"Bob." Came Danielle's answer, definitive as always. "We'll call him Bob."

"Why *him*?"

This was Jane and everyone glared at her, unaccustomed to such assertiveness. "Why not..." she retreated, "Betsy?"

Marla bounced and clapped. "The Betsybob!" she proclaimed, and her laughter echoed through the woods.

* * * * *

When it comes to planning, Randy's hopeless. With schedules and budgets, too. Never the professional type, she was happy with a string of low-demanding jobs—retail buyer, real estate broker, receptionist—that gave her the time and flexibility for T.J. But then he got sick and there were specialists to consult, hospitals to grapple with. Bills mounted, trash cans overflowed. Way beyond overwhelmed, the last thing Randy needed was to organize a trip to a wilderness up north and for women who, though close childhood friends, had long grown up into strangers.

Secrets can do that to people. Bind them tighter or nudge them apart. A source or sapper of strength, secrets can be borne in any manner of ways, with pride, humility, or dishonor. Somehow they knew that back then, slipping into the dining hall and taking their places for lunch, barely exchanging a look, that their relationship was forever altered. That each of them, as people, had changed. By the light of the Betsybob, they'd seen themselves for what they really were and wanted. That knowledge, those desires, would soon bear them far from Willowbrook, across the country and to lives propitiously different. Accomplished women, they'd have little time to spare for Randy's whims and even less for traipsing through forests.

And so she plans, meticulously. Reservations at the hotel their parents used to stay at the night before visitors' day, flights for Jane and Marla, and a conversation with Danielle's driver, giving him pinpoint directions. Dinner that evening, perhaps some drinks, and the next day, at dawn, setting out. The entire excursion will take an hour or two, she figures, and then they'll say their goodbyes. By evening, Marla will be back to her stand-up and Jane to her congregation, Danielle restored to her heights. And Randy will return to the hospital, to the sanitized room with its instruments bleeping like a rocket ship's and T.J., strapped in and tube-fed for blast off.

Only now she will not merely watch. Doctors could pump him with antibodies and nurses might lessen his pain, but Randy will provide him with what none of them ever possessed. A wish. No longer for a pony, dappled or otherwise, but for the miracle he needs to survive.

But first she must find that forest, the clearing, the cave. Stand once more in the energy and the music and beseech that being with the sunspot eyes and smile. She must let the light envelop her and assure her that, if only she'll make it, this time her wish will be granted.

Yet time is what she lacks. The reunion must take place this week, the last in October. Any later and the snows will begin. Later, she knows, is too late. Feverishly, Randy completes the schedule, addressing every question but one. Will they again meet the Betsybob?

* * * * *

At least the hotel is unchanged. Decorated in faux-New England colonial, powder horns and muskets on the walls; its anemic light brings out their weariness as they enter. Randy can see that greeting them, not only the fatigue of their trip but a depleted look, vitality drained from their faces. Danielle in a mauve cashmere coat, Marla in pink lamb's wool, and Jane in an oversized ski jacket, all looking like refugees, but from what Randy won't guess. She only imagines how she must seem to them, a husk. Yet none of them lets on. They hug one another, girlishly scream and fuss, as if arriving at another summer in camp.

But summer is over, and Willowbrook's closed down, and the reason for the reunion is too painful to mention. Instead, they learn about Marla's gigs around the country, about the redneck crowds that squirm at words like boobs and pussy, and the college kids waiting to pounce on any heresy. About Jane's work with inter-faith groups and the homeless, assisted by Sarah, her wife. Over a dinner in which everything, even the appetizers, are fried, they hear stories of private equity, of IPO's and M&A's and the markets that Danielle manipulates. Randy listens as attentively as she can, nodding and smiling and doing her best not to think about tomorrow's trek. Struggling against the sense that not every wish, not even her friends', gets granted.

But the intuition intensifies through two martinis and a snifter of local cognac. Inexorably, the truth seeps out.

"Boobs and pussies are funny on twenty-year-olds, less so at forty." Marla runs meaty hands through redder curls. "And campuses today are courtrooms." Turns out, she hasn't had a major contract in over a year, not even a nibble, and even her agent's stopped calling. She's had her fame, her late-night appearances and specials, but the world belongs to younger comedians, fatter and dirtier. For once she doesn't say "whaat," doesn't laugh, but instead downs the remains of her cognac.

Danielle, too, opens up, confessing between anxious peeks at her phone that her entire world is imploding. She's still statuesque, coldly beautiful and dominant, with eyes reflecting a sky, but success has made her a target. At this very moment, a coup is underway—the terms "buy-out" and "take-over" are spat—a plot to push her out of a top-floor window. "Let 'em try," she rallies, raising both fists in defiance, but briefly. "The ceiling's not glass, it's the floor," she laments. "Step on it with your heels and"—her ringless fingers unfurl—"bam!"

This leaves only Jane, vying with Randy for silence.

"And you?" Marla prods her. "What could go wrong, with all that God on your side?"

Danielle addresses her glass. "I could use a bit of your God…"

The dessert, churros and crullers, is set on the table but Jane merely stares at it. "I have my community. My choir. They swear I'm a good guitar-player, the liars." The women, even Randy, titter, then issue collective "awe" as the rabbi adds, "And I'm in love." But she says this joylessly as the others dig in, her brittle face growing more vulnerable, her sloping shoulders stooped. "With Seth."

The name is repeated, rapid-fire, with puffs of powdered sugar. "A member of your temple?"

"Worse," sighs Jane. "Its president." Pinching the bridge of her nose, she shifts her head ruefully, back and forth. "They'll fire me when they find out. My daughters will disown me. And Sarah, who converted for me, gave up her career, she'll kill me. Already, she suspects…"

The conversation staggers after that, with Danielle reminiscing about her wildcat days on Wall Street and Marla badmouthing Hollywood. Jane goes on about this Seth—bald, skeletal, a CPA—who's upended everything she thought about herself and believed, and all the while Randy's thinking, "This is a terrible mistake."

A stupid, unconscionable mistake, bringing together women who no longer have anything in common. Who are preoccupied enough with their own problems without chasing some chimerical solution for hers. Better to call it off now when she can, apologize profusely to each of them and thank them all for trying. Speed to the hospital that very night and sleep by T.J.'s bed, holding his frigid hand for as long as they'd let her, until they tear her away.

"Well, this has been enlightening," Danielle states suddenly, "and nutritious, but I think we'd better get our rest." She is once again the boss, their captain, leading the way through the woods. "It'll be dawn in a few hours, and we can't keep the Betsybob waiting."

Jane and Marla gawk at her. Randy, too. It's the first time any of them has spoken that name in decades, since that day they snuck back into the dining hall. The first time anyone admits remembering it.

"To the Betsybob!" Marla raises a toast.

"To the Betsybob!" Jane and Danielle join in.

Yet Randy hesitates. For the first time, she's wondering if her friends have really come to help her or rather only themselves, each with her own new wish. And she's questioning whether she is still that little girl too timid to ask for a pony, or an adult now, a mother, asking for the life of her son. "The Betsybob," she says finally, uncertainly, and clinks her empty glass.

* * * * *

The sign says "Willowbrook Condominiums—Buy Now and Save $$$," and behind it there is only mud. Bulldozers and backhoes line the entrance, waiting for their drivers and the day's construction. Dawn breaks over what had once been their camp but is now unrecognizable. The playing fields, the archery range, the cabins—all are erased, the pond scum-covered. The silence of the birdless sky is matched only by that inside the rented SUV, where Danielle's hands turn white on the wheel and Jane wraps an arm around Randy. "Aw, Sweetie," Marla mewls, but Randy remains silent. All she says is "Drive on" to Danielle who, for once, seems open to instructions.

Through puddles and debris, the vehicle waddles, but to where none of them can tell. Shorn of landmarks, they might be in the middle of the parade ground, where once they raised the flag. A consensus is gathering within the car that this is a huge waste of time, that it's better to turn around now before the tires sink. Danielle is already circling when Randy calls out "look!"

She's pointing to what is still the area's only hill, to the half-demolished country house and its off-kilter porch. That is where Samantha

Shapira used to watch them from, Auntie Sam with her cigarette and binoculars, sallow and godly.

"Go forward. Straight ahead."

Danielle frowns in the rearview mirror but does as Randy insists. Past a slag heap and a pile of rebar, toward tree trunks emerging from the mist. The forest. And in front of it, rusted and chipped, the remains of a boiler and loading dock. "It's still here!" Randy cries. "We're here!"

Stiffly, grunting, they pull themselves from the car and stand in the late-autumn chill. "What now?" Marla shivers, but Jane, even in her parka, is too cold to speak. Randy looks at Danielle who, after a regretful glance at her coat, relents and says, "follow me."

They do, along the tree line to the remnants of what once was a trail. Danielle turns inward, tripping and cursing, while Marla worries out loud about hunting season. Jane, struggling in the rear, distracts herself by telling Randy a story. The four sages who went into the woods.

"Nobody knows what they saw there—the Talmud doesn't say—only that one of them looked on it and died. Another became crazy and the third lost his faith.

"And the fourth?"

"Became the greatest scholar of all time. A genius."

"Sounds like they found what they were looking for," Randy says, while impatiently peering through the trees, as the forest thickens around them. Multi-colored leaves still cling to the branches, painting the sun as it climbs. The ground, pressed by loafers and hiking shoes, emits a musky fragrance, and a woodpecker sounds a tattoo. For a moment they're campers again, pre-teen and carefree, far from fathoming the immeasurable depths to which any life can lead. Even Randy, an early initiate to pain, later its priestess, feels lightheaded.

But the giddiness soon passes as the thread of a trail dwindles to a fiber, and brambles, once knee-high, tear across their chests. "I think we're lost," Marla ventures and Danielle doesn't disagree. Jane's arm is on Randy's shoulder again, hugging as she puffs, "We tried..."

They did—Randy can't deny it—took off time that they could hardly afford, traveled, and *shlepped*, and all to indulge her delusions. Because of her, they can't find their way out. Disappointment and guilt bandy in her brain as she flails behind the others. And anger. For she knows now that she would have made that wish. If only they'd reached the clearing, she would have demanded it. Plunged into the cave and grabbed the Betsybob or whatever it was, throttled it if necessary. Anything for T.J.

Anything, and yet she's abandoned him. How could she have left him like this, Randy agonizes, alone, and for what purpose? Just to prove to herself that for once she wouldn't be passive?

"Help!"

Suddenly, Jane is rushing past her, around Marla's bulk that largely obscures Danielle no longer looming before them but down and clutching one knee.

"It's twisted," she growls. "That fucking stump…"

She points at the guilty obstacle but there is more than one. There are many, in fact, interspersed with partially submerged boulders. The trees have retreated in a symmetrical arc and in the center of the clearing, a knoll. A cairn, ancient perhaps or older, composed of moss-encrusted rocks and densely cloaked in ivy.

Randy runs. Danielle, too, oblivious to her knee as Marla is to her weight and Jane to her frailty. They sprint, scarcely aware of the absence of energy in the air, of music. No bolts of radiance beaming. They reach the knoll and pause for a moment, winded and gaping at one another, wondering who will do it. Randy steps forward, clutches the vines and yanks them apart. And then falls back in horror.

In grief. The cave is there, the grotto—they now know the word—littered with broken whiskey bottles and moldy cigarette butts, the remains of what might have been a magazine. Otherwise, it's empty. The Betsybob, if it ever existed, is gone.

Danielle explains, "We probably made it up," and Jane consoles, "Hell, we were only kids."

Marla sighs a decrescendoing, "Whaat," followed by an acerbic laugh.

Randy says nothing, but her body begins to shake. Shoulders, hips, uncontrollably heaving as someone, maybe her, sobs. She can't feel the embrace of the women who were once her friends and are now her mourners. And she's unaware of those around her peeling away before the crunch of approaching feet.

Not feet, it's soon revealed, but hoofs. Trotting out of the bush and into the clearing to brush a dappled flank on her arm. To tickle her neck with a silky mane and nestle a soft, moist nose on her cheek. Randy strokes it as the others look on enchanted. She caresses it and weeps, this vision of a wish long granted. Her magical pinto of hope.

The Night Archer

We've never met, yet you join me every night. Your name is unknown to me, though John would be a fair guess, and your last name Fletcher or Bowyer, in acknowledgement of a skill long forgotten by your descendants. I have never imagined your face, never needed to, but let's just say that your cheeks are stubbled, your remaining teeth black, and your eyes—pale, cold Saxon eyes—at once dull and flinty sharp. Still, as I said, your name and face remain irrelevant to me. Only your filthy fingers reaching down into the mud and grass of Agincourt and selecting one from a batch of arrows.

A life-long insomniac, sleep has always been my enemy. Where most others see an in-gathering of angels or sheep, the harbinger of peace, I glimpse an army bristling with lances and blades clamoring off to war. I have tried all the soporifics, natural and narcotic, the therapies and meditations. I have counted backwards from one hundred thousand and mentally erected skyscrapers from toothpicks. I rid the bedroom of the digital clocks whose clicking panels pound in my ears or whose faint blueish light penetrates even the thickest eyeshades. Nothing—no drug, no routine, nor any pre-emption—worked. Until I found you.

How and why that discovery happened, I have no idea. I'm a history buff, yes, and what history buff doesn't harbor a quiet yet insatiable obsession with the battle given in 1415 by superior French forces to the invading but enervated English? Whose head won't resonate with paeans to "We band of brothers" and cheers of "Kiss me, Kate"? And the prurient sadness of recalling how the flower of French knighthood was cut down by King Henry's archers? I know the length of your bow—six feet, on average—the yew trees it was cut from, the thirty-inch arrows tipped with tempered steel and provisioned in batches of twenty-four. I know its immense 150-pound power and the years you spent amassing the body-strength to draw it. I even know that the two fingers that haul the notch and fletching to the corner of your mouth will become—so the legend claims—the "V" sign raised by future Britons.

I know all the facts—the armor worn, the weapons—but one. Why you? And why each night when I wage my hopeless war with consciousness, do I turn to you for reinforcement? It is not your smell, which I imagine to be prodigious, the sheen of your helmet or the weight of the mallet you pack to drive the sharpened stakes against cavalry. If I try, I can feel the home-spun weave of your tunic. But I do not try.

Instead, I watch from a position just behind and beneath you as the bow hoists into the air, and you take aim the way you have since childhood, practicing first on toys, not by yanking the string back with your arm but, on the contrary, by leaning forward, your torso thrust into the curvature. So the arrow inches to your lips and lingers there momentarily. I see no knights, no clay-churned field or rising mounds of bodies. I cannot hear the cries of the pierced and the amputated, the pleas of prisoners soon to be executed. No, there is only the creak of a hard-bent bow and its drawn, flaxen string. There is only the peaceful sky so unlike my bed which, thanks to my thrashing, now resembles a battlefield.

How many hours have passed? More, I hazard to think, than the entire span of Agincourt. Your right shoulder hitches, almost imperceptibly but enough to expand the range another dozen yards. A cheek muscle throbs. And then, with a spring-like motion too fast for the human eye, your fingers open.

Launching, the arrow soars. Its shaft contracts into a dot. Impossibly high, improbably graceful, the projectile grapples with altitude and gravity and yields to them finally. A perfect parabola of death.

And the arrow finds its mark. Straight in the head if not through the heart, its target emits snores, not sighs. Already you are reaching for your next shot, while I remain fixed to my pillow. Once again, you have carried the day, brave archer, and dispatched me gratefully into night.

Acknowledgments

There is only one thing scarier than facing an empty page, every writer knows, and that's sending a completed page to readers. And as hard as writing can be, honestly criticizing that work is more difficult still. For that reason, I am singularly indebted to all those who read these stories and judged them candidly. I wish, then, to thank Jonathan Rosen, Stefanie Pearson, Jamie Gangel, Mark and Erica Gerson, Charles and Arielle Zeelof, Betsy Madway, Rachel Moore, Jeremy Herman, John Krivine, Orly Genger, Helen Katz, Gil Troy, Jason and Dianna Perkins, Alison Nager, Lisa Schoenberg, and David Ehrlrich, of blessed memory.

Sending stories to relatives is especially stressful, but my family members always came through. To my children, Noam, Lia, and Yoav Oren, and to my sisters, Aura and Karen, and their husbands, Fred and Arnie, thank you. And a special note of gratitude to my parents, Marilyn and Lester Bornstein, age 92 and 95, who read all these stories and assured me they liked them.

I am especially indebted to my editor, Adam Bellow, for his vision, courage, and friendship. Heather King, Managing Editor at Post Hill Press, was unswervingly dedicated and professional. My deepest appreciation goes, as always, to Leslie Meyers, without whom this collection, and the freedom it represents, would not be possible.